CROWN OF STEEL

LOLA MALONE

Editing: Heather Caryn

Proofreading: Charlotte, Nicole, Amy, Jen and Dee

Cover design: © Dream Echo Designs

Formatting: Lola Malone

AUTHOR'S NOTE

Welcome to Saint-Laurent Boarding College for boys.

Welcome to the world of the privileged, of the wicked, of those who love power and won't back down until they have exactly what it is they wanted in the first place.

Thank you for picking up this book. Before you proceed, I would like to state that this is **not a standard romance**. This story is raw and has a decent number of unlikeable characters who have been portrayed to add character to the golden cage that is Monterrey Castle. Or perhaps it is a silver one, designed to keep Régis in place?

These boys are treacherous, forged by money and promises, burned pasts and fear. But no matter what, time will tick by and they are the only ones who can determine their future. Their destiny.

The brotherhood that is housed in Monterrey Castle is dangerous and nasty, reeking of power because they operate in a group. Their behaviour might shock, but their real influence, the one that we only touch lightly, reaches disturbingly far. Like in real life. The things we are capable of, when given the opportunity... are tragically vast.

TRIGGER WARNINGS

Crown of Steel is strictly a work of fiction that includes darker elements. During this story, one of the main characters struggles mentally with the abuse from a parent, and with the loss of another parent. He has severe mental scars from these years and his grieving process, as well as those moments that we see him taking shelter and hiding, may be hard for some readers.

Trigger warnings include, but are not limited to: dub con, use of alcohol, masks, hooded men, bondage, abuse by a parent, loss of another parent (not through death), explicit scenes with multiple members of the brotherhood, prostitution, sharing sexual partners (main characters are not involved), mental health.

Please proceed with caution. If you need any clarification or have any questions, do not hesitate to contact me at lolamalonewrites@gmail.com

Bienvenue

You, our brother, who carries his heritage with dignity and pride, who walks this world with his head high, searching—not quite finding—to belong. And belong you shall, brother, because today is the day that your life will change.

You are invited to become part of the inevitable, the circle of gold that will keep your spine straight and your dignity intact. To melt into a group of people who are like you, brother, who were once searching but who found—found—what life really means.

Loyalty.
Respect.
Tradition.
Sacrifice.

And tonight your Initiations shall begin.

"And now here is my secret, a very simple secret; it is only with the heart that one can see rightly, what is essential is invisible to the eye."
Antoine de Saint-Exupéry

This is for you, my three bright flames. You are my everything.

And to Charlotte and Nicole. One my creative outlet, the other one my rock. Your presence has put me up when I felt down and has made me shed tears of joy and sadness at the same time. Thank you for digging with me.

PART I

REJECTION

"Alpha Fraternarii. *Our world. What started as a sacrifice, a way for our ancestors to survive the carnage commoners forced upon us during the French Revolution, has evolved into the devotion of a sacred brotherhood. A second bible. A way of life and a code of law.* Our *code of law. The one we must obey."*

"Obey." *The cloaked figures who formed the brotherhood echoed.*

"And obey we must." Elder Jacques hummed as he led the initiations. The words sounded like a silky, firm command as he strolled through the dim light of the cool, airy space. He too was completely blanketed in a dark cloak and a hood that was draped over his head.

Darkness seeped in through the windows, countless square metres of glass, as if they were captured in a transparent sphere. Only to go up higher, deforming its shape as they reached for the universe. For the obsidian cosmos that was waiting for them at the ceiling, filled with dense air and stars.

In his gloved hand Elder Jacques carried a wooden cane, one he pounded into the ground as he suddenly came to a halt. He tipped up his head, only to reveal a golden mask that lit up in the flickering of the fire. "We obey. Even when we feel that this path, is not the path we would have taken. Because we are brothers of Alpha Fraternarii." He spun around, surprisingly fast, and lifted up his arms, the cane pointing toward the sky. The three hooded figures that were lined up right in front of the Elder watched along with those who stood behind them and formed a broken circle, had their heads tipped behind their colorful masks. They too looked at the stars, at the bats that flapped around, their squeaks forming an ominous backing track to the soft piano playing from the corner of the Atrium.

"We are loyal. Are we not, brothers?"

"Loyal," *they boomed. And then they all held their breath as they gawked at the cane that landed right between two of the hooded figures that stood right across from the Elder, the curve of the wooden ending teasing between their two shoulders. Mocking. Choosing, without picking.*

"We have respect, right?" Elder Jacques murmured. No one replied.

Instead, the place turned eerily frigid from their silence, the soft melody of Chopin being the only sound left as the pianist held his tune.

Silence before the storm.

"There is no more respect," the Elder mumbled, his tone a strange combination of remorse and agitation.

A harsh creaking sound of the door, then someone entered the room, the faint rustle of a cloak the only indication of his languid approach.

"Monsieur Z." The Elder didn't look up, his stare locked on the cane.

"Elder Jacques." The man's voice was barely more than a high-pitched scratch. "Thank you for the invitation."

"Bien sûr." Finally the Elder turned his masked face to tip his chin at the newcomer, his dark, glimmering eyes void of any emotions. And yet... His gaze swept across the room and toward the far corner to where the pianist was still playing. Dark lace blinded the musician's eyes, but it didn't stop his fingers from flying over the instrument, his body swaying slightly to the music.

"He's mine." One of the hooded brothers right in front of him took a menacing step forward, blocking the Elder's way. His voice was nothing but a smooth rumble, but it was enough for the musician to miss a note and for the hint of a gasp to echo through the room.

The Elder stared at him. "Then who." Not a question, but a command. He resumed whipping the cane from one shoulder to the other. "For the Alpha Fraternarii is nothing if we can't follow our traditions. For centuries, our brothers initiated, funded and directed the largest corporations in this country. We successfully implemented a governmental system that keeps the commoners happy, or happy enough—" A handful of cloaked figures in the outer circle muffled a snicker at that insinuation, making the Elder's lip twitch faintly. "But we have always leaned heavily on our rules. If we want to pull the strings and keep everyone in check out there, *we need to make sure that in* here, *new brothers are initiated according to our rules to obey. It's for our best interest. Now—" He increased pressure, and the cane left a soft thump on each shoulder it touched. Eenie meenie miney mo... "Which one of you will it be?"*

Nothing. No one dared move in the Atrium. This situation had never occurred. Never before had the most powerful family in the brotherhood been challenged. Until now. Because this matter and the entire reason for tonight's gathering, was all about that family.

There was another screeching sound of a bat just outside, then some more rustle of garments. And then one of the brothers took a step forward, head dipped under the heavy weight of the cloak. His intentions were clear, but before those words could leave his lips, he was grabbed by the shoulder and pulled back by the other figure. "I'll go instead."

"Non."

"Si."

Under their disguise, these two men shared a striking resemblance, their hearts and minds intertwined. Out there, they had each other's back. But right now, in here, they were about to be punished for something that hadn't even happened yet.

The ways of the Alpha Fraternarii were extraordinary.

"Well, well, well," the Elder crooned, and with a loud thud the cane rested on the man's shoulder. "Aren't you a lucky one. You two—" He jutted his chin toward the two remaining figures. "Go and join your brothers." After one final hesitation, the two brothers retreated and restored the outer circle of bodies, leaving the third one on his own.

The Elder used the head of his cane, a golden crow, to push the man slowly backward and propel him onto a chair that was decorated with the same, indistinguishable lilies as the ones hanging around in the Atrium. The very ones that curled around the many windows.

"I need you to listen carefully, brothers," he soothed, then crooked his finger to yet another cloaked figure, the one know as Monsieur Z. At the gesture, the man languidly came forward. "Alpha Fraternarii received a most unusual request by one of our founding families. We have been asked to allow a new member into our brotherhood. Someone they have only recently welcomed into their family, and who

needs to be guided onto the right path." Monsieur Z slowly approached the chair, head ducked and chest heaving.

"This pupil will receive an invitation shortly. An invitation to join our initiations and become a brother," Elder Jacques continued.

Monsieur Z stopped right in front of the seated figure who looked more like a golden apparition in the shimmer of moonlight.

"This pupil might be a deviation," Elder Jacques boomed, "Because he was born with the blood of a commoner. But he has been taken on by one of our most valuable families! So we shall treat him with honor."

He unabashedly used the golden crow of his cane to dip in between the sides of Monsieur Z's cloak, unveiling a thick, hard cock. Wet, the veins a little swollen, quivering and tense, just as his owner.

"Mon frère." The Elder whispered. It was all he needed for the brother on the flower chair to shuffle forward and open his mouth. Two hands brushed the black, silky garment that covered his hair as the man put his lips around the eager cock. "You give yourself so beautifully, succumb so gracefully. Power and sex. Sex is power in the Alpha Fraternarii."

"Putain," Monsieur Z gasped, fisting the glossy material, and a nerve ticked in his jaw.

They all stood there in silence. Even the piano had stopped playing, the musician staring across from them into the void of lace with a rigid spine.

"Because we can be kind," The Elder continued.

Monsieur Z grunted, his eyes turned into slits while he watched the bobbing mouth as if in a trance. He was already close.

"We can be gentle, if needed. So I want all of you to be good to your new brother." A cruel smile tipped up the corners of his mouth. "He will embrace his glorious fate soon enough. We will help him adjust and show him home. In the name of loyalty—"

"Loyalty."

Monsieur Z let out an unhinged groan while his body started convulsing,

"Sacrifice." *They boomed, watching the throat of the volunteer work as he drank him down.* "Respect. Traditions."

Their chant sounded as if their voices were hypnotized, their tones a concert of a monotonous mantra, repeating itself again and again. And all the while the Elder hissed, and cackled, then boomed—

"The future! You are the future! Built from the past, ruling tomorrow's world. Because we rewrite the future. You are a blessing, my brothers. And blessed you shall be."

1

RÉGIS

Before

Torment. Its tentacles slither along the length of my body, clutching at my expensive, shimmering, filthy black suit, wrapping itself tightly around my skin. It's suffocating and nauseating, but it does its job of pulling taut around the scarred parts of my entrails. This torment is the keeper of my over-sensitized mind and the part of me I keep safe—*safe*—from the prying eyes of this godforsaken world.

My shame.

My hurt.

And I won't share.

Today we celebrate my mother and Jean-Luc Deveraux's wedding outside on the large patch of grass that's outstretched behind the castle. Sitting warm and fuzzy under the luxurious heaters, I take in the sight before me.

Monterrey Castle.

One of the most prestigious castles in the South West of

France, originally built in the 16th century, with its typical impressive towers and large gardens. We are surrounded by a forest—huge, imposing oak trees and thick, endless shrubs—as if we need to be protected from the rest of the world.

Or perhaps it is *they* who need to be protected from *us*.

The thought brings a chuckle to my lips, its sound turning a little strained when I catch sight of an annoyed flick of onyx eyes. It's one of the twins.

Gulping down the last of my good mood, I clear my throat and give Arthur Deveraux a slight nod. For a moment, his gaze lingers, heavy and unblinking, on mine. It's not the first time he's watched me like this, with that silent accusation palpable in his onyx glare.

My stomach tightens with something potent. Then, right when I want to look away, he curls his lips—a smirk or a sneer or a combination of the two, I can't tell. He leans into his twin, and with his eyes still locked on mine, whispers something in Louis's ear.

Everything, from their thick, dark hair to their tall, well-built bodies covered in expensive, exquisitely fitted clothes, scream perfection.

Scream: "I am rich, you are not."

Scream: "I am better than you are."

Scream: "You don't belong."

They have a point. I mean, until four days ago, I lived in the 30, one of the biggest *cités* of Nîmes. Until four days ago, I didn't want to move out of the pigsty Dad and I lived in. It didn't matter that I owed my tormented mind to the place I called home. Didn't matter that *home* had turned me into a slave of fear. Of agony. Like a virus seizing my muscles, freezing my heart. *Home* is my penance. My shame and my hurt are mine, and mine alone, to bear. I won't let anyone see these hidden parts of me.

Not my dad, the source of so much destruction. Oh, how I hate and love him in equal measure.

Not my mother, who claims that leaving me was her biggest regret in life.

And certainly not the Deveraux twins, *my new stepbrothers.*

Arthur's still looking at me, his charcoal eyes unyielding. Silently challenging me to unravel, to do something stupid.

"It's now time for the vows."

The words yank me out of my reverie and back toward the scene currently dominated by my mother and her husband-to-be, one of the wealthiest men in the country. The way they smile at each other, with pure adoration—*it's nauseating.*

My stomach churns. My anger, currently repressed, but dangerously close to the surface, sits heavily on my chest.

Thirteen years I lived without her. Thirteen years I lived in that fucking pigsty with Dad until she decided she wanted to be a mother, after all. My chest tightens thinking about the day she showed up like some Princess Charming to get me away from Dad and save me from the poverty she'd abandoned me in when I was just a fucking kid.

Thirteen fucking years too late.

My future is already carved out in stone, waiting for me at the doorstep. I have no interest in altering that future. Not anymore. I'll be eighteen soon and the plan had been to leave my past behind. Walk away from it all and build a new life somewhere far away.

But the weight of guilt is heavy in the pit of my stomach today. Because of Dad.

When the judge decided four days ago that it was in my best interest to go home with my mother, I should have said no. *No!* But I couldn't, my throat sealed with invisible glue. Because somewhere deep inside of me, I was relieved. It scared the shit out of me, but it was true. Even after thirteen years I couldn't escape the flicker of joy that she hadn't forgotten me.

After all these years of wondering, I now knew. I used to wonder if she would recognize me if she ever saw me again. After all, I'm no longer the toddler she left behind. Now that she's here, the shame of knowing that what she got, instead, was a pathetic, older version of that sweet little boy is a bitter pill to swallow.

My eyes shift to the twins. Why would she want me when she can have the twins? They're more suited to her: Sophisticated. Educated. Rich.

Me, I'm quite the opposite. Some days I'm too scared to walk into the the light, other days I'm afraid of that same darkness and the punishment that lurks there.

Over the past few days I've locked myself up in my new bedroom, staring at the bare walls, longing for my iron bars. For *home.*

It's ludicrous, I know that. But it's easier to look back to the comforting burn than look ahead of the unreliable sting.

"I finally got you out of here, chéri. Finally got you back with maman. You're safe now."

She's wrong.

I don't belong here. This suit feels too stiff, my curls a slick, itchy mess.

I don't belong here. It's hot and crowded and I don't know these people around me.

I don't—

Something inside me snaps.

"I don't want to be here." A breeze of whispered words, their implication stifling. No one has asked me what *I* wanted.

So what do you want?

I want to get out of here.

The material of my suit is surprisingly compliant as it stretches around my muscles. Because I run. The wooden folding chair, decorated with red flowers, lands with a muffled thud into the grass when I take off. I ignore the gasps around me as I rush down the aisle, but then—

Someone is *laughing*. A raspy chuckle that thunders through my ears. The sound of disapproval. The sound makes me run even faster in my attempt to get the fuck out of here.

I should never have let them take me. Damn them, I just want to go home.

But there is no more home.

It was destroyed right in front of my eyes. My dad taken to court, and then to jail.

Justice will *serve.*

Those were the words the judge used. What justice? Serve who? I didn't ask for this.

Two pairs of broad shoulders and thick arms are waiting for me at the end of the aisle, smoothed in that identical shiny garment that's wrapped around my own limbs. Mom's bodyguards, butlers, or whatever you want to call those people who keep the peace. They advance, blocking the exit.

"*Chéri, chéri?*" My mother's panicked voice crackles through the microphone while I wrestle with the men trying to keep me from leaving. "Why don't you go home with Amadou and Didier and get ready for the party?"

I don't want to be at a fucking party. I don't want to be here at all.

"Behave, please," the bigger of the two men pleads. Amadou. He's their usual watchdog—big, bulky and bold. He places a firm hand on my nape and squeezes, and it's just enough to get me out of my stupor. "Don't give them a show." I'm surprised by the compassion in his tone.

Behind us people applaud, the sound muffled in my head as I grunt and struggle in his hold. "I know," Amadou murmurs while tightening his grip on my wrists, before pulling them tight in the curve of my shoulder blades. My grunt becomes a wheezing protest, legs bucking when my feet are forced to pick up their walking pace and head for the big SUV parked around the corner of the castle. Our crunching steps onto gravel create a screeching sound in my mind.

I don't want to—

"Get in the car," the other guy, Didier, orders. He reminds me a bit of Dad with those eyes in a permanent scowl and that deep furrow on his forehead. "Please."

I step inside and let him give me another shove until I'm right where they want me—in the back of the car like some caged animal.

"Now, put your seatbelt on before I put the child lock in place," Didier grunts when he plants his ass on the driver's seat. His eyes land on mine through the rear mirror, as if secretly challenging me to disobey. Pursing my lips, I swallow my snark down. I won't give him the satisfaction. Besides, I have been trapped my entire life, pushed around like some spineless fuck. Up, down, left, right, black, white, Mom, Dad. I won't show him how his little power trip has me intimidated.

Didier's stern look somehow transforms into tired wrinkles — like Dad's—as it collides with mine, making my chest tighten. *Let me out!* I want to yell. But the words dry up in my brain, overtaken by the viscous swell of fear.

Dipping my head, I eye the fakery that is my expensive suit. The shiny jacket feels too tight around my rigid shoulders suddenly. I wriggle out of it because I need to just fucking breathe.

Agony. *Home* is my penance. My head spins with the memories.

He can't hurt you anymore.

But the words don't give me any sense of comfort.

Amadou does, for some inexplicable reason. When he sits down on the passenger seat, speaking to someone on the phone, I relax a little. There's something about this big guy that sets me at ease.

His muffled voice parrots short words of agreement. Responding to commands. Like the rest of us, he too must blindly obey the director of this play—the Deveraux family.

The subjugation keeps my fury alive. I make sure I never lose sight of the total domination exerted by the Deveraux's because without my anger, there's nothing left of me. Then I might as well rot away in the deepest corners of my mind, or in fucking Castle Monterrey.

The car slowly hobbles over the gravel toward the exit at the end of the long driveway, turning its back to the castle. We've barely taken off when the car suddenly stops on a squeaky brake, sand evaporating around us like sprinkles of fine dust.

Didier softly swears, but before I understand what's going on, both back doors are opened simultaneously. My eyes flutter but I keep my gaze straight ahead. I don't move, despite the sickening sensation of something crawling up my spine and tickling my skin with unease.

"Little rebel Régis," one of the Deveraux twins drawls as they both get in and take a seat on either side of me.

To the untrained eye they look the same. But I can tell the difference. I can *feel* the difference. I tilt my head to the side to watch Louis pull out a bottle of drink from his jacket. "A gift from the lovely girl at the bar." He gives me a wink, then shoots out the cap with a loud pop, followed by a fizzing sound. He puts the bottle to his lips before any liquid can shoot out, and takes a drink.

"Hmm, very good."

Amadou watches us from over his shoulder with a scrutinizing scowl in his black eyes.

Wiping off his mouth with hand, Louis throws Amadou a kiss. "What? It's a party, right?"

"Mister Régis is too young to drink," Amadou clips, but no one stops Louis from handing me the bottle.

"You think I won't take care of my little brother? Especially since we've only just met?" He gives me a cheeky grin—I'm not sure if he's teasing or if he really cares—then murmurs, "I can't believe they kept you a secret for so long."

Amadou's gaze lingers on mine for a second longer, as if silently asking me what I want.

What *do* I want? I want to go home. Home to the 30, to our cramped two-bedroom flat, to my small bedroom with that single bed and the wrinkled sheets. Home to shattered glass and slurred shouts. Because that is where I belong. It's what I know. Rather the devil you know that the one you don't.

I push away that sudden feeling of homesickness, shoving it down to where it belongs, hidden deep inside my heart.

Then I put the bottle onto my lips and take a careful swig. I'm not used to alcohol, but they don't have to know. It's acidic, bubbly, and horrible.

"Yeah," Louis rasps, his eyes still glittering with mischief, "little s-brother likes the cheap stuff."

"Tss," Arthur mocks from the other side of me, his husky tone laced with amusement. His body heat seeps into my core, warming the cool stiffness it finds there.

Louis is right, but I won't give them that. I only know the cheap stuff—I could never buy anything unless it's on sale and even then, I'd bargain for an even lower price. Grade A cheapskate.

I'm so lost in my own thoughts that the soft brush on my thigh has my limbs jerking before they pull taut as a string. It's swift, but warm, private and very, very out of place.

"You know what I think, bro?" Louis chuckles breathily from my other side. "Cheap or not, I think our little stepbrother here knows all about throwing a party. Ain't that right?" He shuffles next to me, and I can feel his dark stare burning into my side. I have no clue how to party, and I'm not entirely sure what he's getting at. But I can pretend. After all, it's what I've done since forever—a mask glued to my face. It's fucking exhausting but it's better than showing everyone my pathetic self.

I let my mask slip the first time I met the twins. I won't make that mistake again.

While Louis and Arthur look alike from the outside, their energy is completely different. It's too early to define the difference, but it definitely has to do with the wicked flare in Arthur's onyx eyes. There's something primal there that I have never seen in another person, even though it's neatly braided around his cool, adept attitude.

And though I don't know the twins well yet, I can sense danger from a distance. Arthur is the Deverauxs golden boy, their empire's future.

I own this world is written all over his face; his behaviour cocky and pretentious.

And yet…

The look Arthur had fired my way that very first time we met had stopped my heart. When I took in those wide, horizontal eyes, framed by thick lashes; that long, straight nose trailing down to his lush, full lips. Raven strands that were slickly smoothed back, revealing his oval face, the forehead prominently visible. . . I must have gaped at him like a fool. Right from that very first moment, hairline cracks began to form along my steel mask.

Even now, with both twins sitting next to me, I prefer focusing on Louis. Despite his rascality he still feels safer than Arthur.

Louis taps my shoulder. "You know how to party, right, Régis?" he repeats.

"S-sure," I stammer, my anger now officially replaced by something else. Something that confuses the hell out of me. Because between the soft, yet persistent brush of Arthur's fingers against my thigh and Louis egging me on, I'm not sure which one of these twins I should be more afraid of. Louis lets out a cackle, the sound making my lips tremble as if they're not sure if they want to shape to a cry or a sob.

"Oh, you're a funny one," he muses.

"I mean, I can party," I try a little firmer, only for him to tilt his head back as he lets out another bark.

"Yeah?" He challenges when he finally has his gaze back onto me. He juts his chin toward the bottle I'm still holding. "Go on then, show us how. You're part of the family now, and your big brothers sure love a good party."

The car leaves castle territory and turns onto the wooden path through the forest. In the front, Didier and Amadou are softly speaking to each other. And in the back…shit, this is happening. I'm stuck here, with my very new, very devious stepbrothers.

"O-okay." I take another swig. Louis lets out an appreciative whistle. See? I can be cool.

The idea of being cool evaporates with a whoosh like Genie in Aladdin's bottle. Arthur's fingertips touch my thigh again, sending my heart into a frenzied race.

My breath catches. People don't…people don't touch me that way.

"I think you might be right," Arthur mumbles. Those words, spoken in that sooty tone, shoos my way, landing somewhere between my temple and my ear, making me shiver with a forbidden rush of turmoil.

I bite my lip as my nerves zero in on those light brushes of his finger. I shouldn't want this. I *don't* –

A puff of air escapes my mouth. I'm so fucking confused. It's like my body is starving for—for what? Arthur's touch? Arousal ignites in the pit of my stomach, blood pumping faster, my body lapping up those heated flicks of his digits. The realization is an electric shock sizzling through my body.

I chug down another shuddering swig of the drink. The

burn sets my throat on fire, its reminder cooling down my body's response to Arthur.

"Drink, boy, show me you're a man after all."

Dad... I miss you. I'm so scared of these people. I don't trust them. Not even my mother. I want to go back home. Let me go back home. I promise I won't try to stop you if you hurt me. Scream at me, punish me. I don't care. Just... let me go back home.

"Pierre Amadou's mother told Dad that they are going to nominate this guy Pascal for the *Prix d'Honneur* as well," Arthur says, his husky sound thick with disdain. His fingers still on my thigh.

"Yeah, so I heard," Louis replies. "He's going to be tough competition."

Arthur's fingers add a hint of pressure on my upper thigh, the only sign that this *Prix d'Honneur,* the most prestigious prize Saint-Laurent yearly hands out to its best performing student, matters to him. "Well, it'll be one I enjoy accepting." The aloofness in his voice is a contradiction to the touch.

Louis snorts, his eyes on his vibrating phone. "Always so humble, brother. Well, I'll come and watch you take that prick down. He's a weird motherfucker."

Arthur sniggers raspily. "That he is." Fingertips brush further up, crawl under my jacket as they make their way toward the insides of my leg, leaving a gentle trace of tingles. When he leans in, his strands touching my temple, I can't help but shiver. He has never been this close before, and I find myself squeezing the bottle in a death grip as I wait for his next move. His mouth smooths over my hair close to my ear.

"I've seen the way you look at me..." His voice is soft as silk, keeping everyone out of our conversation. "Is this what you want me to do, little stepbrother? Does this make you feel hot?" His words are sharp as a razor, and they make my insides shudder. The bottle in my hand trembles when I put it against my lips again. Ignoring the mocking chuckles and encouragement from Louis, I drink. The taste is sharp on my tongue and even more bitter in my throat, but I can't stop.

"Oh, yes it does make you hot." Arthur's chuckles are velvety while his fingers creep over the bulge in my pants, making my body jerk at the touch. No one has ever touched me there, no one apart from my own hand. And he—what's he doing? I place my fist over my jacket and on my lap, in an attempt to make him stop.

He doesn't.

Instead, his fingers pop the button of my dress pants, and before I realize what is going on, Arthur is unzipping my fly. I whip my head to the side and our eyes meet. His are dark, a little hooded as he watches me intently.

When his tongue peeks out to lick his lips, my gaze drops to catch the movement. Somewhere in the back of my mind I can hear Louis chuckle at something on his phone, and in the front the two bodyguards are quietly talking between themselves, purposefully ignoring what's going on here.

I can't help myself. I have never allowed myself to look at *anyone* that way before, but now that he's got my attention, I can't seem to undo this electric tension crackling between us. A wolfish grin tilts his mouth.

Stop. I want to tell him.

Louis's phone vibrates again. "The ceremony has finished. Why don't you start the party, we'll shortly be there. Dad." Louis reads.

Arthur releases a low chuckle, sending chills down my spine. "Seems that our little Régis here has already begun," he murmurs. I watch in fascination how his mouth moves.

And then his hand dives into my boxers and he grabs hold of my dick. I'm hard, I realize with a flush of embarrassment. My hand squeezes the jacket while I swivel my head back and stare straight ahead. I can't—but he—I can feel his eyes on my face, leaving a scorching trace of pure, shameful desire. This is my *stepbrother*.

And he strokes me leisurely, secretly, under the jacket on my lap. I reach for the bottle, but Louis snatches it out of my hand. "Uh uh, don't want to get you all wasted at the party, *little bro*." He takes a swig and sends me a filthy wink. "I hope Marie's going to be there too. Please tell me that Marie will be there too."

"Marie will be there too," Arthur deadpans, his hand keeping a steady stroke. It's too slow for me to climax, I think, but it's enough to make me slowly lose my senses. I clench my jaw forcefully in an attempt to keep any gasps from tumbling out of my mouth. I won't give him that. Won't give him anything.

But my hips buck when his fingers graze my balls.

Oh God.

He rolls them in between his palm and my own nails now dig into the flesh of my palms, my fingers clammy and aching from the tight fist they are scrunched in for too long.

His fingers skit up over my shaft to where they form a tight ring for my leaking tip.

"Yes!" Louis cheers next to me, his eyes still glued on his phone. "You were right bro, she's coming."

"You sound a little desperate," Arthur murmurs, his words only meant for me. The raspy sound trickles through my ears and spiral right through to my cock.

Oh God oh God.

"I—" I heave, then clamp my jaw shut. But my hips…I can't make them stop as they grind into Arthur's fist, now serving as a perfectly shaped fucktoy.

"I can check what time Mademoiselle Dujardin arrives, sir?" Amadou asks.

Oh God oh God oh God.

"I think any minute now," Arthur whispers. "If I don't stop." It's so soft, I'm sure no one else heard. And then he removes his hand, leaving me shaking and out of breath, my body balking in confusion. I let out a startled moan and bend forward, desperate to compose myself from the unrelenting high Arthur has left me in and keep the frustration of being prevented from climaxing at bay. I need to safeguard myself from this brutal attack on my carefully built defenses. No one gets this close to me. No one gets to crawl right into my skin like this. How has Arthur managed to breach my defenses? How could I have allowed it to happen so easily?

I wanted it.

The thought has my face and chest heating with embarrassment.

My shame.

My hurt.

And I won't share.

Louis barks out a sarcastic chuckle. "Wait, does he need to puke?"

"No, he's just fine, aren't you, little Régis?" Arthur wipes off his fingers on my jacket, then pats my shoulder as he leans in. "Welcome to the family, *stepbro*."

2

RÉGIS

Present

Saint-Laurent Boarding College for boys.

Adieu to all those years that together form my past. I've held onto them so tightly, dug my claws into the crumbling stones that once forged the walls of my life.

I didn't want them to let go.

Turning over my shoulder, I eye the large gravel driveway that stretches all the way up to the iron bars that form the large gate of Monterrey Castle. Once I'll pass those gates, my past will be left behind, and the present will be mine to design.

When Jean-Luc, my mother's husband, offered to pay my tuition fees for one of the most privileged boarding colleges in Europe, I knew it was a chance in a lifetime.

I bite my bottom lip while my mind replays that memory.

"I love your mother and we both want what's best for you."

"Please, call me Dad from now on. I'll try and be a good father to you."

"If it's up to me, that monster will never leave prison."

"Graduate in four years time and change your own life."

I—I wanted to reject...but I couldn't resist.

More and more cars now line along the drive, limos and SUVs, as they make their way to the main entrance to drop off students for the beginning of the school year.

Groups of students start dotting around, laughing and chatting as they reunite after summer break. They are second, third and fourth year students, already formally dressed in their school uniform of navy-blue pants and jacket, a cream-colored shirt and dark-brown shoes.

First year students had their introduction last week, but I didn't go, I was still too busy visiting childhood memories. Thankfully Jean-Luc informed the college of my absence during the first week.

Ever since my mother burned my past and brought me into the large villa she lives in with the Deveraux family, I managed to stay out of their claws as much as possible.

They are loud and confident. Beautiful and privileged. And they make me feel everything I'm not, everything I'll never be. It makes me want to hate them. Because they make me want something that's simply out of reach.

Those first months were easy, because my *lycée* was in Nîmes and they thought it would be better for my mental state that I finished my Baccalaureat there. If that meant leaving early in the morning and coming home as late as possible? Yeah, I had no issue with that. Besides, the Deveraux mansions by the beach —multiple houses, yes, because of course they have multiple houses that are occupied by the entire family of aunts and uncles and even a grandma—are big enough to avoid each other. And I have become a master at that.

A faint smirk touches my lips. I like that self-proclaimed title. I like—

"Master of Evasion," I mutter, tasting the words on my tongue

that suddenly feels dry and too big for my mouth, when I recognize the bright red SUV.

The twins.

My stomach churns at the thought. I have only seen Arthur a handful of times after that glorious stunt he pulled last year. He never once mentioned it again, how he touched my weeping cock and almost tipped me over the edge, tearing through my dignity and vulnerability. But every time we saw each other, which was mostly here, at college, he has been nothing but provocative.

A destructive, cocky, sexy nightmare.

"Master of Evasion," I mumble again, needing strength. But the title has already lost its punch, dread filling the pit of my stomach.

The first weeks of summer break I stayed out of everyone's way, with the massive gardens of the Deveraux mansions giving me shelter. It was beautiful, a labyrinth of plants, shrubs, trees and flowers. So many of them. Most of my days I spent hidden between the greenery, reading, reveling in silence. But when the tension in the house filled with anticipation of the twin's homecoming, I knew I needed to be far gone. Granted, both brothers spent a fair amount of those two months away, doing god knows what, but still... I couldn't be there.

Arthur makes me feel... haunted. He has an uncanny way of finding me wherever I hide. That trepidation suffocates me right now, knowing that he's so close to me after too many sleepless nights, just like during the summer. It created a foreign storm of homesickness that raged deep inside me like some twisted inferno.

I had to get out of there.

Needed to fucking *breathe*.

This world I'd been thrust into had become claustrophobic. Too much too quickly. Too overwhelming. I needed the familiarity of home. In some sick way, my need to be surrounded by the only life I had known, made me wish I could see Dad again.

So before the twins arrived home, I fled the property without a note, took the earliest train and just *left.*

They changed the locks of our old house, you know? When I tried my key for the third time, some fat guy looked through the kitchen window with a pan in his hand. Told me to get lost.

I did. With a mixture of shame and sadness.

What was even worse was finding Amadou in the parking lot waiting on me in one of the family's SUVs. I didn't want to get in, I swear, but I suddenly felt so fucking tired.

So. Fucking. Tired.

This is how Amadou and I ended up spending the past few weeks together while he silently took me to all the places I wanted to visit.

My old school.

My grandparent's grave.

My dad in prison.

Now, my breath comes out in a hesitant shudder as my chest clenches at the memory. I have called Dad every other day since he has been in there. Sometimes he won't talk to me, or sometimes he blames me for him being there. And maybe he's right. But no matter how many times I flick through my recollection, I can't recall the moment that I asked my mother to come back into our life over the past five years. Can't recall the moment she came barging back into our life to claim me back.

I grimace at the thought. I may not have grown up with money, and *their* money might have brought me to this college, but I'll show them all. It's the only reason why I accepted Jean-Luc's expensive gift, apart from my hunger for knowledge. I'll be better than they could ever have anticipated. I'll be the best fucking student here in rich-kid college. They'll never see it coming.

The doors of the red SUV open and I find myself staring

with unblinking eyes at the one stepbrother who now climbs out of the car. The one stepbrother who has my emotions scattered all over the place.

Of course he'd be here, what were you thinking? I'm a fool to think that I could escape from him.

As if he can hear my blurry thoughts from afar, Arthur tilts his gaze my way, onyx eyes burning into mine—unapologetic and intense. A flash of annoyance crosses his face, before he tips up his chin and curls his lips into a cruel smirk.

I scoff, then grab hold of the suitcase between my legs and jog toward the glass door entrance, ignoring the way my treacherous heart is hammering violently in my chest.

Two seconds was enough to conclude that he looks spectacular. I bet the sun warmed his skin just in the right places, gently emphasizing that tanned texture on his flesh. His hair is a slick, raven mop, the strands far shorter than my messy, wavy hair. I should have gone to the hairdresser.

"Hello there, how are you?" Some guy grins at me, holding a notebook and a pen, the first two buttons of the shirt of his school uniform open, revealing a strip of pale skin. "I don't think we've met before, I'm Pierre. Are you new here? If you are a first year student, I'm sorry to inform you that your introduction started last week."

"No, I'm not. Sorry, I mean," I correct, offering a small smile through my frigid expression. Even without looking, I just know it will come out as a grimace. I'm so bad at this. "Yes, I'm a first year student, but couldn't make it during the introductions last week. I wanted to get here just before the program started. Anyway..." Biting my lip, I wring my hands nervously. Stupid stammering. Gives it all away. Pierre shoots me a funny look, but doesn't say anything. I nod toward the papers he's holding. "Is that the list of names assigned to the dorms? I should be there. The name is Deveraux."

"Excuse me?" He looks up with wide eyes, appearing genuinely baffled.

"Deveraux," I repeat. Then both Pierre and I turn to the door. Of fucking course. As if they waited for that fucking moment to make their grand entrance, the twins walk through the glass doors in a haze of excitement that's picked up by everyone who follows them, hot on their tail. People are chatting around them, begging for their attention with smiles and jokes. I whip my gaze back to Pierre, clutching my backpack a little tighter over my shoulder.

"Listen, can we make this quick? I am looking for a single dorm. Can you check and give me the right key?"

The guy Pierre stares from me back to his notebook. "The Deverauxs all stay together in a shared dorm," he mutters sheepishly.

"Yeah, so I've heard. But I don't want that, *d'accord*? So I need you to change that for me, like, now. *Now.*" The twins have nearly reached us. Pierre's eyes dart from me to the list, to someone who's now creeped up behind me. Someone who's hot breath hits my nape. I groan.

"I'm afraid, I mean, I don't know—" He stammers.

"Pierre, how are you, pretty boy?" Louis quips from behind me. I don't hesitate, instead grab my suitcase and fling my backpack over my shoulder, then walk straight on and into the corridor, absolutely not knowing where I'm heading. I don't care. Anywhere away from there will do for now. Fuck Louis. I'll wait for them to get their key first, then I'll talk to Pierre again. Surely this huge castle has single rooms. I nearly grin at the thought, forcing myself to see the irony of the situation. It works, because I start to calm down. Unclenching my fists, I take a deep breath. Yeah, no biggie. I'll just…

"Régis? *Salut*, how are you?"

"Jesus," I yelp, body jerking from the sudden voice. I take in a deep breath of air, then slowly make my way around, letting my poker face effortlessly slide back into place—a boring scowl I have mastered over the past months. But Dominique, Gaël's boyfriend, somehow has a way of looking right through my facade. Not that he'd say anything of it, he would never. He's too timid to do so, or perhaps just too much of a nice guy. The few times I've met him, he has come across as friendly, and I have no clue why he is with Gaël, the twin's cousin. The master of puppets. Talk about a devious character...

Dominique's leaning across from me in the other corner, surrounded by heavy suitcases, his dark hair mussed and an apologetic look in his eyes. The school uniform suits him well, and if I hadn't known he is a scholarship student, I would have thought him to be a rich prick just like the others.

We've met a few times over the past months, here in Monterrey Castle, when my mother wanted me to come over and "get used" to my new surroundings. A hot flash zaps through my insides, feral and unwanted.

I toss both thoughts mercilessly into the emotional bin in my brain and grab tighter hold of the strings of my backpack. Now's not the time.

"It's room twelve, by the way," he says.

"Come again?" I ask. Dominique gives me another reluctant smile, then holds up a dangling key. "The dorm we share. In case you were wondering?" His face flushes and he nibbles on his bottom lip as he looks away. When his gaze finally flits up, I shake my head, needing to clarify this misunderstanding.

"Oh yeah, no. No, no. Thanks for letting me know, but I'm not sharing a dorm with you guys. It's nothing personal, but I just need my privacy, you know? My peace and quiet."

Dominique frowns, looking genuinely surprised. "Is it the piano? I can move it out and play in the designated rehearsal rooms..."

"Absolutely not. It's just that I have no intention of—"

“Ah, there you are!” Someone calls out, and I take a step back as the others approach, my back hitting the wall.

“Well, well, well, if it isn’t our little stepbrother.” Louis’s dark, wide eyes are set on mine, and with a tilt of his head he grabs my chin between his digits. I try to jerk away from his hold, but it only seems to tighten. “We haven’t seen you for ages, dude. When you weren’t at home during the summer, I wasn’t even sure if you were still going to join us this year.” His gaze sears through me, searching in their strike, and I flinch, the gesture making me feel small, and vulnerable. “But it’s good to have you here now, little stepbrother. I say we start the year off with a party.” He sends me a fat wink, taking us both back to that moment in the car on a whim. Licking my lips, I shake his fingers off. This time he lets me.

"Yeah well, I came here to study,” I mutter.

Louis gives me a pout. “Come on man, don’t be like that. We don’t want another Arthur, do we boys?”

Some of the guys snicker, their unfamiliar faces making my stomach dip with nerves. They’re all looking at me, and I’m still with my back against the wall.

Grabbing my suitcase from the floor, I shoulder my way through the crowd, practically bumping into Gaël, who’s the only one not wearing his navy-blue college uniform. The long fur coat is obnoxiously soft when I collide with it, his stare fiercely green with black eyeliner to create cat-shaped eyes he uses to gaze at me over the edge of his tipped-down sunglasses. The color reminds me of my mother’s eyes. The thought has my heart stuttering and it’s making my nerves even more on edge.

His eyes roam over me then move to behind my head where they linger, shimmering brightly. “There you are, beautiful, I thought I’d lost you,” Gaël sings, latching onto Dominique and pulling him in and against his fur. He murmurs something, the words being lost by the soft kiss he plants on his lovers’ lips.

“Come on, guys, let’s go.” Louis pushes himself off the wall and walks back toward the reception hall, not bothering to turn around to check and see if we follow. He doesn't have to either, with Gaël operating as some goose herder, admonishing his flock to follow. As if receiving the unspoken message, their friends all dart off once we're back into the large entrance, leaving us once more together.

When I catch sight of Pierre, I wave at him, determined to fix this misunderstanding here and now.

"This way." Gaël motions to me, his face cracked into a smile that doesn't reach those painted eyes. It's one of those predator smirks I know all too well. But no matter how, they always have the same effect on me. I feel small and insecure, and the need to puff up my chest and defend myself, skyrockets.

"Pierre will get me a single room," I bluff indignantly, forcing myself to keep his stare. The suitcase feels heavy in my palm, and the backpack stings the flesh of my shoulder, but I don't look away.

"Yeah, he told me to let you know that there are no available single rooms," Louis says. He grabs me by my other shoulder and pushes me forward. "Now come, let's go. Leave your suitcase here, little Régis, Amadou and Didier will bring them up. Room twelve, right?"

"Uhm, yeah," Dominique replies, flashing me an apologetic look as he hands over the keys to Gaël.

Ignoring my sputter, Louis simply pushes me forward and toward the large, double spiral staircases. When he also tries to pull the backpack off my shoulder, I grab the strings and squeeze them tight, not ready to let go. Unlike the expensive suitcase carrying equally expensive clothes, the bag was a gift from Dad for my sixteenth birthday. It's mine.

The hand on my shoulder squeezes a little tighter, lightly pushing me forward and onto the stairs. Louis doesn't insist, and with a final crooked smile, he grabs the keys from Gaël and starts climbing the stairs. I stumble at the realization that this is not the same touch as the one from before, the one who's holding me steady. No, this one leaves a mark of heat and tingles.

"If I didn't know any better, I'd say you were hiding from your big brothers," Arthur mumbles right behind my ear, brushing his lips against the tender skin there as he steadies me onto the steps. Goosebumps erupt and I swallow thickly while keeping my stare ahead, more of the straps of my backpack now cramped in my hand. "Don't worry. I'll find you anyway."

His words are followed by the ghost of a chuckle, or perhaps it's my nerves imagining it. Whatever it is, is enough for my defence mechanism to kick in.

"Leave me alone." I snarl over my shoulder. When his hold doesn't loosen, I turn around, only to find Arthur's brow winged up, his mouth twitching as he holds back a smirk.

"Really? You already want to start a scene?"

"No, I—" Shutting my mouth tight, I send him another glare, then turn back, making a show of taking in the elegantly designed halls of the castle instead. Obnoxious fucker. He's right though. Now's not the time to express my disdain. The place is quickly filling with navy-colored uniforms as students make their way through the corridors, casually chatting as they're getting settled in, followed by butlers who try to keep up, carrying trolleys filled with luggage.

Numerous paintings and framed pictures hang on the wall, and shiny sconces that once carried candles, are now equipped with light bulbs. Still, even in its full glory the place still looks pretty grim, or perhaps it's my own reflection that's causing my limbs to feel cold and tense.

I need stones to build my home. Steel to melt the gates. Silence to calm my mind.

But I'm not getting any of that with that provocative grip on my neck. The walk seems to last forever, the hint of that malicious chuckle distorting the silence, until finally, we halt.

"Well, here we are." Louis and Gaël are the first ones to arrive at the large, wooden door that has number twelve engraved in a small, silver insignia. "Our home for the foreseeable future."

Louis turns the key, an intermittent grating sound that rattles through my mind. This shared dorm will be a nightmare, and I have fought tooth and nail. Yanking myself out of Arthur's hold with a grumble, I follow the others inside into what looks like a communal living room. Two leather couches face each other, a glass coffee table standing in between. Stacks of magazines have been placed on two side tables, as if the person designing this space didn't quite know what topics to choose. From what I understood, the place got renovated into an apartment kind of dorm to accommodate all of us. I reluctantly have to admit that they have done a good job—the lounge has all the elements to make it look cosy. Cream-colored carpets with similarly colored walls on which family portraits are hanging. Wardrobes filled with books and kitchenware lead to a kitchen island, stools dotted around. A few lights have already been switched on, giving the place a warm and homey vibe.

It's a trick.

"Nice," Louis hums satisfied, sending me a wink. I scowl in return, grinding my teeth when he just cackles the venom away, and looks at the row of doors instead. The bedrooms. They each have a number on them, as if we won't be able to remember which one will be ours. Although... my stomach flutters with nerves again. There are only three numbers.

Gaël's already standing by the one in the corner that sits right behind the kitchen. He swings open the door, revealing a spacious bedroom with an ensuite bathroom. "So, me and Dominique will sleep here."

Louis wolf-whistles at the sight of the large double bed and flat screen installed against the wall. "That big enough for you two love birds?"

Gaël lets out a huff of amusement, but otherwise, flips his cousin off. Tipping his head to his lover, he points his hand toward the opposite wall. "I was thinking of putting your piano here, *trésor*?"

"Yeah, sure—" But Dominique looks my way, unease thickly scrunched into his dark eyes, and now all three heads turn my way, making me groan inwardly.

"What?" I tilt my chin and force my gaze at Gaël, whose green eyes have become bright slits. "I haven't said anything about the piano."

"He hasn't—" Dominique rushes. "I just thought—" But Gaël places his hand subtly against Dominique's chest, pushing him gently back and toward their bedroom.

"I know this is all new for you Régis—" He clasps his lips shut as if swallowing the rest of that phrase, instead watches me for a full ten seconds with those piercing green eyes. I feel like the tension is rising in the room, and it makes me inwardly squirm.

Punishment.

"Which is why Régis didn't mean anything with it. Drop it, G." Arthur's voice is soft, yet sharp enough to cut glass. No one speaks, as if we're all waiting for something to happen. I can't bear the tension, eyes slumping until they catch sight of my feet. When Gaël chuckles, they shoot up and instantly collide with his. He looks amused, shrugs then tips his head. "I'll see you in a bit for lunch."

And just like that, the door slams shut.

"Right, now let's see what else they've got planned for us." Louis turns on his heel, not bothered by that awkward moment in the slightest, as he simultaneously swings both remaining two doors open. Peeking inside, he throws his duffel back onto the bed in the middle of the room. "Nice." When he turns around, he eyes me with his usual laid-back smug, then waves toward the corner. "There's your room, little s-brother."

"Thank you," I clip, squeezing the strings of my backpack tight as I make my way to my bedroom. Nerves make it hard to breathe, but I definitely feel my shoulders dip when I peek inside. It looks…nice. With the knob safely clutched in my hand, I turn over my shoulder. "Thank you." And then I quickly close the door behind me. Carefully locking it with the key, I need a moment to regain my composure before I turn around and lean my back against the door, sagging into the cool material. And then I let out a deep, desperate sigh.

This year will be hell, I can fucking feel it. They will make sure of that, my two stepbrothers. Closing my eyes, I allow my rattling mind to slow down, screeching and creaking as it slowly comes to a halt. "This too will pass," I mumble to myself. "I've come all this way."

I'll keep my head down and give this my best. I'm good at that. Studying is all I've ever wanted to do, and it's the only reason I accepted Jean-Luc's proposition. I let my eyes fall around my new room. Why does it feel like it's not going to be that easy?

Because nothing ever is.

Right?

"You know I love you."

My eyes fall closed as thoughts of the past take over.

"It's not my fault you're useless."

My hands form fists by my sides and I take in a shallow, ragged breath.

"Useless boy. Get in there."

"Dad…"

The air leaves my mouth in a narrow whoosh and my heart throbs frantically inside my ribcage in an attempt to beat the hurt. The memories. There are too many of them, too many moments lost somewhere in time, like fluttering fragments I wish I could obliterate. And yet I want them to stay. Close around my frame, clutching me from this prevailing sensation of loss.

Because I am lost.

My secret.

When I open my eyes again, I take a closer look at the room. A real look. A single bed with a bedside table, a closet to put my clothes. The tiny fridge I specifically asked for. Seems like my mother was listening after all. Although...when I open it and inspect its contents—a pile of cereal bars and energy drinks—I know who's behind this.

Merci Amadou.

There's also a desk and chair. I make my way toward the wooden furniture where my fingertips seek the smoothness of the material. It's not as serene as steel, but it fits my environment. The window is closed, but the curtains are drawn, revealing the breathtaking forest of Monterrey.

I remember the last time I was in that forest...

Large oak trees fill the horizon with their glorious autumn palette of yellow, with red and some streaks of brown. Not quite the same view we used to have back home, where other apartment blocks painted the sky. France's hidden poverty really isn't that hidden—it can easily be found in the *cités* that frame about every single outskirt of our cities.

But then, what's poverty to an outsider's view, is reality to us. It's our life, our neighbors, our shops and businesses, our crime.

I gingerly place my backpack onto my desk chair, then slowly zip it open to take my new Apple laptop out. It feels too shiny around my palms, too expensive in my calloused fingers.

Mom insisted that I'd be equipped with good study materials. And now I'm here, in Saint-Laurent Boarding College for boys. And Dad is locked up in some pissy prison close to Toulouse.

I place the computer on my desk, together with the book I

took with me when I moved—*Le Petit Prince,* by Antoine de Saint-Exupéry. He has always been my tiny regal friend when I'd sit by myself, protected by steel. I used to read the chapters out loud, overthinking the questions the little prince asks. About life, and people. About choices.

As always, the thought brings a smile to my lips, and I stare out of the window toward the twilight view of the forest, while I let my mind slumber. Only to startle when there's a soft knock on my door.

"Régis?"

My hand flies to my pounding heart, and I need a moment to compose myself. Jesus, get a grip. It's only Dominique, his voice hesitant when he calls out my name again. "It's nearly one in the afternoon. Did you want to have some lunch with me and my friends?"

I'll need to eat. Apart from a *croissant* and a cup of coffee, I haven't had any other food today. The thought invites a rumbling sound through my stomach.

I—I don't want to come out, is my first thought. Not yet. Let me stay here just a little more. But there are no iron bars here, no touch to soothe me from reality, it's just me, and my bedroom, and the *others* out there.

And so there's nothing else to do but to put back on my inscrutable mask and head for the door. I swing it open and give Gaël's boyfriend a forced smile. "With you and your friends?" One sweep through the room proves my thoughts—the others have left. They're probably already in the canteen. "Or you and your friend, your boyfriend and my stepbrothers?" I try to keep my voice void of the sneer I feel, but judging by the way he snorts, I can tell I didn't really succeed.

"I get it, Régis, I do. Which is why I thought you'd appreciate being introduced to some cool guys. My friends. You've already met Maxime when you were here last time, and I'm sure you're going to love Jo. He's a bit of a jock, but that's not his fault." He grins. I don't think he even notices the way he puts the emphasis on the word *my*, as if to make it clear to himself and the world that he still has his own life. I can't blame him. If I'd have such an all-consuming partner, I'd also feel the need to assert my autonomy. "We also play chess and go for hikes during the weekend. Pretty please? Come join us?" He bats his lashes playfully, and laughter bubbles up from my chest.

"Alright then. Thanks for asking me," I add on a practically inaudible mumble then make a show of locking my door with my key. But when we make our way through the narrow corridor and toward the double spiral staircases, Dominique muses, "You're welcome, Régis."

3

RÉGIS

This place is… enormous. Grand, luxurious, mystical… fucking *impressive*. With its endless, narrow corridors wrapped in carpets and framed by mysterious paintings, its faint light and those unique, double spiral staircases that lead us down into the centre of the web that is called Monterrey Castle.

"You coming?" Dominique asks. He's already downstairs where groups of guys are leisurely hanging around, ambling around as they move through the large reception, generating a gentle buzz with the occasional chortle. It's…nice?

Such a treacherous thought. I know by heart which subjects I'm taking, plus the extra ones I've picked, have prepared conversations in my mind in case someone wants to work on a project with me. For months I have done nothing but prepare myself mentally for this change. I prepared for every worst case scenario, convinced myself of how much I'd hate it here. Imagine that.

"Hi, how are you?"

"I'm fine. Sure, I'd love to work with you. Thank you so much for asking me!"

Never once did I consider this place could be fucking *nice*. Where students chatter and share, where they enjoy being. I grind my molars, staving off the pleasantness of the scene before me and digging my heels in about this place. It's not nice. It's weird and fucking creepy. It's a trick.

A *trick*.

"Régis?" Dominique's deep brown eyes look up in their search for mine, filled with a curious glance. *You coming?* They ask.

"*Oui*," I clip, blinking away the sudden chaos in my mind. I replace it with a new wave of determination as I drag my feet down the stairs and force myself to keep my cool. Pursing my lips into a fine line, I bypass Dominique in silence, my head dipped and my pace picking up, already dreading this fucking lunch we're about to have. I should have said no. Should have gone to the canteen myself. My muscles tighten at the thought. Why did I say yes? Why did I—

"It's okay to be nervous," Dominique murmurs from behind me. He's close, his voice soft, filled with a husky edge of understanding. He's too close. "I was too."

Part of me wants to snarl at that, wants to tell him to back off. Yet another part of me imagines reaching out, lacing our fingers together and just breathing. In. Out, and in again.

A yelp, then someone gets in my path on a dash, nearly making me stumble as he bumps my forearm in an attempt to pass me. It's a guy I've met before, with ginger locks, a bright smile and a piercing voice that radiates both innocence and infatuation, and he throws himself at Dominique, who grabs him and holds him flush against his chest.

"Sunshine! It's so, so good to see you." Their spontaneous hug is a sign of affection that has me glue my mask of indifference even tighter around my cheeks, my forehead, nose and mouth. It feels a little cramped, as if the sizing isn't good, as if it can crack with one wrong movement. But it's better than imagining what it would be like to have someone hug me with such warmth.

The guy peeks up at me from Dominique's dark mane. "Hey there Régis. I'm Maxime, Dominique's friend. Remember me?" I do. We met a few months ago when he was worried sick about Dominique. We somehow ended up in the forest with Gaél and the twins and some cloaked guy who had had a love affair with Dominique's brother. Weirdest. Night. Ever. One that no one has ever spoken of again.

I give him a jut of my chin, but Maxime just clicks his tongue in disapproval. That's the only warning I get before he grabs my shoulders and pulls me in. His face, pale with sparkling freckles that seem to spring up as he smiles, is close to mine, his gray eyes wide and innocent as he pulls me close. I stiffen, the hug seeming to last like fucking forever. "So you are the stepbrother," he hums thoughtfully when it's finally over. "How's that going for you? Glad to finally properly meet you."

"Maxime—" Dominique warns.

"What?" He teases, gaze lingering on mine. It stays there for a beat, as if they want to pry inside and seek out the secrets that I keep behind metal. But I won't give it up.

My shame.

My hurt.

And I won't share.

"You know they're not the easiest." He gives me another smile and a pat on my shoulder. "But not to worry, we've got you."

Shaking him off, I growl, "I don't need protection. I am capable of keeping them at a distance myself." Maxime's smile turns into a cackle, all cheerful and shit, but I don't miss the way he winks at Dominique.

Flipping them both the bird, I stalk toward the food corner. It's well after one in the afternoon, so there's no queue anymore, lunch hours limited to half past one. I quickly grab a tray, consider leaving the other two, who are still chatting and laughing behind me, and find myself a quiet spot in some corner. But by the time the canteen employee hands me a full plate with lasagne, water and bread, I change my mind. Instantly.

Because I hear *him* laugh. A rumble through the closed space, floating its way through the air and right at me. It's a raspy sound, low and taunting, as if it's a private chuckle brushing past my ear. My fingers clench and I inhale deeply, inwardly preparing myself to get ready to turn around and face Arthur like the inevitable sin he is.

"Can I take my food upstairs?" I ask the canteen lady in my most convincing voice and a flutter of my lashes, but she just crosses her arms, glances from my tray back at me, then shakes her head. "No food in the dorms, I'm afraid. But there's plenty of space and you still have half an hour."

I fail to hide my disappointment when I nod in understanding. Then Arthur laughs again, and I grind my jaw. I need to get away from here, but my feet won't move, body rigid with apprehension. Exhaling a woosh of air, I puff out my chest. Fuck this shit. My stepbrother might be obnoxious and provocative, but he won't get to me. I will *not* let him get to me. No one can get to me. Swirling around, I bite the insides of my cheek and let my gaze wildly flash around in search for a free table in a far corner.

"Régis. This way." Dominique stands half way through the canteen, already waiting for me.

I frown. "How did you—" He lets out a smile, looking unfazed by my inner turmoil. He stood behind me in the queue. Eyeing the seats he mentions, I find Maxime is waving at both of us.

"You blacked out for a moment. We took advantage," he grins, poking out his chin toward a table in the corner. "Especially him. Maxime's a king at finding the best seats. Come on."

"Right," I mutter, then force myself to follow him. I am not that stammering, blushing kid anymore. He's gone. But when I nearly reach Dominique, I hear my name being called out.

"Look who's there. Baby stepbro, why won't you come and sit with us?" It's Louis, who's waving at me, his voice carrying all the way through the canteen. Making heads turn. I grind my teeth at the sudden attention. He is surrounded by guys who now eye me curiously, guys I don't care about. Next to him, Arthur sits with some dude on his lap, who has his face buried in his neck. Arthur's raven hair is all slick and styled, the pants of his school uniform snug around his well-developed thighs, his smile sensual and secretive while he murmurs secret words in the guys ear. I feel my face heating at the sight, puffed chest slowly deflating as something tightens inside. Why am I so affected by this guy? My throat feels dry, and no matter how hard I try, my scrambled mind just can't come up with a sneer. Still my lips part, ready for combat though nothing but a pathetic wheeze comes out.

Dominique claps a hand on my shoulder, leans in and muses, "Get used to it. Whatever rule this school has? The Deverauxs don't have to obey them. Their family name is sacred here. They are powerful." He pulls back and sends me a wink. "That means you too." Letting go of my shoulder, he cocks his head to the public display at the table right in the middle of the canteen, and quips, "I'm afraid you're too late."

At the sound of Dominique's voice, Gaël whips his head around, platinum hair shimmering in the light as his gaze flies up to mine. It makes me fucking squirm. *He* is...oh well, the three of them have that same effect on me. Next to me, Dominique doesn't seem to share that feeling, because he nods my way, catching my wide eyes. "Régis is having lunch with us today. I'm trying to recruit him for our chess club."

"Are you now, beautiful?" Gaël scrapes his chair back as he stands, catching the attention of other students. People stop and stare, their hungry curiosity now fully focused on us, making me grit my teeth. So much for staying low.

Arthur drags his gaze from the guy on his lap, only to sweep that dark stare right onto my face. It's enough to make my legs go wobbly and for my skin to itch. Sinking my teeth in my lower lip, I nibble the soft, plush flesh while my spine turns rigid.

Gaël approaches, his large, painted eyes focused on Dominique. Fuck, everyone in the canteen is watching the show. When he stills right in front of his lover, they eye each other intently for a beat, before Gaël dips his head and brushes his mouth over Dominique's neck, licking its way up to the corner of his mouth.

"*Bon appétit, trésor,*" he purrs. "I'm sure you'll successfully recruit Régis. Save some appetite for later." With his lips connected to Dominique's mouth, Gaël's eyes flit to mine. He stares at me, and then he smiles against his lover's delicate skin. He gives him one last kiss, then snaps his fingers. One of his friends lifts his backpack and holds it out. He snatches it out of his hand and throws it around his shoulder, ready to leave the canteen. "I'll see you later, beautiful."

We watch him leave, then Dominique rolls his eyes at me. "Always so dramatic," he sighs, his voice thick with amusement. "You'll get used to them. Come on."

Maxime's already waiting for us by the time we make it to the quiet corner, eating and smiling brightly while he chats with some other guy, visibly unaware of the show we accidentally just put on. Maybe we weren't as obvious as I suspected after all. Although that does nothing for my rapidly beating heart. Shit, that was weird.

"Hi there," I clip, feeling stiff and even more agitated. I should have not come down here, because now I'm standing like some god damn wooden fool who can't fold his body in order to sit down.

"Here." Dominique quickly pulls out the chair next to his, as if nothing happened. "Come sit next to me. Jo, I'd like you to meet Régis. Régis here is Louis and Arthur's little stepbrother. He's new here."

"*Stepbrother*?" The guy named Jo blinks his pale eyes. His longish blond hair is tied back with what looks like a navy-blue pre-wrap that matches the color of our uniform, giving his square face even more sharpness. "The Deveraux twins have a stepbrother?" He huffs out a laugh, then draws a cross with his index finger. "God bless you, dude." Every single nerve in my body freezes, except for the one I feel ticking in my jaw. I should get up—*get up!*—but can't get myself to move. I'm glued to the damn chair. Right when I feel like I should say something, anything really, even if it's a pitiful stammer, he stretches out his hand. "It's nice to meet you, Régis. My name is Jonathan, but my friends call me Jo." He smiles. "Just stick with us and you'll be fine. Plus—" His smile widens as he juts his chin toward Dominique. "We've got him, and Gaël's boyfriend keeps them all in check."

Said boyfriend huffs out an amused chuckle. "Oh, come on guys, they are not as bad as they'll have you believe."

Maxime lets out a snort.

"You're right," Jo smirks. "Besides, Louis is a decent football player."

"Oh, come on," Dominique chimes. "He's more than that. Louis is a good guy, kind and hospitable. A great cook."

"Cook?" Maxime perks up. "Who would have thought that any of the Deveraux boys could cook?"

"Hmm," Dominique nods. "That's right."

"Just get used to them being very present at college," Jo says, cleaning his plate with a last piece of bread. "I think that we're all familiar with the concept of 'popular kids'. Well, consider them the popular, loud ones. So, you just have to stay away as much as you can."

"Which is not easy when you share a dorm with them," I mutter, not missing how Maxime and Dominique exchange a private look. I should talk to that guy Pierre again.

"They have their own friends anyway," Maxime adds. On queue, I hear Louis bark out a laugh at something someone said.

"So...how about you joining our chess club, Régis?" Dominique, who has finished his lunch, pushes his plate aside and gives me a pleading look that makes me let out a nervous chortle. But before I can reply, Maxime groans.

"Now that, my friend, is a poor pitch. Haven't they taught you how to be more convincing? Coming with arguments and all that?"

Jo huffs out a chuckle, then steals a piece of bread from his friend's plate. Maxime pats his hand, but only after the bread has disappeared into Jo's mouth. And then his light gaze is back on mine. It's making me fidget.

"Uhm—"

"We're really cool guys," Maxime says.

"Well, I'm not sure—"

"And we're one guy short," Jo adds.

I sigh in desperation, a smile creeping up my face. I've never been asked for anything and it feels kind of flattering. I like it. "Why don't you just ask one of your friends?"

Jo laughs. "We already did. But—"

"But we want you," Dominique interjects with a firm voice. His coffee-colored eyes stare right into mine. Calm, and confident. "Because I like you. Because you and I are both the black sheep slash extension of the Deveraux family and we need to stick together."

"I thought you said he knows how to beat Arthur in chess?" Maxime asks sheepishly.

"I did," I reply. Once. I've only played a few times with him when I was here in Monterrey Castle, "getting used to" my new environment. "But the asshole plays seriously good."

Maxime's smile widens as his flush deepens. "So you'd be a great asset to our little team. You look like a nice guy, and Sunshine here likes you." He points toward Dominique.

"And since Pascal got kicked off the team, we could do with a new member," Jo adds drolly.

"He wasn't kicked out," Dominique balks.

"No, you're right. He was kindly requested to leave by Gaël and the Deveraux twins."

"What happened?" I ask. Maxime sends me another bright smile while his fork dangles in the air. He's the only one still eating, of course. "The guy got too touchy, so Gaël had him removed."

"He didn't—he wasn't," Dominique stammers.

"Yes he was, sunshine," Maxime deadpans, his eyes still on mine. "Anyway, just join the club. We're cool dudes, and you and Dominique could teach me and Jo how to improve our skills."

"Speak for yourself," Jo snorts.

"We play every Wednesday evening. But we're flexible," Maxime continues, ignoring his friend.

"Yeah. And if you don't feel like playing chess, but rather play cards, or just want to hang out, that's cool too," Dominique says. The others nod.

My hands tremble in my lap and my knee shakes frantically. I shouldn't—"I'll do it. Yeah." My mask cracks and crumbles. "I'll be really busy though with school, but I'll play. I'll do it."

"Yay!" Maxime fistbumps the air. "So cool. Now we can finally double again."

"Learn from the best."

"We should totally try that pool bar in town one day."

"Pool bar?" Dominique quirks a brow.

"That's a whole different ball game, bro." Jo laughs.

"I know," Maxime huffs. "But I don't care."

Dominique grasps my forearm and squeezes it gently. "We'll see about that, my friend. But hey, I'm really happy that you're joining. I'd like to be friends."

Friends? The word echoes in my mind, heavy and deceitful. I don't do friends. And I don't hang out with people. Everyone I love goes away.

"T'es une merde, Régis."

Dad's words rattle through my core, blanketing my heart with the familiar sting of pain. Pain is easier, easier than this feeling of hope. Because that's what this is. Pathetic, loathing hope. Still I can't help but croak, "Yeah. Me too." And I mean it.

I clear my throat. Suddenly I'm feeling warm. Opening my collar with trembling fingers, I try my best to keep my face in check, holding on to the dull stare I have permanently engraved into my blue eyes. "Well, thanks for the invitation, guys, but I have to get going."

Across from me, Jo stands up as well. "Yeah, I've got to head out as well," Jo says. "First football practice, so I'd better not be late."

Dominique and Maxime wave us goodbye, and at the exit of the canteen, Jo leaves me with a salute, then jogs away. I barely have time to contemplate what to do next when my phone vibrates in my pocket. Checking the caller ID, I practically jog through the corridor with my finger hovering over the keyboard, searching for a quiet corner. My heart suddenly thumps wildly in my chest. Is something wrong?

"You have received a phone call from an inmate of the Toulouse prison. Press 1 if you want to..." The familiar female robot voice rattles, and I wonder why on earth Dad would call this early.

The surprisingly quiet corridor is adorned with plants, with benches being placed against the walls. While I wait for the connection to establish, I head over to the one by the window, eyes admiring the collection of exotic green. Of course

Monterrey Castle doesn't have normal houseplants, but needs to have something exclusive.

My fingers reach out and gingerly play with one of the leaves of a giant white bird of paradise. This rare version sure is a beautiful sight, with its towering height, broad leaves, and striking bird-like flowers. "Aren't you a beauty," I murmur. They remind me of the ones I used to keep in my bedroom, although they were by far not as pretty as this one. Still, they did a great job in brightening up my tiny desk and looking pretty wrapped around iron. Their presence always managed to grow and bend itself around me, protecting me and my restless mind. Like a silent friend.

"*Régis.*" Dad's low, distasteful voice suddenly booms through my ear. My fingers instantly let go of the elegant leaf as if just the sound of it through the phone feels like it can contaminate the plant with all the acid that's leaking from his heart. It bounces gently through the air, before it quietly stills back in place.

"*Oui, papa? Comment vas-tu?*" Shifting my body, my eyes roam the large window with the outside forest, blanketed in clouds. It's not even late afternoon, but already the sky radiates darkness. Probably the lack of rainfall, with humidity forming heavy, murky clouds that intermingle with low mist. Dad lets out a grunt while my eyes adjust to the reflection through the glass. Instead of seeing the darkening forest, my gaze catches the lights behind me. Tomorrow, I tell myself, tomorrow I'll head out and discover the woods.

Dad talks about his daily routine—the depressing cool shower, horrible breakfast, and uninspiring tasks they equip him with. I should head back to my dorm and take this conversation somewhere private, but I don't want to, now I have discovered these green beauties. My temporary safe haven.

Dad talks and I watch. When I catch my own reflection, I stick out my tongue playfully, then pull it in immediately, gut filling with guilt as I zoom back to Dad's monologue. But then, when my eyes flick up again, it's not my own reflection I collide with. No, it's another pair of eyes. I blink, then blink again, but those eyes still watch me intently, its gaze unyielding and arrogant. My heart stutters in my chest and my lashes flutter, but my eyes can't look away.

I squeeze the phone against my ear shell, making my dad grunt inside my head. "*Ah, oui?*" I comment sheepishly, unnecessarily. Dad's talk falters for a moment, and I pray that he won't ask me anything. He doesn't, grunts instead, picking up where he left off. Dad's presence always makes me feel inferior, incompetent, but now, with another predator standing less than three meters away from me, I feel cornered.

My heart thumps wildly in my chest. And still my eyes can't look away.

Through the window, Arthur thumbs his bottom lip.

"Régis?" Dad finally belts, sounding impatient. I clear my throat forcefully, but my throat is too thick for a reply. Sweat breaks out and I can feel my knees tremble.

This is important, you fool! I tell myself. But I can't focus.

"I asked if you spoke to the lawyer," Dad grumbles. Guilt washes over me at those words. I haven't. I should have, but—

"*Oui*," I whisper weakly. "He's not very positive, but still looking into the case. I'll speak with him again in a few days."

Through the window, Arthur languidly takes a single step forward, and in my attempt to create a bigger distance, I practically fly against the glass. I can hear him chuckle, the fucker. He's taunting me. It's working. I'm so pathetic.

"Good. Your mother is a lying bitch, you know that, right?" Dad spews. I squint my eyes, though they never leave Arthur's dark ones through the window, his words echoing through my rattling core. "She doesn't love you, my son. She doesn't love you, and she tried to separate us. She's the true criminal here."

Dad isn't a monster.

Yes, he is.

No.

Yes.

"I know that," I choke, because his words are suffocating. "The lawyer said that he thinks nothing can be done, but we'll get the confirmation in a few days."

When Arthur takes another step forward, I turn around and face him, ready to bolt for the steps, the phone in my hand like some weapon. But my body feels sweaty, stiff and weak. And it's leaving me there, locked up, to face the person who torments me in my dreams. The source of my confusion.

From up close, Arthur looks flawless as always, his tall frame tightly fits into his school uniform, his dark, thick hair tousled. His smoldering eyes keep mine hostage, making me tilt my chin a little higher and pinch my lips. His tongue peeks out as he wets his lower lip, while Dad barks something at the same time.

"*Quoi?*" I ask, the word coming out as a dry rasp. Arthur grins and I catch that obscene movement in utter rapture. Fuck, he's gorgeous.

"God damn it son, are you even listening to me?" Dad shouts. "I said, if he can't do anything, then find another lawyer. That useless piece of shit. I'm sure as fuck not going to rot here for the rest of my life. I'm old, Régis, I'm your father. Perhaps we should trade places, your body is younger. I mean, there has to be something that they can do for fuck's sake!" My mind blanks. Cold sweat on my back now mingles with the coolness of the glass, because I've pressed my shaking body against the window. And all the while this voice continues to reverberate in my head.

"Dad will stay locked up. Nothing can be done."

Nothing. Arthur's raven hair tumbles to one side and my phone trembles against my ear.

Nothing. He opens his mouth and everything has begun to move in slow motion while I wait for him to speak.

Nothing.

"Finally on my territory, little Régis." He finally drawls, voice thick with hoarseness. "Shall we go?" Awareness prickles on my skin and I swallow, and swallow again, but the lump won't go away. Arthur grins and I grab the phone tighter, but Dad's long gone. He's hung up on me, because he's angry. He must be so disappointed in me. Maybe he's right and we should trade places. Maybe that would make everything a little easier.

I scowl and gesture to the phone, pretending to be having a conversation, but it's clear that he's not going away. "I'm not going anywhere with you," I grate, my throat feeling paper dry.

"Oh yeah, that's right. You don't read Mom's messages." Arthur gives me a wicked grin, then points a long, slender digit to my ear. "You can hang up now, little Régis." Amusement laces his undertone. "I can hear the disconnected tone from here. Or are you afraid?"

"Afraid?" I spit out a huff, and my face flushes a little before I pull the phone away and back into the pocket of my jacket. "I'm not afraid of you, you narcissistic punk."

Liar.

"Narcissistic punk," Arthur mouths, then wiggles his brows at me. "Wow. In a normal situation, I'd be impressed. Right now, not so much. Because you see, little Régis, you and I have a problem. Dad's here, and he wants to talk to us both."

"Why?" I breathe, sudden panic churning in my chest. Of course he'd be here.

Arthur shrugs. "I can think of a few reasons. You not being around during most of the summer break being one of them. After all, Dad's paid over twenty thousand euros in tuition fees for you just to be here for six months, Régis, so stop pretending you don't understand." Pressing my lips together, I roll my shoulders in an attempt to puff my chest up. *Dad.* That man's not my dad and he never will be. He's the man my mother married. The man she left me for. The man I have more or less successfully avoided over the past nine months, ever since he barged into my life with his expensive suits and even more expensive lawyer.

"He'll want something in return, little Régis. If you want to attend this college, you agree to play the game. Want to hang out with the big boys? Let's see if you can keep up."

Grinding my teeth, I send him an indignant huff and a shoulder bump while bypassing him toward the hall. "Oh, you've got nothing to say to that?" Arthur laughs as he catches up with me, guiding me further into this maze that is Monterrey Castle. It's a warm, honey, sexy sound that has me seething. Because he's laughing right the fuck at me. Seeing me as some little shit he can wipe off with the heel of his foot. Well, I'll show him that he's wrong.

4

RÉGIS

"Boys. It's good to see you again." Jean-Luc Deveraux stands to greet us when we finally make our way inside the grand room. Our silent walk felt almost as though we were stuck in a maze. Wandering down one narrow hall to another in this secretive castle that's filled with narrow corridors and plush, thick carpets. With endless walls, decorated with glorious golden scones and large paintings.

I have no idea where we are.

"Come in, come in, we've been waiting for you." He holds out his hand, a warm glow in those dark eyes that are so similar to his sons. His smile seems genuine, though it still feels like some pitfall. Some sort of test that I have promised myself to pass. Taking his hand, I give him a clipped nod, and while my core may shudder from the inside, I won't give him a single centimer. My tight smile plastered to my face.

"Dad." The single word falls heavy off my lips, though Jean-Luc doesn't seem to notice.

"Hello, son." He takes his time keeping my hand firmly clasped with his. "I hope that you've settled in alright?"

"Sure." I tighten my lips.

Jean-Luc smiles. "That's good to hear. And the sleeping arrangements? Did they do a good job renovating the rooms?" His gaze turns to Arthur.

"Yeah, it looks great, Dad," he answers with his usual husky tone. "Right, Régis?"

My throat clicks when I swallow thickly. This is the moment I've been waiting for. This is where I stand up and say I don't want to share a fucking dorm with these assholes. But now that we're here, I can't form any words. Because if I speak up, they will know. Know that these so-called arrangements affect me, know how humiliating it is to have no control over your own life. To stand outside of yourself and watch these untouchable elitist people direct every aspect of your life and there is nothing you can do about it.

"Régis, my love, we've been so worried." The voice of my mother is sharp right before it breaks. "I didn't even know if I'd see you here today. You haven't replied to any of my messages or phone calls. I was afraid that you'd just disappeared on us, *chéri*. You can't even imagine how relieved I was when Arthur texted me that you got here safe and sound." She takes a step forward. "I'm so glad to see you again, Régis." Still carrying that hesitant look on her face, one that surely matches mine, she lifts her hands slowly. It's enough for my body to go rigid, and I stumble backward, nearly toppling over a chair.

She's not angry.

"I'm glad that you're glad," I mumble meekly.

Are you disappointed?

She's got to be, I have hardly spent any time with her ever since she locked me in their mansion.

Am I too stubborn?

Mom's face falls, then she drops her hands.

Is that why you left me?

Dad's touches have shown nothing but pain. I don't like pain.

Jean-Luc turns her way and gives her a tender smile. "It's okay, *amour*. It will come. We'll give him time. This place can be overwhelming, am I right, Régis?"

"Yes, Dad," I mumble, interlacing my clammy fingers. It still feels so double to address him like that.

"But we're very happy to see you, son. Happy that you're here, in Saint-Laurent, with your brothers and cousin." He waits a beat, then, "So the sleeping arrangements are to your satisfaction?" I hesitate, then nod. He sends me another one of those soft smiles, looking a little relieved. "We missed you, Régis, your mother and I. Did you just decide to head out one day? Just like that?" My eyes jump at those words, meeting his, and I nibble on my bottom lip while I wait for something to say. But my mind short circuits, panic rising through the creases of my nerves. Jean-Luc doesn't appear angry, but I can't know for sure. "Amadou told me about your trip to Nîmes," he says through my silence. "Did you find what you were looking for?" I stare down at my sweaty, interlaced fingers with a frown while I contemplate his question. Did I find what I was looking for? I don't know. I'm not even sure I know what I was looking for in the first place. Good memories? Or was it an ache I searched for? Raw, undigested pain to blame?

I spread my lips, but my stubborn throat convulses. Instead I swallow for good measure, making sure that the words will stay hidden.

"Well, perhaps you'll share it with us one day." Jean-Luc gestures to the couch of lush, rich velvet. "Please, sit down. You're here now, and that's all that matters." And then he grabs Arthur by his forearms and tugs him in for a hug and a kiss on each cheek.

"Can't say that I haven't seen you for a long time," he jokes, "But I'm also happy that you're here, my son."

I let them have their moment and glance away, taking in the luxurious office. There's a colossal fireplace with crossed epees.

A massive, wooden desk sits by the window. Against the wall, the head of a deer, multiple photos framed in gold. Thick, heavy drawn-up curtains, colorful pillows and elegantly shaped side-lamps that make the room float in gentle light. It looks like Jean-Luc's office. But why would he have an office in Monterrey Castle?

"Boys, the reason why we came here today, apart from making sure that you all made it safely to Saint-Laurent of course, is to discuss this coming school year."

Arthur joins me on the couch. The moment his weight dips, my muscles tense and my stomach tightens. He's close, the heat of his skin slowly crawling inside my core like the thickest of liquids. Shaking my head inwardly, I watch as my legs automatically squeeze together, remembering that veiny hand and those long, slender digits crawling up my groin too well. I've wished it back there way too many times.

Pathetic.

"Monterrey Castle. Houses one of the finest boarding colleges in the world. Stands proudly at the top of that list for Europe. Now, I know this change hasn't been easy for you, Régis," Jean-Luc drawls, as if tasting each word in his mouth before spilling them into the room. My head jerks up, startled, as if my stepdad has just caught me on my filthy thoughts. His voice turns soft. "You were used to living with your father, and must have felt like your mother had abandoned you." I grind my teeth hard and my jaw clenches. Because she *had*.

Mom shifts in her chair, but doesn't speak.

"We already told you all this, but I want to tell you this again, so you won't forget. When I met your mom, I fell in love with her gentle character. My boys never had a mother, she died way too young—" He falls silent for a beat and I don't miss the way my mother curls her smaller hand around his. "Anyway. Your mom made me promise that I would do everything that's in my power to get you safe and sound to where you belong. With her.

With *us*. Though admittedly, it has taken us longer than expected." He clears his throat. "For the twins, learning that you exist also came as a surprise. We'd never told them about you before, and I want you to know that is not because you don't matter. You will always matter to us. But this situation was delicate, and I am trying to do the best thing for everyone." Arthur lets out a disapproving snort that echoes through the room, its sound making me cringe. Jean-Luc's eyes flash when they collide with his son's. An unspoken conversation passes by in a sigh, then his gaze darts back to mine. I quickly look away. "I hope that you've grown to like our family home. Your room there will always be your safe haven, Régis, I want you to know that." He pauses to pinch the bridge of his nose, then continues. "I know that the journeys to school were long and boring, but they paid off. Me and your mom are very proud of your results."

I finished top of my class. Graduation with honors. A daily ride with Amadou so I could continue the same public high school. Yeah, those past months have kept me a prisoner behind a different kind of steel, and it has made me miss the familiar, cool iron between my fingers.

Home.

"This here, is a different world, Régis." His voice has gone a little softer. "This here, is a choice we made together, you and I. You could have said no to Saint-Laurent, but you didn't. You chose your own future and your mother and I are proud of you for making that tough decision." Big words that somehow contain a sharper edge and a double meaning. Still he's right. No one forced me to enter this college but myself.

I'm no longer caged.

I can come and leave as I wish.

And still...I can't. Because books have always been my shelter, my security. Have always functioned as the perfect distraction to reality. Because I'm a good student, and Saint-Laurent is the best. Besides, I've already survived a lifetime with my dad. Surely I can add another four years?

I jerk my chin in agreement.

"This here is about traditions, Régis. About loyalty. Respect." The room has gone eerily quiet, and when the curtain bulges up from an unexpected gust of wind, I startle. Next to me, the whisper of a husky chuckle. "This is about being part of the best, for life." Jean-Luc sighs heavily and squeezes my mother's hand. "Nathalie, I don't know if—"

"I can do it," I blurt, filling the emptiness with a shake of my voice.

No one speaks for a moment, but there's a change in the air. It's as if it's filled with something sharp, something heady. My spine turns rigid with anticipation and I feel Arthur's gaze burning into my cheek, but it's not like before. No, something has switched, and I can't quite put my finger on it.

"I'm a good student," I add on a whisper.

Jean-Luc sighs again. "Oh, I know you are, Régis. We have been following your educational career for years and have been provided with your school reports. You know this, because we've never wanted us to have any secrets within the family. Which is why this—" He clears his throat. "We would like to see you join the family business one day. Perhaps, with time, you can become a top executive?"

Next to me, Arthur sucks in a sharp breath. "In the family business? *What*? Dad?" Jean-Luc turns to face him.

"Let me finish—"

"But you can't possibly…he's not blood…he's not even—"

"Arthur." Jean-Luc's voice clips. "Nathalie is like your mother, so Régis is like your brother. I understand your concerns, and I know it's a big leap. Which is why I have spoken with the family."

"...And?"

"And the family has requested that Régis show his true value."

"True value?" Both me and Arthur stammer at the same time.

Jean-Luc nods. "To the *family*."

There's that silence again.

"I see," Arthur hums. It sounds...*off*, and I swear I can feel something crawling its way right down my throat, creating a lump that I can't swallow away.

"Arthur will guide you," Jean-Luc continues. "My son has been working toward his future for years. He's exceptionally intelligent, and after his graduation Arthur will be finalizing his practice years before becoming the CEO of Deveraux Holding." When I open my mouth to protest, he simply lifts his hand, and waits for me to close it again. I don't. Because I— "I don't need Arthur to guide me," I huff, ignoring that silky snicker next to me. "I don't need anyone to guide me. I'm more than capable of creating my own life here."

"Arthur is your brother and he will be your chaperone, at least for the first months," Jean-Luc repeats, and this time there's a finality to his voice. He presses his lips. "You will also meet up with a counselor that has been personally appointed by me—"

"But I don't want to talk to a psychologist."

Jean-Luc gives me a wry smile. "I know. That's why this man is not a psychologist, but someone who will listen to you. Someone you can confide in, should you want to. Régis, I have listened to your wishes, but together with your mother, we try to do what's best for you. The past years have been hell for you. We want you safe in your body and in your mind."

"I—" My throat chokes up, the lump too heavy to swallow.

"That's the decision the Deveraux family made, and you are a Deveraux, Régis. We look after our own."

"No!" I want to scream. *"The fuck I am not."* But if I'm not, then what am I? The son of a burned past? The son of a man

who's behind bars? It's devastating how the tables have turned. *It's him now who's locked up behind steel.*

"Can I count on you, Arthur?" Jean-Luc asks.

"Of course Dad, I'll make sure that Régis will feel safe." Arthur's voice is still breathy, the remaining tremors of shock adding a rasp to his voice that makes his tone even more sensual. Or perhaps it's his words that make my chest clench.

Jean-Luc stands, followed by my mother. "Good, that's settled. Régis, you can trust Arthur. And trust me when I say you will need him. Being a member of our family comes with certain other obligations. It should have been me to guide you through, as your father, but since the family decided that you must prove yourself, it will be up to you to discover this by yourself. Go to Arthur when you need something, get to know each other a little better. Freely discuss things with your counselor. Please, use the tools that we're handing you. You're not alone. We want you to feel safe." The thought makes me grimace. He doesn't see, his eyes already on his real son. "Arthur, this is his journey. Guide him, but do not demonstrate."

Demonstrate? I think, shifting uncomfortably in my seat. What the hell does that mean?

Arthur casually runs a hand through his hair and nods. "That won't be a problem, Dad."

"The future of this family lies on your shoulders, my son. Everything you have worked for, that we have worked for over the past years, together, is about to happen after you graduate. I need you, Arthur. The world needs you. Please don't let me down."

There's that weird vibe again. Shaking it off, I bristle, "You know, I'm not a kid. If you wouldn't have barged into my life, I would have gone to university, and I wouldn't have had a *chaperone* either. Or a counselor. So don't make this any weirder than it already is."

"Régis." My mother murmurs. "The past years have been so hard for you, so—"

"Hard, yeah. I get it." I too stand up, limbs tight as a string and my breath high in my chest, locked up but too proud to let go. I can't face her. Haven't been able to ever since we were reunited. "I'll wait for the counselor to get in touch with me. If you'll excuse me, I'd like to get settled. Classes will start tomorrow." I mean to pass Arthur and get the hell out of this crooked room. God, it feels like the walls are scratched right off its foundations, only to tumble down—*and down, and down.* The entire place feels like it's spinning, taking my crashing thoughts into some weird spiral.

But Arthur takes that moment to sweep himself off the couch, right in front of me. Our chests are almost touching when he effectively blocks my way. He's taller than I am, by at least ten centimeters. Rolling my lips, I tip up my head and gaze right at him.

"If you'll excuse me," I mutter, then press forward, but he won't budge, leaving us standing even closer than before. Sucking in a breath, I try to focus on anything but the heat radiating off his body. Embarrassment coats my cheeks.

Arthur blinks, raising his eyebrows, and fuck—he must have said something that I completely missed. Slamming my jaw together, I give him a subtle push against his chest, the connection bringing a zap of electricity right into my stomach.

"Since I'm your new chaperone, let's get you back then," he mutters, eyes still on mine, before he flits them back to our parents. "Bye Dad, bye Nathalie, see you soon. Sorry for the abrupt goodbye."

"Good luck tomorrow. Have yourselves a fantastic start to the new school year."

My mother asks something, but I can't hear her words through the whooshing of my ears. I don't know what has taken me out of balance. Perhaps this weird talk of true value and family, perhaps seeing my mother again after all these weeks of hiding. Perhaps it's the way I can feel Arthur following me, stalking me like the prey I am. Whatever it is has my skin prickling in trepidation.

"This is something he needs to do himself, Nathalie," I hear Jean-Luc say, his voice slowly dimming because we're now across the room, facing the door.

Need to do what? I want to ask. Study? Earn my place in their fucking family? I never asked to be part of their family, nor do I want to work in their business. I never asked for my mother to come back after having left me with my dad.

But you wanted to.

Oh, I did. So badly.

Night after night I'd wait for her to come home. And I wondered, oh I wondered.

Why did you leave me?

Espèce de merde.

Did you stop loving me?

Useless boy. Get in there.

Why didn't you take me with you?

And you'll only get out when I fucking say so.

You left me with him.

The door clicks closed behind us, but we've hardly taken a few steps, before Arthur snatches his fingers around my neck and jerks me against the wall. I flinch at the touch and at the need to shake him off. My chest clamps tight, but I force my chin to tip up and stare back.

Punishment.

"You're shivering." He tilts his head, watching me with flicking eyes. "Why?"

"Perhaps because your hands are wrapped around my neck like a fucking collar?" I snarl. He's right though, I am trembling. It's…a lot. All of this. Seeing my mother again, being instructed to confide in Arthur. I hate the way I react to his presence, to his warmth. It's confusing, and forbidden, and it makes me feel even more fragile. He's my stepbrother of all people. "Stop treating me like a dog."

"Not a dog," Arthur halts and turns to face me, his fingers still dug into my skin. "Miaow." He grins, crooking his fingers like the paw of a cat, scraping his nails against my flesh. "I can hear your heartbeat, kitten."

Pushing him hard, I let out a grunt when his fingers won't budge. "Let go of me."

His chuckle is hoarse. "Not quite the same reaction you gave me the last time you and I were together."

I tilt my chin, teeth ground together. "That was a mistake. And it will never happen again."

Arthur slowly tilts his head, a dark gleam shining in his eyes. "Yes, it will. The only thing that has changed is the situation."

"What the hell's that supposed to mean?"

He shrugs. "Just like I said before, you're in my territory now. My world. And *you* will play according to my rules."

I let out a huff. "Okay, this *game,* or whatever you feel like calling it, ends here." Running a frustrated hand through my hair, I take a moment to choose my words carefully. "I don't need a babysitter, Arthur, and I sure as hell ain't your competitor." The words have barely left my mouth when I feel his hand squeeze tighter around my throat. Arthur thrusts me firmer against the wall and presses his fingers into the tender skin between my collarbone and ears, nails scraping my flesh.

"Wrong. The moment Dad said that there would be a place for you in the family business? That's when you became my competitor, little Régis. Or should I say, my future colleague," he scoffs. His breath fans against my forehead, then lower when he dips his head until our eyes meet. Anticipation rustles through me like a breeze, and I bite my lip—a movement he follows with his onyx eyes. From up close I notice a tiny sparkle of golden flecks in those dark irises, but when his gaze moves back up to catch mine, it's gone. Swallowed by the black depths of his pupils and his fury. "You see, I don't share my future. Not with anyone, and sure as fuck not with you."

"I—I won't get in your way," I wheeze pathetically, hating myself a little more. His hold stays firm. "I'll refuse the job in your family business. I'll show my worth."

Arthur leans in and our noses brush. It's barely there, and it's only the tips of our noses, still I try to pull back, against the mercilessly unrelenting wall. His smirk is subtle, but visible enough.

"You don't get it, do you? You have no idea what's coming at you. And like some little, innocent boy, you're bringing out the worst in me." He murmurs, using another of his sophisticated riddles he seems to enjoy. "You are going to need me in the next few months. And I'm going to need you to be grateful for my help. You think you can do that?" My entire body goes rigid when his lips scrape my neck on their way to the corner of my mouth. Goosebumps break out, and sparks of pleasure tingle my insides. Still, I won't back down. Not when he considers the battle won without having to put up a single fight.

"I don't need a fucking babysitter." I hiss, but due to the lack of oxygen the words miss their punch. My throat burns, very much like the desire that blazes through my veins. Pain and pleasure create the most electric combination. Just like Arthur himself. Hot and cold, black and white, gentle and cruel. His fingers on my throat hurt, but his lips on my sensitive skin are gentle. Making my cock buck.

Arthur chuckles my words away, his teeth still connected to my ear, his claws around my neck. "You're in a lot of trouble, little Régis," he sings in a murmur. "A lot. Of. Trouble. So if I were you, I'd be nice to your stepbrother. Show some gratitude. And maybe, just maybe, he will protect you." He drops a soft kiss on the corner of my mouth, making my inside shiver.

"Fuck off," I seethe through gritted teeth. He pulls his head back, but still stays close to my face. Too close.

He tips up the corners of his wicked mouth, then releases the pressure on my neck and moves to massaging the skin with warm, soft fingers. I take in big gulps of air while I try to calm down. I think he wants to say something else, but movement in the narrow corridor cuts us out of our haze.

"Oh, there you are!" Louis appears in our line of sight with swagger. "Am I too late for the party?" I expect Arthur to let go of me, perhaps even spill the beans and tell his twin about their father's intentions for my future,, but instead he remains quiet and keeps one hand around my neck, while the other one cups my cheek. Louis, dressed identically like the both of us, gives Arthur a funny look, before his eyes roam over my face. He huffs out a laugh.

"Looks like you've already started your own private party. Yeah, I get it, bro." Tilting his chin toward the door, he adds, "You coming? Mom and Dad wanted to see us. Sorry, without you little s-brother."

Mom... the word makes me cringe. She's not their mother. But she's not mine either, not anymore. I'm too caught up by his word choice that I can't even feel offended by Louis's meaning.

When Arthur finally lets go of me I make a show of straightening my clothes and with an indigent huff, ignoring my raging hard-on as I flip the twins off. Fuck the entire Deveraux family, my mother included. That thought brings a smile to my face. Yeah, that's right. Screw them all. I came here for myself, and for no one else.

But when I nearly turn the corner, Arthur calls after me. "Oh, Régis? Go back to our dorm and wait for me. I'll come and see you very soon. After all, we are connected now. You won't forget that, will you?"

5

RÉGIS

Oh, I won't forget. Not for a single, freaking minute that's left in this dreadful day. It's the only thing I *can* think of. Because the entire conversation feels distorted—like a trick. Something to catch me off balance so I underperform.

Connected, he said.

Am I being punished? No one shows up after so many years and just throws around all this money for a child they don't know and never wanted to begin with. If my mother did love me, why did it take her thirteen years to come back to me? And why would Jean-Luc want me to join their successful family business?

That conversation replays in my mind like a scratched record player on loop, again and again. But no matter what, I come up empty, though that persistent feeling of calamity still lingers. Jean-Luc always comes across as sincere, just like the words—though absurd—that leave his mouth. Ambling through my room, I contemplate my options.

Arthur as my chaperone. The thought has me huff in annoyance and my chest flaring with heat.

There's no way I'm going to sit here and wait for Arthur to

just show up. After all, I've been pretty clear that I don't need a chaperone and he needs to respect that. He needs to understand that I won't be menaced, nor am I scared by all their mysterious words about loyalty and traditions. Fuck that shit, I don't want to be a part of this. I'm no competition and I don't want to get my heart burnt. I just want to prove to myself and the whole world that I can do it. That I can graduate from Saint-Laurent. But that's not what's happening right now. No, I might not know Arthur well yet, but he does come across as awfully stubborn. If he has decided that I am his rival, then I am.

"I'll come and see you very soon." Those words are enough to convince me that I should do what I do best.

I'm getting the hell out of here.

Arthur thinks he's smart, but he won't know where to find me. Besides, if there's anything I have learned about Arthur Deveraux, it's that he's a fucking proud bastard. He won't come searching for me in public.

So all I've got to do is lay low and stay the hell away from him. And maybe, just maybe, this whole thing will just pass. Good thing I know exactly how to do so.

Climbing out of my window is not as easy as I'd hoped, but with a bit of help from the rain pipe and the soft grass landing at my feet, I'm outside my room in no time. It's already getting close to seven, so most students will be heading down to the canteen soon. Me, I'll be on my own outside in the woods.

The sun will be setting shortly, the faintest sprinkle of red glimmering over the large oak trees. It's a beautiful sight. And right now, with those colors in my face and my fingertips brushing gently at the plants as I make my way through the garden, fresh air invades my lungs and finally, *finally,* I can relax.

The winding gravel path takes me to the edge of the gardens, from where I can see the football field. A few guys are jogging over the grass, and Jo sends me a wave when I pass them on my way to the woods.

When I turn my back to the college and head for the darker cavity of trees and shrubs, it feels as if the temperature drops. God, it feels peaceful here. Crisp and silent, with the occasional sound of a chirp or a breeze. We're still in the early autumn days, but this year gifts us with plenty of sunshine. Sand replaces gravel as I follow the path through the trees. The woods are wrapped in brown, yellow and red leaves. Most are still attached to the trees, but here and there they have already fallen onto the ground of sand and moss. I pick one up and hold it against my nose, inhaling deeply.

Flora wrapped around iron.

I start collecting them, piling them up, in an attempt to make a start of my sanctuary. It's pleasant work, one that keeps my mind occupied without it going into a panic mode. "I don't need a chaperone. What the fuck do they think I am, a baby?" I scoff against the growing pile of leaves. "I've got to prove myself. But I can't keep them out of my life." Not accepting this situation means not accepting my studies. And I'm not ready to give that up. Meaning there's only one solution left. "I've got to beat him."

Moving on to searching sticks of wood, I overthink that option. My fingers tremble when I pile the wooden sticks once more, all the while searching for a place to store them. I'll first need to find a sheltered place, one that is dry. Gazing around me through the shimmering woods, I don't exactly find that, but I do find a hole that's been dug into the ground at the base of a tree. Perhaps a nest of some sort, though it's empty now. Making sure not to close the hole entirely, in case animals make their way through during the night, I neatly store the sticks on one side and the other. It clears my mind, and when I'm done and even find some space for the colorful leaves, this whole situation doesn't seem so dire anymore.

"I will show them." I will show my value to the Deveraux family, even though I'll need to make it clear that I have no desire to work within their company. Traditions, loyalty, and whatever the rest Jean-Luc mentioned...that's not really my thing. But if that's what it takes to keep my place in college, then I'll show them something. I'll be the best fucking student Saint-Laurent has ever had.

An image of my smooth talking stepbrother flutters though my mind. "Why him? He's nasty and arrogant. Why does it have to be him?" The desperation makes me angry. Arthur is rapidly turning into a two-faced fiend with words razor-sharp and fingertips soft as a breeze. His words I can fend off, no matter how intelligent he is. But his touch is another story.

Touch is my weakness. I can deal with pain, with punishments, and have taught myself to endure, to hang in there until agony dims. But the way he makes my core tremble when his fingers rake over my body, has me utterly shattered. Defeated. He's got to know the effect he has on me, with the way he stares right through me with that smug grin and those golden eyes. With his caressing touch he sucks in all my emotions, undoubtedly storing them somewhere to be thrown back at me some day. To be used against me.

The worst thing? I can't stop my body. Can't stop trembling when his hands are on my flesh, can't stop desire flooding my nervous system when he teases me with that raspy voice. He takes away my mask and unfurls my true identity—the stammering, timid, virgin.

Damn it. Patting off sand against my upper legs, I look at the result. Not bad for a first day. I'll have to find some equipment as well, but with the professional gardeners Monterrey Castle employs, that shouldn't be too hard.

There's another sand trail a little further down, surely taking me further into the woods. I shouldn't follow it, leave it to tomorrow as I'd originally planned, because it will be dark soon.

But then my eyes stumble upon a small garden a little further down that path, and my hesitation slinks away.

Are those...Grabbing my backpack I take a few steps, then curl my lips into a smile. Flowers...I stroll deeper between the trees and take a moment to admire the small garden. It's small and sweet and brings a smile to my lips. Flowers have never let me down. Green is peaceful, patient, understanding.

Leaves rush gently in the wind, making my mind stop—*stop*—from spiraling.

Somewhere in the background, church bells chime. Eight o'clock. My stomach tightens. I wonder if Jean-Luc and my mother have finished talking to the twins by now. I wonder how soon is soon.

I walk for another few hundred meters, until where the shrubs part and give way to what seems to be yet another opening in the woods. I look behind me. Yeah, this is a different route from the one I took when I got here.

Inhaling deeply, my lips curl up when I catch the vague, but unmistakable sweet scent of lavender. It's a herb garden. Yes, this spot will do.

Searching for the source of that luscious scent, I find the small evergreen shrubs with gray-green hoary linear leaves and plop down next to them and onto the ground. Opening my backpack, I grab my dinner for tonight—a few protein bars and a can of energy drink. I also made myself a coffee in the small kitchen we have in our dorm, and though it has cooled down a little the drink still tastes divine—well-roasted with a touch of freedom.

I look up at the castle from my well hidden spot in the forest. Trace its elegant architecture of towers and white stones, its painted decorations where large scorns are set against the walls, lighting up the drawings against the walls. Closing my eyes, I remember Arthur's scorching gaze from before, his tilted head. What would it be like to have a guy like that kissing me—

"Oh stop it, for fuck's sake," I grumble. "It's a trick, don't you see?"

Always. A trick.

I take an angry bite of the protein bar, but no matter how harshly I chew, I can't seem to swallow that persistent, nagging feeling away. It's something I can't put my finger on, unfurling right beneath my lashes, but I can't grasp its texture, can't seem to estimate its weight. But it's there. Perhaps it has been ever since I met my new family last winter, when my mother brought me to the Deveraux mansion that very first time. When I was introduced to my two stepbrothers.

The look on his face. On his devilishly handsome, arrogant face.

He called me "Little Régis", but the twinkle in his onyx eyes wasn't tender, far from it. No, he took his time scanning my face, looking for flaws, looking for anything that his wicked mind could use against me. I knew then, I just knew. That Arthur was going to be bad news. Bad, bad news.

And still, I—I couldn't look away. Though I wanted to. I wanted to tell them all to fuck off and run away, back to the past, back to safety of the known. I had wanted to scoop up all the shattered pieces of my memories in my trembling hands and keep it there, keep it with me, and cherish them.

And then there was the wedding. Heat floods my cheeks, despite being on my own in a dimming forest. The memory of Arthur and his hand, down my boxers, and me being so hard for him…I'd never felt so hot for anyone. The way he consumed me with his brooding stare, the way he defiled me with his wolfish grin.

The way he humiliated me with his imperious actions.

My mother cried that night during the party. "Tears of happiness," she called them. That finally, after so many years of doubt, of trying, of not wanting to barge into my life, we were finally one, big family. The dream she'd always had.

They gave me my own room in their mansion. My own bathroom. A lock that I used despite my mother's wish to keep the door open. I couldn't explain to her that I wouldn't use the bed to sleep in.

They brought me to therapy, but I had nothing to say. They brought my mother to therapy, but they told her to give me space. She did. And I took that space. Used it to drive around with Amadou, avoiding everyone in that mansion.

I let out a long and heavy sigh as I finish my coffee. It's starting to get cool out here, the sun now fully set, leaving nothing but darkness in its retreat.

I check my phone, it's a little past nine in the evening. I can't believe I've been sitting here, on this spot, for over an hour. And still, I'm not ready to leave, the peaceful trees blanketing my whirling thoughts. One episode of *Dark* on Netflix turns into another, and just to stay on the safe side, I watch another one. It's no hardship. How soon is soon?

Finally, I stretch out my arms above my head on a long yawn. It's a little before midnight now, and I'm not used to going to bed late. I'm sleepy. And a little scared.

"He's just scaring you with empty threats," I tell myself, but the truth is, with Arthur you never know.

Tomorrow I'll tell him that he can chaperone me from a distance, end of story. He doesn't need to be in my room for that, even Jean-Luc will agree.

"But I'll still beat you," I decide.

By the time I leave the gravel path and the grand reception comes into view, the door is being swung open from the inside, revealing the porter, Claude.

"Mister Deveraux." He dips his head, and waits for my shivering self to make it inside, before he closes the door behind him. Everything changes on a whim. I'm no longer on neutral territory, surrounded by silence and flora, but I'm back in the maze that's filled with menace, and I can already feel it creeping under my skin. I wonder how he knows my name but I don't ask, unsure if I'm ready to hear his answer.

"Good evening sir," I give the porter a clipped nod. "Apologies for staying out so late."

"Not a problem, Mister Deveraux. Good night."

I mumble a reply, then scoot upstairs to our dorm. In the deserted corridor, I linger, not wanting to head in. I should really get some sleep, with classes starting tomorrow. But instead, I stare at the framed images that decorate the walls. Some of them are old, with young men standing in a formal line, all dressed in the same school uniform.

The years go up all the way to last year, and I find myself searching for one particular raven-haired guy with onyx eyes. The moment I realize what I'm doing, I send the wall a scowl, take a deep breath and unlock the door. It opens with a slight creak and I flinch, body turning rigid with anticipation. I hope I didn't wake up anyone. With a few solid strides I make it to my own bedroom, opening and locking the door behind me. Once I'm alone, I practically melt against the cool wood.

"You're alright," I whisper through the darkness. "You can do this." I will start this college and graduate in four years time, and I will do it by keeping my head down. I will keep my head *down* by doing what I do best—by studying. By honest, old-fashioned studying. By keeping my dad in check. Wiping the sneaky tears from my cheek, I decide that I should really follow up on that lawyer. I owe it to Dad. No matter what my mother said. No matter what those police officers said, or those psychologists. Tomorrow. After school.

My phone buzzes in my pocket, making me jump in surprise. It's too late for Dad to contact me, him being the only one to ever call me. I blindly reach for the closest side lamp that bathes the bedroom in a faint light while I check my phone. The message is from an unknown number.

Anonymous: "Game's on. What's your next move?"

Something flashes in my chest before it tightens in bewilderment.

"What—" I look up and scan the room. Everything looks the same. The desk by the window on which I left my computer bag. The door to my closet stands ajar, which is how I left it right before taking off earlier. And my bed…my heart ruffles fast in my ribcage. On my bed is a chess game laid out. *My* chess game, the portable one I always carry with me. Two armies, one black, the other one white. A black pawn has been moved forward, opening the game for the queen and the king bishop. It's the most aggressive opening in chess.

The King's Pawn Opening.

If that doesn't show Arthur's true colors, then I don't know what does.

6

RÉGIS

I end up staring at the chessboard half the night, tossing and sweating in my new bed. It's too big, the challenge somehow too real, and mixed with my unwanted attraction toward my stepbrother, it creates a toxic vibe.

At some stage I must have fallen asleep, because when I wake up the next morning, my groggy state and tired eyes need a moment to adjust to reality. I am still lying in bed, somehow managing to stay there, in my new, *shared* dorm, the chess board staring right back at me.

"Fuck you," I grate raspily, my voice still tired. Still my hand grabs the pawn right in front of the bishop and puts it two places ahead. He wants to play? There.

Sicilian Defense.

The quick shower in my small, though luxurious, walk-in bathroom helps me to feel fresh and chipper enough to face the new day, despite the early hour. I've always been one to rise early, but where discomfort used to be the reason for that, it sure as hell will be the comfort in this place. The bed's too big, too plush. Too…much of everything I'm not used to.

The only thing that the past and the present *have* in common is what I do right after I get up—I study. Best moment of the day. And with the glorious library this school has, I have high hopes for being left alone a decent number of hours before I have to present myself in the canteen.

I get dressed in the navy-blue colors of Saint-Laurent, making sure to put on the golden brooch that carries the emblem of Monterrey Castle. After a quick glance in the mirror, I head back to my bedroom, make my bed, then grab my backpack. Outside it's still dark with the hint of morning rise that showcases dark red and golden glimmers through the trees. It's beautiful.

Swinging the bag over my shoulder, I purposefully ignore the chess board, make sure that all windows are closed, then leave my room with a turn of the key. There, locked. As in, stay the fuck away from my personal space.

I wonder if that will truly keep him away.

Outside, the communal space is bathed in darkness, and it takes me a moment to find the lightswitch. It flicks, putting the lounge into faint light.

"Already heading out, little Régis?" A hoarse rumble makes me jolt.

"Jesus," I mutter, trying my best to keep my cool, then throw my gaze around the communal space as I keep on walking. Where the hell is he? There. Arthur is sprawled out onto an armchair, his eyes raking over my presence, a small smile curled onto his lips. Clutching my hand tight around the door knob, I snarl, "That's not your business, is it?"

"Ouch." He slowly unfurls his larger body as he gets up. It's not even six yet, still he looks immaculate—his school uniform melting around sculpted muscles and a well-developed chest, thick hair slick and brushed back, the top mussed. He pulls a hand through those raven strands before he grabs the school bag at his feet. "You see, this is where you're wrong." His voice drips with sweet sinfulness, and he shoots me an amused wink when I scowl at him.

"It's a little early for your presence, Arthur." I open the door before he can say anything else and step outside, into the narrow corridor.

Unsurprisingly, Arthur catches up with me in less than three steps. His schoolbag slumps off his shoulder, and it bumps against my forearm. When I pull away, he simply chuckles. "You're not a morning person, I presume?"

"Fuck off," I grumble. "Not when the first thing I see is you."

We round the corner together, Arthur's mocking wolf-whistle lingering in the quiet air as we make our way toward the double spiral staircase. Balling my fists, I inwardly prepare for the next thing to say. Part of me wants to run and hide, but I'll be damned if I let him scare me away. Besides, he's got some explaining to do.

"I locked the door to my room yesterday, so I'd appreciate you giving me back my key."

He turns to face me, creasing his brow. "And why's that?"

"Stop playing games, you know what I'm talking about." We halt at the edge of the impressive stairs where the rising sun with its glorious reddish and golden colors reflect through the immense arched windows.

"On the contrary. We've only just begun playing games." He drums his finger against his temple. "I can't wait to see what your opening defense is, *future co-worker.*"

"Stop it," I snarl, somehow feeling caught. I shouldn't have moved that pawn in the first place, shouldn't have accepted the challenge. "We don't work together and you aren't the boss of me. I don't want you coming into my room snooping around, leaving games on my bed." My voice shakes a little. "I don't want you around."

With one surprisingly fast movement, Arthur pushes me against the railing between the stairs. "Don't you now?" He smiles a little, but every spark of humor has left his gaze. Instead, his eyes glower like fireballs that make me flinch. As if in slow motion, his long, wispy fingers tilt my chin to face him fully. The touch is light as a feather, but every single inch of my nerve system is lit. "You do remember who I am, right?" He drawls. I want to throw him off and tell him to get lost, but I'm finding myself speechless. My veins are pumping blood south, and my cock is filling rapidly, which is absolutely terrifying.

"I don't need guidance," I rasp, my throat thick with trepidation. I fucking hate myself for it.

Arthur's fingertips trail a little further over my face, brushing over my lips while he curls his own into a lazy smile. "Let me clear up some things. If I want to get up early to accompany my baby brother to his first class, I will get up early and do so. And if I want to go inside your bedroom, I'll go inside your fucking bedroom. Whenever I want to, little Régis." He dips his head, his mouth teasing the shape of my lips, then he nips at my bottom lip. His gaze narrows when he watches my smaller hand grabbing hold of his, in a lame attempt to free myself. "And I'll do whatever the fuck I want to do. Now, say sorry for not being in your room last night."

Pursing my lips, I shake my head.

He grins at that, then slides a hand around my throat and lifts me up. Eyes bulging, I look down, to where my feet have left solid ground.

"What the hell? Put me down!" It comes out as a breathy plea that makes his lips tick up even more.

"Fuck, you sure are sweet, little Régis. And a little naughty. Now, say sorry to your big brother."

"No." Arthur places his legs around my dangling ones, caging me in, then slowly brushes a curl out of my face, not giving two fucks about the way I'm literally hanging here, back arched around the cool wood, clawing on to him for dear life. "You son of a bitch—" I sputter, the effort of those words causing my cheeks to flame. I tap on his knuckles, and he wiggles his brows.

"Oh, you want me to put you down? Or would you rather me toss you down the stairwell? I wonder which set of stairs your pretty head would hit." My body shivers at the thought. We're on the second floor, and those stairs are a complexity of wooden art. That means a lot of hard material that could bash my head in.

It's a trick.

Though I can't be sure.

"Fuck you," I wheeze, swearing some more when he simply tilts his head back and lets out an obscene bark. My throat is burning, together with my eyes that are itching from the lack of sleep they've had. It's too early for this shit, and the worst part is that my hardened cock is filled with misplaced arousal.

Arthur glides two fingertips over my burning cheek. "If you bite, I'll throw you down the stairs." It's the only warning he gives before he slips them inside my mouth. I'm too surprised, too indignant to fully understand what he's doing, but when I feel his digits connect with my tongue, I nearly bite on them in my attempt to stifle my groan. Wiggling like a fish in his hold, I sputter, my hanging foot coming up to kick him, only to have the force taken out of me when he tilts my head further back. His eyes stare intently at my mouth, tipped into a cruel grin while he pushes me further over the railing. Pain flickers through my back, and I grunt, feet still trying to catch a hold. I'm completely at his mercy. And all the while, his fingers play with my tongue.

"So here's my father wanting to take care of his new stepson, little Régis. And he wants me to help you while you're on my territory. And since I'm the heir of our family business, I'll oblige and look out for you. And you, my sweet little stepbro, will be grateful. Now, I told you that I'd come and see you soon, yet you failed to be in your bedroom. As your *chaperone,* I'm not pleased." He chuckles lowly.

Tears sting in my eyes when my lungs constrict, a dull ache forming in my throat.

"Please—" I whimper between his fingers, my hand on his no longer feisty but turned into a limp rag.

"Hm. Not quite the word I was looking for, but I like the way it rolls off your tongue. Out of your sweet mouth that's stuffed with my fingers." Arthur steps forward, but instead of yanking me deeper against the wood, he glues our bodies together. I dip my gaze, cheeks heating with shame. He can feel me, *he can feel me,* echoes through my mind. And there's not a damn thing in the world I can do to make it stop. "Are you going to let me guide you, little Régis?"

I nod, desperate now for him to back off.

"Good. Open your pants then."

My eyes widen, all earlier bravado now officially thrown out of the window. "Wh-wh—"

"Your. Pants." The curl of his lips is feral and he watches me intently.

"No," I stammer, my tongue colliding once more with his fingers. It nearly makes me gag. "No."

He pulls me back over the railing, feet dangling in the air in less than two seconds, and I yelp while I grab hold of his clothed thigh.

"*Now.*" It's nothing but a hoarse whisper, but it feels like a heavy, heavy defeat. Why isn't anyone out here right now? Surely, it isn't that early anymore? Or is it—

Arthur gives me a dirty smirk. "No one's here to save you now. Now, let me guide you."

My fingers tremble when I finally pop the buttons of my school pants. I can't believe I'm doing this. I can't believe my cock is hardening despite the insanity of this situation. But I can hardly breathe, and Arthur is even more of a crazy fucker than I'd suspected.

"Good. Good," he croons after he's squeezed me back against the railing again. Slowly he pulls out his fingers from my mouth, then plops them into his own. When I eye him in suspicion, he just grins. Then they disappear from his mouth and dip inside my boxers. His hold on my neck becomes less firm, and I suck in a deep breath of air that comes out on a confused, shaky moan when he wraps his hands around my cock. "All hard for me already, little Régis. Tell me, does that make you hot?" Arthur purrs. "Having your big bad stepbrother nearly choke you to death? You like it when I threaten you?" He bends his head to breathe in the skin of my neck, greedily humming when he does so.

"You smell good. Do you like the shower gel I got you?"

What?

"Fuck you," I want to tell him, but nothing leaves my throat except for a filthy moan, while my mind scrambles to remember what I used earlier under the shower. Eucalyptus. He got that for me? His hand feels so damn good, as it slowly, teasingly makes its way over my girth. He comes up to my tip, swirls his thumb into my wet spot, whispering all kinds of filthy things as he does so.

"You really are a kitten, little Régis. A *chaton.* You claw and hiss, but underneath that self-defense you really are sweet, aren't you? So innocent."

Pressure builds in my stomach and balls and my fingers dig into the wooden railing, into his clothed thigh, into his shoulder blade. His rhythm picks up just that little bit, but those filthy words, that husky sound…it drives me fucking crazy. White hot pleasure shoots through my veins and my balls draw up even further, readying themselves for release. And then I come on a startled cry, squeezing Arthur tight as my body shivers in pleasure. I am in ecstasy, famished from all those secretive dreams, those wicked sins that haunted me at night. Fuck, I've dreamt of him ever since he layed his hands on me the first time in the back of that car. But in real life, his hands on my body are so intense, just like my orgasm that seems to last forever. My body quivers as it empties itself, pouring my cum onto my stepbrother's waiting hand. My *stepbrother*.

Oh my god.

"That's it," he rasps into my ear, hands wrapped around my trembling shoulders. "That's a grateful, little stepbro." He slowly drags his fingers over my shirt, all the way up to my chin, leaving a wet trace of cum on its trail. "You act as though that's the first time someone's touched you." He cocks his head as his charcoal eyes take me in, searching for the truth. Either the orgasm hasn't really finished or I'm sick in the head, because my mouth goes dry and my thighs tremble.

"Yeah, it was."

He gives me a wolfish grin. "Don't worry, I'll guide you through everything. You and I are going to have so much fun." I can only stare asphyxiated when he pops his cum-stained fingers between his own lips and suckles them down. My mind has gone blank, the power of my orgasm having wiped out all reasonable thoughts. After one last dart of his tongue around his fingers, he pops them out.

"You—what about you? Don't you—" The outline of his hard cock looks devilishly obscene through his uniform. He smirks.

"Don't worry, we'll get to that in the next round. This one was for you, in exchange for your beautiful gratification. Now, let me look at you." Pulling back, he takes his time eying my disheveled state with a wicked twinkle in his eyes. "Your pants," he finally rasps. I look down, horrified by the dirty stains on my clothes. The wet trail from my shirt down to my clothed crotch, that has smudges of cum on them. "Leave them on. I like watching you covered in your own release, knowing it was me who tipped you over the edge and made you come." He lazily brushes his wet fingers over them, as if to rub the evidence of my weakness even more in. I haven't received my other sets of uniforms yet, is the first thing that comes to mind. The thought makes me even more furious.

"Now that you have proven to be the strongest, let's quit here and now." I snarl.

"They'll all know, little Régis," he sing-songs softly, his voice laced with mischief. "Every single one of them."

Tipping up my chin, I bristle, "I'll show you wrong, Arthur. You cannot control me, no one can."

He clacks his tongue, smiling. "You and I were made to compete, and we both know it."

"I don't want to fight you!"

"No, but you want to win the prize."

"*What* prize?"

"Hmm." He curls his lips into a sarcastic smile. "You'll find out all about that."

"What's that supposed to mean? I don't—"

"Oh, but I do," Arthur winks salaciously. "I'm a greedy bastard, little Régis. I want it all. And you know what?" He chuckles, the sound soft, but his touch in my hair is anything but. "I always get what I want." He lets go of me to straighten his jacket, looking fucking perfectly calm.

"You're such an ass," I seethe. Then, without a single second of hesitation, I lunge for him, ignoring the way my heart thunders in my chest, and shove at his firm chest. Hard. He lets go with a groan, but I don't turn around to see if he's hurt. No, I practically dive for the stairs, needing to get the hell away from him. The step is lower than I think, and I yelp when I lose balance. My arms lunge in the air, readying for a deep dive, while my entire body follows in slow-motion. Shit. My feet don't even touch the first one, before Arthur plucks me like a strained cat and presses me against his warm, firm chest, while he keeps one hand clasped around the back of my neck.

"Careful now. You don't want to get hurt." His kiss on the crown of my head is featherlight and as lethal as his threat. He settles me gingerly on the highest step, where I stay while I wait for the tingles to disappear. Stupid, treacherous body.

I don't know how long I'm there for, just standing and staring into nothing. But finally, the air around me clears and students come into view, passing me as they make their way downstairs and to the canteen.

Arthur is gone, I know he is. But then he isn't really. Because I've gotten myself into some serious shit. He's not going to let this go. He's going to use this as the perfect distraction.

Focus. Just fucking focus. Arthur will only be here for one more year and then he has graduated. He'll be gone, ruling his empire from god knows what throne.

But I can't. All I feel is this clawing desperation in my chest cavity telling me to run. Run from all of it. I won't let him touch me ever again. It's not right and it shouldn't affect me. Shouldn't... fuck, I'm going to be in so much trouble.

The first bell rings, announcing that breakfast will finish in fifteen minutes.

So I have been here for a while. Time I could have spent on studying.

"Damn you, asshole," I grumble, picking up my bag, my breath and dignity. I blink, catching sight of the large painting that hangs in the staircase. It looks like a portrait of hell, with a group of cloaked figures watching a golden crow that flies in the air. A fitting image for this nefarious place.

"Hey!" I bump into Maxime while having my last-minute breakfast. He gazes at my filthy clothes, taking his time to take it all in, while I shovel the last bite of a croissant in my mouth. Trying my best to ignore his unspoken questions, I swallow my food away with a sip of coffee that practically burns my tongue. Motherfucker. "Bad start of the day?"

"You can say that." I try another swig. Yeah, definitely too fucking hot. And by the looks of the other students, passing us as they make their way to the main hall for the official start of the school year, I know my time's up. Placing the cup back on the table with a sigh, I pull my backpack over my shoulder, only to realize that Maxime's still there. Waiting for me. With a shit eating grin on his face.

"Are you looking forward to kicking off your college career?"

"I definitely prefer being down here than up there in my dorm." It comes out a little crankier than I meant, but Maxime still chuckles. "Touché."

I bump his shoulder playfully. "Now, let's just get this over with, shall we?"

We follow the other students into the noisy large reception hall where the official kick-off of the school year is about to take place.

"So what's your major?"

"Business Administration."

He nods. "Any extras?"

"Global Management and Data Analytics. And they also do a few classes on the history of Monterrey Castle that I thought would be fun."

"So you didn't try out for the football team then?" He shoots me a wink and I can't help but grin. Really, this guy is impossible. We're about the same height, around 172 cm, and equally slender built. We're not really small, but most of the guys around us are still taller. Dominique is, and so is Jo.

Around us, the whispers and agitated chortles slowly dissipate, leaving us all standing here in the increasing silence. Waiting for the air to be filled. It doesn't take long before a voice rings through a microphone, welcoming us to the new school year.

Maxime points toward the stairs, to where a middle-aged man stands with the microphone at his lips. "That's Mister Dupont," he whispers. "He's the director of our school. You'll probably only see him today." A pristine suit shines in the faded light and grey hair is slicked to one side, neatly tucked behind the man's ear, that frames his face together with the legs of a pair of silver glasses.

Dragging my eyes from the older man with the sturdy voice, I narrow my gaze at Maxime. "Only today?"

He lets out another one of his typical innocent chuckles that makes the corners of his eyes crinkle a little. It's so gullible and so misplaced in a world like Saint-Laurent, that it makes me nearly wonder if it's genuine after all. He nods, then grins some more. "That's what they say. That he's never here during the school year."

"...You're such bright students, the country's most privileged young men. And I'm honored to welcome you home..." The director continues, but I check out. I know that Saint-Laurent doesn't have more than 150 students, but still... With all of us crowded in the reception hall, the lounge no longer feels spacious, cramped instead, making me feel light-headed as if I can't breathe. My chest constricts when that thought lingers, as if giving me exactly what my mind believes it needs.

Swaying a little on my feet, I feel sweat dripping from my forehead. And that makes me think of earlier. Christ, the day hasn't even started yet, and I'm already filthy with fluids. My knees buckle, and I open my mouth to inhale a sharp breath, no longer focusing on that voice that continues to resound through the open space. Here and there students cheer when being called out, but for the rest, it's just oppressive.

Until finally, *finally*, it's over. People start moving.

Maxime grabs me by my arm, and I bite the inside of my

cheek to stop myself from leaning into him in an attempt to regain my balance and recharge my battery. I'm not sure if he's aware of my inner turmoil, but he doesn't call me out on it. Instead he gives me a beaming smile. "So, how does it feel now you've officially started? Want me to walk you to your first class? My god, I remember how nervous I was. So?" I look around me, forehead drenched in sweat, at all the people around me. Their sounds are muffled, as if I'm not really here.

I sense Arthur's gaze on me before I see him. Tall, menacing, the way he watches me from where he's standing next to Louis, who's chatting to some random student.

"Régis?" Maxime asks again.

"No—" I turn my head to face him, making sure to keep my facade on. "I'm fine, thanks. See you." And then I take off, having absolutely no clue where the hell I'm going. I accidentally end up in the wrong wing, then walk into the wrong class.

Their eyes are on me, I can feel it. On the messy strands that tumble around my ears, on those blue eyes that work so hard to glare indifferently, and on my filthy clothes.

I can't believe I let him do that to me.

Other students are polite, but distant, and I can't help but wonder.

They'll all know, little Régis.

I can't believe I wanted him to do that to me. Because I can ignore it as much as I want, but some dark, shameless part of me wanted what Arthur did. Wanted my stepbrother, the guy I've been crushing on ever since I met him in their mansion by the sea, to touch me. To blanket me in his wickedness and mark me as his. Even if it's just for that moment...it felt so good to be captured by him, to be clutched between his claws and held against his firm, warm chest. It made me forget about everything else—about the man who once kept his son a prisoner, only to have become the prisoner himself. It's striking how the tables have turned.

There was only Arthur and the undivided attention that he lavished on me. Those onyx eyes glued to my face, those full, curvy lips teased into a smirk, and those long, slender fingers wrapped around my cock.

Fuck...

I need to calm the hell down. This is college. And not just any college. It's a place for rich, stuck up guys who all now stare at me with that knowing look. Because they know it, just like I fucking know it. I don't belong.

This place shouldn't make me want things I can't have.

Apologizing thoroughly when I finally make it to my own classroom, I scurry into the furthest corner, relieved to find an empty seat. Thank god for that. Luckily I'll be stuck in this room for the next three hours, so that's sorted. I can finally breathe. And with a tentative smile on my face, I open my bag and grab my books, chest slowly deflating. I can do this.

As it turns out, I am right. Because despite my constant trepidation, classes are interesting. And despite my own hesitation, one day melts into another.

Apart from the chess board on my bed, where a new move is revealed every evening, nothing remarkable happens. I guess letting Arthur come into my room and play his game is my way of accepting his presence, even though we don't cross paths anymore.

He's a good player, but I knew that, challenging me to switch from an attack to defense, and back to attack. Our white and black army falters, sighs, then continues its tauntingly slow march toward the end of the game. And I find myself looking forward to that moment every night, when I come back into my bedroom to see what his next move has been.

Around me, everyone else seems to slowly fall into their rhythm as well, as the season picks up from before the summer break. Football practice has started, meaning I hardly bump into Louis. Projects are announced for this school year, and that means that Arthur is practically never in the lounge room of our dorm.

It's nice to settle down. To find a flow of my own standards, a cadence I choose because I can. I like to get up early, spend as many free hours as I can in the library or outside between the quiet and peaceful green.

It's nice. Perhaps it would be even better if people would actually come and talk to me, aside from staring. Because I can feel them watching, ever since that first day when I joined Maxime with my cum stained clothes. But they won't talk to me.

That evening, and despite my premonition that he'll be in a foul mood, Dad's actually talkative on the phone. He asks me how school has been and even seems to care about my answers. Sitting crossed-legged on my bed, I'm listening to Dad moaning about the poor quality of his food and the lack of hygiene. About the horrible showers and the constant, constant fear for safety. Our phone calls are not allowed to take more than five minutes, and the judge decided that Dad can only contact me every other day. That includes me contacting him.

He tells me about a visit he had from our lawyer, who really is stil a graduate student, because he's the only one we can afford. After he met up with Dad for the first time, he decided to take on our case, despite having an enormous law firm breathing down our neck. Such an ambitious fool.

By the time our conversation is automatically disconnected, I feel completely empty inside. Guilt and remorse flood through the void of my core. Because no matter the outcome, I'll probably always wonder if this whole mess Dad's in is my fault.

Perhaps I wished too hard for her.

Perhaps I wasn't the perfect son he wanted.

Gazing out through the window from my bed, all these scenarios flood through my mind, trying to suffocate me.

A knock at the door makes me flinch. It's soft enough to

make me realize that it's not someone standing at my door, but at our dorm door. I wait for a full ten seconds in the hope that someone else miraculously appears and takes care of it. Then curiosity kills the cat and I sneak out of my dorm and walk toward the door. When I swing it open I stand face to face with Claude, the porter.

"Uhm, hello?" I stammer.

His oval, pale face is blank. "Régis Deveraux?" He asks rhetorically since he knows who I am.

"Uhm, yes?"

"You have received a letter."

"A letter?" I ask, flabbergasted.

"*Oui.*" He hands me a cream-colored envelope. "For you." Then he turns on his heel and walks away without a single word.

"Uhm—" When he disappears around the corner, I dip my gaze to look at the envelope clutched in my hand. With an ink pen my name is written on it in curly letters.

My hands tremble a little when I tear the casing open to take hold of a letter, the words written in that same, curly handwriting:

BIENVENUE

You, our brother, who carries his heritage with dignity and pride, who walks this world with his head high, searching—not quite finding—to belong. And belong you shall, brother, because today is the day that your life will change.

You are invited to become part of the inevitable, the circle of gold that will keep your spine straight and your dignity intact. To meld into a group of people who are like you, brother, who were once searching but who found—found—what life really means.

Loyalty.

Respect.

Tradition.

Sacrifice.

Soon, your Initiations shall begin.

Hell no. I'm not going there.

PART II

DENIAL

A spicy, resinous scent flooded through the darkness. A darkness that was merely lit up by the flickering fire and those decorative torches that occupied the corners of the small space. They were hidden in the dungeons of Monterrey Castle, in a room with wooden flowers on its ceilings. Bars outside the small windows were used by flapping bats that squeaked into the night.

Rumor had it that this part of the building was deserted save from a handful of teachers who resided here.

They were lies.

The truth was that the south wing was kept desolate for history to slip through the cracks of the ancient wooden flooring and its stone walls. To make sure that what was done between these facades would never be forgotten in time.

The rebellion that shook the streets of Paris back in 1789. That revision of destiny to those who made it here, in this castle. They had been the lost elite, but after a few years of hiding, they were ready to be found again. Ready to reunite, to strike. To become unforgettable.

What kept them together?

Loyalty.

Respect.

Traditions.

Sacrifice.

"One of our pupils has not shown up tonight." Elder Jacques commented, his voice merely a slither like a hissing snake, filled with disappointment.

"Despite accommodating the request we received to accept a commoner amongst us, and the invitation that he has received to join us for his first Initiation, he has decided not to appear. He is a deviant, though I'm not sure why. Perhaps it is because of the lack of dignity in his blood?"

Someone whispered behind his heavy, golden mask, the unintelligible words sounding more like a gentle touch caressing the air, the words light and heavy at the same time.

"What to do brothers?" Elder Jacques ambled through the room,

cane booming in their ears like thunder, its intervals slow and threatening. "What do we do to pupils who forsake their own destiny? An invitation to join the Alpha Fraternarii is a tremendous honor. One that can't be ignored, nor refused!" He snarled.

Tonight, the first rituals had taken place. With five new pupils, instead of six, it had been busy in the small dungeon room. But my, oh my...had it been satisfying for the most senior brothers. In a few months things would change, once the pupils had completed their pledge to the brotherhood. Then they'd all be together, and able to discuss the future and the way they could alter it. But there was something very special about those first months, when sex was power and pupils were eager to please.

"We need our deviation to show soon, we promised the founding family to bring him home." Elder Jacques breathed, and his voice turned soft again, regretful. "He needs to embrace his altered future." His cane boomed again, annoyed. "He can't ignore his destiny!"

"Priviledge," hooded brothers chanted.

"He too shall become powerful."

"Loyalty."

"He too shall become influential."

"Traditions."

"He too shall belong."

"Respect."

Elder Jacques tilted his gaze, his stare empty from behind the golden mask that covered his face, and watched the group. "What happens to a brother who is lost?"

"We bring him back," someone muttered with a low voice and a dipped head.

"And what if he doesn't want to be brought back?" He spread his arms wide, silently requesting everyone to join in on that answer that would give each and every brother a flutter through their chests.

"We hunt him down," they chanted. "Hunt him down. Hunt him down. Hunt him down..."

7

ARTHUR

"Hm, yeah, just like that..."

Slumped back onto the armchair, Louis has his head dipped backward, pointing toward the ceiling. Not that he's watching the colorful coffered panels or all those tiny details. Nah, he's got his eyes closed. His lips are parted, his chest is heaving and his hand is lightly placed onto the guy's head. That guy is our favorite sex worker, who's currently on his knees and between my brother's spread legs, blowing his cock.

"Fuck, baby boy, how I missed you," Louis groans. Grabbing hold of the escort's light strands, he tugs at them, dipping his head to take in the action. He winks when he sees me glaring, then starts thrusting his hips. He's getting close, and I really don't have to see the outcome of that show. Unlike most siblings, Louis and I are not shy about watching each other having a good time. We've found ourselves in similar situations more than a few times. But that doesn't mean that I have to see it through until the end.

Getting off the couch, I head for the shared kitchen to make myself a drink. Classes resumed earlier this month, and I've got one hell of a year ahead of me. This is my fourth and final year, and with my future outside school lurking closely over me, it will be a challenge to combine all of it. Once I graduate from Saint-Laurent, I will start my traineeship within our family company. The goal? To become the future CEO of the Deveraux Holding.

Destiny. My life has always been wrapped around my future. Every single careful step I take is in the name of my family. We currently manage six business units, and as part of preparing me for my future, Dad has allowed me to co-manage the merger of a chain of winehouses in Spain. So far, it has been both interesting and exciting, as well as a reassurance that this is what my brain was meant to focus on. Business, money, the future of our family. That was…until Dad and Nathalie got married.

I mean, no surprises there. They've been together for pretty much as long as I can remember. Even though she and Dad only officially moved in together when me and Louis started college, she comes as close to a mom I have ever had. Before she finally agreed to live with us by the sea, she lived in a beautiful penthouse closeby. Their love has always been solid. We were happy, the four of us. That is, until the day Dad told us about Régis. Our little stepbrother.

No, that's not true either. I guess that I was surprised and curious about these sudden events. Where the hell did he come from? And where was he when we were living our lives together? Why had she never mentioned him before?

Behind me, Louis's urgent pants are a sign that he's about to come, but I switch off his sounds, focusing instead on the Nespresso machine Gaël insisted on getting. There's a disarray of colorful cups that hurt my fucking eyes. Too much choice. Since I plan on putting a few more hours in studying, I settle with the yellow cup, the espresso *Volluto*. Whatever, as long as it does the trick. It's the final one I allow myself for the evening. After nine I only drink herbal tea or water, unless it's Friday night. My mental planning doesn't allow for me to have any social outbursts, my public appearance always monitored.

I am the one they all count on. The one who will secure their future. Which is why I can't afford to make any mistakes.

"I thought you already finished your homework?" Louis asks on a ragged breath. His cheeks are flushed and he licks his lips while his eyes flutter, staring at my coffee.

"I'm still working on that final report for Dad." With the coffee in hand, I flip them off, sauntering back to the bedroom I share with my twin. They did a great job renovating this dorm and turning it into a place for five. Our room is spacious with two single beds, two desks and a shitload of space for us to get dressed, complete with walk-in wardrobes and a standing mirror. Behind the changing area is a private bathroom with a tub and a separate shower and toilet. It also sits right next to Régis's bathroom, and it didn't take me long to realize that I can hear him in the morning. Meaning I know exactly when my gullible, snarky little stepbrother gets up for the day. He's an early riser like myself, which I appreciate.

Can't afford any mistakes, though.

But there's something about my little stepbrother. Something that has me spending far too much time thinking of him. Something that has me behaving like a bull, ready to devour its prey. It seems I can't stop touching him. There's something about him that makes me want to dig deeper and pry inside, like I'm studying some exotic animal. I don't know if it's got to do with his skittishness that borders on some social anxiety disorder. Or the way he freezes when he catches sight of me, a horrific deadpan stare on his handsome face. Perhaps it's the way he practically melts into my hands, submitting to my every touch, that scowl burning fierce in his blue eyes.

It makes me wonder what goes on deep inside that delicate mind of his. He's all sweet, smooth, innocent and shy, with that delicious bite in his words.

My competitor. Because if the family has decided to bring him into the family business, who's to say they won't make him CEO one day?

No, I can't afford any mistakes.

But fuck, do I like him rattled and spitting foul words at me. It's dangerous, the way my body reacts to his presence. From that very first moment he scurried inside our house, all shy and prickly, with that haunted look in those bright, blue eyes. Something in my chest pang, and I fucking hate it.

Fucking hate the way he toys with my heart and my future. Yeah, he's got to pay for speeding up my heartrate.

Sitting myself down at my desk, I take a sip from my coffee, then open up my laptop. I start with checking what my calendar looks like for the remainder of the first semester. Wrong choice, because the number of ticked off time slots is kind of depressing.

Despite my morning work-out routine, Gaël insisted that I take two meditation moments per week. He has even already marked them off my timetable, his classes scribbled down with a bright yellow marker. My eyes catch the golden crosses that Louis marked on the calendar. One for last month, and one for next month, the date approaching rapidly.

The Initiations of the brotherhood have officially begun and those first months always take more time. Not every brother has been decently prepared by their dad, and sometimes the unknowing can lead to tensions. Just like in Régis's case, where Dad can't guide him through this procedure and has given me free reign instead. Although during their first gathering, this group looked promising. After all, there was only one pupil who didn't show up for his first initiation.

My little stepbrother, telling the whole world how he doesn't need a chaperone with his chin tilted and that distant, cool look on his face while his shoulders slump in anxiety.

Mon chaton, do you have any idea what mess you're walking into?

I mean, he's clever, the little shithead. But small, fragile, innocent, quirky Régis makes me do all sorts of things I should regret. Like groping his dripping cock in the back of an SUV and making him quiver. Fuck, so alluring. All dainty and feisty, with imaginary claws and all. It brings out my biggest asshole-y side, and trust me, he's an even bigger asshole than I usually am.

Guzzling down the remainders of my coffee, I stare at the report on my computer screen, suddenly not so inspired anymore. I shouldn't have taken that coffee after all. I'm feeling agitated, and distracted, mind filling with things I shouldn't want. Perhaps I need to get my dick wet, or get that misplaced distress milked out of my system.

Dominique once asked me if I like it that people are afraid of me because of the reputation our family has gained.

Yeah, I guess I fucking do.

My little stepbrother being a fascinating creature shouldn't be an obstacle. Call it unethical, I don't care, but I could fuck him good and be done with this weird fascination. But Dad wants him in the business? Yeah, there's a problem.

My little stepbrother is—alluring. Which makes him dangerous. And dangers need to be eliminated.

Grabbing my mug, I head back to the living area, suddenly hoping that my brother is nearly finished. I need him around. But when I make my way toward the kitchen, I see that he's still in the middle of his play, as breathless chuckles filling the heady space. No one else seems to be around. Since I'm tempted, I check Régis's door. It's locked, I know—he always locks it—but I carry a spare key to his room. I've used it over the past weeks to make my daily move on the chessboard, and the fact that he has let me, that he has even taken on the challenge, shouldn't make me feel as victorious as it does. But still... Knocking on his door, I wait for a full two seconds before I use my spare and undo the latch. A few seconds later the door swings open.

The faint scent of eucalyptus invades my nostrils—it's his shower gel, which I got him. For some inexplicable reason I felt the need to choose it, and given the fact that he loves plants, I made the right choice. Still, I'm strangely relieved that he hasn't thrown it away out of pure spite. No, he's using it, and fuck me, if it doesn't smell good on him.

Régis is well organized, his stuff neatly put together on his desk. Pens in a glass, books all nicely stacked together, his laptop folded and waiting to be used. Behind the table on the window sill, he has placed a few small pots with mostly just potting soil.

Giving his view a quick glance, I turn around and eye his bed.

My next destination.

The sheets are drawn, pyjamas waiting on his pillow. The pillows are missing, but I know that he doesn't use them and leaves them in his closet. I still haven't figured out on which side he sleeps though, neither appears used, the chess board switching sides far too often. Today it sits on the far end, right by the window. I glance it over with a satisfied huff. I knew he was going to go for my knight. He has tilted it to the side, taken by his bishop. It's a risk, and a pretty bold one, since I now prevail over the left side of his board. Rather than going for his rook, which I technically can, I decide on moving forward a pawn, letting him decide what strategy to take.

His wardrobe is only half full, but whatever clothes he has are nicely stacked together or hung on coat hangers. They are mostly clothes from his past, the ones he already carried when he came into our lives a little under a year ago.

He still goes back to that shithole in Nîmes, despite Dad's successful efforts to have the place rented out to another family. Still goes back to visit his old school, though he didn't meet up with any friends, assuming that he has any. Still visits his grandparent's grave. Still visits his dad in prison.

I fucking hate it. Amadou does too, which is why it didn't take too much convincing for him to spill it out. The place is too big, too dangerous for someone like Régis. Inwardly groaning, I head for the windows and look outside to where thick, dark clouds are gathering. It's only early evening, but with heavy rainfall on the way, the sky is darkening rapidly, blanketing the glorious woods in all its true, autumn colors.

After a quick check in his shower to assure myself that he still has enough bath gel and towels, I lock the door behind me and return to me and Louis' bedroom. Outside there's a bang through the overshadowing sky and the treetops seem to tremble in anticipation.

Behind me, in the living room, Louis and the escort talk in hushed voices as they say their goodbyes, but with my gaze glued to the glass, I blink in surprise, then tug my eyes into a frown. Is that—

It is. Régis is walking outside, following the garden path toward the football field. I check my watch—nearly seven. What the hell's he doing there at this time? It will be dark soon.

"Our little Régis..." Louis mumbles when he moves to stand next to me, his eyes following my gaze. "Is in trouble," he sings. Identical, dark eyes gaze up to meet mine, his usual, playful grin tugged at his lips. "Whatcha going to do about it? Our brothers are getting restless."

"Hmm." He's right. Jitters of turmoil have swirled through the brotherhood lately like some mutual agitation. A hunger for more wickedness. For play, for more power. It has made it challenging to keep everyone concentrated. Our little deviation from Régis not playing his part right now is only making things worse.

"You need his stubborn ass in line for our next initiation." I grind my teeth and Louis snorts out a laugh. "Although, I have to say, I was a little surprised that Dad chose you, of all people, to guide him through the next months. He clearly doesn't know of your rather…" He flashes me a wink, "Naughty thoughts. I was tempted to tell him and Nathalie how I was sure that you'd take real good care of our little s-brother."

"Fuck off," I growl.

"Nope, not me. It's you who has his grumpy, possessive gaze all over Régis, not me. The poor guy doesn't even stand a chance. I've seen the way he looks at you. I bet you could get him on all fours in no time. With a nice firm collar hanging around that long, curvy neck, the leash nice and tight, and that cocky mouth of his at work."

"You're such an asshole," I grunt, throwing a playful punch at his shoulder. Though that sounds…my stomach clenches and my dick perks up.

Louis pinches the bridge of his nose. "Seriously though, we need to be careful. Look at how Elder Jacques managed to stir up the situation. We don't want things to escalate."

"Wouldn't he like that? The old pervert."

"He's an ass, agreed." We both snort at that. "Are we sure that Régis actually got the invitation? He hasn't mentioned it to anyone."

"Which is why I've put Julien on the case. He's a brother, and being Dominique's brother's ex-boyfriend, he knows all about difficult lives." I wiggle my brows. "I may have promised him an evening with you for every bit of useful information on Régis's whereabouts." I huff out a laugh when Louis chokes out a grunt of something close to contempt. Or amusement. Perhaps it's both, I'm not sure.

"You did *what*?" He grumbles. "And he agreed?"

"Of course he did. His dick is permanently dripping for you, man. So far his information has been useful, but not good enough for him to earn his prize." Although my brother would jump at any occasion to plough that twink's tight ass, despite his protest. Dominique's cute friend, all giggly and bratty, has been sweet talking to Louis ever since we started college.

"Apparently our little stepbrother enjoys spending an unhealthy amount of time outside in the forest."

Louis shrugs. "So, he's a treehugger? Who cares? It's a beautiful forest."

"I want to know what he's up to, brother. And I will, even if it's with the help of an outsider. And one of these days, I will find out, despite Régis avoiding me like the plague."

Louis's grimace blooms into a shit eating grin. "So you really have lost your shit? Marking your territory all over here, knowing exactly what our little s-brother is up to. Damn, bro, I knew you had it in you. All these years of being the perfect son, but there he is, my evil twin. I fucking love it." He shakes his head, chuckling to himself, ignoring how I'm visibly boiling with anger and fisting my hands. "Our little stepbrother," he mutters again, and it's enough to make me explode.

"I'm too busy for that shit, bro." I say in denial.

I can't afford any mistakes. " Though leaving Dad's office and shoving Régis against that wall while my hand itched to get inside his pants? Yeah, that was sort of a mistake. It was irresponsible. The need to get him all flustered and stammering fucking *feral*. Although having my twin catching me in the act? Not so clever. Thank fuck he doesn't know about what happened that first morning of classes. Flutters of what happened between us at the top of the stairs ravage my mind. Of having his neck between my fingers and his feet off the ground. Pushed against the wall. My cock jerks and I rake a frustrated hand through my hair.

"Yeah? So what are you saying, you're not fucking him?"

I snort. "Of course not."

"No?" Louis wiggles his brows playfully. "Want me to ask Dad to put Régis under my care?"

A rumble shatters through my chest, and I squeeze my hands

even tighter, frantically chasing the sting. "I've got it under control, bro."

"I just thought, if you're too busy finishing this year on top of your class, and winning the *Prix d'Honneur,* I can volunteer. It wouldn't be the first time that I cover for you."

"I said, I got it under control," I grit through clenched teeth, ignoring the way my brother cackles at that, his eyes glimmering, knowingly. He was handed to me, my sexy, little stepbrother. On a fucking platter. *Me,* of all people. Fuck, if that doesn't make me feel hot and powerful. Touching him, that full package of perfect innocence, made me feel more aroused than I have felt since a long time. Though... I eye the other option, my brother. Louis is the sturdy one out of the two of us. He's a tough dude, a bully, the football player, the loud one, the popular guy. He's my other half, everything I am not, and I love him to bits. Together, we fucking slash it.

"Well, whatever you have in mind, get it sorted. I'm not lying when I say that something's going on. Our brothers need a change, and the other Elder hanging around with his obscene fantasies is not helping either. What did those three guys do together during the Initiations?"

"Yeah, man, that was brutal." I saw that. It was fucking hot as hell, can't deny that. Louis doesn't say a word, but I know that our minds have drifted off to the same thought.

"We hunt him down. Hunt him down, hunt him down, hunt him down..."

And they will. They are hungry, powerful guys who believe they are entitled to any form of entertainment they choose. If Régis continues to ignore his destiny, things might get out of control. Because they will bring him in and onto his knees. They will play with him until he begs to do his pledge.

Outside, the wind has picked up, toying with the heavy clouds while the treetops stream. And with that, the shadow of Régis disappears into the woods.

"We need to bring him to safety first, Arthur." Louis muses. "If you want to play with him afterwards, that's fine. But we won't give him away. He's part of our family now."

Those words...they bring a soft rumble to my chest and a throb to my dick. I hate how I like the sound of them. How I want them to become my reality. The thought of having Régis on his knees and with my cock between his wet lips is fucking thrilling. The thought of claiming that gorgeous, curvy ass and burying my dick inside, victorious. And the thought of him being part of the family has no business sounding as sweet and melodic as it does.

Louis's gaze radiates triumph when he turns to face me. "Well... since I got you to be quiet, I seem to be hitting the mark." Leaving me there with a dry throat and a sneer on my face, he turns around and stalks back to the shared lounge.

He doesn't even seem surprised when I pass him with a raspy snarl as I march to the rack to grab my coat. Louis is right though, Régis belongs to us. To *me*. After all, Dad made me promise that I'd guide him, and right now, I need to guide him to his fate before our brothers do.

"Are you going somewhere?" He asks innocently, lashes fluttering with amusement.

"Yeah. I'm gonna pick up that little shit."

"In the forest? In your sweatpants and cashmere?"

I don't care about the pants, and after giving my Louis Vuitton coat a quick once-over, I shrug. Fuck it. Buttoning up with agile fingers, my hand lingers on the tiny bag that contains the rain coat provided by school. I shake my head in annoyed surprise, pull it back, only to snag the coat off the rack right before I open the door.

"Catch you on the flip side, bro."

"Call me when you've finished?" Louis asks.

"Yeah. See you in a bit."

Autumn has a way of fooling us. Of making us believe, when we're still standing behind glass, that the sunshine and the fluttery, colorful leaves will shower us in gentle weather.

Wrong.

The wind is surprisingly cool and stings my cool hands and face like a bitch when I make my way outside the gardens. Despite the school employing multiple teams to maintain the acres of land that belong to castle territory, there never seem to be many students outside. Or perhaps they are, but I just don't see them.

Perhaps they're just like me. Over the past years, I have spent the occasional obligatory class outside, or have been for casual walks whenever I couldn't avoid them. But mostly I spent my time either in the gym, or in class, or in the library. I'm a creature of habit, one who lives on a fixed plan that tells me how many hours I sleep, what I eat and how I spend my time. Order is imperative in order to excel.

For my future and for my family.

But right now… my hands fist in frustration. This path that was laid out for me ever since I was a teenager is in jeopardy. Because of the sweet, golden-haired kitten who's walking less than fifty meters from me at this very moment.

I caught up with Régis pretty quickly. Where my footsteps are measured, light and fast in their determination to find my target, his are slow and casual. His blue gaze searches all around us, through the twilight, making me seriously wonder what it is that he's so eager to find. He's completely oblivious to my presence, that's for sure, because he wouldn't be so chill if he knew that he was being hunted by the big, bad wolf.

A growl escapes my throat and my cock jumps at the thought. Yeah, I like the nickname the Alpha Fraternarii gave me. Big, because of my size, and bad, because Louis is right, I can come up with the filthiest of activities for our pupils to do during their Initiations.

Ahead of me, Régis stops and stares between the large oak trees. We have nearly reached for the cultivated part in the woods, where Gaël and his cronies keep their herb garden. If we keep on walking, less than two hundred meters from there, Régis will stumble upon the stables, hidden in the shrubs.

The sun dips behind the trees, pretty suddenly bathing us in darkness. Even from this distance I can feel his shiver, even though my vision of him is quickly fading. It's really getting dark.

"H-hello?" He suddenly squeaks. The air fills with a different kind of breeze as it intermingles with that sweet aura that surrounds him—fear. So he is afraid. The realization makes my pace quicken. Another rumble involuntarily leaves my chest.

I can smell him before I realize that he stopped walking. Eucalyptus and burning wood, mixed with his own, unique scent, engraved in his flesh. It settles deeply in my stomach when I breathe in a thick waft of air. He smells divine.

I take another step, and my foot steps on a twig, the crunching sound echoing sharply through the chill. Shit.

"Are—are—" he wheezes, and then I hear his rapid footfalls.

"God damn it," I mutter. The fucker is running away, right into the darkness. I don't hesitate, but give chase. My breathing picks up and a familiar feeling nestles in my stomach...excitement. Fuck yeah, Régis is not just a plaything for the brotherhood, or a deviant as Elder Jacques calls him.

He's about to become my little plaything.

Mon chaton.

8

RÉGIS

Something rustles behind me. *Creak*...another twig crushes under a foot, this time closer.

Someone's following me.

Someone who's slowly creeping up behind me.

I try to expand my chest, try to breathe deeper through my nose, but fuck... I can't. I'm scared. Which is completely ridiculous, since I'm close to Monterrey Castle, to my dorm ... but I went looking for something to keep me feeling safe, something to help me through those dreamless nights. Now I'm feeling all perilous, and the darkening sky isn't helping. Neither is the threat to another heavy rainfall.

Creak.

"Hello?" I squeak as I fist my hands. I don't dare turn over my shoulder, too afraid to stumble and fall. Oh god, I don't want to fall. "Who's out there?"

Is this about the invitation? I mean to ask, but I'm running out of breath quickly, and my eyes are still fighting to adjust against the rapidly obscuring blanket draping over the trees.

A low chuckle, far too close, rushes through the wind. It brings instant goosebumps to my neck and forearms. Flutters of chainsaws and knives molest my mind in a fraction of a second, before I can feel a whoosh of air behind my nape and ears. I swear it ruffles my hair, like some invisible hand that brushes through my curls, pulling me in by my hair, toying with me, teasing me, showing me who's...

The wind gets torn out of me when I stumble over the uneven ground and crash to the ground. Roots from the large oak tree unflatten the surface when I blindly search around me, fingers clawing as I try to get up and position myself. My knees feel wobbly and I'm panting heavily, the echo of that raspy chortle lingering in the air.

"It's all in your head," I soothe myself when my flat palm reaches the tree trunk. But when I reach inside my pocket to grab my phone, the first softened pitter patters descend through the trees. It's making everything achingly calm, like some threat preparing its arrival.

There's another snapping sound, this time way too close. Dropping my phone back in my pocket, I make a blind run for it, speed fueled by horror. I try to stay on the sand path, that's now rapidly turning into a muddy path, the clear sounds of footsteps behind me. When I throw my gaze over my shoulder, I make out the clear silhouette of another person giving chase, and it ignites my agony into something hot and sticky.

Disoriented and afraid, my breathing is way too high, making me splutter and pant as I keep on racing. I'm not going to make it. I don't even know where I'm heading for anymore.

The rainfall is picking up, making my wet jacket glue against my freezing skin. A growl cuts through the air behind me, low and raspy. Then, a hand grabs me by my hair, making my head whack back. An instant sting flares through my skull and I wince in pain. Before I know what's happening, I'm being spun around, my back yanked flush against the closest tree trunk. When I hit the tree, the sudden dull ache spreads all the way from my already stinging scalp down to my spine, through the back of my legs to my heels. A strong hand curls around my neck. My teeth clammer and my eyes bulge, hands flying up for protection. Those fingers...they are too tight around me, squeezing off my breath. When the dark shape bends his head, I am caught in the onyx stare of my big stepbrother.

"Arthur? What the hell are you doing here?" I pant through my ragged breath. My nails dig into the hand he uses to squeeze my airways, scraping until he lets out an annoyed hiss. "Let go of me."

"Well, well," he rumbles, "Look who I had to save from the woods. If it isn't Little Red Riding Hood."

"What are you talking about?"

"Spending more time in the forest than he does in his own bedroom. Even when it's raining outside. What the hell were you doing here anyway?" He squeezes my neck tighter as if that annoys him, and my nails claw deeper around his skin.

"That's none of your fucking business," I hiss. We're both panting now. From the race, or from the building pressure that snakes itself around us. I'm not sure.

"Oh, you bet it is my business. I'm here to guide you. If our parents find out that you got lost in the woods at night on my watch, they'll come for my ass."

"I don't care."

Arthur lets out a dark chuckle, eyes flaring with something fierce. "But I do. I care a lot more about you than you think." His fingers crawl around my neck, swiftly replacing that earlier, sluggish feeling of being smothered, with something else. Something that has my stomach tighten and my eyes widen. Because they are so soft. His fingertips, dragging over the tender flesh of my throat, the only exposed skin I have since I'm still wearing my school uniform. His grip is possessive, and it makes me shiver with something I don't even want to label.

"You're delusional," I seethe, though right now, I'm not sure to whom that is more applicable, my own thought being far from appropriate. They have taken me back to that disgraceful morning not so long ago, where Arthur had me dangling above the stairs with his hand in my boxers. God, he made me feel so good.

Fury coils through my blood. Lifting a foot, I try to kick him in his crotch, but he dodges me with a last-second shift of his hips. A grin lifts his lips. I should look away. Shouldn't think about the way he's using his attractive looks as a weapon in these games of destruction I've somehow called upon myself. But he's so handsome. So cruelly beautiful. I could stare at him all day.

"And you, little Régis, are in my way." He has dipped his head, his warm breath caressing my cheeks. I snort as best as I can, but his crawling fingers have now moved down to the collar of my jacket, and it's creating a crazy sizzle that goes all the way down to my cock. No no no.

"I don't want you following me."

"What were you doing here?" He asks again. He has lowered his chin and tilts my head to the side with his agile hand, giving himself access to my exposed neck. "You were hiding, right?" He insists when I don't reply, his voice nothing more than a low rasp.

"No."

"Always hiding. I can't help but wonder why." His tongue darts out and connects with the tender skin of my neck. "Hm," he rumbles against my ear when his tongue lifts all the way from my collarbone to my ear. "It doesn't matter anyway. "

And then his other hand is on my chest, on my furiously beating heart as it pounds against my ribcage, unable to handle the exertion from running, from being chased, from being caught...

"I've found you." He lowers his hand to pop the buttons of my wet school jacket and leisurely slides down to my stomach. I tremble, chilly air gripping my senses, just like something else does. Something unwanted, like arousal to his touch. Thick, burning need for Arthur's fingers to continue brushing over my chest, my stomach, my cock… I bite my lip, drawing blood as I do so.

Arthur's fingertips sneak in between the distance of my shirt, and I jerk when they connect to my naked skin. With one hand still steadily wrapped around my neck, he uses his thumb to tilt my chin and look up at him. From up close, I see him clearly. Those eyes, pupil-dilated and dark with hunger, as he stares me down. Then he swipes the blood from my bottom lip and suckles it between his own. I swallow a groan, cock bucking in my pants, while my mind scrambles for words.

"I need to go back," I rush on a tremble. "I don't—"

"You really are adorable," Arthur purrs. Both darkness and amusement lace his tone. "Fuck, *chaton*, your nervousness turns me on."

I shake my head. "I'm not a kitten. And I sure as fuck don't want to be caught up in your game."

Arthur laughs at that. A low, husky rumble. "So much denial."

That word stirs a new fire in me. "Denial?" I growl, and my knee kicks up again, hitting his thick thigh. "I know that you are not happy with me in your life, but guess what. Neither am I." I give him another kick, this time using my hands to squeeze his upper arms. It's a total chick move, but with his hands wrapped around my neck, it's the only thing I can think of doing. Besides, I don't care, because the more I speak, the more my words make me fume. "I have never denied anything, you privileged son of a bitch. You have always had everything your heart desired—"

My mother.

"You have always had plenty of friends—"

My mother.

"Your brother, your cousin—"

My mother.

"Your, your castle!" I spit. My chest is heaving as I'm running out of words. I'm so fucking ready to curl up into myself and hide behind iron bars. Suddenly, I'm feeling exhausted. But I can't relent now, not with Arthur still holding me in a chokehold, a grip that's tightening because of my words.

"Castle?" He asks, and the corners of his mouth tip up wolfishly.

Yeah, okay, castle may not have been the right word for the Deveraux mansion. I tilt my head, ignoring those possessive fingers on my throat, or the way that my breath comes out in wheezy puffs. "You know what I mean. Your family's houses by the sea. Point is, I am not scared of you. And I'm not in denial. And I don't need you following me around like some sniffing dog—"

"Sniffing dog?" He barks out a clipped laugh. "Try a sniffing wolf." He lowers his head and nips at my neck, and oh God... my cock jerks again. Thick, succulent desire drips through my core, all the way down to my stomach. "Hm, you taste good, *chaton*."

"I told you, I'm not a fucking kitten. Get. Off. Me." I push him back, but his hand dips down from my stomach to my cock, cupping my erection. My jaw closes on a thud when I fight to keep the moans from spilling. I've never been touched by anyone else before Arthur, and it's making my body responsive to the faintest caress.

Arthur rumbles another chuckle, his dark gaze devious. "Ah, look at that. Kitty's trying to fight. But secretly he's loving it, aren't you, *chaton*?" His hand brushes my cock, and I groan. "Yeah, you do." He sounds pleased, the smug fuck. But then his eyes turn a little softer and he presses our chests together. His voice turns soft. "We've already had this conversation, and I don't like repeating myself. I promised Dad to guide you." Our noses brush, and I press my back further into the wooden trunk in an attempt to avoid him. It doesn't stop him from bringing our mouths close.

"I know everything about everyone like the sniffing wolf I am—" his breath hits my lips and creates gooseflesh in its wake. "And you are a problem. You are a threat to my future. But you're also no match." He kicks my legs apart with his thigh and I jump when his hand dives into my pants to grab hold of my thrumming length. "Look at you, little boy. You like this?" His thumb swipes over my crown, collecting pre-cum that he uses to brush over my shaft. I grind my jaw even further, not wanting to satisfy him. Arthur just chuckles while continuing his touch, slowly driving me crazy. I can feel my toes curl, my knees buck, my lips parting in desperation.

"I want more..." My sinful conscience begs, but I keep my mouth shut.

"A sweet slut for my touch, aren't you?" He drawls.

"I told you before, I won't get in your way," I gasp. "You will be the next CEO of your family's business, I don't want anything to do with it. I'll be far gone before you know it, and right now, we can tell your dad that you have been guiding me and that I'm doing fine."

"Hiding time is over, little Régis. You see, Dad wants you to be part of our company. He loves your mother and she insists."

Despite my fogged mind, those words cause a tremble. I jerk up my gaze. "Maybe I don't want to be found."

His dark eyes flash, grin widening a little when he speeds up his stroking. "Oh, I'll always find you." He gazes down at my pants that hang halfway around my thighs. At his own stroking hand in my boxers. A long, thorough once over that doesn't intend to miss a single centimeter of my flushed skin even as rain cascades over us. I feel warm, despite the coolness, flesh hypersensitive and adorned by goosebumps. "I might even keep you as my own pet," he mumbles so softly that I'm not even sure if I heard him well. The words, if correct, are so appalling that I'm internally readying myself for another offence.

"Now let's talk about that invitation." He casually changes the subject to one that has been living in my brain for the past few days.

"Invitation?" I screech, peeking up at Arthur through my eyelashes, my heart thumping wildly when I catch him staring at me.

"Yeah. The one that requires your presence." His voice comes out lower, raspy like there's an edge to it. I shiver. He continues to stroke my cock, toying with my crown, my balls, with the speed. He takes it slow, squeezing my shaft and balls on its way down, then moves up faster, circling my slit.

Licking my lips, I prevent my knees from buckling while I think of an answer to give. My mind has gone all fuzzy, invaded by pleasure and by this increasing need to spill.

"You see, *chaton,* when you decided to attend this school as a Deveraux..." Arthur's mouth grazes my lobe, and he lets out a soft moan. My entire body whimpers, begs, and my hips rock into his touch, pleading for more. "You chose to be part of our family. But we also have another family, and your brothers would love to meet you."

"Brothers?" I moan, balls feeling heavy as they draw up for release. The pressure inside me is building, and when Arthur opens his expensive looking coat, and pops the buttons of his pants, only to take out his own hard, throbbing cock, I swallow thickly, eyes bulging. I've never seen another hard cock before in real life. But this... and his...

"They were waiting for you, but you never showed up," Arthur croons. And then he takes both our cocks in his large, calloused hand and starts stroking furiously. "Don't worry, your big stepbrother will protect you."

His lips brush over mine and I hiss at the touch, cool, and commanding. I watch in fascination when his lips part and his tongue darts out, tracing the outline of my lips. The corners, the seam. He pokes his probing wetness against my firmly pressed lips until I yield, opening my mouth to let him in. He groans at the victory, his tongue dipping in and coming out for mine. Head falling back onto the wooden trunk, I accept our mouths melting together and our tongues playing around. It feels so fucking good. The bliss he brings with his mouth, his sound, his smell. Our hard, dripping cocks intermingle inside his unyielding fist, erasing our earlier dispute. His tongue plunges around with adamant determination, and I break apart, falling when my body mollifies into his. Moaning, I let him claim my mouth, my body, as I gyrate my hips against his, feeling desperate, overwhelmed, and so, so hot.

"Ugh, oh fuck, oh god," I muffle into his mouth, nails digging deeper into the material of his coat, not even remembering I put them there in the first place.

And then I explode. Everything around me vanishes, apart from Arthur and me. I clutch on to him, sinking into the orgasm being wrung out of me. At some stage I hear him let out a choked grumble, then his warm release touches my cock. It shouldn't be sexy, but it fucking feels that way. Here he is, Arthur Deveraux, one of the most popular guys in college and my stepbrother. So handsome, so nasty, and he wants me.

Time stands still when our breaths fill the air. Rapid puffs and rattling hearts that take a moment to calm down. Then—

"Clean this for me," Arthur whispers, holding out his hand in front of my mouth. "With your tongue. Like the sweet *chaton* you are."

I stare at him, as if trying to figure out if it's a joke. But I only see his dark eyes and that waiting hand. Its long, slender fingers that were wrapped around me just before. It's dripping from our combined cum. This shouldn't... But it does. So my tongue darts out and I start licking his fingers clean, one by one, suckling them into my mouth, my eyes locked on his. I've never tasted cum before, and it's warm and salty, its texture a little different.

"Good boy," Arthur purrs, a satisfied glint intermingled with cockiness in those onyx depths. His free hand pets my hair, plays with my curls, while I continue to lick and clean. Because those words of praise flutter in my stomach and make me want to finish the job even better. When I have cleaned every single centimeter of his palm and fingers, he moves his hand, and I need to fight the strange urge to follow him and get his fingers back into my mouth. That gentle caress in my hair.

I can't, I *shouldn't*. It's too much, and I can't fall for that hoarse voice telling me that I'm doing a great job. Instead I switch back to the normal Régis, to the one I have carefully moulded. The one who's even more annoyed now for wanting something he shouldn't want.

Arthur closes his pants and reorganizes his coat. "Get yourself dressed." When I finish by pulling the jacket a little tighter around my shoulders, he clicks his tongue disapprovingly, then grabs the raincoat with the typical Saint-Laurent marine-blue and caramel color from his pocket and folds it out. "Put this on as well, it's getting chilly."

"Fuck you," I want to say. But I don't. Right now, I need him to get me out of the dark of this forest and back to our dorm. So I obey like the pathetic loser I am, letting him pull the sleeves around my wrists and over my arms. He eyes me over, then nods.

"Good. Now, you are not going to like this, but there is no escaping from that invitation—"

"Oh, like hell there is. I never applied to some frat house."

Arthur shakes his head and lets out that *tssk* again. It's fucking patronizing and makes me fume inside. "How many times do I have to tell you that the rules are different here? We are not some public university, Régis. If that's what you wanted, you should have gone to study in Toulouse." He waits a beat, as if he's expecting me to protest. When I don't speak, he continues. "You've got to set your own, small mindset to the side. For this college, you are a Deveraux. And we are wealthy and very, very powerful. And as such, we act like it. So, man up, little Régis, and come with me. I'll show you about the brotherhood. You can ask me your questions."

Biting my lip, I look away. I don't know what to think of this. If it's a prank, it sure is a complicated one. I mean, he's right, it is getting seriously cold in the woods. He could have easily done it inside our dorm. But a brotherhood? I mean, seriously... I did not see that one coming.

"On one condition," I decide, feeling brave.

"On one condition?" Arthur rumbles, sounding amused. Yeah, I guess I would be too if I was standing in his shoes.

"No touching." My face flushes at the insinuation.

There's a beat of silence, then, "No touching?" Arthur lets out an incredulous bark, then gestures at me to follow him. And like the pathetic wimp I am, both curious and too scared to be left alone in the woods, I follow him deeper into the pitch-dark forest. Long, slender digits curl around my smaller hand. "Régis, if I want to touch you, I will touch you. If I want to tease you, I will tease you."

For a second, I fear that he's seriously going to leave me behind in the darkness. He doesn't. Instead, he turns around and moves onto my chest, tipping up my chin with a featherlight touch.

"And if I want to fuck you, I will fuck you." His voice is nothing more than a smoldering grumble. "Are we clear, *chaton*?"

"Fuck you," I spit.

His lips curl into a nasty smirk, then he leans in and brushes his lips against mine. "Good boy, Régis. Now, let me show you what's lurking for you in the darkness."

9

ARTHUR

We walk through the darkened shrubs for what feels like hours. There are no lights out here apart from the murky glow of the moon that glitters through the oak trees, illuminating the sand path ahead of us. Not that I need it—I know these grounds like the back of my hand from the numerous nights I have spent out here with the brothers.

Next to me, Régis is mostly silent, aside from the occasional swear word that leaves his mouth on a mutter as he makes another misstep. Anxiety rolls off his shoulders in thick waves, his spine rigid and his shoulders tense. Perhaps I should try to comfort him, make him feel at ease. But during the ten minute walk, the stubborn fuck won't speak.

Until now.

"Wow…" Régis suddenly halts, stumbling into my side. I can hear his breath hitch as he stares right ahead of us. Casually, I curl my hand around his limber waist and squeeze him a little closer. Before I can think things through, I've already turned my head to inhale a waft of his enticing scent.

Right across from us, in the middle of a sphere created by trees, shrubs and grass, combined with more sand that takes us directly to its heart, stands the Atrium. The building that, according to the official paperwork of the Alpha Fraternarii, was built by the nobles once they set foot inside Monterrey Castle and was meant for *soirées* organized by the brothers.

"Pretty impressive, right?"

We still use the Atrium for those *soirées*.

"What is that?" His voice is filled with fascination, sprinkled with a layer of...dismay? The thought makes my heart rate speed up. I have been discovering more and more sides to my little stepbrother, each and every one of them fascinating. But the part where he's afraid? Yeah, that definitely makes my blood heat up.

"This is where the brothers celebrate," I answer. He jerks himself free of my hold, his shoulders almost touching his ears and his eyes wide and clear as he stabs a finger into my cashmere chest. "You're fucking with me, aren't you?"

I chuckle at his word choice. "Trust me, you'd know it when I was fucking you." Not taking the bait, Régis flips me off with an undignified huff, and continues to search around him.

"I'm not some naive college kid, you know? I know when I'm being pranked."

Now it's my turn to feel indignant. "I'm not some low-level asshole who'd go all the way into a rainy forest in the fucking darkness, just to mess with you."

His gaze lands on mine. "No, you are so much more, aren't you? Daddy's precious son, his future heir." He clears his throat, and my gaze drops to where his Adam's apple bobs delicately. I want to bite him there, taste that delicious wet skin of his. "So why did you bring me here?"

"I thought you'd never ask." I step right next to him. Looking at the glass building with its fine lines of silver curves and exotic greenery, I try to imagine what it's like to see this for the first time. Even in its current, sombre state, the shapes appear regal, even somewhat dramatic. "Come."

To his credit, Régis hesitates only briefly before he allows me to grab his hand and guide him closer. "This trail is known for its treacherous little stones, and I don't want you to end up spraining your ankle in the pitch-dark forest."

Around us, the narrow path adorned with oak trees melts into an opening where the shimmering light of the moon finds us once more. Slowly we walk toward the Atrium, Régis's smaller hand feeling strangely cool and fragile in my palm, the physical connection making my heart gallop inside my chest. I set it aside immediately, nodding my chin instead toward the building.

"This is the heart of the brotherhood, Régis, the Atrium. It's for celebrations." We get closer to the glass building with its symmetrical shapes. *When soft music mingles with the chatter and moans, slaps and hisses, cackles, light as a feather, floating through the heady air.*

"I told you that the invitation you received was meant to be accepted. If you had, this is where you would have come. To meet the others." I don't bother telling him how he would have met them. Some things are better to be experienced than to be described. Like gatherings. Because people change when they operate in a group, fascinatingly so. It's cruel to see how they can play with others, show off their supremacy as they reign, together, while others are kept in captivity.

If people are depraved, rich people are the devil. Because we take what we want—and trust me, that's a lot—while we ruthlessly cut down those who stand in our way.

Régis knows this. Knows what it's like to be lifted and repositioned as if it's nothing, while the soil under his feet is falling away. Although in his case, I wonder what was hidden under that soil to begin with.

Right now, his golden wavy hair glimmers in the dark, and some stupid part of me is glad that he didn't put the hoodie of the raincoat over his head. I like his curls, how sweet and innocent they make him look, how they beautifully frame his face. *Mon chaton.*

My brothers already know that he's been claimed by me, I've made that very clear during our last initiation, despite him not being there. A mistake on my end, since I didn't think I'd have to make sure he'd come downstairs and into the dungeon, where our first initiations are always held. A mistake I won't be making again.

But Louis is right. There's something in the air, as fluttery as it can be threatening, and it's making our brothers restless. They are waiting for a moment of weakness, and if I don't pay attention, they will strike, like the group of hyenas they are. They will seize the opportunity to nuzzle through our defenses and use their canines to tear them apart. They will come for him because he is fresh meat. Because he is not used to our ways of life, and because the Elder will let them.

My little stepbrother will be present during the next Initiation, I'll make sure of that. For his own fucking safety.

Régis shivers next to me. "And how..." He clears his throat, but doesn't finish his phrase. Because he's afraid, or because he simply doesn't know what to say.

"Come, let me show you." Despite the gentle rainfall, we slowly cross the path that lies all around the building, careful not to slip and fall into the wet, rough and prickly shrubs.

"I can't believe I haven't seen this building before," Régis grunts softly when we finally stand in front of the darkened building, sounding displeased, his hand still in mine despite the now flat surface.

We reach the door, that's equally made of glass and silver. Reluctantly, I let go of his hand and try the handle, inhaling a quick breath of air in relief when I find it locked. Which means it will be just me and him. This place isn't open to the public, unless they have been invited, but Dad gave me an extra set of keys so I always have access, should it be necessary.

The door falls wide open, revealing the beautifully decorated open space, an elegant invitation to come forward and drift toward the heart of its foundations—the Great Hall, as we call it. We amble forward over tiles carved into a mosaic pattern. They are colorful, I know, but right now, it's too dark to catch their vibrant yellow and moss greens.

Behind me, Régis lets out a gasp, and I turn around. He has found the plants, of course he has. In the entrance alone, tens and tens of plants have been placed against the glassed walls, their branches curled into one and other as they form a green strip.

"Is that a—" he mutters, his crystal blue eyes filled with a softness I have never seen on him before. They make him look so young, so passionate… so fragile. "It's a Monstera Deliciosa Aurea," he mumbles into the silence. "This plant is so rare, I've never seen one before. They have a fantastic collection in this school." His fingers brush the lime, full-moon shaped leaves, gently and caring as if it were a lover.

It makes me annoyed as hell. "Can we stop the plant fucking and focus instead?" I grunt, perhaps a little too harshly, but fuck that. At least he immediately drops the branch, and as it bounces back, the leaf gently brushes his cheek. His chiseled, but soft, wet and flushed cheek. My hands itch to touch him again.

Turning back ahead, I snort, "Jeez, Dad really should have prepared you." At least that part's true—he could have told Régis at least *something* of what was waiting for him, instead of leaving him as food for the predators.

"I'm stronger than you think," Régis bristles as he catches up. "Why don't you tell me something about this place instead of walking around like your usual arrogant self?"

"Hmm." I flick on the faint light, then march toward the Great Hall, gesturing to him to follow me as I step across the threshold and into the heart of the glass building, further and further, until I reach the round stage. High and proud, obscene in its promise to fulfil many things. Régis follows, until he stands right by me at the foot of the set. "The Atrium used to be the center of a house's social and political life. Back in Ancient Rome, this is where the male head-of-household would receive his clients on business days." I turn to watch Régis glaring at me.

"And why are you telling me this? Is this part of your non-existent prank? I already know that. I know a lot of things."

"I know you do." My lips split into a small smile. Leaning in, I make sure to keep his gaze as if I'm about to spoil a secret, then whisper, "If not, Dad wouldn't think of you that high, regardless of his love for Nathalie."

Régis purses his lips in annoyance but doesn't blink. He's waiting.

"Look around you." I spread my arms. He does, his blue eyes darting around as he takes in the surroundings of this beautiful place. Magical, with its glass and silver. With all those plants and flowers that grow everywhere, some even as high as the endless ceiling. Dotted around us on those ceramic tiles are plush pillows and low stools, their colors a warm ochre, brown, green and red, matching outside's autumn glow.

"What's the stage for?" Régis finally asks.

"Hmm, the stage," I drawl. "What do you think it's for?" Fuck, I shouldn't be doing this, shouldn't use my little stepbrother for my own pleasure, but he's just so quickly disturbed, his mask so easily cracked. It turns me the fuck on.

"I don't know?" He stammers. Like a light switch, the mood has changed into something less hostile, something more heady, I can't put my finger on. Well, whatever it is, my limbs tighten with anticipation.

I take a few steps up the stairs, fingertips tracing the shiny cherry wood of the stair railing. "We use them for performances."

"Performances?"

"That's right. Come further." I wait for him to reach the spotlight, while blood continues to fill my eager cock. Dripping anticipation has my body coiling with heat. This place was designed for one thing and one thing only.

For power. And tonight I will use it just for that. I'll show my little stepbrother who gets to toy with him. Who gets to tell him what to do and when. Who makes him understand that he better not get in my way.

Mon chaton, my little devil whispers. And only mine. Fuck. How did it come to this, so soon?

Régis reluctantly follows me, the first cracks already beautifully forming in his large, clear as blue, stoic glare. He's nervous and fuck, if that doesn't make me hungry. But I continue explaining, because this part needs to be clear. I want him to know what he walks into, need his full conscience.

"During the French Revolution, when Paris became one big warzone, many elite families fled to neighboring countries, such as Switzerland, and Italy. Some came here, to Monterrey Castle, where the monks promised to keep them safe. They kept their word, and the privileged families stayed in the south wing for years, *together.*" I flick my gaze back at Régis, then guide him to a wooden chair. The only thing on this stage. He languidly follows me.

"I still don't understand what this has to do with me, nor with this brotherhood."

"They *are* the brotherhood, Régis, the very same one that sent you an invitation to join. The Alpha Fraternarii was founded by our ancestors, the elite who fled the capital when the streets of Paris were burning down."

He blinks, then blinks again. Then he lets out a strained chuckle. "This is... Why did you bring me here anyway?" His gaze turns serious once more and he shifts uncomfortably as he looks around him. "To scare me?" He takes a step back toward the stairs, the mask on his face cracking a little more, making him even more vulnerable. My chest tightens a little, but I shake it off. Shake it the fuck off. "I have to go soon, it's getting late," Régis mumbles.

I grab his shoulder before he can climb back down the stairs. He turns over his shoulder, surprised. In the faint light I catch sight of his large eyes. He's afraid.

"No. This is about you not being a pussy and standing here and listening to what the fuck I have to tell you, little stepbrother." I squeeze his shoulder a little tighter, but it comes off as some weird gesture of affection. I drop my hand. "When they stayed here, in Monterrey Castle, our ancestors formed a pact based on communal values. They vowed that history would never repeat itself, that they'd never again be taken off their thrones by commoners. Because that's the thing with the people, Régis. *Le peuple.* They believed in the French Revolution. Believed that things would really change for them. That their voices would be heard, that they would pay less taxes, be more protected and safe from disease and other destruction. But they can't take what's ours. Not then, and not now."

Régis flutters his lashes, his lips parting, then closing again as he visibly searches for words. I wait, suddenly curious about what this kitten thinks about the Alpha Fraternarii. He doesn't speak for a few minutes and we end up just staring at each other.

"That's absolutely sick," he finally settles with, his luscious lips curved into a sneer. "You are—do you know how poor some people are out there? How many people work their asses off, only to barely get by? And you...you just, you just—" He shakes his head. "I'm actually speechless."

I snort. "No, you're not. You're judging, based on two lines I gave you about something that happened over two hundred years ago in a different time, a different life. Like all the other sheep out there, who are too lazy to inform themselves. They speculate, that's all they do." He doesn't smile at that, but remarkably allows me to sit his ass down onto one of the three chairs that stand on the stage. It's Elder Jacques's chair, I notice with a satisfied grimace.

This one's for you, old man.

"But, you know what? The brotherhood agrees with you. We understand that times have changed, that commoners are valuable and should be rewarded for all their hard work. Which is why we give a lot to society."

"Stop calling other people commoners, it's disrespectful!" He seethes through clenched teeth.

"Why?" I shrug. "There's nothing wrong with showing some respect to those who make sure you get your monthly allowance every month. To make sure that your child goes to a good, public school. That you can be treated in a hospital when you are ill."

Régis lifts his chin, glowering up at me, his eyes a darker blueish glitter filled with indignancy and fire. "And you're saying that your brotherhood is responsible for that?" I expect him to honor me with another show of disbelief, or anger. Instead he lets out a long sigh, then rubs his forehead, visibly in thought. "What exactly are you talking about?" His voice trembles a little, as if his brain is slowly connecting the dots that he doesn't want to connect.

"I'm talking about loyalty, *chaton.*"

"Stop calling me—"

"I'm talking about sacrifice, respect, traditions." I continue, ignoring him. I'll call him what the fuck I want to call him. "They are the backbone of our world. Our ancestors believed so too, which is why they created the secret brotherhood. To provide a safe environment for themselves and all future members." I pause when Régis raises his brows.

"But why keep it secret?"

"Because not everyone has to know."

He snorts. "Yeah, I understand what secrets mean. But I mean, why—"

"Because it's not for everyone, little stepbrother. You can only join upon invitation."

His eyes search mine, flitting from one eye to the other as if searching for any information I will give up anyway at this stage.

"Then who can join?" He asks slowly. Finally, now we're getting somewhere.

I dip my gaze and our eyes collide. "The elite."

"The…" He sucks in a deep breath, and nods multiple times as he scrunches his gaze. "Now I get it. Fuck, this is like one of those elite society clubs."

"*Bravo*, little stepbrother," I snicker. The words make his eyes fly up and scowl at me once more.

"So why me? You know I don't belong here."

"Yes, you do."

"No…I mean, I'm not like you. I don't want this."

"Then you are a fool, *chaton*. You want to have a career, right? You want to make a difference in life?" He nods carefully, but doesn't speak. "Then you've come to the right place. The Alpha Fraternarii is everywhere, Régis. You can't outrun us even if you tried. We'd track you down and bring you back. We are the future our ancestors redesigned. For us. And we recreate destiny, every year, for ourselves, for *them*."

A heavy silence falls between us, as my little stepbrother stares at me.

Then, "What do you mean?" He looks around us from his seat, then visibly flinches when I take a step closer. Damn, if that doesn't make my cock feel heavy beneath its restraints. There's something so fucking sexy about having him look at me with those big, blue eyes. I don't know if he truly fears me, or if he's just confused by his physical reaction to my presence. I meant it when I called him a little virgin. Whether he's never been with anyone or just with a guy, it's obvious that he doesn't know what to do with himself.

But none of that matters because I'll teach him. I've already started. I'm a hunter who loves the chase. There's this need, heavy and solid in my body, to capture and claim. My favorite toys know that. They know exactly how to please me, but fuck me...I have never played this game with someone who is as innocent as Régis. I shouldn't, there are so many reasons why I shouldn't. But as we stand there, facing each other, him on that chair and me looming right over him, they all melt away.

"What do I mean?" I repeat his question. Régis looks away, but his eyes don't divert further than my chest. From there, they dip lower until they land on my hardening crotch. He clears his throat, then licks his lips, but his eyes stay put. "You're such a clever guy. You know what happened during the French Revolution. Well, we change that outcome, every year. We rewrite our destiny. And you will too, when you become a brother of Alpha Fraternarii."

"How many times do I have to say that I don't want that? I don't want this...brotherhood. I don't want to get in your way." His eyes are still on my cock. On my growing, hungry cock.

"That's not an option, little stepbrother. Unless you already want to quit college?" When he doesn't reply immediately, I taunt, "I never took you for a quitter."

"You know nothing about me," he snarls, eyes finally flying up.

I chuckle, holding up my hands in fake surrender. "I didn't mean to offend you."

"Yes, you did," he mutters to himself. Still, he doesn't move to stand. And I don't move to make him stand. When silence falls upon us again, I continue.

"Our family is a direct descent from one of the founding families, which is part of the reasons that we are this powerful. Remember when you accepted Dad's generous offer to attend this school, and he said that the rest of the family needs you to prove your value?" He jerks his face in a nod, and I can't help but smile. Finally, we are getting somewhere. "This is what they meant, little stepbrother."

Régis takes in a deep, ragged breath. His—*defeat,* is that what this is?—is intoxicating, and has my cock painfully buck in my pants. I'm desperate for some relief. *Again.* When he licks his lips once more, I decide to challenge him a little more, and trace my fingers along the waistband of my sweats. Régis clears his throat. His lips might be nothing more than a tight frown with that ticking nerve in his jaw, but his pupils are dilated, his gaze fixated. On me. Yeah, he wants this too, my pretty *chaton.* No matter how hard he mewls. No matter how sharp his little claws.

I take my time toying with the strings, slowly loosening the material until I can dip two fingers inside. "They want you to become a brother of Alpha Fraternarii," I mumble, needing to hear it myself, again and again.

Mine mine mine.

"They want you to come home and embrace your altered future. A guy like you—" Both my hands grab the sides of my pants and I slowly roll them over my hips. Régis shudders beneath me. "Would normally end up right where you were born. In the slums. But thanks to your mother, thanks to our family, you are given this opportunity. A second chance." I brush my fingers over the exposed black boxers where the tip of my leaking cock already salutes Régis's big, blue eyes. His waiting, wet mouth.

Fuck, I should not be taking this any further. Sure, I'm fucking evil, but this... I should stop myself, this is not what Dad meant when he wanted me to guide this sweet boy. But it's too late for that now, a train derailing and heading right for hell, because I slowly lower my boxers and my cock plops out eagerly. It's hard, the veins clearly visible in its sharp contrast to the pale skin and the flushed crown that's glistening pre-cum.

Régis swallows thickly. "You don't know that. I'm smart," he rasps, his eyes focused on my cock.

"Yeah?" Brushing a finger over the wet slit, I slide it between my lips, then let out a long hum. He gasps, the sound making me throb all over. "*Smart* doesn't buy you the luxuries our family has, *chaton*. *Smart* buys you an expensive F2 in Paris, from where you can commute nicely every day into work and do as your boss says. Every, fucking day until you retire. And who makes sure that you get your pension?"

"The government?" he grinds his teeth, as if annoyed that he's even replying to my question. Brushing a curl out of his face, I let my fingers linger on his cheek. His skin is soft, and hot.

"That's right, *chaton*, the government." I pause and eye him expectantly. Surely he must get it now. But instead he lets out a snort.

"You're lying."

"I don't lie." He bristles at that. "Alpha Fraternarii is the elite, Régis. I told you before, we are everywhere, and we truly are. We rule large firms, operate in politics. We *control* this society and by doing so, allow others to be part of it too."

Another bristle, though his lips are still firmly pursed.

"Our families donate huge amounts of money to good causes, to research centers for disease, to shelter associations looking after the homeless, to educational organizations that provide decent schooling. We protect those who depend on us."

"But you look down upon them," he rushes to snarl. His eyes flick between my eyes, sending me scowls, then drop to down where I am now leisurely stroking my cock, contemplating his accusation. My cock, that is only a few centimetres from Régis's delectable mouth. "I don't look down upon them," I finally say, meaning it. "But I won't be replaced."

"No, you just throw them a bone every now and then to keep them satisfied," he snarls, his words making me smile. And horny. My hands curl around his nape and he gasps.

"Spoken like a true poet."

He ignores the irony. "I don't want to be part of that." My cock jolts at those words, laced with sweet, sweet loss. Because we both know how this is going to end.

"Careful what you wish for, sweet boy. Not many people are given this possibility." I rock my hips forward a little, and Régis lets out a strangled "*Non.*" Then his lips part a little more. "I've never—"

"Ssh." Brushing more of his curls out of his smooth face, I press my crown past his waiting lips, slowly sliding inside his mouth. It feels like fucking victory, and I let out a groan at the sudden sensation of silk and warmth that wraps around my dick. His eyes widen and lock with mine, a mixture of surprise and pride. My fingertips brush his cheeks, then move to where his lips are stretched by my rigid length. "So beautiful, *chaton.* Your lips are perfection wrapped around my cock. Does it feel good?"

He blinks, flushes, then nods on a jerk.

Fuckkk...

"Soon, there will be another Initiation and I need you to be there. There are only a few gatherings, but they are very important, because we will explain what is expected of our future brothers. Then, in December, we celebrate *Réinvention.* It's a celebration after pupils have done their pledge and become a brother. After winter break, we will start integrating our new brothers with the outside world, so you understand what Alpha Fraternarii does for the world. And you, sweet little stepbrother, will be part of it. Or...if you don't want it, you will pack your bags and leave this college and return to the slums. Is that what you want?"

Régis shakes his head fervently, his mouth still stuffed with my cock.

"Oh, so you do want to stay?" His eyes shoot daggers, spit dribbling down the corners of his lips. I trace it with my fingers, then smear it back onto his stretched lips, and let out a satisfied moan.

Régis nods one time, then flutters his eyes shut.

"That makes me so happy. We want you to stay as well." Grabbing his chin between my fingers, I grind a little further inside and head for his throat without reaching it fully. His eyes fly open and he splutters a string of no doubt, *objections,* but the words are muffled in his full mouth.

I tilt my head back and laugh. "Oh, *chaton,* still complaining. Even with your mouth filled with dick." I gaze back down on him, smoothing my fingers over his curls. His eyes roll back at the touch. His cheeks are flushed, nostrils flared. He loves it, needs the praise, but is too stubborn to admit it. Always so fucking stubborn. If that doesn't turn me on. "Suck it good, baby, yeah..." I let out another moan and arch my back and neck until I gaze up again. "So fucking perfect."

Eying the glassed ceiling, I see countless stars, shining bright in the dim light. It must be well past dinner time by now, but fuck me, do I care? And we're using the Elder's chair... My lips curl into a wicked grin. I might be the Bad Wolf, but I'm also the brains. My reputation is always at stake, especially with graduation around the corner and Dad peeking over my shoulder, as impatient as I am to head for the big world.

Which is why having my beautiful, innocent, annoying as fuck little stepbrother sucking my cock, is a terrible idea. But I don't care. Because I have him right by the balls, and he knows it.

"Don't worry, I'll guide you." Pulling my throbbing cock out of his mouth, I make a show of smearing it across his mouth, making it one big mess of saliva and pre-cum.

"I don't want to go..." Régis splutters.

"Yes, you do." Pushing my cock right back between his shiny lips, I pat his cheek. "And you will. You agreed, remember?" He scowls at me, his blue eyes darkened with need. "I have a mask specially made for you. You'll love it. We'll also wear a black cloak, because the brothers like to participate in their carnage without being recognized."

His gaze flickers.

"Oh, you want to know what I mean?" I let out a grunt when Régis licks around my crown, hands still clenched at my hips, hanging on for dear life. "Although I must warn you, there will be a lot of sex, *chaton*. Our brothers are horny fuckers, and we use sex not only for pleasure. We also use it to show our power. Money and sex are the engine to it all." Pressure builds leisurely inside me and I grind forward, picking up speed. "Keep up with me," I rasp, and my hips dig further, and further, making the tips of his mouth leak even more. "Don't stop." My balls become heavy with need, drawing up even further when I hit the back of Régis's throat. He whines, then digs his nails into my clothed thighs and pulls me in, unexpectedly, and it's enough for me to erupt. I let out a strangled roar when bliss curls up all around me, pressing me tight, warming every centimeter of my flushed skin. I pour my release into my little stepbrother's mouth and he drinks it all down, his throat working as he keeps my cock between his moist, puffy lips, his lashes fluttering. When the shudders have finally settled down and my toes have uncurled, I pull out, tuck myself away, then crouch in front of Régis. He looks properly debauched—face flushed, eyes drooping, lips still wet with spit and cum. Fuck, he looks perfect like this. Used by my cock, he has a glance of satisfaction around him that is so peaceful.

For once, no objections. Until he finally tilts his gaze. I don't know what I was expecting, and frankly, with him, you never know, but it certainly wasn't this cold, tenacious glare that has replaced that warm, soft expression he carried just before.

"I fucking hate you," he grits out, though he still makes no effort to stand. Just sits there, sagged back, sending daggers. He looks exhausted, but something tells me it's not just from the blowjob.

"Why?" I ask, still crouched in front of him.

His stare turns glassy, empty. "*My* secret. And I don't share." The words are nothing but a string of incoherent whispers, not meant for my ears. But I hear them. And they make me raise my brows.

"What? I'm not following."

Régis sighs, exasperated. "Perhaps you understand ancient language better, *stepbro*. I'm a commoner, not an elite. I'm that guy who works his ass off his entire life and commutes every fucking day to a job he doesn't want to be at just so that his boss pays him at the end of the month." He suddenly stands, making me inadvertently stumble backward. I catch my weight with my hand, but by the time I'm back on my two feet, Régis has already made it toward the exit. Fuck, isn't he a courageous little fucker. He's still wearing my raincoat, I notice, and it makes me feel a little stupid. He actually blew me while wearing that stupid garment. Not the usual attire my pets wear. But then Régis is not a pet, is he?

Yeah, he fucking is. But only mine.

Mon chaton.

And fuck me, isn't he a delight to play with?

By the door, he turns over his shoulder, and hisses, "You know what? You're right. I will change my destiny, and there's nothing in this goddamn world that you can do about it to keep me from my opportunities. I will graduate from Saint-Laurent, and if that means becoming a brother of your elite club, I fucking will. But just, stay away from me. You know that I can't resist—" His cheeks blush right before he turns away, and my chest foolishly constricts at those clumsy, gullible words. "I need to focus on my studies and do what's expected of me. I don't want trouble with you or your brother or your cousin. So fine, I'll play your game." He walks out, then halts. "But don't touch me again."

"Because why—you can't resist me?" I shout out after him, nostrils flaring with annoyance. He stills in the hall. Fuck yeah, I want to hear him admit that again. I don't want him to walk out on me. "You were practically begging for it, *chaton*, parting your lips and waiting for me to stuff your mouth with cock." Straightening my clothes, I descend the stairs, perhaps straightening my cool as well. Because him saying words like that makes me feel a little giddy. But he wouldn't be my little stepbrother if he wasn't a champion in crushing that vibe with three, tiny words.

Turning over his shoulder, he sends me a furious glower. "*Connard*." And before I can do anything else, he runs off.

10

RÉGIS

I can't sleep. My limbs are tense, muscles sore and my heart thumps furiously in my chest, making me clench up. I'm cold, but after I've finally found the courage to grab the extra pair of blankets from under my bed, my body warms up too fast. With clammy fingers I peel down the thick, plush cover, only to feel myself cool down too quickly once more.

Huffing in annoyance, I roll onto my other side and stare outside the window, to where I put small pots with cuttings of the herbs from the herbal garden they keep outside in the forest. There's also a vine of the white bird of paradise they have downstairs, I hope will flourish.

Outside my room, I hear Gaël barking out a laugh in reply to a muffled voice. It's probably Louis, they seem to be particularly close. Tuning out their sound, I focus on the faint sliver of light instead that peeks inside my room. I pretend it'd be beckoning me outside and into the forest. Part of me wants to do just that. To climb out of this suffocating room and run for freedom. To the promise of iron bars waiting for me.

The garden staff hadn't questioned me when I finally found the courage to ask for a metal shelter to be brought into the forest. As if such a request is an everyday occurrence. The cage, at least, will bring the promise of better nights in solitude... like it used to. But, is it enough to protect me from the Alpha Fraternarii?

My stomach flutters treacherously at those thoughts. My mind is a traitor in its attempt to keep me off guard. It throws in flashes of Arthur and me in the woods, of him pinning me down against a tree, of him taking me to the Atrium...

Being alone with him is like being claimed by a lion. His approach calculated and dangerous, yet careful. His words a constant stab to my brain and heart as they make me reconsider many thoughts I grew up with. Thoughts that have always been shared by the community I lived in. Before. Not now. Now, everything is different and I'm barely hanging on. Still I crave his attention and I can't understand why.

So I focus even more on my studies, which isn't a hardship. I love those long days when I can zone out of my surroundings and purely focus on classes and piles of homework. Though I'm no fool. I see how the other students look at me. How they talk quietly behind my back but not straight at my face. How they won't work with me unless there's no other choice.

"They'll all know, little Régis. Every single one of them."

I figured that was more a figure of speech. Another method Arthur uses to frighten me. But as the weeks at college progress, I am still finding myself void of contact with most other people except from Dominique and his friends, Maxime and Jo. He's kind, and brave, for stepping up against the Deverauxs and inviting me to social activities organized by college. Such as the first, monthly film night that we all attended together with Maxime and Jo. That was nice.

Still, whatever I do, nothing erases that restlessness. No busy days, no walk in the woods, no mind breaker over a chess game, can wipe out what seems to be shifting inside me like a gentle breeze. That night in the Atrium started a conversation like I've never had before, started a physical hunger I've never felt before. Fuck. It isn't normal to want to be ordered and cornered by your stepbrother. But I'd loved every single minute of it, and hated it at the same time. Hated that I gave him even more power. Hated that he could take it away from me so easily. Hated that he let me leave and hasn't contacted me a single time since.

Hated that I want him to.

Alpha Fraternarii. A secret brotherhood founded during the French revolution. It sounds like the scenario of a bad horror, or a suspenseful thriller. I let out a huff at the thought. Some twisted version of a fraternity and their ominous initiations. It's not...reality. Right?

Tossing under the blankets, I fight off the shivers. It's a trick. My lids feel heavy, yet my thoughts prevent me from drifting off. I'm so tired, yet I can't fall asleep.

"Fais dodo, Colas mon p'tit frère Fais dodo, t'auras du lolo..."

Maman. I miss you, miss who you used to be. When you sang this lullaby, your voice soft and sweet. Sometimes I wish that we skate back in time and remain frozen there.

I drink into the memory of the song, eyelashes fluttering, needing to be tipped over the edge and falling into the emptiness of the night. Let me fall...

A voice thunders through the air, loud and angry, rattling my insides. Suddenly, I am back in my old bedroom, crawling in agony, my knees grating the floor as I hurry for cover.

"Met-toi dedans!"

I don't want to go inside the cage.

"Tu étais mauvais."

I don't want to be bad. I'll be good. I'll be better.

My heart thuds wildly and my eyes fly open. This fucking bed's too big. I can't breathe. The flutters slowly evaporate my foggy mind, making me see clearly again. Half past twelve. My tired gaze sweeps over the chess board that lays on the other pillow, and I blink at my latest move. My knight stands strong between an equally white pawn and rook, causing a direct threat to the flank of his army. I wonder what he'll do next. A small, tired smile spreads across my face. It's a strong move.

Outside my room things have gone quiet. Everyone has gone to bed. I've had a few weeks now to map out everyone's habits. Despite his wickedness, I've noticed that Arthur doesn't go to bed late, and like me, he likes to wake up early. But where I like to have a quiet hour in the library before I head for breakfast, to prepare for the day and collect my books, he goes to the gym. Avoidance is key, and our little chase of shadows is working pretty well. Sometimes I even wonder if he too avoids me on purpose. Since our revealing night in the Atrium, we haven't crossed paths. That excludes the lingering hint of his presence, here in my room, where he sometimes shows up every day to make his move on the board.

That thought brings flutters in my stomach. To know that he comes in here, in my personal space, should piss me off, especially since I'm such a private person, but it doesn't. Instead it brings some confounding sense of meaning, as if I'm somehow worthy of not being forgotten.

Louis spends most of his time either in class, or on the football grounds. I doubt someone like him could go professional, or would even want to, but he doesn't seem to spend much time in the library, studying. The same goes for Gaël, but from what I understood from Dominique, his parents just want him to graduate before he can join his mother in developing their beauty line. Which is why Dominique writes most of his papers.

Yeah, I guess that despite it all, I have fallen into a convenient daily flow. A convenient habit of avoiding them. Perhaps they are simply letting me live my life completely separate from them. Or they don't care. The Deverauxs have plenty of friends and admirers.

That should bring some peace to my exhausted mind, but it

doesn't. Loud voices occupy my conscience, keeping me from falling asleep at night. The past clashes with the present, Dad with my mother, a cramped bedroom fights against the sight of this large dorm, with its stylish interior and its oversized bed.

And through all these intermingling thoughts, my stepbrother forms the common thread. His eyes are glowing in the dark, the corners of his lips tipped up in a seductive smile. And his hands...

"Stay the fuck away from me," I growl into the darkened void. No one answers. Exasperated, I exhale a sigh, then grab my blanket and head for the closet. It's a narrow, dark space, so I fit perfectly. And with the door locked and the closet ajar, the blanket wrapped over my shivering core, I finally fall into nothingness.

"Sir? Sir!" Fumbling with my backpack, I race down the hall and toward our new teacher of International Business. "Wait up, please."

He turns over his shoulder, eyes widening when he sees me. "Régis? Régis Deveraux?"

"Yes, I—" I pant, taking a few big breaths before I get my voice under control. My teacher smiles as he gestures with his hands for me to slow down. I can feel them staring, the other students. Always fucking staring, without talking.

What the hell are you looking at, huh?

Brothers, they could be *brothers.*

The thought makes me cringe.

"I'm sorry to disturb you, sir, but I wanted to ask you a question."

"Sure. Follow me, please." We continue a short walk through the hall, avoiding groups of students who mostly go the opposite direction as they head for the canteen. As soon as we turn around the corner, he points at the closest door, on which he has written his full name on a piece of paper. Noah Montague. It's not a common policy for a teacher to communicate his first name, or hang up sticky notes on their doors, for that matter. When he sees me staring, his lips tick up. "I ordered a wooden nameplate that matches the color of the door, but it hasn't arrived yet."

I don't reply, instead give him a weak nod. For a flash of a second, I wonder if I shouldn't just drop this stupid idea and get the hell out, but when the door closes behind us on a quiet click, I know that I've run out of time. That should probably make me curl inward like I usually do, but when Mister Montague stares at me with a warm glow in his eyes, I can't help the puff of air that leaves my mouth in a whoosh, and my shoulders sag in relief.

The room's got a functional size, with a desk and chairs, and a bookcase overstacked with books. Piles and piles of them. Against the wall, a painting of Pythagoras and a quote from Newton, and on the window sill, a small pot with a cactus. That makes me frown.

Catching my trail of sight, Mister Montague shrugs, but doesn't answer my unspoken question.

"Please, sit." He gestures to the dark-leather chair across from his desk, and waits for me to sit down, before taking place at his desk. I take a seat and pull my bag on top of my lap to mask the ticking of my knee. I'm nervous.

I have been tense ever since I woke up to a message on my phone from a not so anonymous caller, stating that tonight's the night. The first initiation of the brotherhood. Over the course of the past ten hours, I have fought back all kinds of different thoughts. From refusing to go, *full stop*, to waves of anger. I have wanted to call my mother and tell her that my stepbrother is bullying me, but then thought better of it. I don't want her to know that her son is even more fucked up than she already thinks.

So I decided that I will go, face it, and survive. Two can play this fucking game.

When the silence continues, Mister Montague gives me a small smile, not trying to reveal his curiosity as he eyes me with surprisingly light eyes that are surrounded by thick, dark lashes and equally dark eyebrows. Still, his gaze seems genuine, and that's all I need.

"What can I do for you, Régis?"

"You are new here too, right?" I blurt. That was not what I meant to ask. My cheeks heat with embarrassment.

Mister Montague's smile widens. "I am. This is my first school year at Saint-Laurent."

"Me too." I wince. "I'm sorry, I'm not a big talker."

He nods at that, lips still curled up. "But you have a big brain. I saw your high school results. They are exceptional."

"Thank you, sir." I roll my lips. When the silence lingers once more, Mister Montague stands up, and walks toward the closet. He's dressed smart casual in the colors of Saint-Laurent, with navy-blue pants and a coffee-colored jumper, unlike most of the other teachers who show up in a suit. The collar of his equally dark blue shirt is tucked neatly over the edges of his sweater, making his slender neck look even longer.

He grabs a few books from its pile. "You are Arthur and Louis's little brother?" He asks.

"Stepbrother," I correct.

"Right. stepbrother. But still new."

"Yes. I—" Inhaling sharply, I continue, "In class you mentioned a prestigious price? I— I want to qualify for the *Prix d'Honneur.*"

Mr Montague looks up from the books. "And so you should. Though we haven't officially communicated the new criteria to qualify yet. We have made some changes of interest to you."

I smile nervously. "Do they make it impossible for me to enter? To win?"

"On the contrary." Mister Montague's fingertips tap on the desk as he seems to think things through. "They are designed to give more students a fair chance to participate. You'll be expected to give a presentation about a relevant topic." Mister Montague plops down onto his seat once more, dropping the books onto his desk. "Can you think of a topic you're passionate about?"

"There are plenty of subjects I am passionate about," I mumble, rapidly overthinking my options. "But I need to work on my presentation skills. This college isn't like any state university, and it's unlike something I have grown up into. I guess…" I inhale deeply through my lungs, fisting the strands of my backpack as my knee wildly taps against the floor. "Do you want to help me prepare for the qualification? I mean, I understand that as a teacher, it's your job to be neutral and all. I get that. And I don't—But it's just, I could use a bit of support."

But then Mister Montague gives me that smile again. "I'd love to, Régis. I understand that this college can be overwhelming."

Silence.

"You would?" I gape, though unsure why I'm so surprised. He is a teacher, after all. He nods, and his widening smile gives me enough courage to say, "In that case, I want to prove to the board that by being smart you can buy a villa by the Mediterranean Sea."

Mister Montague frowns, clearly in thought, as he uses his pen to tap against his wooden desk. "I'm not sure I follow?" But the look in his eyes contradicts that. There's another silence, though this time I can feel tension. It's subtle, like the swirl of a feather, but it's there. Right when I think that I may have made a very wrong call, he adds on a murmur, "I take it you don't come from wealth?"

I slowly shake my head. "I don't."

"Okay," he draws out. "Perhaps I have some ideas, if you would like..."

"Yes."

We spend the next half hour discussing different arguments. Mister Montague is not very open about his own background, though I enjoy collecting the few puzzle pieces of his past as he casually throws them around in our conversations. Turns out, we're pretty similar. We surf through various topics, sharing knowledge of articles or documentaries, defending our arguments with facts and research data.

Needless to say, when we part half an hour later, I'm feeling pretty elated. Because it's only the start of working on this project, and it's already quite something.

Walking through the hall, I can't hide the wide grin on my face and for once I don't care about the trailing eyes. Fuck them. I'll get through tonight, through this ridiculous prank that might not be a prank, and then, tomorrow, I can continue working on these topics Mister Montague and I discussed before. Mister Montague borrowed a book about French Economic History, which is extremely relevant to my choice of topic. I can't wait to dive in.

Crossing the hall to the far end, to where the collection of plants is placed, I plop down on the furthest bench, the one with its glorious view of the garden. Then I take out my phone to call Dad. The first thing I stumble across though, is that treacherous message I received this morning.

Anonymous: Little stepbro, it's time. At midnight I'll leave your cloak in your bedroom. Put it on, with only boxers underneath. I promise you won't be cold...

At those words, my thoughts start wandering, unwilling to listen to my mind. I am here to graduate. I am here to show them all that I'll fight them. This is *my* future.

This too will pass.

But my lips suddenly feel dry, despite the saliva that forms inside. My mouth on his cock. Fuck, the thought is enough to have my nerves back on edge. Flutters confiscate my practised cool, and form a tickle inside my stomach. I haven't seen Arthur in too long. Have only heard that taunting, husky voice in my mind.

What will he look like in a cloak? Sexy, I bet. Fuck yeah, he'll look hot and cold, sweet and evil at the same time. I can be evil too.

My notes burn in my backpack. The ones I just formulated together with Mister Montague.

Those thoughts are not convenient. Not with Arthur, not this desire, not this...but will he let me touch him again? Chase me down in the woods, wrap his hand around my neck, let me choke on his cock...fuck... Then I can finally let go. Like the helpless little boy coming out from behind the iron bars, even now, I just want to please. To touch, smell, fucking bury my nose in Arthur's skin, because I want to be seen, want to matter, want to be good.

I fucking hate him for playing me this way, for making me feel like some helpless pet. But no matter how hard I ignore it, I want his attention, even though I know I shouldn't. The thought comes on a shudder, though it's true. I want him to claim my attention with that husky timbre that's his, let it slowly overtake all my senses. Despite his spiteful words, despite the revolting sensation they bring to my core, as they go against everything I believe.

I want him to know what it's like for people like us. Want them *all* to know. I want them to understand that because of this self-imposed division of rich and poor directly from birth, we will never be able to understand each other. They—this brotherhood, or whatever it is—would never know what it's like for "the commoners", as they like to call us. I doubt they've ever considered what life must be like for some of their employees, like Amadou, who came here from Senegal for something better, and Didier who came from Martinique.

And then there's me. *I* want to be heard. Hopefully the *Prix d'Honneur* will offer the right space to challenge topics that are heavy.

Surrounding flora doesn't give me their usual calm, and I get up again, swinging my backpack over my shoulder and heading toward our dorm. I call Dad as I climb the stairs, who's in a particularly foul mood. Some other inmates stole his towel and clothes and left him like that in the showers. The guards had to come and save his ass. When I admit that I still haven't been able to get hold of the lawyer, he starts shouting and swearing, calling me all kinds of names. I need to force my knees not to buck and crawl through the corridor when the need to find an escape overwhelms me.

There are no iron bars here.

Dad calls me useless, swears that my mother will throw me back into my old life any time now, and I know I can just hang up, knowing that he can't get to me. I know that. But I don't feel it. It's engraved in my past—that inked cross meant to make me remember. Degradation. Punishment.

No freedom.

When he hangs up on me, raging and frustrated, we still officially have two more minutes. I know he can still call me back later, he sometimes does, and perhaps that's why I feel even more vulnerable, and agitated. My earlier state of elation is long gone. The corridor is too narrow, the paintings too close, with faces, so many of them, watching me, taunting me.

I need to get out.

Out.

When I practically stumble into someone, I flinch. It's Dominique, and he eyes me cautiously. "Hey, Régis, are you alright?"

Rubbing my eyes, I grumble, "Yes, I'm fine. A little tired.

Happy that the weekend has begun." The lie rolls easily off my tongue. "If you don't mind, I really want to—"

"I think you should come down with me." He eyes our dorm, then looks back at me. "Let's grab a drink in the canteen, yeah?"

"Sorry, I'm just going to lounge a bit." I slip past him and grab my keys from my pocket.

"Régis, come on." He's followed me back to our dorm. Trepidation wins from my earlier enthusiasm, and in kicks the claustrophobia. My thoughts tumble.

"Régis!"

"Espèce de merde."

The door bursts open and bangs against the wall, making me freeze on the threshold. All gazes turn to me.

Lounging on both couches are the twins. Louis is still in his football gear, long, muscled legs unfurled as he occupies the entirety of the sofa. Arthur's on the other one, his laptop and books lying next to him, his arms crossed behind his head and his legs pulled up against his chest. Next to them, on one of velvet armchairs, sits Gaël, crossed legged, inspecting different kinds of oils from a shipping box. Soft music is playing, but I can't hear what it is since blood is pumping so loudly in my ears. Their chatter dies on the spot.

"There he is," Louis exclaims, a little too cheerful. "Our little, lost s-bro. We were just talking about you." He taps his foot on the seat of the couch. "Haven't seen you for ages. Come and sit with us. After all, the weekend has begun." He wiggles his brows, and something pangs in my chest. It's tonight's events.

Behind me Dominique enters the room, and by the sound of it, Maxime's right on his tail, as he babbles enigmatically with his bright voice.

Louis seems pleased with himself when I amble my way toward his couch, but at least he has the decency to pull away his feet so I can sit. Lithe as a cat he climbs off his seat and peddles toward the kitchen. "Finally all together. Now there's a reason to celebrate." He reaches for the fridge and takes out a bottle of champagne. I recognize the label immediately.

"I didn't know you'd be the kind of guy who enjoys celebrations with a cheap bottle of drink," I mutter bitterly, remembering that comment all too well.

A short silence follows, in which Louis looks genuinely flabbergasted. Gaël snickers and I feel a nerve tick in my jaw, but refuse to look away. It isn't until Arthur snorts out a laugh that I'm seriously caught off guard. My trepidation returns in full force. I think...I think I made a wrong move.

I catch him winking at Gaël, who spreads his arms to welcome Dominique who swipes the tiny bottles of oil from Gaël's lap and straddles his sculpted thighs. Our gazes meet—his cheeks flush, probably from this public display of affection, matching my own awkwardness from being caught staring in the first place. But then he smiles at me, and it breaks the tension. For some inexplicable reason it feels like a heavy weight is taken off of my deflating shoulders and I can breathe. I don't know if it's because of him, or because of Maxime who has a natural gift of being so casual. So...nice. Even as he inspects the bottle of champagne with a suspicious frown. "Uhm, I wouldn't call a 2010 Rothschild cheap."

Licking my lips, I decide to keep it quiet for now. Which is the right thing to do, because Louis swaggers back, another bottle in his hands.

"It's a private joke, my man." He winks at me, looking amused. "A family joke. Right, Régis?"

"Sure," I grumble, and that causes another wave of laughter, that even...yeah, even makes *me* smile. Though I still wonder if he's fucking with me.

"There we go." Louis opens both bottles in two rapid pops. "Since we can't walk on one leg." He offers me a glass, but right when I want to take it, he pulls it back. "Or do you prefer drinking straight from the source?" He laughs at his own joke, but before I can come up with a snarky answer, he hands the glass over. "Just kidding."

"You're awfully funny tonight, Louis." Maxime joins me on the couch. He has already exchanged his school uniform for a more casual look of sweats and a hoodie.

"I know. It's because I'm happy we're all together." Someone switches on some music and I watch as Louis walks around the room, topping up glasses as he offers a casual reply or joke here and there. I'm still unsure if he's messing with me.

From what I've begun to understand, people often can't tell the twins apart. It's true that they have an identical build and physical appearance. They even have a similar swagger and overall confident way they carry themselves. They're devilishly smug with their dark, twinkling eyes and lush, full lips. When I first met them, I wasn't sure who was who, though that changed rapidly. The difference, for me, is in the air. Louis gives off this electricity, waves of snapping energy. He demands attention. Arthur, however, radiates a soothing balm edged in darkness. There's a false sense of softness tinged with a promise of challenge. When I'm around Louis, I feel like he might trick me, but he is otherwise innocent. I definitely don't feel attracted to him. When I'm around Arthur though, a sensation finds its way around me, blanketing me with arousal and desire.

"Jo says that the football team will finally play in the local competitions this year?" Maxime asks.

Louis smiles. "We will be. It has been ages since we were out there, but with some good new players, Coach believes we have what it takes to make regional again. We don't really have what it takes, but most of the guys are not that ambitious anyway. We just want to play."

"Don't we all," Arthur mutters quietly, privately.

"Well, you should let us know," Maxime insists. I don't know if he heard Arthur's comment, but if he did, he blindly ignores him. "We'll come and watch you play."

"Sounds good." Louis stalks over to where I'm sitting, and when he holds out the bottle I tilt my chin to meet his gaze.

"Want some more?"

"Sure." My hands tremble a little as I watch him pour more of the glittery liquid. Part of me expects him to do something unexpected, something wicked, but he just mumbles, "*Voilà*, little s-bro," and sends me a dopey grin. I relax a little, deciding that I am going to survive tonight.

"Absolutely. By the way, have you met that new teacher, Mister Montague?" Maxime asks, wiggling his brows. "I heard he's one of the members of the committee for the *Prix d'Honneur.*" He looks smug when his eyes land on Arthur. "And in my class, he announced that things will be done a little differently this year."

"Different how?" Louis asks, bottle in hand. "I mean, not that I care, but I know someone who does."

Maxime shrugs. "He didn't say. I think they don't know yet. I mean, it's not the sort of thing you can just change, with all the traditions and such."

"He told us that from this year onward, all students need to do a qualification presentation first," Dominique adds. "For the entire board."

"*What*?" Arthur nearly jumps out of his seat. "What happened to qualification upon invitation?"

"Perhaps they also want to give other students the opportunity to come forward. Invitations are very scarce, and from what I've heard, are played out on a high level."

"And you believe that crap?"Arthur snarls.

"I don't know," Dominique stammers. "It's what I've heard."

"That's bullshit!" Arthur punches his fist onto the coffee table, and his onyx eyes flash in rage when they collide with Dominique's, who visibly flinches.

"Arthur," Gaël warns as his hands reach for Dominique's

sides. "I know that news doesn't make you happy, but don't take it out on Dominique. That shit scares him."

Arthur blanches. "Damn." He brushes an annoyed hand through his thick mane. "I'm sorry man, I didn't mean to scare you."

"Wow..." I mouth, but when I feel Arthur's fury unexpectedly land on mine, I can't hold myself back. Perhaps it's the drink talking. "Is the big, bad Arthur Deveraux making an apology?"

Someone cat-calls, as more snickers follow. They are all watching the show. *Us*. Fisting my hands, I puff up my chest, readying myself for yet another conflict. But rather than descending his predictable wrath on me, he lets out a laugh instead. And coarsely kicks Maxime from his seat, before he plops down next to me.

"I guess I did. Tell me, how did that sound?"

"That sounded fucking awesome," I admit. It's not a lie.

"C'est vrai?" Is all he says, eyes gleaming with mischief. For a brief moment it feels like there's nothing else around us, just him and I. "You better cherish this moment, because I'm not a fan of apologizing. Definitely something you won't hear again."

I snort. "Why am I not surprised?"

"Were you looking for an apology?" His gaze narrows, eyes searching.

"Maybe?" It comes out a little breathless, and my stomach tightens with something unfamiliar. Arthur's tongue darts out and he slowly licks his plush bottom lip.

Around us the guys have moved on to another topic, goading Gaël about something he doesn't agree with. Not like I care. Every single fiber of my nervous system is focusing on Arthur and his perfectly curved lips. On his dark stare, as it takes me in.

"Yeah?" He rasps. His voice has dropped, and he leans in a little. "What's that for?"

I shrug. "For the trouble you're gonna put me through?"

He chuckles at that, shaking his head. "Whatever you think that you'll be going through tonight? You have no idea." God, his voice. "An innocent lamb like you?" Another raspy chuckle, followed by a click of his tongue. "No. Idea."

The others bark out in mutual laughter, Gaël huffing out some words in disdain.

Nerves ripple through my veins, together with some weird form of bravery. "But will my big brother protect me?"

"Maybe. If you're good to him." He has dropped his voice to a murmur.

Oh God, why does this turn me on? Why do these words...

"Like the other day?" I whisper.

"Hmm, he would like that very much. And you?"

The memory of his hands on my body causes toe curling tingles. Of his cock in my mouth...I salivate. I'd die for another taste of him. But I can't forget my past, my iron bars. Can't forget my future, altered since I set foot in this college.

Forever intermingled with his, even if he doesn't want it.

No, I've got to be stronger than this. But it's becoming so fucking, hard.

"I—" Probably still wouldn't have had a clue what to say, but my phone, vibrating in the pocket of my school pants, shuts off any other thoughts. I check the caller ID. "Oh, shit."

I fly out of the couch before anyone can stop me, then give everyone a little wave. "Thanks for uhm—I need to go. I'll see you later." Pressing the phone against my ear, I grab my bag and head for my door. "You have received a phone call from an inmate of the Toulouse prison. Press 1 if you want to..."

The knock on my door doesn't come as a surprise. Neither does my response. Squeezing the silky material of the black cloak a little tighter, I ignore how my body tingles with nerves. This wait was killing me. Whatever it is they have in store for me, I can't escape. Not tonight.

This will pass too.

But when I open my door, I'm suddenly not so sure anymore. The jitters jump violently inside my stomach when I take in the view of the twins and their cousin who are standing by the door, wearing identical cloaks to mine. Smooth, black velvet hangs loosely around their broad shoulders, tied at the waist.

Perhaps Arthur was right all along when he said that I have no idea what kind of trouble I am in.

It's a prank, I tell myself. We're students. There will be drinks and music, and the promise to keep the wild things of the evenings a secret.

No one smiles. No snickers or taunts, no wickedness or sins. In their hands they carry Venetian masks, their fingers wrapped in velvet gloves.

"Are you ready?" Arthur asks. I swallow, blink again, then nod. "Good boy. Now, an important rule, we have to be quiet in the corridor. I told you before, but there are many students out here who don't know about us. If you talk, I'll do whatever I can to get you expelled from this school. *Tu comprends?*"

"Yes," I hear myself mumble. Anger builds inside my core, slow and hot as it unfurls, together with a wicked idea. I promised myself I'd fight them all. And no matter how much they've got me cornered, I won't back out now. I'll find a way to have Arthur on his knees, to make him listen.

"Good."

"*On y va.*" Louis takes the lead, followed by Gaël. Arthur pushes me in front of him, and as we head out of our dorm and onto the deserted, narrow hall with its soft, velvet carpets, I can't help but wonder if this was all made for this reason. To be quiet, secretive, and hidden.

11

ARTHUR

We shuffle barefoot through the narrow corridor, a silent procession on its way toward the hidden stairs that will take us all the way to the dungeon in the South Wing. According to the papers on the Alpha Fraternarii, these stairs were only made back in the mid 18th century, when the monks left and Monterrey Castle became Saint-Laurent Boarding College for boys.

The breeding ground for the brotherhood.

It's also the most distressing part of the night. I don't think there hasn't been a single time that I don't fear for any random door to open by accident.

To be seen in our cloaks. To be caught. Despite the tremendous repercussions, the thought is fucking thrilling.

In front of me, Régis follows the others. Though the smooth garment wrapped around his frame, I catch the way his shoulders are drawn-up. He's nervous as hell. That too, is fucking thrilling. And has my cock fill with blood and arousal. I squeeze it through my silk. Not yet, big boy. But soon.

In the front, Louis places his flat hand against the wall and feels for the opening to the secret passage, hidden behind the wallpaper. He slides open the door, letting Gaël through, then follows him, and again, Régis is third in line, with me as his gatekeeper following close.

Down the stairs.

Innocent lamb, it's time for the initiations.

We descend the stairs all the way down toward the dungeons, which are dimly lit with torches for tonight, as they guide us toward our gathering. The entire castle has dungeons, and while some are used for storage, others have been designed as communal areas where students can hang out, play some pool or darts, or even organize their monthly movie night. Not South Wing though. Officially, this is where personnel sleeps. Unofficially, it's where the founding fathers keep office. It's where my dad has his office. It's where the Alpha Fraternarii rule. There are four other families, but their sons have already graduated from this college.

We are the final ones. I eye Gaël and Louis as they wait for us to catch up.

In front of me, Régis stumbles on the final stairs, and while he probably won't hurt himself should he trip, my hand is fast as it reaches out. I grab his neck to steady him. Not his shoulder, nor his arm. It's his neck I claim. Because I can. He flinches at my touch, but is too proud to turn around.

"Ready?" Louis asks when we've all reached the concrete floors of the dungeon.

"*Oui*." They both pull down plain, white masks that cover their entire faces, only to leave room for their eyes. We have other masks, smooth rubber that comes only down to our nose and leaves our mouths free for other tasks, but we won't be wearing those tonight. No, tonight's for the pupils to show their value.

Most of the brothers will be coming in black and white tonight. Watching them move forward, I squeeze my fingers a little tighter around Régis's silky neck, then pull him closer to my mouth.

"I hope you'll like your mask. I had it made especially for you." I mutter. Not able to resist, I unwrap the glove from my hand and pull my fingers back around his neck. He lets me. Its shape is slender, beautifully curved the way it dips toward his shoulders. Flesh warm, smooth. I wonder what he tastes like. I know what he *smells* like—of eucalyptus and burning wood, mixed with that unique scent that is Régis. And right now, of fear. It's heady and thick, and I want to lap it up, savour its flavor and devour it all at once. I want to hunt, then bring him to a plush corner and have my way with him. His breath comes in strained puffs, and I'm not sure if he's about to coil away like the skittish guy he is, or lash out like the naughty kitten he can be. He doesn't do either, just stands there, and I'm a little disappointed. Though he's right, now's not the time to play. That doesn't mean I can't provoke him. Just a little. "You won't need it tonight though." When he still doesn't react, I add, "Pupils don't get to wear their masks, but brothers do. We can watch you, recognize you, question you, play with you... But you won't get to return the favor. Not yet anyway."

That makes him jerk his head. His lips are pinched and his eyes are large. But he still doesn't fucking take the bait. Yes. He is afraid. But he's too much of a stubborn, hotheaded little shit to admit such a thing to anyone.

"Good luck tonight," I breathe. It comes out a little raspier than intended, but fuck me, he's burning me up. With one gloved hand, I reposition the hood around his shoulder, my other fingers still viced around his neck. They don't want to let go, it seems. "And enjoy the fucking, because there will be a lot of it."

Now *that* has him reacting. He yanks his grip around my wrist. "Arthur, please." Licking his lips, his eyes dart from me to the narrow hall behind me, to where the other disappeared to.

My little stepbrother begging me for something? If that doesn't harden my cock. Flaring my nostrils, I dip my head to look him in the eye.

"Yes?"

"You—I've never..." He splutters, then clears his throat, his Adam's apple bobbing against my silked hand. Hmm. I fucking *knew* it. My *chaton* is still a virgin. And while I usually stay the hell away from inexperienced dudes, the thought that I will be his first, has my cock throb behind my black briefs. "I didn't mean—it's just, you know—" Régis backpedals, but the harm's already done.

Pulling him flush against my chest, I muse, "I told you not to worry, your big brother will protect you."

Movement behind us has him flinch, before the look in his eyes turns hard again. He's protecting himself, shutting everything and everyone off. That annoys me more than it should, and I squeeze his neck, forcing his attention back on me.

"Now, if you want to say something else, I suggest you make it quick."

"Fuck you," he spits.

"That will do. Now, let's go." Régis bristles at my words, eyes flaring with embarrassment, and rage, that I ignore. We'll have more time for this later on. His disdain evaporates gradually when I pull up my white and golden mask and his eyes flutter when he takes me in. I know what I look like in that black cloak, because I see my reflection in him, but I know the effect of a mask is huge. Camouflage changes everything—even when you know the person. When you don't recognize them anymore, everything is put in a different perspective.

Régis now thinks he knows what my mask looks like. But I like to keep my little stepbrother on edge, it will have a bigger effect on the surprise. He won't see me coming until he's already kneeling right by my feet.

Sliding my fingers from his neck to his nape, I push him

forward and through the narrow hall. Behind us, more brothers descend the stairs, their voices nothing more than a hushed whisper. The torches only offer a dim light, but it's enough for the paintings at the wall to flicker, the portrayed people giving a gloomy glower as if they are about to walk out of their frame.

Régis obeys, taking the final steps toward where two other masked brothers are waiting. Their gazes land on my little stepbrother, then back to mine, followed by a little nod. When I let go of him, Régis doesn't waver and the look he throws my way is one of anger before he is being set right next to the other pupils, who are already waiting, cloaked and visibly nervous. Right before I step inside the room, I dive into the shadows, where I change my mask and slip on my other glove. I'm now completely in black, exactly like the villain they want me to be.

Inside the room, my brothers are waiting, forming a line of silent anticipation. They watch me come closer, pass them slowly, as I make my way to the front, right beside the window, to where the Elder is already waiting. He dips his head in a greeting, a formality I return.

We don't know who's who, which is part of the allure of the brotherhood. No matter what we represent in the outside world, how powerful we are, how much money we invest and spend at the same time, these gatherings are mystical, anonymous nights with one theme—sex. And power, though to me, that comes in one. In one, erotic, package.

Someone rings a bell, all brothers are now here.

The door closes behind us.

Elder Jacques pounds his cane onto the floor with a loud boom. "Brothers. It's time."

Night has fallen and the dark stakes its claim, casting a nefarious energy over the woods. We listen to the dimming sounds of flapping bats as they make their way from the windows and back into the forest, where they linger in the twilight. Like always, the fire's already crackling, the corners of the room decorated with plush cushions and torches. It's nothing like the Atrium, but the anticipation that's coiling in my stomach, doesn't care.

"And what better way to start, then with another peaceful evening." His dark, piercing eyes scan the room and linger a little longer on mine. Not for the first time I wonder if he knows who I am. "Before we ask our pupils to join us, I would like to take a moment to remind you that national elections will take place in two years. I am pleased to inform you that Alpha Fraternarii has managed to be welcomed with the staggering number of twenty brothers in the Élysée." His voice turns into a crescendo, louder and more urgent, chasing the next words. "We are growing, our numbers increasing steadily. The world is a better place with us in it. By growing our businesses and organizations, by respecting nature and charity, Alpha Fraternarii has never been as wealthy as we are today!"

Brothers applaud and cheer, their masks crevicing as they smile.

"*Oui!*" Elder Jacques sweeps the mood up, bangs his cane onto the rhythm of their clapping hands, as his never faltering gaze stretches across the group, taking in every hoot and howl with his dark, observant eyes.

Unmistakable, our pupils can hear us from the corridor. While my hands clap and my throat works, sending cheers into the room, I think of Régis. Waiting. Fearing.

Let him be afraid. That's the price he should pay for getting in my way.

"Let our pupils come forward!" Elder Jacques roars. Crescendo turns into an explosion as the door opens on a loud clunk, sending in a gush of chill. Of excitement, of consternation, of fucking sexual arousal. Six cloaked, unmasked first-year students stand in the corridor, nicely set up in lines of two.

The Elder must be in a particularly good mood, because they

didn't get the same treatment during their first initiation. But then they weren't *all* there.

Watching my little stepbrother walking inside, followed by some guy who looks like he's about to start crying, makes my cock harden instantly. Knowing that every single brother is watching, Régis has carved his face into his usual aloofness. For a brief moment he looks up, eyes flitting around, never resting on one of the staring masks, before he dips his head again. I wonder if he's searching for me. However, he won't find me, since I changed from white to black. It's a better match to his pale, smooth skin and those golden waves of hair. To those big, blue eyes and those lovely, wavy lashes that flutter swiftly when he gets anxious.

Like now.

"Pupils. I'm thrilled to see that you are all here, all six, brothers-to-be. Welcome home." Father Jacques eyes Régis, who looks away, biting his lip. My cock throbs behind my cloak, so ready for action. "You have all been chosen by the Alpha Fraternarii, and in these next weeks, we will show you who we are, what we stand for, and what it means to be a brother among us. We will familiarize you with our values, and you will not always learn in the easy way. You will go down on your hands and knees and show your respect, and will take out your chequebook to make that royal donation to one of the many thoughtful charity associations that make our country so prosperous. After all, we respect our commoners. We want what's best for them, even if they don't realize what that is. We will guide them, will protect them, will keep them modest. So we can shine, bright and big, and keep the power between ourselves."

"*Respect.*" We all boom. Elder Jacques's cane bangs into the wooden floor and Régis flinches.

"*Loyalty.*" All brothers line up in an outer circle that keeps our pupils inside. Régis turns around and takes a few steps toward the door as we start to shuffle and chant at the same time.

"Traditions." We keep on shifting, keeping the circle intact as the values of our brotherhood are sung on repeat, on a similar rhythm that perfectly matches the booming of the cane. Régis seems to panic, now clawing at a random brother in his attempt to break the circle and bolt for the door.

"Régis Deveraux," Elder Jacques suddenly roars. Everyone stops, and even my little stepbrother freezes on the spot, before he turns over his shoulder. The cloak is too big, and honey curls peek out from under the large hood. It makes him look even more fragile. Still, he manages to radiate a biting fierceness. He stays rooted to his spot inside the circle, close to one of my brothers, right across the door. So close, yet so far away.

"I'm glad that you could make it, though you will need to learn that you can't always come and go as it pleases you. We operate as a family, and as such, we value trustworthiness." Elder Jacques uses his smooth voice. When Régis doesn't reply, he asks, "Do you understand what it means to be relied upon by your brothers?" Régis's eyes dart around the room, but again, they don't linger long enough to see.

He can't find me.

That makes me both hot and cold, but my cock still thumps against my garment. He has clearly made up his mind.

Régis shrugs.

"In here, we answer with words," Elder Jacques croons. "So what's your answer, Régis?"

The tension rises with each second he doesn't speak.

The bell rings, and someone clears his throat, then the door opens and another brother enters. *Monsieur Z.*

Shit. I know what's about to happen now. We all know the procedure, but I'll be fucking damned. Régis is mine.

Monsieur Z languidly moves inside the circle, his mask a brilliant red, and makes his way to the window in the front. When he reaches Elder Jacques, they exchange quiet pleasantries, as if he hasn't just disturbed an extremely awkward situation. The longer it lasts, their mumbles creating a soft buzz as it floats on silence, the more I think they will just step over the unfortunate situation my little stepbrother has created. It is his first time, after all. But right as the first brothers start to dwell in impatience, Elder Jacques rises his arms and reaches out to Régis.

"Come here, Régis." Still glancing from over his shoulder, he nibbles his lips nervously. Both cloaked figures are now watching him, together with the rest of us. "If you're not sure, I'll show you how you can become trustworthy in our eyes."

Régis takes another step back, hitting the chest of my brother, who gives him a firm push back into the circle. Régis stumbles, then turns, a furious glower on his beautiful face. He looks haunted, shoulders deflated, jaw tightly clenched, but dazzling at the same time.

"Very well," he finally mutters. It's his damn pride that makes him listlessly move, the cloak gently brushing his slender frame. The other pupils step aside and watch him come forward, most likely relieved it's not them who have been called upon. Régis doesn't stop until he stands right in front of the two predators and the thick, wooden cane that carries the logo of the Alpha Fraternarii.

The golden crow.

"Good." Elder Jacques purrs, then he palms Régis's cheek. "Members of this family say what they do, and do what they say. Do you understand?"

Yes. Just tell the old hag that you understand.

"Nothing? Hm?"

He doesn't reply.

"Very well." I can feel the smile on Elder Jacques's mouth, and it makes my skin crawl with something cool and slimy. *This is exactly what they are looking for.* It makes me want to jump out of my own flesh. I can't see his face from here, but when the

Elder and *Monsieur Z* soothe my little stepbrother onto his knees, I feel my own body go rigid with agony. Clenching and unclenching my fists, I try to fight the urge to run forward and beat the hell out of them. And maybe it's in my mind, but for a flutter of a moment, I feel like everyone agrees. Why wouldn't they? Every single brother in this circle knows that I claimed Régis as my own. And like hell will he be taken from me. When Régis's knees hit the wooden floors, it's like the rest of his body collapses. He looks so fucking small right now, despite his head, tilted up, chin brought forward, eyes no doubt sending daggers. But that little act of bravoure is not going to protect him.

No, I am.

Isn't that what I told him? Isn't that what he literally asked me earlier tonight? I bite my lip until I draw blood. This is for the best. Régis won't stay after tonight. He will leave, and my future will be secured. My cock vaults in my boxers, disagreeing.

He's mine. My little devil growls. But my brain wants to overrule anything else like it always does.

Go get him.

Needlessly, I take a step forward, but when the first heads tilt my way, I freeze. And then, right when I get my limbs to move —*move!*—someone else does.

A brother breaks the silence and rustles all the way forward, until he stands right next to a kneeling Régis. Sliding down onto his haunches, he tilts his chin and reaches a gloved hand across Monsieur Z's crotch, visibly waiting for permission. Both predators seem to be taken aback for a flitting second—this is *not* part of the procedure.

Monsieur Z dips his head, chest heaving from arousal as he watches the stranger cup his cock. Yet, nobody moves.

"*Sacrifice.*" Elder Jacques finally rasps. He jerks his chin and my anonymous brother carefully opens the cloak. I can't help but wonder who it is. "Watch him." He pushes the guy, who has lifted his mask to reveal his mouth, forward with his cane. I can't see his face, just the back of his hood. And Monsieur Z, as he grabs hold of his thick shaft, then pushes it into the waiting mouth. Elder Jacques pats the kneeling brother's head, then peers up at us again. "This is also confraternity," he decides, sounding pleased. "To help out a brother in need. Sex is power, Régis. And power is what this brotherhood stands for. Sharing values and respecting those, is what has made Alpha Fraternarii big and powerful. Get your hands dirty. Your mouth." He turns his gaze back to Régis and lets out a dirty chuckle. "Who wants to show our pupil how much we value our traditions?" This time I don't hesitate. I'm already halfway there by the time the others realize what has been offered.

When he sees me coming, the Elder dips his head. "You hungry, brother?"

We both turn to face the ground where my little stepbrother is still kneeling, and my cock leaks behind its restraints. Régis doesn't look up, but that doesn't stop the shudder from running through my body. Hungry for him? Fuck yeah.

I give Elder Jacques one firm nod.

"Very well." He reaches out to get Régis up, then places his smaller hand in my gloved one. Even through the velvet material I can feel that his is ice cold. He won't look at me, not even when I guide him toward the furthest, flickering corner of the room while Elder Jacques continues talking to the other pupils.

It's not until I sit him down on the pillows that he looks up, his eyes large with fear. Gone is the earlier bravado. Honestly, I can't blame him. "Do I know you?" He whispers.

Something clenches around my heart. I should tell him it's me, but I can't. Tens and tens of eyes are on us—watching, calculating, judging. They don't know who I am, although they probably suspect, since they know who he is.

The only guy who logically stands between me and my future. Régis is smart, angry, and traumatized. That makes him unpredictable. And that, ultimately, makes him dangerous. He reaches out a hand and brushes gently over my covered, black lips, making my heart hammer in my chest.

"You're not going to talk, are you?"

I shake my head. Incense is set alive around us, creating clouds of sandalwood and dragon's blood. Somewhere a bell rings, this one a high-pitched sound that indicates the end of the formal part of tonight. Pushing Régis flush onto the pillows, his back colliding with the plush material as he lays down, I widen his legs and place myself on my knees between him, then stretch my gloved fingers around his neck. They instantly know how tight to squeeze, having already mapped out those delicate curves leading down to his collarbone. He swallows thickly, the feel of his Adam's apple bob deliciously wicked.

"What's going to happen now?" He licks his bottom lip as he watches the scene behind me through hooded eyes. I don't need to turn to know what's going on there. Sex. Raw, unforgiving sex. Escorts come to entertain us during our nights with our brothers, and pupils are more than welcome to join. Normally I enjoy having some time with our favorite boy, but tonight he can be all Louis's. I have more than enough on my hands with my little stepbrother. Leisurely tracing a velvet finger down his clavicle and between the sides of his cloak, I take in every single flicker in Régis's stare. His eyes are on mine, wide and curious, nervous as he flutters his lashes. When my fingers finally reach his stomach, he shivers.

"W-what are you doing?" He whispers. He looks so young like this, so innocent. All brothers are scarcely dressed below their cloak, but I wouldn't be surprised if Régis was too fucking stubborn to take off his pants. The thought makes me growl in impatience, and I practically rip off my glove, feeling famished. This is what I wanted tonight. Fucking *him* at *my* mercy. Not with that old fart, or that twisted dickhead who only ever comes to get his cock sucked. I want Régis for myself.

My stepbrother.

My obstacle.

My rival.

Carefully teasing the silky sides a little further apart, I catch a glimpse of light, glimmering skin and smooth valleys of sculpted muscles. Around us people openly moan and hiss, chatter and croon, but when I slide the cloak a little further open, Régis grabs my hands.

"No! I mean—" He nibbles his lip and looks away. I don't catch his flush in the dim light, but I'm sure it must be something fierce. When he looks back I tilt my head, silently asking for more. "Arthur?" He whispers. "Is that you?"

Don't let him get to you.

I snarl at him, then place my fingers on the warm, naked skin of his stomach. Fuck, he feels good, all warm and soft. Hard in the right places, though his body isn't as muscular as mine. His is more slender, more lithe, pearly white and delicate. I need to swallow a guttural groan. He's taken my instructions to heart and is only wearing black boxers that reveal his thickened length, his crown already peeking out from the material.

"Please. I've never, I mean I have s-sucked, but I have never —" Been touched before. Apart from that one time in the woods when I got us both off simultaneously.

He stands between you and your future.

Ripping off his underwear with a snatch of my fingers, I wrap my hand around his engorged cock. Fuck, he is hard for me, his slit wet with pre-cum. I start stroking. Slowly, from tip to base, my fingers curl around his soft balls as they rest in my palm. Régis's breath hitches and he flutters his lashes some more.

"You don't have to—" He chokes, and then his hips start to move. Fuck me, if that isn't the hottest thing I've ever seen. Sitting on my haunches between his spread legs, I watch Régis slowly lose control. He's so responsive to my slightest touch, it's fucking mesmerizing. I lean in and trace his balls with the coolness of my mask, and he shudders. I grab hold of them while my bare fingers work his cock, and he keeps on gyrating into my palm, his head writhing on the cushions as he does so. He's restless, wet lips parted, as his head goes from left to right. He has closed his eyes now, but his voice, soft and breathy, form the sweetest of sounds.

"Oh my god—oh..." he stifles. His eyes pop open, hooded and glassy. "I'm going to come if you k-keep, oh fuck..." I don't need another single warning to dive forward, rip the mask from my face and pull my mouth on his cock, eagerly sucking him into the back of my throat. Hot fucking damn, he tastes amazing. All slick and sweet, aroused and desperate as he convulses around me with unintelligible shouts. His hips come up one last time and he stutters, then fills my mouth. I swallow around him, and milk him until he spills his last drop. Slowly pulling off, I make sure that he can see me, lips on his dick, before we finally part. Quickly, I slide my mask back on my face, not wanting to risk any suspicion around me. I look up, but the other brothers are still too busy pleasing themselves. Elder Jacques sits on his chair, two red cloaks lapping at his cock.

When I look back at my little stepbrother, he looks dazed, mouth agape, nostrils flared. Then, surprise turns into anger. "It's *you*." It no longer sounds like a relief, more like an accusation, and I narrow my gaze, inwardly backtracking.

"Yeah, well, who did you think?" His cheeks flush, and his lips pinch close, eyes shiny with irritation. "What, you wanted me to be someone else?" Now that thought has me fuming.

Régis tilts his head, watching me. "Perhaps."

I huff out a laugh that turns into a growl. "*Perhaps*? What the fuck is wrong with you?" He looks away, anger melting into something else. Something more vulnerable. His gaze dips to where my cock is begging to be taken out for a treat. He blinks. "You want me to give you—" He nudges his chin toward my crotch, then lays back onto the pillow with a lazy curl around his mouth. I bet he doesn't even know how sexy he looks like that. "Come on, let me make you feel better."

I shouldn't, not with Régis going from hot to cold, from angry to vulnerable. He's got something up his sleeve and I can't risk it, not with everyone looking. But fuck them, I know what I want. *Who* I want. So does my dick.

Fucking *him*.

"Yeah," I growl. Shoving all thoughts aside, I climb over his exposed sculpted stomach and pecs, then straddle his shoulders. Opening my cloak, I lower my boxers and my cock springs free, wet and impatient, its veins clearly visible. Régis eyes it without a blink, then swipes his tongue at my slit, then licks his lips. And then he smiles.

I blink, something prickling on my skin. What the fuck?

"You're right, I had hoped it was you," he murmurs. And before I realize what the hell that means, he suckles the crown of my dick into his mouth with a visible hum of pleasure. I groan through a clenched jaw, unable to stop the hot, sticky pleasure that glides through my vessels. Régis looks up, blue eyes filled with mischief, with that fucking glimmering challenge. Alarm bells go off, but when he takes me in deeper, my hips can't stop from grinding, from wanting more friction. His hot, tight mouth is glorious, but I don't miss the way we seemed to have tumbled back into our usual fighting stance. Only this time—

"Fuck," I growl when my cock hits the back of his throat. "What the hell's gotten into you?"

Only this time he's got me by the balls.

Régis pulls off my cock and I hate the needy whimper that leaves my mouth. Where the fuck did that come from? How is this happening?

Swirling his tongue around my slit, he keeps a firm grip on my shaft, eyes flicking up to meet mine. "I told you before, and

I'll tell you again. I don't need your guidance, I can protect myself." His tongue laps up the fresh pre-cum that has gathered, then licks all the way down to my balls. I shudder, thighs clenching to keep it together. I falter when his mouth suckles in one ball, fisting my cock as my insides roar with lust.

"I'm very capable of surviving here at Saint-Laurent, big brother." He suckles in my other ball, and I clench my jaw again as I tremble. "Wouldn't you agree?" He whispers against my balls, then puffs some more air on my shaft, as he moves his lips back to my tip. Fuck, oh fuck... "I'm going to make you come, then you're going to leave me alone, and I will tell Dad that you are being such a good, big brother to me. Okay?"

"No." I grumble, sounding desperate. He chuckles hoarsely and I shake my head. This little bitch. Who the fuck does he think he is?

"I won't get in your way if you don't get in mine. Now, why don't you give me a little nod so I can finish what I started?" He flicks at my crown, fast and light, making my skin burn with desire. My balls draw up, feeling heavy and so ready to spill, but my mind is not ready. He was supposed to be *my* plaything.

Then Régis pulls my cock away and gives me a pout. "Oh, I must have misread. You don't want to come?" He starts to wiggle under me, as if he wants to leave, and that's all it takes for me to lose it. I push him down onto the cushion, ignoring his cackle, only satisfied once I've stuffed his mouth with my cock again.

"I won't be blackmailed, you little rat," I grumble. His mouth is like heaven, but he doesn't...he doesn't... "Get your dirty mouth back on my cock, *chaton*." I need it. Need to come. Need it. My grinding becomes sloppy in my desperate search for release. "Oh, fuck," I rasp when I can feel it close, but not close enough to reach. "Suck it, come on." Our eyes collide. His flicker knowingly. "Okay," I whisper, then roll my hips again. "Okay, damn it. I'll give you space. But you can't, I won't—" No one else. You can't have anyone else. I swallow the words before I make an even bigger fool out of myself. Régis shakes his head, his gaze softening. Then he hums around my cock, and I moan in the air when he picks up on his perfect suction around my sensitive flesh. "Fuck…yeah." I'm not going to last. "I'm—" I gasp, and then I explode. Scorching hot licks of fire buzz through my veins, making my body hot and cold at the same time as I roar, flesh sensitive, first from the orgasm, then from the aftermath. Because the intensity of my emotions makes me feel vulnerable, and that is a whole new sentiment to me. I don't like it. Don't like the way Régis licks his puffy, wet lips, and smirks at me.

"If I catch you doing that to another guy, I'll have your ass on a fucking plate," I threaten. Am I too possessive? Absolutely. And I can promise him this, he hasn't fucking seen nothing yet.

His smirk turns into a full-blown smile. He looks so handsome, which annoys the shit out of me. I don't even know why that makes him smile. Seriously, he can't believe his own bullshit, right? He should know me by now. There's no way in hell that I'll stop guiding him if that's what it takes to insure my future. If he really thinks that this is all it takes to get rid of me, he's stupid.

Suddenly I'm no longer in the mood for games. It's late and I'm tired.

I have not lost this fucking round. I get up from his luscious body and reorganize my cloak. Then, ignoring the curious look from my brothers—most of them in much more compromising positions—I head for the door.

Then why does it feel like I have?

With a clipped bow to both Elder Jacques and Monsieur Z, who are still talking in hushed voices by the door with their cocks being serviced, I leave.

12

RÉGIS

That night, the three of us make it back to our dorm in utter silence. I can't believe Arthur left right after we…after I…my mask cracks at the memory. Too many thoughts in my mind.

What the hell just came raging right at me? What…who *are* these people? These…these brothers? I'm not sure what I really expected from tonight, not after Arthur warned me so thoroughly. But…not this. This was truly creepy. Everything from the cloaks to the masks. The chanting and the heaving. That man with his cane, and the other one with his dick out. That was nearly me there, nearly me on my knees with a stranger's cock in my mouth. My chest constricts at the thought, gut churning with something close to panic as I follow Gaël through the narrow maze and back to our dorm.

Someone had come to my rescue. Someone who had offered his services instead. Who would do such a thing?

A strong hand claps my shoulder briefly, making me jump from the chaos in my head. Turning over my shoulder, I gaze right into those perceptible, onyx eyes. It's Louis. He doesn't utter a word, but the goofy grin he shares is one that has my shoulders relax a little.

This too will pass.

I can't believe I did that. Can't believe I had the actual balls to intimidate Arthur the way I did. But when they caught me in that circle, something snapped inside me. Call it survival instinct, but I needed to get away from under this heavy wing of control. This unyielding corner he's got me backed up in. It felt suffocating, and he won't listen to me, he never listens to me... so this felt like the only way out.

Perhaps now he understands that he and I don't have the same goal.

But that night, when we got back to our dark and quiet dorm, something changed irrevocably inside of me. As I watch Louis close the door shut behind us, and Gaël shimmying out of his dark cloak before he makes his way to his bedroom, I know that I won't ever be the same. I wonder if Dominique's lying in their bed, asleep and blissfully unaware of the whereabouts of his lover. Did Gaël participate at the carnage tonight?

Tonight's events were no prank, no frat joke to show their new members how to have a good time. No, tonight was a display of pure control, of raw dominance.

Exactly like Arthur had said it would be.

"If ever you need to talk about tonight..." Louis stands on the doorstep of his bedroom, his cloak curled over his forearm. He's already wearing a black tee, meaning I must have blacked out at some stage, lost in my own thoughts. His breathy voice makes me jump, my mind already heavy in debate. When I look up in surprise, he gives me another of those dopey smiles. "I'm not as good a talker as Arthur is, but I can listen pretty decently." Without waiting for my reply, he taps softly on the wooden door, then clears his throat. "Anyway, I'm exhausted. See you soon."

"Yeah." I watch him close his door, still in my black cloak, suddenly feeling extremely ridiculous in the silken garment. "Sure."

My bedroom feels strangely safe when I lock the door behind me, despite the knowledge that there is something out there, in Monterrey Castle, that's raw and strong, that has the capacity to give rise to tens and tens of masked and hooded members.

Alpha Fraternarii.

I still can't believe it. Arthur wasn't lying when he explained more about them. And I… fuck, I still had the courage to disobey the clearly laid-out rules. How long will this ceasefire last? Perhaps he has decided that I'm no longer a target, now that I have surrendered and joined their little club of rich perverts.

The chessboard on my bed shows our intermingled armies, black and white pieces all scattered in our everlasting battle. It has been like that for weeks now, our game advancing excruciatingly slow. I take a step closer, and draw in a heavy breath of air. Something twinges in my chest. In the middle of the board are both kings, black and white, tumbled on their sides.

Game over.

After that night, life picks up as if nothing has happened. October quickly turns into November, and things slowly continue to fall into place. Weeks are filled with courses and side projects, with visits to the woods and evenings of playing chess with the guys. With avoiding Arthur.

It should be a relief that he's no longer entering my room, invading my space, or surprising me in general with his obnoxious presence. But it doesn't.

Something has shifted inside of me.

That first night with the brotherhood replays like a tape inside my head, and there are moments I itch to share my thoughts with someone. Despite our obvious different opinions, the brotherhood is fascinating. Their history is linked to mine, much like many of their ideas of respect and loyalty. My initial trepidation has melted into a more solid sensation of curiosity, and I have questions that I want answers to.

I put them aside for now and focus on my studies. My first grades are better than I could have imagined, despite my restless nights. Still, I'm not able to sleep well. Not even the luxurious bed can offer me a full night's rest. It's. . . too big, the bed, but the narrow closet doesn't feel right either. I find myself longing for the familiarity of the iron bars.

Punishment.

Locks.

Darkness.

I fucking need those.

Need to stay safe.

Still, solitude is a focus, and I've got plenty of that. I have met up a few times with my counselor, a middle-aged mediator who keeps his own practice and has been hired by Saint-Laurent for one day per week. Students walk in during the morning hours, and in the afternoon he works on appointments, with the likes of myself. He's a nice enough person, though, quiet and observing as he lets me speak. I mostly stick to my activities at college, and so far, he seems to be okay with that.

And Since Mister Montague has agreed to help me prepare for the whole nerve-wracking process of standing tall next to the other qualification presentations, we have weekly appointments. So far, we've chosen my topic and I've been practising on presenting them to him in a convincing way. Something that's not easy when I feel his prying eyes on me while my brain searches for plausible arguments to his questions.

I like being around the young teacher. He seems to be one of the first to offer me real friendship while maintaining a level of professionalism.

However, no matter how hard I've been working and no matter how things have been around school, I can't help but notice how things have also been awkwardly quiet.

By day, a silence like that before the storm hits surrounds me. By night, a rage of heat spins me round and round, like some fucking lottery machine. Arthur's tight, hot mouth wrapped around my dick, his black mask ominous and taunting at the same time. My first, astonishing blow-job, a mind-shattering experience.

Power. He smelled of power. And he wanted me.

And I had... *No.* I'm not going to finish that thought. But whatever it was rattled my core deeply and fuck, if it had been anyone but him, it would surely have me crawling back for more.

"Dude!" Maxime huffs from across the table. We're sitting in the empty canteen for one of our infamous chess nights. "Is that..." He picks up his king, ready to put it down.

"Wait, *wait...*" Jo holds his hand, glaring at the board. "Never give in too easily."

Maxime stares him down. "Too easily? I have been hanging in there for half an hour. At least! When you played against him, he had you checkmate in less than 10 moves."

Jo lets go of Maxime's hand and stabs his chin in the air with fake defiance. "That's because I wanted to do him a favor."

"Guys," I give them a little wave. "I'm sitting right here."

Maxime leans his elbows on the table and buries his head in his hands. Letting out a grumble, his eyes dart over the board. "If I move my knight. My bishop...no. But what about..." His hand hovers over a piece. "What about this?"

"You can't move your pawn back, it's against the rules." I deadpan. He looks up at me and bristles.

"Really? I mean, you still have nearly all your pieces and you won't let me move my pawn back? It's not like I can do much damage anyway with that thing," he adds in a mutter, then looks at Jo for support.

"What about your rook?" Jo picks it up carefully, then mimics a few moves with it. "What if you tried..."

Voices behind us announce Dominique's return. He brings a tray of hot drinks—hot chocolate with school-made biscuits—and someone else. Another person who has my heart thump faster in my chest on instinct. Fuck. I instantly glare back at the board, but somehow the scenario has entirely lost its earlier satisfaction. My skin starts to crawl with unease, the flesh on my back heating with every step Arthur takes forward. Around me the guys chatter away, but I'm caught in my usual lockdown. I fucking hate it.

"Ah, our favorite butler," Maxime grins, then hurries to get up and help Dominique with the full tray.

"You're too kind," Dominique grins and blows him a kiss.

"That's because I want something from you. Will you please, please, *please* stay the night? It's Friday, and we can have another slumber party. I'm sure your hubby won't mind. He's not here anyway, right? Come on, like the good old times. Pretty please..."

Before Dominique and Gaël got together, he shared a dorm with Maxime. From what I've understood, Maxime requested Saint-Laurent to keep their place in the exact same state, just for the nights Dominique and he stay together to relive their good old times.

"His parents, my uncle and aunt, have come for the weekend to see how Gaël is doing," Arthur answers instead, his smooth timbre hot and coated with that usual raspy edge. Too close. He's already too fucking close. I try my best to focus on the board and block out the conversations, mentally calming myself down.

He agreed, that little voice soothes. *He'd back off and leave you be.*

It doesn't stop my body from going rigid, from sweat to bead in the crevices of my forehead, of annoyance with myself to build in my stomach. He shouldn't be here in the first place.

No. It shouldn't fucking *matter* to begin with.

"So, the rook really is the only piece I can move?" Jo, clearly certain to take over the game, still sits across from me, his face curled in a wrinkle as he gazes at the pieces. "Or am I missing something?" A warm, firm hand lands on my shoulder.

"Hello, little stepbrother. Long time no see." He crouches down right beside me, and the arrogance in which he so casually breaches my comfort zone, has me fuming. "Know why I'm here?"

"I don't, and I don't care. Now's not the time," I snarl, eyes still on the board.

He chuckles, the raspy sound fanning the tender skin under my ear. I shiver, dry eyes glued to the board as I force myself not to squirm in my seat.

Hooking his fingers against the edge of my nape he turns me to face him. A slow smile spreads his lips. "You really don't know why I'm here?"

My cheeks burn from embarrassment and something else. "Other than to make my life miserable? No, I wouldn't have a fucking clue. Now get the hell away, I'm playing chess with my —" But Jo's not sitting across from me anymore, the king nicely put to his side.

Check mate.

"Friends?" Arthur chuckles, his typical rasp ticking my throat. "Nah, they've had enough. Look, they've even moved to the bar to give us some privacy."

I glance over, stomach dropping. At least Jo has the decency to send me an apologetic wave when I look his way. No one can beat a Deveraux, and whereas I seem to struggle with that concept, the others clearly don't. Dominique and Maxime are still sipping their drink, and they have clearly already moved on to their slumber party mood, unaware of my predicament as they laugh and giggle like a bunch of school girls.

"Mom and Dad called and texted us a few times over the past week to let us know that they would be here tonight. If you had bothered checking your phone, you would have known. Instead, you decided to ignore them. Per usual."

I swallow, refusing to let his words make me feel anything close to guilt. He's right though, I have ignored their phone calls. Their messages.

"Just like you've been ignoring me." His lips brush against the shell of my ear, making my breath hitch. Making my everything hitch when his true meaning hits my brains. My body feels heavier as arousal slowly rises from my toes to my thighs, then settles in my groin. My body remembers, craves Arthur's possessive and filthy words, but my mind rebels. Of course I fucking do, he was supposed to leave me alone.

I shift my head, only to hit my nose with his. Fuck, he really is too close. I try to pull back, but his hand is faster, cupping the back of my head and pushing me forward, closing the distance.

"Please." I breathe, hating how small I sound. Hating how he always seems to affect me. "What do you want?"

Arthur narrows his gaze. "Please?" He parrots, tauntingly. "Really? That's all you can come up with? Where has my nasty, wicked Régis gone?" He pulls back and pretends to search around my face with an amused, narrowed gaze. "Hmm, not here."

"Oh, fuck off," I grunt.

"No, *you* fuck off." Like a switch of light, gone is the amused smirk. Instead his onyx eyes shoot daggers and his grip on my head turns more rigid. "Here's the thing, *chaton*. You're really,

really messing with the wrong guy. Did you think that you could bribe me like that?" He kicks the chair and grabs it tightly as it tilts on two legs, turning it smoothly until I'm fully facing him. He's still crouched in front of me, our faces now on the same height, his muscular thighs around my legs.

I tilt my chin, swallowing away arousal and trepidation. "I need you to back off."

"Uh uh." Arthur clicks his tongue, then slowly stands, keeping me trapped with his legs as he reaches for my belt. His other hand pulls my head back and when our eyes meet again, I realize that I've really pissed him off. His dark eyes glower, the golden-brown color of his irises practically swallowed by the black depths of his pupils.

"Back off," I hiss again, this time through gritted teeth.

"No." His answer comes in a short huff, making my entire body buzz with anticipation, blood flooding south at a disquieting speed. "Not anymore. You wanted some space, I gave you some space. But guess what? I got impatient, and I really started to miss you. And on top of that, now we're back in the game now, with Dad waiting for us." He unbuckles the leather, and pops the buttons of my pants before I realize that's happening. My hand flies to his.

"What are you doing?" I seethe, but he just tilts my head even further, making me arch my back until my knees are wrapped around his thighs and I'm practically facing the ceiling.

"Nothing that you don't want me to do." His fingertips linger on my hardening cock and squeeze my crown. Pain and pleasure ripples in one, long shudder and my knees start to tremble, just like my voice. "My friends are here. They can't see us, not like this."

Arthur's grin is low, and thick. "They already know, *chaton*. Don't you realize by now? Everyone already knows. I told you this. It seems that you are the only one who's a bit slow." His fingers, those cool, slender digits, crawl inside my boxers and grab hold of my throbbing cock. Groaning, I try to squeeze my knees together.

"What do they know?"

Suddenly, he's looming over me. Keeping me steady on my chair, practically horizontal with my feet in the air, his other hand plunges into my boxers and starts to work my dick with firm, quick strokes. My entire body trembles. "That I've claimed you, little stepbrother." A lazy grin lifts his lips. Straddling my thighs, he continues to take me apart. "In a minute, we're going to see our parents, and they will want to know how these first months are going for you. What are you going to tell them, hmm?" He swipes the pre-cum of my slit with a brush of his thumb, then licks it into his mouth. The gesture is so obscene that my eyes roll back, and I start to pant.

"Hgh—that everything's going fine," I wheeze.

"Hmm." Bending forward, Arthur licks his way up my neck and to my mouth. I tense in his arms, not sure what to expect, but certainly not the way he dips his head and closes his mouth around my upper lip, breathing in. "So good," he nuzzles against my face. "You smell so fucking good."

He does too. The scent of aftershave and something spicy makes me widen my nostrils and inhale deeper. Arthur nips at my mouth, brushing his lips against it, and moves down to graze his teeth over my lower lip. I gasp, sliding my hands up and around Arthur's neck as he licks inside my mouth, stealing our first kiss. My first real kiss.

"We don't have much time," he murmurs. Voices around us make my body go rigid, but Arthur just chuckles as he continues to stroke my cock. We're in public, just like last time, touching and groping each other for the whole world to see. Although in his defense, Arthur has draped his large, heavy body over mine, so there isn't much to see I guess. His hand feels heavy on the back of my head, from where he pulls it exactly where he wants my face, my mouth. He nibbles on my lips, bites and suckles on my tongue and swallows my moans that are becoming more and more frantic with each forceful brush of his hand.

It's like all my carefully built-up defenses crumble down into one, big pathetic pile of grit. I have missed him, and I fucking despise myself for it. But it doesn't change the way my mind melds into his, purring when my flesh connects to the tips of his fingers and the softness of his mouth. I can't stop it.

"Don't try to cross me again, *chaton*, because I'll always win," he croons. "And come now in my hand like the good boy you are."

No, I want to scream. I won't! But Arthur's playing my cock like it's some fine-tuned instrument and he knows all the right places to pluck. He places his open, wet, hot mouth at my ear, then lets out a moan. It's a low, husky, vibrant rumble that makes my toes curl and my balls erupt.

"Oh God..." I cry. And then I come. Like an awoken volcano on a deserted island, I fucking explode. Arthur's lips are on mine once more, swallowing my mewls and wails as I fall apart for him. Again.

When I finally come down from my high, he moves to stand up and grabs a towel from his duffel bag. "Come on, get cleaned up. We need to go, they're waiting for us."

"Start without me, I'll be right there," I snarl, feeling defeated, sated and furious at the same time. "You don't have to chaperone me to them. For fuck's sake."

I'm fuming as I set myself right again. Because I underestimated his poison, believing that I'd had him by the balls this time. Because he knows just exactly where to attack me. I just can't swing those flutters away that he always causes. Whenever he's close, my body is filled with tiny fireflies. And it's exhausting.

"Mewl," he goads, and I snap. He's fucking infuriating and he knows it. Grabbing the towel, I lunge for him. I miss and he runs away with a howl, fleeing the canteen.

"Oh no, this time you won't get away with it," I growl, giving chase. "You believe you're untouchable, just because of your name! Well, guess fucking what. You're not! You hear me?" I run after him, and while he increases the distance, he turns on his heels to run backwards, laughing and howling as he avoids the swinging towel. I'm on fucking fire, fury coiling through my veins like thick lava with every missing pitch.

"Apparently I am," he mocks, taking yet another turn and taking us deeper into the castle.

I lose track of time and place as I chase him down, zigzagging through Monterrey Castle and its countless hidden narrow corridors. By the time he finally halts in front of the office, I once more have no clue where we are. Right now, I don't care either, not when I can finally take my revenge. Arthur props himself against the wall, arms wrapped around his chest, as he barks out his laughs and tries to avoid the towel. I get in a few whacks, to my utter satisfaction, until he grabs hold of the edge of the towel, pulling it in. Pulling *me* in. Before I can let go, one large hand cups my nape and squeezes, while his glistening, charcoal eyes take me in.

"Behave," he whispers against my forehead before planting a chaste kiss there that makes my toes curl.

What a fucking asshole.

"Arthur, Régis." Jean-Luc stands up the moment we enter the large study, a smile on his face. He's got the whole suave look—handsome with a touch of elegance, his square jaw nicely shaved, putting emphasis on his tan and those dark eyes. The twins definitely look after him, though Jean-Luc misses that cockiness that both guys possess. But then, he's older now, and with my mother…

She's standing behind him, wearing a colorful, expensive

looking dress with flowers on it. High, dark brown leather boots and a scarf that hangs loosely around her neck. Her hair is tied in a bun, but a honey-brown curl dangles next to her cheek. Where the twins look after their dad, I look like my mother, a curse my own Dad often spewed over me over the past years.

"Régis, *chéri...*" She gives me a careful smile. Her lips tremble a bit, as if that was difficult to say. Maybe it is. Dad never called me something sweet.

"Useless boy. Get in there."

"Mother." My spine turns rigid and her smile falters. Great, that took a full twenty seconds.

"Arthur," Jean-Luc gestures toward an open door in the back of his office. "Let's give Nathalie and Régis a moment. Care for a drink?" They walk away, casually chatting. And I'm still here.

"Mon fils." My mother's voice is soft, familiar, though I baulk at the memories.

Fais dodo, Colas mon p'tit frère Fais dodo, t'auras du lolo...

"Why are you here?" I can't help but ask.

"I wanted to talk to you." She gives me a sad, lost smile. "I've been wanting to talk to you ever since I finally got you inside your new home, far away from your father. They told me to wait, that you weren't ready. But now that you've moved out here, and I've sort of lost you again, I need you..." Her throat clicks on a swallow. "I need you to understand, *mon chéri*. Will you please—I know you don't reply to my messages, and I don't mean to pry—" She cuts herself off, clearly looking troubled, "After all, I know what happened to you before, my son. But I want you to know about us, please. About everything that we once were, until we weren't. About everything, I'd love for us to become once more."

I blink. I can only stare at her, into those remarkable eyes, into the frown that reflects our mutual anxiety. Hers water, the moisture creating a shimmer in those green pools, turning them into shiny emeralds. She must take my silence for an agreement, because she slowly continues.

"Before, a long time ago, your dad and I weren't exactly a happy couple, though that might not surprise you. He had a bad temper, a foul mouth, and little patience. I—he—I wanted you so badly, Régis. But the pregnancy was a challenge and the actual delivery a nightmare. You were perfect, so sweet, my little angel. Such a sweet baby." She sniffs and something clenches in my chest. "Still I—I wasn't the same anymore. I was young, didn't have a job, your father was the way he was…I got depressed, couldn't see a way out. I couldn't leave, because I had no support system, no family, no job, no money to take care of you. The doctor gave me medications, but they only made me feel more miserable. Useless. Life wasn't at all what I'd imagined. And after another fight—" She shivers as a tear finally rolls over her cheek, "Something broke inside me. I—I couldn't anymore. Forgive me, my love."

My chest constricts violently at her words and despite myself, my hand reaches out, searching for hers. "You left me." My throat locks around the lump formed in my throat.

Left me with him.

She jerks her head in rapid nods, sniffing as more tears roll down her face. "I know that, I know that, *chéri*. I didn't think—*Enfin*, I left home, turned to live on the streets, feeling sick of being away from you. I watched you going to school, on the playground. I used to follow you around, not wanting to let go." She chokes on a sob. "You were so precious. Such a sweet, little boy."

Sorrow floods through my core like an ice-cold slither, and I lick my dry paper lips, unable to speak.

"Then one day, three days after you had turned nine, I met Jean-Luc. He was walking through the streets and asked me for directions. Just like that, as if I was a normal pedestrian and not a stinking, homeless person." She shivers. "We talked a bit, then talked some more. I fell in love with him, Régis. And he became my way out."

"No—" Her words make me convulse. I was thrown away, replaced, just like that. Abandoned, just as I'd always feared. Fucking abandoned like some stray dog, not wanted anymore.

"I don't want to hear this," I croak.

"Please, my love. Let me explain. Please? Please, Régis."

I breathe in, willing myself to calm down, and breathe out. We're still barely standing inside the room, and I reach behind me, feeling the door. *I can leave this place if I want to,* a voice soothes. It's a choice, not a trick.

Not a trick.

I nod weakly.

"Thank you," she breathes, then continues, "Jean-Luc and I dated for two years before I met the twins. Those were happy times, the boys sweet, but still—" Her face contorts as if she didn't mean to share that hurtful, stinging piece of information. "I never lived with them, Régis, I couldn't—not knowing that my own son lived in Nîmes without me. There were times that I believed that I was given a second chance. That you were happy and that things were better like this. That I should stay away from you instead of standing on your doorstep one desperate day. Perhaps you had forgotten about me. I..." She takes in a deep breath and her gaze stutters before it dips. "With time, I started to believe that. It was better this way. You were happy without me, and the old me had somehow exchanged my boy for a better life. Was given two in exchange." She chokes on those final words, and a grieving wail explodes from her mouth. She shakes her head, eyes leaking with tears. "But I missed you so much, Régis. My *child*. It started to eat at me from the inside, the feeling of loss becoming bigger and heavier, and I started to doubt my earlier decisions. What if you wanted to be found? What if we were meant to be together, despite my horrible mistakes? Apprehension sucked me in and I couldn't take it anymore." A tentative, fragile smile flares onto her lips. "When Jean-Luc asked me to marry him, I knew that was my call. I was tired of living with my self-inflicted reality. Part of me wanted him to prove me right. That you wouldn't want anything to do with me. That you were, effectively, the child I had lost. But he didn't. He actually wanted to know about you. He...gave us that second chance."

"You mean getting me out of the slums like some charity case?" My chest expands from the built-up pressure. Inside, anger and sorrow squeeze tight against each other, snarling and growling as they battle for dominance. "I bet that looked good on your social profile, despite the fact that you were, what... ten years too late?"

My mother lets out another sob while her hand squeezes mine. "Please, *chéri*. I know we were too late at starting to look into your background. You were already seventeen, nearly an adult, and I'd been gone for over ten years." She closes her lips tightly, rolling them as her throat constricts with guttural sobs. "Nearly an adult. But you...we started looking into your background. Through Jean-Luc's connections we got hold of your school reports and your medical visits. That's how I found out that you were seen by a psychologist..." She pauses, and when she speaks again, her voice is low with withheld emotion, on the verge of a breakdown. "Everything changed for me that day. There are no words to describe how sorry I am for taking so long to get you out of there, my love. I have wondered many, many times why it took me thirteen years to get you back. Wondered many times that if I'd stayed, with your dad, with you, life would have ultimately been better for us. My ulterior motive that you were better off without me tarnished when we found out the truth, and bitter resentment for my own lack of actions filled my cup of regret instead. I had left you there. With *him*." Another guttural choke leaves her rattling chest and she raises a hand to cup her cheek and rub the wrinkles of repentance away. "The more information about you we dug up, the more I needed to be triple sure that we'd be successful. That your father wouldn't have any secret weapons in court. You were suffering so much. Jean-Luc assured me that with his contacts, we'd have nothing to fear. But I did. I feared every single second after our lawyer sent out that first letter to convict your father." She pauses, lost in her own thoughts for a moment, before she continues, "I hated myself. And I wouldn't risk losing you in that process. After we'd had all the risks covered, we went in hard and fast."

They had. And in their wake, they had burned everything to the ground.

Fisting my hands, I snort at the thought. "I never asked you to regret leaving me, nor to come and get me. I was nearly eighteen, I could have left him by myself."

Mom shakes her head tragically. "But you and I both know that you would have never left him. You would have stayed, and he would have continued his abuse. After his formal arrest, when the police cleared the home you shared with your father and you'd already been taken to live with us in the villa, they sent me the photos of your room. That's when I found out about that cage, Régis..." She puts both her hands in front of her mouth as she lets out another deep sob. My heart freezes, humiliation combined with fear making my spine rigid with something fierce.

"I wasn't sure, but did he make you—"

"Yeah," I rasp, cutting her off. I can't hear her say those words out loud. Can't bear the memory.

Her hands rub her mouth, her green gaze wet. "Oh, my god, *chéri*, I am so, so sorry."

My fisted knuckles have turned white through the pressure. "Does anyone else know?"

She hurriedly shakes her head. "No, I would never have told the twins."

"But Jean-Luc does?"

"No. Not of the cage. I would never share something so raw, so hurtful, with anyone else. But I'm hoping that one day you'll open up and share your heart with me. I will always listen to you, my son, will always love you, no matter what."

I suck in a deep breath, and let it linger in my constricted chest. My heart is bleeding, my mind broken, yet I can't get myself to hate my mother.

But I am feeling lost. Small. Unloved. "You threw me into this world of the rich."

"I had to. You are exceptionally bright." Flashes of masked hoods and orgies breach the emptiness inside, rattling my over-sensitive brain. "I wanted to give you the best possible future."

"After taking away my past? You, *maman*. I needed you. And you weren't there for me. You left me. And all these years, I wondered what I did wrong for you to just pack your bags and go. I searched for you, I—" I hold my hands in the air, desperation flooding deeply through my veins. My lips are trembling, cheeks scorching, and when I press my hands against them, I notice they are wet. "The memory of your voice kept me up every time he put me down. When he threw me in there and—" I swallow thickly, throat clicking but bile sticking too tight against my pharynx. No matter how hard I try, I can't get it away. "Maybe if you'd stayed, he wouldn't have become such a monster. Maybe he wouldn't have gotten the cage."

My mother shakes her head. "He won't see the daylight again, *chéri*. Please..." Her hand brushes past my shoulder, but I'm too caught up in my thoughts, too distressed, to stop her from cupping soft fingers around my cheek and tilting my face toward her. "Let him go, Régis. Stop calling him. What he did to you was the worst kind of crime."

I huff, but it comes out as a broken choke. "And you? What you did, was that a crime?"

"I'm doing everything in my power to make up for those lost

years, my love. Everything. I want to give you the world. A father, two brothers, money, a fantastic house, the best education you can imagine."

My eyes flick between hers. This is by far the most we have spoken ever since she forced her way back into my life. I want to shut her out—*need* to shut her out— but I can't. Because I want her so badly, her loving words and soft smiles, her praise. Her love. After all those years of wondering, of suffering, I am getting my answers. I am getting my mother.

Back.

"Do you think you can ever forgive me?" She whispers. "I so, so wish for you to forgive me."

"I don't know." It's the truth. But I want to. God, I beg for a day where I'm not afraid. Where I can simply love and be loved.

The door opens and in comes Jean-Luc, followed by Arthur. I instantly look away, swallowing the excuse to get the hell out and flee. There's nowhere to go now, and this conversation has left my emotions too raw, my heart bleeding.

I won't show them.

Inhaling deeply through my clenched chest, I force my hurt away. It takes me a few, sharp puffs of air, but by the time I have myself back in shape, my mask has been placed across my face, fitting tightly. Hurting a little. It will have to do for now.

"Do you care about joining us for a glass of Moët?" Jean-Luc holds up the bottle of champagne, a small, tense smile on his face that makes it clear that he sees that I've been crying. He doesn't comment. I silently thank him for that.

"Sure, *amour*. Régis?" My mother gives me a hesitant look. "Will you stay?"

I release a shuddering breadth. "*D'accord.*" There's no point of running from this anyway.

"*Merci.*" My mother gives me a smile that has no business of making me feel as precious as I do, but still. The soft kiss she plants on my cheek makes my insides warm again.

Immediately after she had me back, my mother would constantly try to pull me in for a hug. She'd cry when I didn't want her touch. It wasn't until the psychiatrist told her that I needed time that she backed off. But time is relative, and I don't know if our definitions are the same. When we all have a glass of champagne in our hands, Jean-Luc slides the bottle back in the ice-bucket before he raises his glass. We all follow suit.

"This is for you boys. Your mom and I are so proud of you. We'll invite Louis in for a drink in a minute, I can't wait to hear what he's been up to. But we wanted to have a brief chat with you two first, to see how you've been doing. *Santé*."

"Wanna sit?" I turn over my shoulder to find Arthur already seated on the couch. When our gazes meet, his narrows into what feels like a silent question, and I drop my gaze, feeling a little too raw to fight with him again. But fresh fire licks my veins when my gaze accidentally stumbles across the crook of that long, slender digit that's rubbing the velvet padded spot next to him.

"Fuck you," I mouth, then sit down anyway, a grimace plastered on my face. I am trying to ignore the way his hand still lingers somewhere behind me, far too close, but it's fucking hard.

"It has been strange to live in an empty house," Jean-Luc chuckles generously, "But we're happy that you're settling in, Régis."

Ooh...there are many, many things I want to say to that. Such as why anyone thought that letting me take part in the initiations of some secret, masked, very privileged sex cult is okay?

"Actually—" I start, but when I take in my stepdad's hopeful eyes, I swallow the rest of the words. It's not fair to put this on him. No, this is on me. My battle to fight. To win. Next to me, Arthur's hung back against the couch, one long, firm leg casually crossed over the other, while he casually comments on my mother's question about the extra subjects he has taken on this year. I knew he was a clever guy, but even I am impressed with the number of courses he has taken, especially with its complicated combination. No wonder he's always studying.

Feeling my gaze glued to his, Arthur turns to meet mine—and winks. He fucking winks. I'm sure no one else noticed, but I did. And it causes my breath to hitch and my boxers are starting to feel a little tight. Swallowing heavily, I decide to ignore him altogether. Confusion created by the hurtful words exchanged with my mother earlier, and the way my body nevertheless burns for Arthur's touch, flare somewhere ferociously inside of me. I force my lips wider and smile at Jean-Luc.

"It has been interesting," I start. "The level of the courses here is amazing, that includes the support I've been getting from the teachers."

Jean-Luc nods, happy with my words. Next to me, Arthur stands to take the bottle of champagne out of its ice bucket. When he's turned his back to me, I quickly gulp down most of the contents of my glass, stupidly not wanting to be the only one who hasn't even started yet. When Arthur refills my glass, we both stare at my shaking, outstretched hand.

"What about friends?" My mother suddenly asks. I eagerly take another sip from the glass, knowing that I need to slow down. Knowing that I need to keep focused now.

"Um, yeah," I blabber. "I've made a few of those as well. I joined a chess club."

"Dominique asked him to join," Arthur adds.

"Dominique, Gaël's boyfriend?" Jean-Luc asks, and my step-brother nods. It makes me puff up my chest with pride.

"Régis has been doing really well," Arthur shares a small smile, sounding like he's my damn psychologist. "We're both very committed to our studies, but I know that his door's always open. I like to make sure that he's feeling happy and safe, right Régis?" He drops the bottle back into the bucket, then sinks back onto the couch.

"Well, we're relieved to hear that." Jean-Luc says. What falls is a small silence, then he clears his throat. "There's something else I wanted to speak with you about."

"Which is?" Arthur counters immediately. Before, I wouldn't have noticed, but having spent more time with him over the past weeks, I recognize the way his tone dips, making his natural huskiness sound a little strained. The touch of his fingers on my lower back falters. Jean-Luc offers us a reassuring smile that is not at all reassuring.

"What's going on?" I find myself asking. I mean, it can't get any worse than him offering for Arthur to guide me through my first months of college now, can it?

"Nothing to worry about," Jean-Luc urges. "It's actually kind of a celebration. You may have already met Mister Montague, the school's newest recruit. There was a big article in the local newspaper about Saint-Laurent recruiting a remarkable teacher who has come a long way through public schooling. By hiring him, the school also achieved an important quota on hiring... less privileged people." His gaze darts to mine before it flicks back to Arthur. "After his trial period, Mister Montague made a formal request to change the criteria for our traditional *Prix d'Honneur* to make it more accessible for different students. The board agreed after hours of debate. It wasn't a decision we made lightly, given the fact that the prize is laced with traditions. It has never changed ever since it was introduced in 1865. But, I suppose our world has changed since then, and we finally decided that perhaps it is time for things to modernize."

"Well," Arthur chuckles lightly, his tone too low. "There are already plenty of rumors making their way around school. Something about a presentation in order to be qualified for the actual competition?" I don't understand why those words sting the way they do, technically he hasn't said anything wrong.

Perhaps it's the way that chuckle vibrates past his sensual lips, pretentious and imperious. Perhaps it's the way my body reacts to that rumble, despite the sting those words cause. I seem to find myself in a free-fall when it comes to Arthur and any unwanted desire. Or perhaps it's because I'm feeling fucking awful now that my heart has been torn out of my ribcage, squashed, and put back. Whatever it is, makes me feel a little bold and a whole lot of game for some competition.

"Oh, that." I force a grin, the dried tears on my puffy skin making my flesh feel rigid and dry. It doesn't make the sudden need to defeat Arthur on his own ground any less strong. "Mister Montague told me about the news himself. Every single student needs to do a presentation to qualify. Referrals no longer rule—" I wrench my hips as I turn my body to face Arthur. "It hasn't been officially communicated yet, but trust me, an official declaration will be announced shortly, right, *Dad*?"

My mother sucks in a breath at that word, and I don't miss how Arthur's eyes flare with something dark, while his nostrils flare. "Care to clarify?" He drawls.

"Well, Mister Montague and I work on different projects together. I highly value his skills and opinion." Jean-Luc lets out an impressed hum. I turn my head and send Arthur an innocent smile. Damn. If looks could kill, I'd be on my way to hell. Arthur's *little* stepbrother.

A surge of pride washes through me.

I do that. *I*'m getting under his skin.

"He's helping me to prepare a presentation that will make sure I qualify for the competition."

Arthur opens his mouth to speak, surely to spew venom, but his dad beats him to it. "That's great to hear Régis," Jean-Luc beams. "Noah is an excellent teacher who comes with a solid list of references."

"Perhaps you want to elaborate on the types of conversations you're having with your teacher?" Arthur hisses through clenched teeth. He's fuming, barely unable to hold it together. But there's also something else there, in those dark depths. Rivalry. Like fucking always, he's trying to challenge me in overplaying my cards.

It makes the bleeding of my heart stop, placing the conversation with my mother to the back as my mask slips back in shape. I can do rivalry, I can do aloof expressions. Because I have the upper hand here.

"He says I have a good chance of qualifying."

"Oh, does he now?" Arthur snarls. It's the first time I've seen him so off his game, and judging by the shocked look on Jean-Luc's face, he's noticed as well. I inwardly purr. "And what else did your pet teacher confide in during your one-on-ones?"

Tilting my chin in the air, I reply, "That it's time for a change. After all, like Dad points out, we no longer live in 1865. Our world has changed, and while people may still be the same, the situations we call ours today, are by no means comparable to those in the late nineteenth century." That's not entirely true, and Mister Montague would never have said such a thing, but right now, the words are already spilled. I can only hope that my hothead stepbrother won't go after an innocent teacher. "And that—"

I am going to win this fucking prize. Arthur's onyx eyes flicker, as if he can hear my thoughts. After all, it was you who told me about it before I even knew of its existance. You told me that we'd end up competing, didn't you? Even more than we already have.

"Your Mister Montague is full of lies and deceit," he sneers, cheeks coloring the slightest of pink.

"Arthur," Jean-Luc chimes. "Those are heavy accusations. I suggest we direct ourselves to safer territory." I think he says something more, but I'm too captured by Arthur's onyx glare, drilling holes inside mine. His jaw is clenched, lips pursed into a fine line, seething in silence, challenging me. When he finally leaves my face with that heavy, mystical gaze, I exhale on a shudder, heart thumping wildly in my chest. Fuck, I won. Again.

"I agree with you and Noah—Mister Montague—Régis. Since I'm part of the board, I can say that we have been looking into ways to make this environment a little less traditional, but never seemed to know how to do so. Perhaps this decision is the fresh air we needed." Jean-Luc turns to face my mother, smiling.

"So you expect me to do an actual presentation in order to be qualified for the prize?" Arthur rumbles in a low voice. "You'll have me beg for it like some...some—"

"Yes, son," Jean-Luc nods. I inwardly fistbump the air while keeping the expression on my face blank. "And before you ask, yes, I have considered giving you a free pass. But I also realize that that wouldn't look good for the family. People will notice, and not in a good way. Besides, you are the most praised student of your year, Arthur. You have absolutely nothing to fear."

"More students will apply," he grunts. It almost sounds like a pout. Something flickers in his voice. It's enough to make me bold and show my polished, cool side. Because it's the first time that I caught a weakness in his solid walls of self-confidence.

"Afraid that someone else might steal your prize? Someone with a less powerful name than Deveraux?"

Arthur shifts to face me, dark eyes blazing furiously. "You have no idea what you're talking about."

Sitting a little straighter, I narrow my gaze. "Oh, *I* don't know what I'm talking about? Let me tell you what I see. A spoiled brat who already has everything he desires in life, and who wants that damn prize on top of it. Just to add to his collection."

Arthur's eyes flare with something fierce. "Is that what you think of me? That I'm some rich ass who doesn't do anything to prove his worth?"

"Régis, Arthur—" My mother begins, but none of us look her way. We're too busy getting back into our staring competition, only this time I see clearly. It's like part of Arthur's mask has slid off, exposing a rawness to his anger. A cocktail of pride, mingled with sultriness and sinfulness. *Ruthlessness*. The realization brings a shiver to my core, and goosebumps freely rise. He won't back off because he is too fucking proud to do so. Too privileged to believe that this could really affect him.

"That's exactly what I think of you," I snarl. "So unless you truly believe that you're too good for us all, show the contrary. Prepare a presentation that rocks our world. Work on—"

"That's enough." The rest of my words freeze in my throat. Jean-Luc has stood up, his hand raised. "You have made your point clear, Régis, and as I mentioned before, there is a reason the board agreed to this. There's room for modernization."

My mother stands too, and we follow suit. My legs are wobbly, anger and sorrow swirling freely inside me. This cocktail of conversations has left me drained.

"You are family, boys. We can disagree at times, but we always stick together." Grabbing my mother by the shoulder, he pulls her in closer. "I'm sorry, but we'll have to leave you shortly, we have an appointment in town. But whenever you want, we can discuss this further, I always have time for my boys."

My boys.

He leans in and gives me two kisses, patting my shoulder. "Before we leave, we'll be heading to the football field to watch Louis during his last hour of practice. You want to come with us and watch your brother play?"

"Thanks, but I'll be heading back," I mumble, fatigue already curling around my mind like fog. "This was a lot." Jean-Luc nods at that, his gaze softening in understanding. "Take good care of yourself. You're making us very proud, whether you qualify for that prize or not."

"Oh, before you leave, Régis, I'd like to go over our Friday meeting." Arthur blinks his thick eyelashes at me, before turning to my mother, sending her a charming smile. "We always take a moment at the end of the week to discuss how Régis is settling in and if there's anything I can help him with."

"What a great idea." My mother beams, green eyes glistening with something suspiciously close to hope. "Thank you, Arthur, for helping Régis."

Gritting my teeth, I force out a smile. *If only you knew.*

"Uhm, yeah, sure." My voice feels breathy, a little hesitant. But that disappears the moment she sends me a bright smile. She's proud, I realize, proud of me. And that does something to my heart. It makes it swell in its ribcage, makes it thump a little faster, makes me crack a smile that we hold together as we drink each other in, carefully clinging to that earlier conversation we had. Maybe, just maybe, it isn't too late for us.

"Thank you," she breathes. I only notice our hands were intertwined when she carefully lets go of mine. "For listening to me. For allowing us to start over. We'll take our time, of course. We will do it our own way, right?"

I'm unsure of what to say, but luckily Jean-Luc chooses that moment to stride toward the door, ending our conversation. "Come on, love, we need to get to the football field. Arthur, half an hour? You know how Louis loves it when you come and watch him."

"See you soon, boys," my mother sends us a final wave. When the door finally closes with a subtle click, my heart rate doesn't hesitate to pick up, my mind raising a red flag.

At first, the silence stretches, while I look at the closed door and swallow. Hard. When I finally have the courage to turn my face and eye to my stepbrother, Arthur's leaned back, his head resting against the board. His legs are planted wide, glass twirling in his hand, his eyes already on mine. God, his stare is intense, dark, and provocative. But it's void of any mockery. Tilting his head, his lips part, but nothing comes out. It's as if he's tasting the words in his mouth, before throwing them out.

"*Chaton*," he finally mumbles, his low rasp making my breath hitch and my mask tighten. He huffs out a hum, visibly lost in thought again, letting the silence stretch. Tipping his head back, he stares at the ceiling. "Did you really just try to screw me over in front of Dad?"

13

ARTHUR

It feels as though the air has been sucked from the atmosphere by my question. Something shifts in Régis' demeanor with a flick, and I blink as I try to understand what's going on. My little stepbrother looks exquisitely freaked out as he turns to face me.

"No?" He squeaks. His earlier bravado has disappeared, though parts of it are still lingering. Pride and irritation battle with that usual skittishness, and it's fucking alluring. His big, blue gaze is wide with something devilishly close to fear, and it makes my heart thump a little faster. Did I just do that? It makes me feel incredibly greedy and indecisive. Because my body craves for nervous Régis, my mind wants to provoke snarky Régis and then there is this other part of him, the one he accidentally revealed, that seems to have captured both my mind and soul. It's a sad, lonely Régis, I think. The part of him he's always so desperate to protect from the world.

Thoughts lock inside my chest. Without a chessboard to hide our play behind, our conversation won't get far. *Shouldn't* get fucking far. Because things have gotten far enough. But catching sight of those eyes, all red and puffy? Yeah, I didn't like that.

What made you cry?

There's no way he's going to unmask that to me without being challenged. And I shouldn't really, but as those thoughts swirl through my mind, my resistance crumbles away, bit by bit. I could poke him just a little, just enough to inflame his exasperation. Then strike.

Curling my lips into that smirk I know he hates so much, I mumble, "Well, I think you just did. You tried to screw me over in front of Dad. Sit." My gaze is tied onto his, battling to catch any flicker of emotion that flutters through those beautiful eyes. Yeah, he's definitely getting annoyed.

Régis eyes the padded velvet seat of the couch, and I expect him to make a show out of rejecting me. He doesn't. He does, however, choose to take a seat across from me on the other couch like the stubborn little fuck he is. Ignoring that detail, I place my glass on the table, then place my elbows on my knees and bend a little forward, cupping my chin in my folded hands. We stare at each other for a moment, silence intermingling with the crackling of the fire.

"Now, tell me, what are you playing at?" I growl.

What made you cry?

"Nothing," he snarls. "I'm not playing at anything."

"Haha, funny." I fake a bark of laughter, only to shift it back into a deadpan glare. "Are you taking me for a fool?"

His gaze narrows, eyes flaring with rage. "What are you talking about?"

"The prize, Régis. Those fucking qualifications. You knew about the changes, and you hid it from me. Dad didn't say anything, but he must have felt that too. You don't keep secrets from your family."

Régis lands a hand through his messy, golden hair, making

my regard dip to take in the curve of his long, delicate neck. "I didn't realize you weren't aware," he finally admits. "I'm just..." Is it me, or does his voice shake a little? "I'm just trying to survive here, Arthur. If that makes us competitors, then so be it. But I need to prove my worth too, and since I don't have the same network as you have, I turned to someone I knew I could trust."

"Someone you could—" I press my jaw shut, taking in a deep breath through my nose to calm the sudden rage that threatens to boil up. "You have that same network now. We are family." Something flashes in those clear eyes and I catch it before it dims. A light.

"Family, right." He shakes his head and lets out an undignified huff. "Anyway, I turned to Mister Montague because I wanted him to help me to be considered for the prize to begin with. I trust him. We started talking, and that's when he told me that the criteria had changed."

He's really serious about this. Seriously thinking of competing against me. That...I don't know what to make of that. I glare at him. "I told you that you'd want to win that prize." Régis is a clever guy, but he's only a first year. If he doesn't win this year, he has another three tries before he graduates, if he makes it that far. And I have three more years to convince Dad that this fondness for his newfound stepson can stop at paying tuition for Saint-Laurent. He doesn't have to offer him a job. Worst-case scenario, he gets a job and I fire him once I'm made CEO. My breath comes out on a heavy whoosh, a breath I hadn't realized I was holding. Things suddenly don't look so gloomy anymore.

"You are thinking very hard," Régis mumbles. When I don't react immediately, he gives me an apologetic grin. "You always get that little frown on your forehead, when you pinch your brows together."

"I do?" The question leaves my mouth before I can think.

Damn it. "Well, whatever," I backpedal, but he just laughs his soft, sleek chuckle and nods.

"You do. It gives you an even more serious look."

Hanging back, I tilt one foot against the coffee table, bending the knee. "Well, that's because there's no nice way of telling you that you're not going to win that prize, so you can save yourself from the effort. Not this year."

"Because this year the prize is yours?"

"I'm glad you're finally starting to understand what we're talking about."

Régis sends me a secretive smile, but doesn't reply. His silence forms a tightness in my stomach. I know I'm being an asshole, but I need him to fight back. Show me his claws and teeth. No one ever does that, apart from my own family, no one ever questions my words. They all take my knowledge for granted because they know about my carefully laid out future. As the next CEO of Deveraux Holding, I could be a powerful ally or a serious competitor, depending on our agendas. And that keeps them in check. Not Régis, no. My little stepbrother is rapidly becoming my fearless, bashful nemesis with his handsome, angelic face. Because I get the growing feeling that the more I piss him off, the more he will get in my way, just to prove me wrong.

He tilts his chin in the air as if he caught my thoughts, lips pressed into a thin line. "Well, you're not the only one who wants to win."

"If you don't want to get in my way, like you told me so on numerous occasions, I suggest that now's the time you take your own advice to heart and stay the fuck away."

"Afraid you might lose?" Régis flutters his lashes playfully, and arousal stirs in my loins. Fucking finally.

"Against you? Not a chance."

He smiles at that, and for some reason I get the impression that he's enjoying this newfound banter as much as I am. "I wouldn't celebrate too fast, *big* stepbrother. You have no idea what I'm preparing for."

"No idea, huh? I wouldn't be so sure if I were you. People like me have contacts in the highest ranks."

"Who's threatening who now?" He hisses, his words making my cock thicken.

Oh, chaton, *you have no idea how I'd like to corner you.* But before I can come up with a sneer, Régis barks out a laugh. "You know, you could just ask me about it, instead of throwing threats my way." He lets out another fit of laughter, the sound clear and round. It's the first time I hear him like this, and unable to control myself apparently, I feel the corners of my own lips tip up.

"Would you?" I find myself asking, suddenly curious to find out more about him and pluck his mind for thoughts. "Tell me if I asked?"

"And what? Have my head bitten off by your cruel judgements?" He shakes his head, still grinning. "No, thanks. I'd rather leave in one piece tonight."

I huff out a chuckle. "Perhaps you're right at that. Though, speaking of judgements," I put my other leg on the coffee table, crossing them at the ankle. "We never talked about your first initiation evening with the brothers." At those words, Régis's cheeks coat with a delicious pink that makes him look even more handsome and fragile at the same time.

"I'm happy we managed to settle things earlier between you and I. But as your guardian—" he freezes at that word and that makes my insides purr with glee— "I want you to know that I'm here if you have questions. Despite our frequent misunderstandings, you can trust me. And the rest of the family."

He blinks and a glint of that sadness flickers through those blue irises. It's gone as soon as it appeared.

What made you cry?

"I have no questions," he clips, all signs of our earlier banter gone. I wonder what made it disappear so swiftly, and probably should say something nasty, something challenging, just to get out that snarky side of him I've come to enjoy so much. But now that I witnessed him crack, caught those red-rimmed eyes laced with that usual look of being haunted, I find myself looking for something else. I'm looking for another piece of Régis.

"Good," I nod, locking away the unexpected sweep of flutters. "It's—" I halt when he mumbles something unintelligible. "What was that?"

"I said I don't trust anyone out here," he repeats, voice firm and chin tilted even higher if possible. God, if that doesn't sound sad. He's alone here, my little stepbrother.

Together alone.

The thought makes my chest clench.

"That's probably for the best. Although, you really can trust our family. I know these first months are a little daunting. The scene unfamiliar, your brother's faces hidden. Just know that this is only temporary. After you've done your pledge in December, the masks will go off."

He frowns in surprise. "They do?"

"Of course." I shrug. "The idea is to know who your brothers are. But we keep our identities hidden until after you become an official brother. Like I've told you before, this brotherhood is only for the elite. We don't share with outsiders."

He nods at that, considering my words. Then he licks his lips, opening his mouth, though it takes a moment before he speaks. I like that about him, this delicate hesitation before he opens fire.

"Why me?" He asks.

Creasing a brow, I eye him. "What do you mean, why you?"

He nibbles his bottom lip, gaze contemplating. "Why are you always after me? I get that I'm your stepbrother, and that your dad told you to look after me. I get that you are waiting for your brilliant future to unroll after graduation, I get that. But you should know by now that I would never take any job in your family business, right? I mean—" He cuts himself off with a shake of his head. His blush reaches all the way down his neck. It makes him look fucking edible, all sweet and smooth. And so troubled. This guy is really getting himself into big trouble. Because I want to keep talking to him. And I don't even like talking to people. Want to claim every single part of my little brother, tuck it in a safe, velvet box that can only be opened by me. Because I want him all to myself.

"Why won't you just leave me alone?" Régis throws into the growing silence, making me even more annoyed. I grumble, showing my irritation, although with myself or him, I'm not sure. Because he's got a point, and I fucking know that. Truth is that ever since I laid eyes on my little stepbrother that first night, when he stumbled inside our home with Nathalie like some drowned duckling, he has caused a swirl of emotions. Like right now, where the entire atmosphere changes just with one loaded question.

Régis is lithe and dainty, with lush, golden wavy hair that lights up in the sun and flops over his ears. His eyes are large, reflecting the color of the sea, and his lips are full and pouty. He's shy at best, but mostly just prickly, snappy. It makes him even more delicate, his smaller size and long, slender shapes emphasizing that.

Yet he has managed to turn my life upside down. Louis has always given me *carte blanche* to step up and become the next CEO of Deveraux Holding. He has never had any business ambitions, just like Gaël won't follow up his dad when he retires. No, the guys have always supported me, have always trusted me with their fate, knowing that I'd prioritize all our interests when the day comes. And I've been counting these days, have prepared myself for a long time with unwavering confidence.

And still… Régis is haunted by his past, and I know I shouldn't, but his agony turns me on, unleashes the beast in me. But it's his intelligence that has my stomach tightening with every ring of closeness, my anger heating with every centimeter Régis gets closer. There's no fucking way that this broken, pretty boy will get in my head.

I make the rules here, not the other way around. The thought should make me feel better, but instead I find myself standing up and slowly making my way toward him, heart hammering in my chest.

Maybe he already is in my head. Because fuck, I haven't felt this alive for a long time, thanks to this feral need to claim. Régis flashes his eyes, blinking slowly as he tilts his gaze to meet my eyes. Halting right in front of him, I revel in the short moment of standing tall and having him gaping up like a deer in headlights.

"Hmm. I'm not sure," I hum. It's probable that we're both at a loss for thoughts here. It's not enough. I need his wrath. "Perhaps because you bring in a sweep of fresh air that is both amusing and irritating. Perhaps because I somehow feel the need to protect you from it all." I crouch down until I can touch the couch with my fingers, spreading his legs as I nestle my body between his thighs.

He hesitates, and I watch in rapture as his wide, surprised eyes morph into his usual sneer of protection. "W—what the fuck?" He snarls, but his blushing cheeks take out the sting of his words. He's so damn responsive to my touch, so damn innocent. It's addictive. Rubbing my hands over his legs, I lean a little forward, until our chests practically touch.

"You have no idea, *chaton*. No idea where you landed. You walk in here, thinking that you're going to change the world, forgetting that people here don't want their world to be changed. We are trying everything to keep things intact, like the way they were."

"But your Dad said—"

"I know what Dad said, but look around you, Régis. Do these people look like they want to change things?" I shake my head. "They're going to devour you." That's not true, I know that. Especially since they know who Régis belongs to. But fuck me, do I like my little stepbrother being this close to me, all scornful and shit.

"So what?" He snarls, eyes flickering with something fierce. "Maybe I want to be devoured. It's better than being a pathetic, rich prick like yourself."

I huff out a chuckle. "You don't mean that."

He puffs up his chest, sending me another of these proud glares I love. "No, you're right, I don't, and sometimes I even wonder why I'm still here. But then I think of all these ambitious, clever people out there who don't have access to the best education, and I remember why I hang in."

"Like an all for one, one for all kind of thing?" My grin widens.

"If what you say is true," he hisses in reply, "And Alpha Fraternarii rules our country, then you know of equal opportunities. You know that now's the time to be generous and open up your doors to let in some of these people?"

I breathe out a disdained chuckle. "And why would we do that?"

"Diversity," he says at once. His eyes shimmer with something bright, making the blue of his irises indigo.

Despite our earlier moment of fun in the canteen, my appetite for my little stepbrother never seems to seize. And do I love to make him talk, and touch, and lose that horrible mask that he wears like his second skin. My nails want to dig into the soft cotton of his suit pants and trace the lines of his firm skin. Want to feel that supple skin against my own, feel it thrumming and give in under my firm kneading. Feel him give in to me. But now's not the time. Because there's something glorious about hearing Régis speak his mind, share his big brain. It's like at those moments there's nothing separating us.

"Back in the Atrium, you were talking about keeping the people happy," Régis muses, giving my hands a squeeze. "Then you need to give them something they want, right? Someone they want. In schools, hospitals, and businesses. In politics."

"What does that have to do with the brothers?"

"Different backgrounds mean a broader, more developed opinion. It creates growth. Don't you want to grow the brotherhood?" His eyes flicker with something close to mischief, and despite it all, I smile. The little fucker.

"Tell me, how would you make those talented commoners qualify for our brotherhood?"

He shrugs. "I have never really given it any thought before."

"No, you've been too busy competing with me."

He snorts. "You're kidding, of course I am. Have you ever asked yourself why you won't give me just that little more space to be myself here at college?"

"Now *that* is a strange question." Strange indeed. Because I've never once asked myself to slow down. It has never been expected from me. I've always been Arthur the clever one, Arthur the competitive one, Arthur the wicked one. And I fucking love to be your worst nightmare. When you try to conquer my king, you won't back off during combat either, will you?"

"This is not some chess game. This is you already being the one and only Arthur Deveraux."

I chuckle. "Say that again?"

Régis snorts. "Fuck you. You know what I mean. You have already conquered all the kings. You *are* the king, here, in college. What more do you want?"

"You." The word leaves my mouth before I swallow it down. Régis's mouth has gone slack, and he just gazes at me, cheeks flushed, lips parted, with that cat-like curiosity. Régis claims that he's not interested in me, but he sometimes stares at me as if he wants to creep inside my mind and place the pieces of my puzzle, too.

"M-me? Why?" He asks, voice cracking. Fuck, he's gone back to skittish Régis again, and I want to bite his lips into my mouth, feast on them with my tongue, and rip them against my teeth.

"This is so fucking wrong," I mumble. So fucking wrong on every single level in my life. I have completely and utterly lost my mind. But when I'm with him, I can't seem to think clearly. He must understand what I mean because he backpedals in his seat, his back searching for more of the backrest while his gaze lingers on mine. "But you're not getting away from me."

Without warning, I bend my head and capture those soft lips with mine. He gasps against my mouth, then lets out a soft moan when I nip at his bottom lip, flicking my tongue and teeth against his plump flesh as I dive in further. Régis tastes divine, all innocent, and shit, and he lets me take control so fucking sweetly, opening his mouth with my lips and flicking my tongue inside his mouth. He's hot, and wet, and deliciously tight, when he lets me come and play. It's an unfair fight, and when my hand reaches for his neck and I crawl my fingers around the delicate skin, he leans back to give me more space, which I fucking take. All of it, every centimeter he gives, until his back is flush against the backrest of the couch, and I'm practically hovering over him.

I can feel his head shake before he manages to push me away. "No," he breathes heavily. He hurries to stand, the thick outline of his hardened cock clearly visible in his navy-blue pants, but when he catches me licking my lips, he scowls, then turns to walk away.

"Yeah, go, scurry away like the fucking little coward you are," I hiss at his retreating frame. I'm fucking fuming, annoyed with myself for losing my cool so dramatically, for the dramatic oblivion on my part. Am I really going to let my little step-brother have the upper hand?

"You know," Régis mutters when he reaches the door, the knob already secured into the palm of his smaller hand. His back is still facing me, shoulders tense as they rise and fall with every sharp intake of his breath. "Everyone I love goes away in the end. I don't..." He doesn't finish that sentence, and it shouldn't fucking matter, but I still find myself looking at the empty spot by the exit long after he has left, my chest constricted and filled with tiny feathers at the same time.

14

RÉGIS

"Everyone I love goes away in the end. I don't want to fall in love with you."

The words echo through my mind while I run through the corridors, heart thumping wildly in my ribcage, making my movements jerky and tense.

This place is a fucking labyrinth, but thank god I'm finding my way around better these days. Before, when I came here as part of the adjustment days the Deverauxs organized for me, Monterrey Castle wasn't anything but a large, beautifully engraved structure from the past like we have so many we have in France.

But now... knowing that the Alpha Fraternarii was created here, that a long time ago monks lived in this place and opened their arms to the fallen elite, the thought alone gives this place something eerie. As if, I imagine it fiercely enough, I can practically see those people floating around those narrow halls. Monks used to wear simple tunics with a waist, it's what the teacher told us during our extra course on the history of Saint-Laurent. It isn't too far a line to draw between tunics and cloaks, although the thick, velvety material we wore during Initiation was far more luxurious.

My insides are tingling, knees wobbly as I keep on running further away from Jean-Luc's office. From Arthur.

I don't want to fall in love with you.

Why me? He didn't answer my question. It shouldn't have been too hard to explain, certainly not for someone like him. Arthur always has a sassy retort to whatever I dish out. The thought that he still sees me as his competitor, despite having done everything he's asked me to do so far, including joining a group of privileged pricks who walk around in cloaks and scare the living life out of me despite them being students. I did that for him. The thought makes my brain stutter, its conclusion bringing a slither of shame. I'd do anything for him.

It's like I have waited for years for someone like him. Someone who is big and strong, someone who challenges me, hears me out, makes me see different things. Someone like him.

Turning into yet another silent corridor, I let my gaze roam the framed pictures that decorate the walls while my mind is trying to wrap itself around my spinning thoughts.

I manage to successfully keep it gone for the rest of my walk back, ignoring the way it lingers in the back of my mind.

It only takes me another three wrong turns and two floors up, but finally, I reach our shared dorm. When I walk in, I find it void of the two other Deverauxs, which doesn't surprise me. With Louis being at practice, that would only leave Gaël, and god knows he's always hanging about.

Still... the faint sound of the piano makes me pause in the doorway. Whisking the final steps on the tips of my toes, I gently close the door, then just stand there, in the empty lounge, with my back against the door. Listening to Dominique playing the piano.

Such soothing notes, such tragic rhythm as the melody lingers around, meandering into my own, private thoughts.

They're all dotted around, a mixture of the past and the present.

My destiny. Arthur's words echo through my mind. Would I ever be strong enough to rewrite my own destiny? The thoughts, the sound, the unexpected peace I'm finding from just standing here after what happened just before… It brings a lump to my throat, and I swallow, throat clicking, but it won't be taken away.

My hand shakes when I bring my fingers to my hair and brush a lock behind my ear. For some reason, the music is making me feel more vulnerable than I should. It's difficult to get my mask back on, like the sizes don't match. Like the glue won't hold. I'm feeling drained. And I guess I could use a friend right now.

I need my iron bars.

They are more solid, more trustworthy. They won't let me down.

The music stops. With a tightening chest, I slowly head for my bedroom. Despite the nights becoming shorter at this time of the year, it's not too late to go to the woods and finalize my shelter. But before I make it to my bedroom, Dominique's door opens and he peeks outside. He's bare foot, wearing a fancy looking pair of track pants that must be Gaël's and a white tee. His darkish strands tumble around his head in a messy mop, as if he's brushed through them too much. But his eyes…

They make me halt. "Are you alright?"

They are red-rimmed as if he's been crying, the coffee-brown irises glossy. He shrugs and I swallow, searching for words. "Is, uhm, Gaël not there?"

Dominique doesn't reply, just stands there. Waiting for something I won't say. My throat feels thick with hesitation. "I like the way you play," I settle with. He gives me a soft smile.

"*Merci.*"

"Would you..." I clear my throat, suddenly feeling uncomfortable.

"Sure." The tips of his lips curl up, knowingly. "Come. I could use a friend as well."

Following him into his bedroom, I notice how spacious and clean the place is. It smells nice here, like some spicy herb.

Dominique gestures to the couch by the window. "Sit. Please feel comfortable." He installs himself in front of the piano, then turns over his shoulder. "This was my brother's favorite song. 'Moonlight Sonata' by Beethoven." And then he starts playing. Yes, it's the same tune as the one he played right when I just came in. It's slow and tragic, and it makes my chest tighten and my eyes burn. I think of Dad, in prison. I think of our small apartment back in Nîmes and my iron bars. Of my mother, who's now watching Louis play football with her husband and her other, perfect son. Of Arthur challenging me, talking to me...

"He made me come," I whisper, voice cracking. The piano stills and Dominique slowly swings around on his stool, facing me, not saying a word. "He—I—" I'm not even sure what I want to say anymore. This was a bad, bad idea.

"He likes you," Dominique breathes after what feels like forever. The tension is heavy, somehow filled with anticipation. Still, his lie makes me huff in amusement.

"No. He hates me."

"Ahh." Dominique lets out a low chuckle and stretches out his long legs in front of him, crossing them at the ankle. "That too. He hates you for getting in his way."

"I don't want to get in his way."

"No?" Dominique tilts his head as he gazes at me. "You don't enjoy telling that smug bastard exactly what you think of him?"

"I—maybe?" Yeah, I fucking do. Dominique barks out a laugh.

"Exactly. So yes, Régis, you are in his way. And you know what else?"

"No?"

Dominique juts his chin my way. "He likes you standing in his way."

That's...not what I expected. "We're rivals, though," I counter.

Dominique nods. "That you are. But rather than being pushed along, you can decide the rules." I can decide the rules? Eyeing the room, I let my brain bend over those words. At first glance, every single centimeter of their shared space is occupied by Dominique's obsessive boyfriend. But when I take a closer look, I see that I'm wrong. Traces of Dominique linger all around us—music books, the piano, his clothes, a signed football that doesn't seem to belong to any of them...

"The Deverauxs are used to having everyone wrapped around their little finger, Régis. They may not know it, but they do. Because they're wealthy, and good-looking, and because they stand tall together."

"I can decide the rules," I repeat, tasting the words in my mouth. I want to tell him that I already tried that, but that it didn't work. "Like you?"

Dominique nods. "You see, Gaël comes from a different world than I do. Everything about us screams unconventional. And maybe we are. Maybe we weren't meant to have life taken on a different course. I would never have met him if my brother hadn't died. But we did meet each other. Gaël is possessive as hell, cool and distant to those he doesn't know, but I have never loved another person as much as I love him. Together, we work on creating our own realm."

"I don't want to be with Arthur," I blurt in reply, heart pounding fast. Something shudders in my chest, making it tighten with a need so feral I didn't know I had that. It makes me confused, and judging from the way my face flushes, a little embarrassed.

Dominique just gives me a soft, knowing smile. He doesn't reply, which is a good thing, since my thoughts are bouncing around, questions screaming to be asked.

"And what about—" I close my mouth. Fuck, it's on the tip of my tongue. I shouldn't mention it, but damn it… I want to.

"The brotherhood?" Dominique cocks his head, then smiles. "Oh, I know about them. You don't think Gaël could keep that hidden from me?" He shrugs. "They sometimes ask me to play during their gatherings."

"What? They do? So you were…" Something furls inside my stomach. "Were you there the other day? Did you see me?"

Dominique nods, then shakes his head. "No. I mean, they won't let me see, I'm not a brother. I just got to play. Blindfolded," he adds, when I crease my brows in confusion.

"*Blindfolded*?"

"Yes."

"And you're okay with that?"

He lets out an amused huff. "Am I okay with that? Am I okay with the simple existence of their brotherhood? I could ask you the same question."

"Now I understand why you called us the black sheep when you first asked me to join the chess club."

"Yeah." He smiles at that.

"I'm not okay with the brotherhood, if you want to know." Feeling a little braver now that this is no longer some heavy, hidden secret, I add, "And I've told Arthur."

Dominique's eyes widen, and he whistles softly. "You did?"

"Yeah. I mean, he's been asking me about my opinion. We've been having discussions about, you know, different stuff." Which has been…nice. I don't tell him that, though. I'm not ready to hear myself say those words. A silence follows as he just stares at me. Then, "Arthur doesn't usually ask people's opinions. He's a bit like the box of Pandora. Enigmatic, unpredictable. But then he is different when he's with you. And he's good-looking, right?"

"Oh, shut up." I wince, and that makes him laugh even more. "He's my stepbrother, Dominique."

"Doesn't stop him from claiming you. They tend to do that, the Deverauxs. They kind of just barge in and make you theirs. Stepbrother or not."

"Yeah, well, that's not going to happen." I stand up, suddenly feeling lighter, despite the topic. "What about you?" I gesture to the piano. "I've only talked about myself..."

Dominique shakes his head. "This was enough for me. Sometimes I get a little too caught up in my head, you know? Then it's nice to have a friend around." Dominique's phone buzzes with a message, and judging from the smile on his face, it's Gaël.

"Well, I better get going. Thank you for the concert."

He looks up from his phone. "Anytime, Régis. You want to meet up and play some chess with the guys tomorrow night?"

"Yeah, that sounds nice."

"Cool." He watches me leave. "Oh, and Régis. What's about to happen is pretty inevitable. So trust me when I say that you want to do things on your terms."

It's quiet in the woods. Football practice finished about fifteen minutes ago by the sound of their team cheer. That means that by now, the Deverauxs must be back inside, doing god knows what.

Cool air brushes gently through my hair as I keep a steady pace over the sand path with its oak trees looming over. Where the path breaks up in two different trails, I hesitate only briefly, searching around my darkened surroundings as I do so. Where is it? Turning my flashlight on, I use my phone as guidance, its sharp light illuminating the dark shrubs with its dancing leaves as the wind blows through them. My gut clenches a little with trepidation, remembering all too well when Arthur found me in those woods.

Before he took me to the Atrium.

I inhale sharply when the light flickers in a dark building hidden off-road behind some trees. Fuck, it really does look more ominous at night. The silence that felt so peaceful just a few minutes ago, feels thick and a little threatening right now, which is ridiculous. At night the world looks exactly the same, there's just a blanket wrapped around everything. Making it more private, more secluded.

My steps pick up as I keep my light steady on the building, breath coming in more steady puffs, heart rate gradually slowing down. I'm in control once more.

"Gotcha," I mumble, when I approach the horse stables. The barn, entirely made of wood, keeps multiple types of saddles, bridles and brushes under its porch. Slowly approaching the place, I watch out for any activity around the place. I'm not a fan of horses, but much to my relief, and despite the storage spaces being filled to the brim with hay, the place appears empty.

"Hello?" I peek through the open space, but no one replies. "Anyone here?"

Slowly I walk onto the porch and open the door toward the stables. Nothing, apart from a flapping flag of a blue shield with three golden fleurs-de-lis.

I think of the iron that the garden personnel left me. I've kept it where I buried my leaves and twigs at the foot of an oak tree. It's not as big as the one Dad kept me in at home, but if I try hard, I'll fit. And when I do, I'll move it here, where it can stay hidden.

My secret.

I look around and take in my environment. Yes, this place

will do. It's covered and deserted. By one of the oval rectangle windows, I crouch down, my flashlight checking for any insects I don't want too close. Nothing. In fact, the place looks surprisingly clean, as if someone sweeps it frequently.

After I've crouched down in the corner, I switch off my light and let my eyes adjust to the darkness huddled around me. It's cool in here, the rainy weather of the past few days having leaked inside the wooden beams. After my initial tremors, something heavy, and soothing, lands over me, draping me in a familiar comfort. This is how I've spent numerous nights. Punished, alone and in the darkness. In the quiet.

Mentally preparing myself for my next step, I press the redial button and wait for the connection to establish.

Dad's clearly enraged when I finally talk to him. Our lawyer contacted him directly and told him that as things stand now, we have no case against my mother. When he mentions her name in a venomous spit, I can't help but remember the conversation she and I had just before. The way she looked at me.

It makes me feel so fucking confused. Yes, I want her love, her pride. I want it so much. But having Dad sit in a rotten prison cell just feels so wrong. It's like I failed him, as if I am not loyal to him.

Loyalty.

Oh, go away.

"I told that psychiatrist that all was good," I protest weakly when he gives me another rumble of protests, remembering those horrible conversations that we had. All those moments she had me relive. I'd just wanted to curl up into a ball and be left alone.

"Yeah, well, your testimony was overruled, remember?" He grunts. "That woman decided that you were not fit to decide." Sarcasm drips off his tongue.

"Yeah, I remember," I whisper in defeat. She'd said that my

trauma was too fresh. That it clouded my judgement on the things that had happened.

"There's no way I'm going to stay here in prison," Dad spews. "No. Fucking. Way. If you're as clever as they all say, find me a solution, son. Don't let your old man die here."

"I won't, Dad. I won't." Though I have no clue how I can get him out.

Let him go, Régis. Stop calling him.

When my mother and Jean-Luc brought me into their home, they told me that they'd make sure that Dad would stay locked away his entire life.

After we hang up, I curl myself into a ball in the corner of the porch, ignoring the cold, as my fingers scrape the iron hinges of the door.

Like a cat.

He calls me *chaton*.

I close my eyes and think the cold away. And I think of Arthur, let the fictive version of my stepbrother soothe my trembling core.

Do things on your terms, Régis.

Don't they see? Arthur already plays me like a fucking violin. He already has me on my knees for him. I shudder at the thought, shudder at the memory of our bodies sighing against each other in sweet relief. I bet his bare skin feels amazing, strong and defined. I bet he smells amazing too, all spicy and male and fucking unique.

I gaze at my fingers, wishing the thoughts away. But no matter how hard I try, that stubborn desire won't leave. Instead, it lingers, heating up in my stomach, where it coils up together, bringing the perfect remedy against my loneliness.

Outside, the woods creak and shudder under the fierce wind. I close my eyes and drift off, never once leaving the cool metal of the hinges. No bars, but at least it's something.

No more punishments. Because Dad is gone.

My thoughts take me back in time, but refuse to bring me to the safety of pain. Of regret and sorrow. Of my younger self pining for a mother who just took off. Instead, it lingers in that mansion by the sea, in the room I'd been given. In the room I could have loved, hadn't I been too busy longing for my past and fearing my future.

Now that future is back in my own hands again.

Opening my eyes with a startle, I realize I must have drifted off. I must have fallen asleep after all. It's cold around me, and quiet.

Or...What's that sound?

I sit up on a whim at the sound of cries. Someone. Someone's out there in the woods. My hand fondles in my pocket, grabbing hold of my phone. Fuck me, it's nearly one in the morning. My head feels heavy with sleep, but my skin prickles with awareness. I need to get the hell out of here.

Squeezing my jacket tight around my shoulders, I quietly leave the porch and try to remember what side I came from. Everything's so dark, I can't see a thing.

There. Again that noise. As if something's seriously crying in the forest, a loud and screeching sound. It's fucking terrifying. I turn on the flashlight. I wince when the shrubs and trees suddenly light up, showing the outlines of two masked, dark cloaks standing in between the trees.

Watching me.

It's a trick.

Walking toward me.

"It's not real," I mumble.

Coming closer.

"Oh, fucking stop it," I growl at myself. The words of their chanting are lost in the wind, fluttering through the air light the leaves. Until they reach my ears in a slow, menacing taunt.

We'll hunt you down. Hunt you down.

"Oh, god." I turn on my heel and run.

With a thundering heart and rapid, shallow breaths, I follow the trail from my flashlight over the wobbly sand path.

Can't fall, not now. Can't fall, not now.

I don't hear that sound again, though the faintest of rustles through the bushes have me freaking out even more, yelping in agony as I keep on running. And then...finally, I reach the football field. It looks eerily big, the way the grass is lit up. For the briefest of seconds, I imagine them standing there, close to the goal, but I jerk my head away and the image is gone.

The gardens don't offer that same feeling of protection they usually do. Instead, the faint branches and bare plants look like sad, gloomy sticks, freaking me out.

When I finally make it to the stone walls of the castle, I peer up, searching for the candle I always light up. My heart is furiously beating in my chest, panic surging when I can't find my room. What if I stayed out too long and the candle finished? I turn over my shoulder, half expecting someone to grab me from behind, but that doesn't happen.

There.

A faint flicker of my candle. It's enough to have me grabbing the drainpipe tight and cranking my legs up, squeezing the cold white material between my legs as I hoist myself up. It isn't usually this hard, but right now, with a thundering heart and a drained mind, it feels like fucking forever. I squeeze my eyes shut at the faintest sound coming from the woods behind me, begging for the life of it that the material will hold. When I finally get to my window, I press it open, nearly knocking the candle out of its holder.

"Fuck," I pant, then throw my shaking legs over the windowsill and hop onto the wooden flooring. With the candle in my hand, I stare through the window and toward the kilometers of quiet darkness that stretch the view.

What the fuck was that? What just happened? Me imagining

things, that's what this was. It's in the middle of the night, of course there was no one out there. Right?

Forcing myself to get a grip, I blow out the candle and take off my jacket with trembling fingers. Safe. I'm safe now.

"You know we use doors for such kinds of things, right?" A hoarse rumble vibrates through the room, and I hit my knee against my desk when I jump in surprise. Reaching blindly through the darkness, I switch on my desk light.

"What the fuck are you doing here?" I snarl, refusing to acknowledge that slither of embarrassment at the thought that he must have witnessed me freaking out.

Arthur's sitting on my bed in nothing more than a pair of sweatpants and a tight, black tee that makes the firm muscles in his biceps bulge. "Why did you come through the window?" He throws back at me. I can see his brow curve up through the dim light, and I hate him for looking so damn sexy in those clothes and his wild mop of raven strands. So composed with those striking, square features and that small curve around his lips.

"That's none of your business. Leave."

"Uh uh." He shakes his head. "Not gonna happen. *Viens*." He lifts his glorious, strong thighs to roll the blankets back, and when I don't obey fast enough, he crooks his finger at me. *"Allez, viens."*

Biting on my lip, I go through my options. There's no way that I can go back into the woods now. At the thought of the woods, I turn around, only to freeze when I see a flicker of light shining through the oak trees.

I blink, but it's still there. I blink again, but don't wait to see. As if the outside danger pushes me in my back, I slowly drag my feet toward the bed, heart thundering in my ribcage. Arthur's eyes flicker with delight. "You're going to tell me where the hell you were just now. Come here, you're trembling." His nostrils flare when I halt in front of the bed. "Now strip."

"Strip?" I sniff. "Absolutely not."

He lets out an annoyed huff, then leans forward, laying on his stomach as he crawls toward me and reaches for my pants. Grinding my teeth, I hate how my cock perks up at his simplest of touches. "You're not going to sleep in your school uniform, are you?" Opening my belt, he opens the fly, and we both watch how my pants drop down my narrow waist until they puddle around my feet. My hand flies out, but I'm sure I'm too late to cover up my half hard dick. Arthur peers up at me through his thick lashes, a wicked grin on his face.

"Where were you?" He pulls on my wrist, and with a grunt, I remove my hand from my crotch to unbutton my cuffs, before taking off my socks and shoes.

"I'm not going to tell you," I grind out through gritted teeth. After I pull my shirt over my head, my hand hurries to get back to my crotch, but Arthur slaps it away. Leaning in, he presses a soft, slow kiss onto my rapidly hardening cock, mouthing the rigid shape through the fabric with his lips, making me stifle a moan when something tight unfurls in the pit of my stomach. When he pulls back and gazes up, something wicked flares in his eyes, and it makes me clench my jaw. The asshole knows exactly what he's doing to me. Humiliation blankets the tightness in my stomach.

"You also missed the conversation I had with Dad while watching the football team practice. I raised my concerns about you, little brother."

"Concerns?" I breathe.

"Hmm." He gives me another one of those innocent looking gazes, lashes fluttering when he blinks. "Dad asked me if, aside from school results, you were fitting in. And you know me, I just had to tell him the truth. Of how you haven't been hanging out with us a lot. Your family."

"That's because I am busy." I hiss.

"I know you are," he soothes. "Come." Grabbing my sides with his muscled arms, he pulls me forward, chuckling when I tumble onto the bed, then drags me under the warm blankets. The warmth makes me shiver again, before my body settles into the pleasant snugness. "There. That's better. Now, tell me what you were doing out there." Warm hands brush my forearms slowly, warming my skin with each firm stroke.

I squint my eyes in frustration. Fuck, I should have known better. "I was with Dominique."

"Outside? Until one in the morning?" He leans his chin onto my shoulder while his hands continue working, and I can feel his soft puffs of air brushing my ear. Goosebumps erupt across my sensitive flesh, making my mind stutter and my eyes burn. Because having someone in my bed, holding me, feels so precious. It brings the kind of flutter that I could fly away on, like thousands of golden fireflies.

"I was—I—" My mouth locks, throat swallowing the words. I can't tell him. Not him. Not anyone. Turning over my shoulder, I catch sight of the golden gleam of the moon as it shines through the curtains. During the random nights that I do actually manage to sleep in my bed, I usually lie facing the curtains with that slither of light, but tonight I'm rolled onto my left, facing the door. "Why do you care anyway? What are you doing here?"

His eyes glow like a ring of dark gold as he peers down at me like a cat, thick lashes fluttering when he blinks. He's so close. Suddenly I don't dare inhale deeply, afraid to inhale his unique scent of musk and Arthur, afraid to lose the shackles that keep me grounded and far, far away from others.

He shrugs. "Couldn't sleep. Why were you crying before in Dad's office? Is it because of something your mom said?"

"That's none of your..." I lock my dried lips, then flinch when he pulls me in closer, his clothed chest burning through the cool flesh of my own skin. Arthur presses a soft kiss on my shoulder, then mumbles, "You know, my mom died when we were three."

"What?" My heart thumps in my chest, my mind temporarily coming up empty.

"Car accident," he continues, his soft voice caressing my ear. "She was behind the wheel when a truck drove into her and smashed her under the truck she was behind. She died on the spot."

"I'm so sorry," I breathe, voice a little husky. Finding his hand under the warm blanket, I squeeze, unable to formulate my sympathy in words.

He shrugs. "It was a long time ago, I don't remember much of her. But I guess it explains why Dad won't let us drive."

"Never?" I finally ask.

He presses a soft kiss behind my ear, the hint of his plush lips lingering when he pulls back. "Never, *chaton*. I don't know if you've ever noticed, but Didier always brings us everywhere."

Turning over my shoulder, I frown at him. "So you can't drive?" Arthur rolls his eyes, his gaze slowly morphing into something that surprisingly looks like amusement. "I didn't know that," I mumble to myself. Silence falls upon us while we lay on our sides, our hands intertwined, Arthur's face glued to mine. "My Dad..." I swallow thickly, unblocking myself from anxiety before I continue to push out the words, "Taught me how to drive. I don't have a permit, but I didn't use the car often."

Arthur snorts. "So you drove a car without a driver's licence?"

"Only to buy groceries."

"My little stepbrother," he teases. "Such a little villain."

"So, what was it like to grow up without your mother?" I whisper after a while. Arthur presses another kiss on my ear, this time on my lobe. It tickles a bit.

"Is that why you cried earlier?" He answers instead.

I hesitate. "Yeah," I finally crack.

"Is that why you hide in the woods at night?"

"No, I—"

Punishment.

Arthur chuckles against my ear while his grip around my wrist tightens, rolling his hips seductively against my back, the sound as menacing as thrilling. I suck in a breath of air as my cock thickens. "*Mon chaton,* you think I don't know where you were?" He lets out a smug as fuck grin that makes him sound both sexy and wicked. Gone is the earlier, softer side of my big stepbrother. It leaves me to wonder if he is struggling as much as I am against this spiralling attraction that I feel for him, sucking me in deeper and deeper until I'll be stuck and defenseless. "You think I got this far in life without knowing where those who are spun in my web are?"

I lick my lips, both surprised and a little shocked. "If you know where I was—" I gulp the rest away. "Then I'm sure you know who else was out there too? They freaked me out."

"They freaked you out—" He draws against the curve of my neck, his breath making me shiver, before I let out a yawn. I never knew it would be so calming to lay in bed with another person, so warm, and snug. Comforting, despite my cock being hard. "And so you came back running and ended up here with me. In your bedroom."

"In my defense, I didn't know that you'd be here. Where did you place the chess board?"

"Relax, *chaton*. I left it on the floor. It's your turn to play tomorrow."

"Okay," I reply sheepishly. Silence falls over us, and I'm left staring at the darkness of my room—the *wrong* side of my room —and, despite my fatigue, awake. When I reach counting to one hundred, he's still here, his breath a steady puff that tickles the back of my ear. And still, the silence drags on.

My body feels heavy against the warm sheets as it sags in relief. Under the sheets, we're warm and snug, and he's still... "Can I ask you something?" I ask, cutting off my own thoughts.

Arthur's reply is a low rasp against the tender flesh of my nape that scatters goosebumps all around my neck. "You already are."

"Are you not going to your own bed?"

"No," he mutters drowsily. "I like it here."

"You..." I cut myself off at the sensation of something warm and tight, that spreads across my chest. I like it too. Like him being here, making the bed less big.

Inhaling deeply, I whisper, "So do you know who was out there, in the woods?"

His hand on my waist tightens as he gets himself comfortable again, purring as he does so. "I know everything that happens around this college. But you don't have to be afraid of that, *chaton*." Thank god he can't see the roll of my eye. Arrogant shit.

"How do you know?"

"Because I know who they are. Restless brothers who want to play."

That...doesn't bring any relief in the slightest. "Play?"

He chuckles. "Yeah. But they can't play with you."

"Why not?"

"Because you're my toy, Régis. Now, sleep, *chaton*, it's late."

"This, us...in the same bed. It doesn't mean that I like you, because I don't."

"I was hoping you'd say that." He presses a soft kiss behind my ear, a strangely intimate gesture. "Now, sleep."

15

RÉGIS

There's a rattling noise, hollow and metallic. It's a snappy, popping sound on repeat as I keep on banging the hammer against the bars.

The darkness makes me lose all track of my surroundings, the only certainty being my surrounding iron.

Let...Me...Out.

Let me out.

Let me out. Let me out. Let me out!

I can't breathe.

Let me out.

"There you are. I wonder where you'd gone."

"Not far."

"Nah, not far."

Enough. Let me out. You're a monster.

A monster.

But there's no door to this cage. Only a lock. And I don't have the key. He has the key. He has it. He has it...

On instinct, my mouth opens on a cry and I suck in the largest gulp of air. Fuck, I feel like I haven't taken a breath for so long. Drained, I'm feeling drained, my chest tightened and my heart beating furiously at the same time. Panting, I open my eyes, blinking a few times to see clear.

Where the fuck—I take in my desk with my reassuring books, my computer, and backpack. Gazing up to the curtains, I catch the faintest of moonlit darkness. My closet…I'm not in my closet. My limbs stiffen at the realization.

Fragments of those haunting thoughts still linger, making my brain sluggish. The past is burned, Dad behind bars, but it doesn't save me from my own mind. Perhaps that's what scares me most. You can change your entire life, but horror always has a way to find you.

It sucks me right back in, making me close my eyes again, falling back into my nightmare. It's different now. The cage is still there, but the threat is dissipated. Instead I'm feeling hot, so fucking hot. It's still dark around me, but somewhere a torch is lit, putting a silvery glow over the cage. There's a soft noise, like a moan, low and smooth, and it's making my body slow and lethargic, as my stomach hits the warm floor. Arousal shoots through me at the next shuddering moan. It takes me a moment to realize that it's my own, pleading voice.

Then I can feel it. A strong hand wrapped around my waist. Rolling my hips back, desire inflames instantly, thick and hungry, as I touch something hot, and hard.

"Fuck, yeah," I urge on a breath. My vision flutters behind my lids. The lock is opened, the darkness fading away. I'm free.

I'm free.

"*Ouvre tes yeux, chaton.*" Open your eyes. A hoarse voice rumbles in my ear, making my flesh explode in goosebumps.

"Hmm." My body rocks into those soothing thoughts, into that liquid heat that runs through my body, faster and faster with every grind of my hips. Dazed, I open my eyes again. Fuck, I'm feeling euphoric. Black and golden light shimmer through the room, and my hips roll slowly while I try to catch my breath. My body is burning with desire, and when I slide my hand down, I find my cock hard and dripping behind their restraints.

I'm wearing my pyjama pants and a tank top, but can't remember when I put those on, nor when I somehow rolled back into my usual side, facing the window.

And that tanned arm, tightly wrapped around my waist, prominent veins and soft, dark hairs.

"Fuck." It comes out on another moan. I'm not alone. Blinking furiously, my thoughts come tumbling back. Last night's meeting with my mother and Jean-Luc, followed by that freaky evening in the forest. Then finding my stepbrother waiting for me, here, in my bed… "You're still here."

My nightmare has left me so vulnerable. Raw and exposed, and ready to be picked up and fooled around with. It scares me. The way my mask has slipped from my face and has wiped off my guard. I'm left naked. It's why I want Arthur so badly it hurts. Want him to braid his strength around me and claim my body and mind, chase away the fear by doing so. Fucking *crave* him to keep me safe.

Arthur's hand tightens around my waist as he guides my hips to skim flush against his groin with every roll. He's hard, like me, his cock teasing the crease of my clothed cheeks with every pound. It makes every single nerve ending come alive, making my lips part in ecstasy.

"Is this what you need, *chaton*?" He rasps.

I moan."Yes. Oh yes."

"Fuck yeah." Arthur lets out an unhinged grunt and his hand creeps up, long fingers sliding around my neck and squeezing. His lips brush against my ear. "Nightmare?"

I swallow, my gaze still focused on the curtains. "I—yeah."

"Got those often?"

I bite my lip, shaking my head only to hesitantly turn it into a nod of my chin.

Arthur lets out a huff, then brings his lips close to mine.

"Well, you won't anymore. I'll kill them all for you. I'll kill your monster." Their touch, featherlight, intensifies my desire.

"You're just saying that," I mumble on a breath, sounding too desperate. *But you don't mean it.* Because when he's like this, all possessive and determined, he's got me desiring things I can't have. Things I usually have carefully stalled in the far corner of my heart.

My secret.

Such as believing that one day I can be freed from my past. That one day I can be freed from the fear of being punished, of being put in place because I deserved it.

It's a trick.

It used to be. I'm not sure if Dad meant for them to be, but they sure felt like it. When he'd ask me about school and listened to my stories, only to suddenly…explode. Right before that would happen, his face would tighten, making his eyes pop and his smile tight. It was as if he was fighting whatever happened inside his mind from bursting free. And though I knew what would come next, knew how within the next few seconds he'd chase me down to my bedroom and lock me up, I'd always just sit and stare. I'd listen to all the horrific words he'd spray down on me, like some toxic storm.

Of how she left because of me. Of how having me had been the biggest regret in his life.

Arthur chuckles on a rasp, and his tongue flicks my earlobe. "I don't just *say* things, *chaton*." Turning over my shoulder, I'm taken aback by his genuine smile. He doesn't get real like that often, and that smile is…the way that chiseled, square jaw takes in those lush, curvy lips. They are glistening with moisture and so beautifully red, full, and edible. And still… his dark eyes twinkle with mischief, as if he still has a secret or two up his sleeve. He probably does. Like the college's hidden quidnunc, he seems to know exactly what's going on around this place.

"Unlike you, I don't shy away from actions but take full responsibility."

His eyes flicker with amusement as he waits for me to react. He doesn't have to wait long, because something about those words beat me right in the chest.

"I don't shy away from things," I snarl, keeping his stare. His eyes flare with something dark, something primal. It's not enough to keep me quiet. "I have never shied away from things. Not from this school, not from your freaky brotherhood. I have never once backed off."

"Oh yeah?" Grabbing me by my forearms, Arthur rolls me onto my back with a harsh plop, then crawls over me. Our warm thighs connect even through the fabric of his sweats, and I growl at the lack of touch. I want to feel his skin, feel his beating flesh against mine, soothing my rattling arousal. I'm exasperated, its flame raging inside me at the thought of his words. Balling my hands into fists, I use them to lash out onto his chest. "Yeah," I grit between my teeth. "You see, I didn't ask for any of this. I was living my life the way I did before all of this came bursting out of the sky and right onto my doorstep." That's not entirely true, but we both ignore that detail for now. Besides, the more I speak, the more my words wind me up, making my skin tremble with fury.

"Living your life," Arthur huffs out in disdain. "You mean in that small apartment where your asshole dad could treat you like shit."

My chest flares up with heat at those words. "That's not for you to say," I sneer. "That's none of your fucking business. I was nearly eighteen, I could have left myself."

Would I have left him?

"Wrong." Arthur dips his head, ablaze eyes colliding with mine. "I'm your stepbrother. That means it is my fucking business."

"Why?" The word comes out on a high shrill. "Why would

you care? I'm an adult, you presumptuous prick. Ever since you've walked into my life, you've been nothing but against me."

He blinks his eyes at that, silent for the first time. Not me, I seem to be on a roll, brain working overtime like some machine gone wild, spewing words as if it's water.

"People have never given a damn about my home situation. They knew. Neighbors, teachers, they all fucking knew. And yet, they decided to turn a blind eye, to look away every time I came face to face with them, their superficial greetings making me cold to the core."

I was so lonely.

My mind trembles at that feeling, those cold tremors making me remember every time I try to create too much of a distance from my past. It's making me relive those moments of agony over and over again, casting iron where it tried to melt, because pain and humiliation are easier than *this*. An unknown future. I'm a good student. But I can study all I like, work those brains to get the best grades in school, the truth is, the rest of me is helplessly lost in a world too big.

"And you..." I glare up at Arthur, wishing his beauty away. "You've been nothing but forceful. Controlling. Continuously dragging me into this...into this—mess. " My voice shivers a little, but it's not because of my words or how they make me feel. There's something else there, something that's far more embarrassing than any cocktail of words could be. I clear my throat, but it's still there, and it makes my body thrum.

Arthur's eyes soften, their earlier annoyance replaced by a look of knowing. He finally trails a hand over my cheek, the fingertips taking their time to feel my flushed skin, neck, then down over my pecs to my lower abdomen. To my hot, throbbing cock.

I sigh, eyes fluttering as the humming in my body becomes stronger.

"You like me being forceful, and controlling," he muses

softly. "You like me pulling you into this mess, challenging you, peeling you off the corners in which you've been hiding for too long."

"I—" Why? I want to ask him. Why am I this defect?

"Your cock is throbbing, *chaton*." The soft touch makes me jerk. "For me. Your body knows what it wants, but your mind is rebelling as always. Always so fucking stubborn."

"I don't want to want this," I admit, eyes opening in a blink. Arthur has moved even closer, his pouty, kissable lips hovering over mine.

"You're scared." He breathes against my mouth. "And when you get scared, you shy away. You crawl back to your safety zone. Tell me, Régis, where else do you crawl back to?"

If only he knew.

He dips his chin and I shake my head. Our mouths brush and my body catches fire, the thrumming of my entire frame trembling at our touch.

"Tell me." His hand slides between my back and the sheets, lifting my hips to roll down my pyjama pants and boxers. "Tell me where you were last night. I need to hear the words from your mouth." He leaves them at my thighs, but it's enough for my cock to jump out, flushed and pink, glistening with desire. Arthur lets out a low growl, then cups my naked ass cheek, fingers tracing the crease as it slides one finger through its fold. It makes me jerk my hips upward and blindly search for friction.

"Not scared," I grit out, my voice sounding restrained. "Not crawling back to anywhere."

"Yes, you are. Tell me, little Régis, what was it like to stand in that beautiful cloak among all your brothers?" He rolls over and reaches for my bedside drawer, where I watch him leisurely own my drawer as if it's his. Rolling back and positioning himself between my spread thighs, he continues to roll my pyjamas down my legs and over my feet with one hand, exposing me in a way I have never been exposed before. I feel the need to cover up my aching cock and vulnerability, this need to run away and hide behind iron. But pride stands in my way.

"You know I will fight you," I hiss as I help him wiggle me out of my clothes. "I will fight injustice and privilege. You know I will join this brotherhood, but will never be a true brother."

Arthur opens his palm, revealing a small bottle of lube and a condom, his eyes flaring with wickedness. "It's time my little stepbrother knows his place."

"And how exactly are you going to do that, big stepbrother?" I clench my teeth and tilt my chin on a glare, but his stare is burning right through me, his brow curiously arched. He knows, and I fucking hate it that he knows. His fingertips trace the sensitive skin of my loins, and I can't help but lift my hips, body overstimulated.

"I'll go slow." Leaning over, his face dips right in level with mine. His lips curl into a wolfish grin. "Dad gave you to me, Régis. All of you."

"You won't have all of me," I growl.

"I'll take what I want, *chaton*," he whispers. Before I can think of a thing to say, he slams his mouth over mine and squeezes my sensitive cock at the same time, making me jolt in rapture. I moan, lips falling open, and with ferocity he claims my mouth, curling his tongue around mine and pinching it with his own. He rolls his hips against mine, and flesh meets flesh. He must have shimmied out of his sweats when I was too busy fighting him off. Arthur kisses like he lives life—a constant battle for power. He flicks his tongue devilishly, playfully, wrapping it around mine, and attacking it with soft nibbles that leave me a moaning, grinding mess. When he finally pulls out of my mouth to take off his shirt, my hands fly up to his naked skin before I can think twice. There are no more guards, I'm wholly uncovered, a panting, desperate mess for his touch.

When he sits back and spreads my legs, I can't help but exhale and peer up at my stepbrother's sculpted chest. Dips and valleys roll around his developed muscles. Spellbinding, the way his lean, tanned skin shimmers so subtly beneath the faint light. Arthur takes hold of my desperate hand and wraps his bigger one around it. Then he slides my hand down his chest, achingly slowly, until I reach a nipple. My fingers brush past it, and he hisses, arching slightly. "Yeah," he grumbles. I do it again, enthralled by the way that bud hardens between my digits. His mouth curves. His eyes glint. "Again," he growls softly. "Both at once."

My lips part at the command. The heavy fog of fear dissipates, replaced by an adored nothingness. It makes me feel weightless.

Adding my other hand, I obey without question. This time, however, I tug both nipples a bit harder and give them a little twist. Arthur growls and rocks his hips, the tips of our cocks brushing. My groin pulses in reaction, dick straight-up humming in its sheath.

"My stomach now," Arthur instructs, his voice like abraded velvet. "Touch my stomach now, *chaton*. Use your nails."

Clearing my throat, I give him a faint nod, then slowly drag my fingertips down Arthur's torso. His lids dip lower. "Harder, *chaton*. I want to feel you ablaze my flesh." I stifle another groan. Complying, I add pressure, dragging five blunt nails down Arthur's abs. Along each dip and clenching swell, until I can't help but pause to admire as his muscles clench and shudder at the touch.

"Lower," Arthur rumbles. "Or are you afraid?" My heart rate spikes faster as I eye Arthur's happy trail, warily following its path with my finger. A path that's made of a tantalizing line of dark hair. His large cock bobs when he lets out a husky sound, its girth a blend of smooth skin and protruding veins. Its slit wet with pre-cum. It's—fuck… it's a mouthwatering sight. Not being able to resist, I dip a finger through the liquid and suckle it between my lips, curious to explore. It has a stringy texture and sweet taste, and makes me stifle a groan. Fuck, that tastes good.

"You like that, don't you?" He murmurs, cat eyes hooded as they stare into mine. I swallow and want to look away, but his fingers tilt my chin right back at him. "Do it again," he orders.

My hand wraps around his cock and once more he places his firm grip around mine, guiding me as he leads me around his girth. Slowly we glide up, and down and up again. My thumb brushes over his slit, collecting some more pre-cum. Arthur's eyes slide closed. "*Oui* ..."

I freeze, distracted instantly. That husky growl is like a shot straight to my groin. Together, we continue stroking his rigid length until we hit his pubic hair. There's a gentleness in his guidance that wasn't there before. Back in the Atrium, when he'd sat me down onto a chair and wrapped my lips onto his cock, he'd slowly fucked my mouth. But this is more careful. This is about me experiencing his body, about that silky skin that feels hot and soft in my palm as I attentively grope his balls, just like his murmuring approval of my touch. When he finally lets go of my hand to open the bottle of lube, fresh shivers race through my core again, anticipation thick and heady.

"Don't stop touching my dick, *chaton*," he rumbles. I comply, brushing and stroking his flushed dick, swiping another plashet of pre-cum onto his girth. He feels amazing, all hard and large and strong. My own dick jerks frantically against his hip, untouched and wet with arousal. I'm too focused to care.

Keeping one palm filled with his balls, I stroke his cock from tip to base, agonizingly slow. A dark, lethal sound rumbles up Arthur's chest. He shudders, then pats my hand away.

"Stop it, I don't want to come yet." Before I can freeze or be embarrassed, he grabs my hand and opens my palm. "Here. Stroke yourself. Show me what you like." He drizzles lube into my hand, then guides me to my own desperate dick. "Touch yourself," he rasps. I watch how he repeats the action with his own palm, fist wrapping around my dick. I start stroking myself, moaning as I do so. Fuck, I'm so caught up in this moment, in the emotion that we've created, that cocktail of words and physical touch, in *him* and the way he watches me, eyes dark with hunger.

"I'm going to play with your hole now, *chaton*. Going to prepare you nice and easy for me to fuck you." Without any further warning, wet fingers trace the lines of my crease, teasing my cleft before dipping a slippery finger inside. My muscles clench, and I let out a surprised yelp, fist still tight on my weeping cock. "Ssh, relax for me, little stepbrother." Arthur halts, keeping the tip of his cool, wet finger against my hole, as he waits for my muscles to recline. With his legs kicked against the insides of my thighs, he keeps my legs wide. "Give me some space, *chaton*," he murmurs. Replacing my fist, he grabs hold of my cock, then drizzles even more lube onto my girth, using it to smoothly glide up and down my shaft. I choke on a shudder, but when his finger enters my ass, my muscles lock up, clenching around him again. Arthur smiles. "Too late, I'm already in. Now, bear down. Push against my finger, give me passage."

I shake my head, feeling exasperated. "I don't know how to do that."

"Yes, you do. Breathe in… and out. And again, breathe in… there you go…" With eyes collided on him, I mimic his gesture, taking in deep puffs of air through my nose. When we find a slow rhythm, he purrs on a hum. "Good boy, for letting my finger into your ass. Can you feel me?" He crooks his digit and I nod. It feels a little strange. So full, uncomfortable with a slither of ache. I emit a choke of air when he collects some pre-cum from my slit, then picks up stroking my cock. My knees tremble, and my head feels heavy on my pillow as I thwack it from left to right, feeling restless and aroused at the same time.

"Fuck," I choke. "More. I need more."

"I'll give you more." My ass clenches at the sudden tightness, and he gives me another of those smiles. "Well done, that's finger number two. You're so incredibly tight. My cock is going to be in heaven."

I swallow, but when he pushes further, he presses against something that makes me jolt in euphoria. My core trembles, cock jumps and I let out a filthy moan.

Arthur chuckles. "Like that, hmm? You still want more?"

"Please." He grins, then he bends his fingers into that same angle, making me cry out. "Jesus, fuck. Oh, fuck," I pant. "Feels so fucking good."

"Yeah, you do." Arthur's eyes glimmer. His fingers work inside me, and that weird feeling of fullness intermingles with pleasure, the combination strangely intoxicating.

That thought gets me even more aroused, stomach tightening and releasing as I shudder on the bed. When he finally pulls them out, a whine escapes my throat. Arthur puts on the condom, then pours even more lube onto his thick cock. Grabbing hold of my thighs, he pulls up one leg and hooks it over his shoulder, followed by the other one. It's making me fully exposed, and my hands snake out to reach my stomach, ready to protect myself.

He's looking at my hole, toying with it with a slick finger. "Fuck, so gorgeous," he mumbles. "You've got no idea how long I've wanted this ass. Ever since you walked into our home with those big, blue eyes and those delicious lips, that delectable stammer. I knew I shouldn't want you, that it was wrong, but fuck…" He licks his lips slowly, catching my hungry gaze. "Did I want to." My eyes flutter and my heart pounds ferociously. Those words do something to me, something they shouldn't do at all. But fuck me, if I don't like to hear how we've shared that mutual feeling of conflict.

"And now I gotta have you." He lifts my knees over his shoulder, then lines up his cock right at my entrance. Rubbing both my ass cheeks, he spreads them apart, humming as he slowly takes me in from head to toe. I'm lying on my back, naked, my back arched as my knees are hooked over his shoulders, ass exposed. I should feel embarrassed, but the hungry, appreciative gaze in his charcoal eyes makes me feel desired instead. "A nice and slick hole for my eager cock. Fuck kitten, you're making me so hot." Tipping the head of his cock right inside my wet hole, Arthur lets out a pleased hum. Time dips when I gaze at the slow motion that is the intermingling of our bodies. Slowly, ever so slowly, Arthur penetrates my ass. When my muscles clench, he halts, fisting my cock until I shudder and pant for more. He continues his invasion gently and thoroughly. We stop two more times because he can't get in any further, my muscles too strained for him to tunnel any deeper.

And then... we let out a mutual shudder.

"So good, little stepbrother. Look at that." My legs have gone slack, chest heaving from exertion. "I'm all the way inside you, Régis. How does that feel, *chaton*? How does it feel to be claimed by your big stepbrother?"

"You haven't claimed me," I balk on a moan. "I told you I'd fight you."

Arthur's eyes gleam maliciously, but his actions are careful. "Come on then, give me your claws, and let me fuck you nice and slow."

He pulls out almost entirely, growling as he does so, then leisurely pushes back in. It feels so full, so impossibly full, and it hurts. I think. Clawing my hands into the sheets, my brain scrambles to understand that he's hitting that same spot again... and again. I let out a cry, my back arching as I search for more.

"Fuck, you're so tight," Arthur growls. "Fuck, *chaton*, so good." He tilts his head and lets out a howl, muscles rippling as he keeps on rocking his hips, plundering and pounding as his cock owns my ass. "I'll teach you to be my obedient little boy," he hisses through clenched teeth, sounding agitated in his ferocity. "I'll have you when I want you, how I want you. You're all mine, *chaton*. All mine to fuck."

"You're delusional," I seethe. Arthur grabs hold of my ankle, using it for leverage to ravage me even deeper. "You're a narcissist punk. You—Fuck!" My choked rambling turns into a hoarse cry, my entire body locking up. Arthur releases my cock, then makes a show of lapping at his palm before putting it right back. Firm and warm around my shaft, stroking me in rhythm with his thrusts. It feels so fucking good. So good. My eyes roll back, and I let out an unhinged grunt. "I'm so close."

"Me too," Arthur grunts. "Fuck." He leans forward and crushes my lips to his in a demanding, heated kiss. Our tongues curl as he works my cock with furious, fast strokes. And my ass…

"Ahhh." I come to a blinding peak, and my legs go wobbly, knees giving out against Arthur's shoulders. I can feel myself clenching around his width as my dick pulses in his hand, scattered heat shooting all throughout my body. Everything seems to happen in slow motion. His tongue in my mouth suddenly feels electrified, and the hand on my hip becomes searing hot. My chest rises and falls with ragged breaths, and warm lips touch the side of my neck. His stubble grazes over my skin, and he groans.

Like a train that slowly comes to a halt, time, sighing and rattling, comes to a stop. My thoughts, my ever spinning thoughts, desist. It's elating. Arthur looks up at me, his onyx stare gazing right through my unguarded fences, and I can only smile. "You're so beautiful," I breathe. It's true. He's the most striking man I've ever met.

He brushes a lock behind my ear, but doesn't speak. Slowly, he pulls out of me, slides off the condom and wraps it up and puts it back into the wrapper. Tossing it on the floor by the bed, he curls the blankets back around us.

"No more nightmares now," he mumbles against my ear. "Big brother will chase them away."

"Shut up," I grumble, but I can't stop my lips from ticking up.

"Gladly so. I'm fucking exhausted and you prove to be a lot of work."

"That's your own fault. You didn't have to take me on as some voluntary project."

"I did."

"No, you didn't." I yawn, and he rubs the skin above my thigh. "And I'll fight you off, every time again."

"Sleep now."

I do, drifting off once more under the shade of the moonlight, with Arthur's arms tightly curled around my waist. "I'll fight you," I can't help but mumble. Can't help the smile to curl my lips upward either.

"*Couche-toi.*" Go to sleep, kitten.

16

RÉGIS

I wake from the slice of light invading the room through the narrow space between my curtains. Fluttering my lashes, I blink the brightness away. It takes me a moment to realize I'm still in bed, though curled up into a ball and naked under the sheets. I'm cold, my body a shivering, wrecked mess.

I'm also alone. Arthur is nowhere to be found, making the bed once more drearily big. And yet…I can't get myself to leave the sheets, my mind too fuzzy, my body still too tired.

Rolling onto my back, I try to calm my rapidly increasing state of panic. He's my stepbrother… What the hell were we thinking?

God… it felt so good. My stomach flutters. It was the most erotic experience I've ever had. And it can never ever happen again.

It's Saturday today, and judging by the voices outside, some time in the late morning. Somewhere a ball bounces, followed by laughter and hoots. Football practice. I imagine Louis being out there, and Jo. I should still go and watch him play. If football is starting, it means tennis too, and that group that always jogs through the forest on weekend mornings.

Yoga, and pilates. Study group in the library. The special bus that takes students into town for their weekly shopping. Somewhere in the background I hear the vague sound of the piano.

It seems like the world has continued and I'm still here, sprawled out in a cold bed, feeling sorry for myself. Because the more I'm here, by myself, the more I hate that Arthur is gone, that he was here in the first place, and that his absence wants to persuade my unstable mind into believing that he was never here in the first place.

He took my virginity, the first person to breach my body and claim me as his.

Struggling to get out of bed, I wince. Yeah, they are vivid memories. My ass stings from last night's intrusion. But damn… it's such a good sting.

Scurrying over to my small bathroom, I turn on the faucet and get my cold body warmed up. At the sight of a new bottle of shower gel that's waiting for me, my fingers pause. Next to it stands a bottle of almond oil, which is, judging from the image of its elongated shape, meant for my ass.

I frown when I hold the two bottles up. I can't deny that this offering soothes something in my heart, just as it no doubt will heal my aching body.

It's a trick.

Shoving all thoughts aside, I check the running water for the temperature, then hop in when it's warm enough. The hot jets of the water feel a little like a rainfall directly from heaven, warming my cool limbs and pumping strength into my core. I end up staying there for a long time, just staring back into last night's events.

I still can't wrap my head around it. What the hell's going on here? What am I missing? Why would Arthur…my chest pangs at that delicate moment when he saw me coming through the window, panicked and trembling from those sounds in the woods. He saw that. Caught me shivering like a fucking leaf as if chased by the devil himself.

Restless brothers who want to play.

The thought makes me grimace.

Why has he told the others that he has claimed me? I just don't fucking get it.

I stay under the shower until the water runs cold, then after drying myself, use the oil to soothe my sensitive skin. It becomes warm on my fingers, and when I apply it around my rim, the oily texture is absorbed quickly, leaving a tingling sensation and a faint scent of a nutty aroma.

But by the time I've put on some fresh clothes, my anxiety levels spike. They have replaced all those soft, secret murmurs and clench my throat and chest.

"I will fight you. I will fight all of you," I murmur into the quiet space of my foggy bathroom. I'll fight all those unwanted feelings that screw me up from inside and make me feel even more confused. My head's already full enough as it is, and I'm not sure if I'm strong enough to make space for my big stepbrother and the intense desire he makes me feel. That intense fire that burns through my veins whenever I'm with him, whether we fight or fuck.

Fight or fuck. I bite my lip, throwing my towel in the hamper. I let him have me, let him arouse me with his filthy words and this misplaced supremacy, as if he could somehow claim some part of me. And I wanted it. Wanted him, his raspy murmurs, his warm hands curling around my frame, pulling me close, his words...god, I love his words. Love when he shares his thoughts, gives me a peek into his life.

And I shouldn't, because if someone finds out, we'll both be in serious trouble. Right? No, it can never happen again.

I can beat this, this...ridiculous infatuation with my stepbrother. Still, I find myself making up the bed, biting my bottom lip when my fingers reach out for my pillow and I press it against my nose, inhaling deeply. Greedily. Fuck, his scent is still there. It's a woodsy musk that reminds me of his aftershave combined with sweat and…him. Arthur's own, unique essence.

After taking another whiff, I scoff out loud, then throw the pillow back onto the floor of my wardrobe, slamming the door shut as if I'm afraid it can somehow get up and break free.

I end up spending that entire day in my bedroom, alone, searching and finding haunting thoughts and letting them control me. I need the hurt, the stinging clench of disappointment, to know how to carry on. We design those shackles we wear in life. And then we melt into them, searing our flesh to chains.

It's easier. Always easier to evoke pain than to hope for bliss, because it's volatile, unpredictable. It will come and go as it pleases…like Arthur did.

He has left me the chessboard on my desk where he started a new game.

My books won't do, and even *Le Petit Prince* can't seem to sprinkle his contagious curiosity over me today. Still, I clutch the book in my hands when I sit at my desk, from where I stare outside and right at the forest.

"And now here is my secret, a very simple secret; it is only with the heart that one can see rightly, what is essential is invisible to the eye."

"I'm so lost," I mutter in reply. "I don't know what my heart wants anymore."

But I know what my brain wants.

I'll protect you.

The thought is reassuring. In the end, the only person I can count on is myself. And when my heart is weak, my mind will give support.

Always.

Once more, I fall back into a rhythm of avoidance.

Between waking up even earlier than before and heading out way before the others do, peace and quiet is secured. Even during school days, the canteen is quiet at six in the morning, and I quickly claim a nice spot by the window as *my* seat. Soft Christmas music fills the lethargic air, even though we still have a few weeks to go before the break. I guess even canteen personnel need those stupid, tacky songs to compensate for the stormy weather that has been tormenting us. It feels like our days have turned into an accumulation of rain and wind, the perfect portrait for my own feelings. It's hard to imagine that this part of the country gets hot during spring and summer.

I've been counting them, those days, mentally ticking each and every one of them off as they go along.

After an early morning rise and quiet breakfast, I head to the massive library to put in my first hours. Then, by the time the building is hustling and bustling with students who wander between their dorms and the canteen, occupying the hallways and the patio for an officially prohibited morning cigarette, I focus on school work. After classes finish, I quickly go back to my dorm to get changed and empty my mini fridge, then head for the woods and work on my metal bars despite the fucking rain, although that raincoat Arthur gave me comes in quite useful.

I carefully make sure to avoid everyone else while I quietly make progress in all my projects, and so far I manage pretty well.

It makes me feel as satisfied as it makes me feel empty. I miss Arthur's touch, and I fucking hate myself for it. Apart from his daily move on the chessboard, as the weeks roll by, he leaves me messages, every evening at nine.

Garde ta porte ouverte.

I don't reply, nor do I leave my door open. Nor does he use the master key to sneak into my room.

No, apart from my weekly meetings with Mister Montague and my chess nights, I am alone. A hidden character in Monterrey Castle's scene. Even the brotherhood hasn't sent me any invitations anymore, for which I'm both disappointed and grateful. Because I know it won't last.

Punishment.

The prison won't let me talk to Dad much. Barely one out of three times when I call, they'll put him on the phone. It's for my own safety, they say, though they have agreed to give me updates on Dad. He hasn't been doing well mentally, and outbursts of violence—though no one will provide me detailed information on those—are the reason we are not allowed to speak with each other at the moment.

He doesn't understand anymore why he's been put in that hellish place, fights it with claws and teeth. If that doesn't break my heart. For him, and for myself. He's angry with me, I know it.

I've let him down.

All those years of neglect.

Get in there.

Dad...

"Espèce de merde."

Please don't stop loving me.

Thoughts corrupt my mind as I make my way through the woods early in the evening, my backpack filled with food and books.

I miss Dad. Continue his punishments to keep his memory alive.

Do I make you proud?

When I finally make it toward the stables, it's already dark outside, despite it being barely six in the late afternoon. Checking my surroundings to make sure I'm still on my own, I light a candle. It might be cold here, but it's dry, and quiet. There are still no horses, but then again, not every student has a private horse. Typical for an elite school to have the facilities nevertheless.

Dropping my backpack onto the cold, stone floor, I continue where I left off yesterday, decorating the enclosure as much as I can with my leaves and twigs. It doesn't look as protected as the one I had at home, but it's better than nothing.

When I'm finally convinced, I carefully crawl inside and let cool metal freeze the clothed skin of my elbows and knees.

Yes. The feeling makes my eyes sting. This is home.

When I pick up my phone to dial the familiar number, part of me hopes they will refuse to let me speak to him. Part of me wants to hear his voice.

"Espèce de merde."

Because I'm afraid. Of him. I guess I always have been, ever since my mother left me there. Alone.

Tightening my hand around the iron bar, I squeeze my other hand around the phone, my forefinger drawing a pattern on my temple.

Dad can't come to the phone. I listen to the brief overview of his week from the guards while exhaling air on a slow whoosh. When I hang up, I just sit there, nothing more than a huddled shiver, as disappointment swallows me whole. I shouldn't be here. Yet, I am. I shouldn't stay here. Yet, I do.

It brings me down. Night after night I find myself in my iron den, juggling between early morning library sessions, school, and total avoidance of everyone. I pretend to myself it's okay, that I'm okay. My grades are fantastic, my sessions with Monsieur Montague fruitful, the start of my presentation hopeful. My counselor insists we talk more about my past, but I don't want to. Not with him. Not with anyone.

But no matter how hard I try, I can't seem to beat my craving for intimacy. And it certainly can't beat the self-loathing I feel because I desire that intimacy. But it's there, screaming the words in my head.

Arthur, I miss you. Miss your warm presence in my bed, your touch, your full attention.

So every evening when I sling myself up from the rain pipes and into my room, my eyes dart to my bed. Arthur is never there.

Part of me knows that he's waiting for me to leave my fucking door open, to make a move. But I won't. Can't give in now. If it comes out that he and I have been intimate, it might put Arthur's future in jeopardy. I'll be seen as the one who defiles golden boy's reputation and they'll all hate me.

I'm not sure if that's the real reason for my silence though. Perhaps I'm just afraid. Always, fucking afraid.

Pathetic.

It's a Wednesday evening when I climb into my room from my visit to the stables, body wet and freezing from the storm that turned the sand path into a mere muddy puddle that I've tried to avoid as best as possible as I raced back to my dorm.

I've barely made it inside my room when the sky flashes up with another thunder, casting an ominous light on the howling treetops. My limbs are dripping and stiff from being folded into the stern position inside my cage in the stables. Fuck, I'm desperate for a shower. Taking off my dirty shoes, I leave the rest of my clothes in a pool at my feet, relieved that I took the time earlier to change my uniform for a pair of sweats and a hoodie.

My body is flushed pink and feels like ice, making me hiss at the first contact with the hot, running water, before I slump back into a state of content. Fuck, this feels good. And damn…I tilt my head and let it lean against the wet tiles behind me. It's as if my exhaustion cracks for the first time, tearing holes in the layer of protection. Because I'm so tired. So, so tired. Of this killer rhythm of waking up early and being out a lot, of asking my mind to focus on so many hours of studying, of my heart for being locked up so tightly.

Tears leak out at the corners of my eyes before they dribble down my wet, puffy face. My tightened chest rages with grief, and nothing—not even my hands as I place them flat against my cheeks—can stop my ribcage from expanding on a desperate shudder. I nearly fold in two when I surrender, allowing for that wail to leave my throat. It's too much.

I cry, shaking as I sob and mumble strengthening words at the same time.

Come on, you're stronger than this.

No matter what I say, that raging storm inside me needs a way out. And so I stay there, leaning against the tiles, panting through my cries, and let go, emptying myself in shuddering breaths.

When it finally stops, I am left a quivering mess. It feels… fuck, it feels good. Quietly humming, I fold my hands behind my back and tilt my head until the warm water hits my face, washing sorrow away. I definitely feel lighter.

It isn't until I'm drying off, that I realize I'm humming "Jingle Bells Rock," some ancient song they always play this time of the year. Laughter bubbles up in my stomach and finds its way outside my mouth.

Christ, I'm going crazy.

Still, I can't help but grin stupidly as I get dressed into a fresh pair of boxers, my favorite pair of pyjama pants and a plain shirt. Brushing my teeth with a chortle clutched in my throat isn't easy, but I still manage. Much to my own… amusement. By the time I'm nearly done in the bathroom, I'm shivering once more, but this time it's not just because of the cold. Or because of fatigue. I'm feeling fucking light, and I have no clue what caused all my misery to just get poured out, like some unwanted venom.

But it feels fucking great.

I'm brushing my hair when my phone buzzes.

It's a message. Turning my back stubbornly to where I placed the damn thing by my towel, I resume humming. But that earlier feeling of euphoria is gone. Instead, the skin on my back itches, as if feeling exposed to my own glee. The only people who send me messages are my mother and Arthur, but right now is not their usual time.

The thought of my big stepbrother brings back bittersweet memories.

Fucking pathetic.

I pick up my brush and continue brushing forcefully through my unruly hair. Fucking phone.

It buzzes again.

"Leave me the fuck alone," I growl.

It buzzes again.

"Oh, for fuck's sake." Throwing my brush into the sink, I pick the damn thing up. It shows three new messages. I bite in my bottom lip while my heart starts pounding faster.

They're images. I suck in breath. It's him, Arthur. Sprawled out on his bed in nothing more than a pair of tight, black boxers. My dick responds immediately as it fills in my briefs. Fuck... he looks absolutely mouthwatering, his chiseled stomach and firm pecs glimmering in the dim light of the bedside table. That very same bedside table that...

"No fucking way." My head jumps up, and I catch my own, wild stare for a brief moment, before I turn around to peer through the open door, toward my own bed.

"Arthur," I gasp. My throat feels paper dry as I stare at him. There he is, on my lonely bed, legs spread. His raven strands are mussed, but his hooded gaze burns with a fury that matches his clipped lips. He must have gotten inside my room when I was under the shower.

"Régis." The word leaves his mouth on a pissy hum, and it makes me feel like I've been a bad kid at school. His eyes darken when he drags them over my body, taking in every centimeter of my flushed skin. When they finally creep up back to my face, his lips tick down, turning into something like a flower. Crooking his finger, he rasps, "Come here."

Shaking my head, I take a step back, for once not caring that I might not come across strong enough. Tonight I'm feeling too vulnerable to fight him. "I can't," I mutter.

"You can't?" He huffs in mockery, clearly pissed. "Well, if you'd have actually checked your messages, you would have read the one I sent you tonight. The one in which I sent you my ultimatum."

I blink, unsure if he's serious or if it's once more one of his pranks.

He raises a brow. "Judging from your look, you didn't even check your fucking phone. Have you actually received the messages I've been sending you? And Mom has been shit worried about you. Because you hadn't replied to any of your messages, I checked in with your counselor." His eyes sweep over the window, then back to me. "You were clearly occupied tonight. And the night before, and the night before..." His voice trails off, and he lifts his hand once more, crooking his finger. "Come here."

Balancing on one foot, I mumble, "I haven't been checking my messages." Guilt wraps itself tight around my heart. I hadn't thought that my mother would get worried about me.

I shuffle to my bed, then linger awkwardly, nails dug deeply into the flannel of my pyjama pants. Suddenly they don't feel like my favorite pair anymore, but a little silly, too colorful and all. My cock is rock hard, recognizing Arthur, and desperate to reconnect. My mind however, is a different story. It rattles and fumes as it tries to make sense of the tumbling emotions. Surprise. Joy. Lust. Fucking rage.

He pulls back the blanket and watches me crawl onto the bed, unable to refuse him now that he's finally here. I've missed him too much. He rolls me onto my side and wraps my leg over his strong thighs, tucking my head in the slope of his neck and letting his hand trail over my shoulder down to my arm, rubbing the clothed skin until I can finally let out a shuddering breath.

"What's going on with you, hmm?" He rasps, his breath tickling my forehead. "You let me into your bed, and then you ignore me for the weeks to come?"

"You were gone when I woke up." Pressing my lips tight, I wince at my reply. It's stupid, and weak, and—

"Is that what this is about?" I can feel how he dips his chin onto my head, feel his jaw work when he says, "I had to go to the library early in the morning. Dad got me a tutor to help me prepare for that qualification presentation." He lets out a heavy sigh after that and then silence falls over us. My stomach coils, a strange feeling fisting tight in its pit, and it's an unfamiliar sensation. "It has been fifteen days, Régis. Fifteen, fucking days."

Something shatters inside me, and I free my grip from his to look up, mind dazed, and slant my mouth against his, scraping his wet, bottom lip with my teeth. Desperation clings around my heart, cradling those steel bars that are permanently ground into my soil.

"Fifteen days of hiding," he mutters against my lips. "And I sent you a text message every freaking day. You never replied. We live in the same dorm, but you've been playing hide and seek for the past weeks. That game has finished now."

"I was—"

"No," he rumbles. "Don't give me that crap. We're all busy here." He licks inside my mouth, his tongue flicking against mine, while his fingers snake up and tilt up my chin, keeping me in position. My entire body roars to life, skin heating up behind the flannel garment, cock lengthening behind its restraints. "I want you to talk to me."

"No," I flatten my hand against his chest to push him away,

then roll onto him, reaching for my night stand to take hold of the lube that he put there. The bottle feels awkward and surprisingly light in my hands as I touch it for the first time. "I don't want to talk." No talking, no thinking, just for fucking once. "I just want to feel."

I've missed you.

"I've missed you," he breathes, and something explodes inside my chest. Crawling on top of him, I plant both hands on either side of his head. I can feel his dick pressing against my ass, and I need to swallow the violent moan that threatens to spill. "This can't carry on like this," he rumbles, his darkened eyes fixated on mine.

"Touch me." I grind into him, our hips connecting, our hot and hungry dicks glueing together as they rock in sync, causing bliss to tingle through my entire body. "If you can't make me forget, leave instead."

Arthur groans deeply, then snatches the bottle out of my hand. "You treacherous little kitten." He opens the cap and squirts a generous amount onto his fingers, rubbing them together as he glares at me. "Fifteen days of pretending." He slips a wet finger under the waistband of my pyjamas and into the crease of my ass. I gasp when he breaches the tight ring of muscles and scrapes unapologetically inside my hot hole.

"Fifteen days of avoiding me." He dips another finger inside my hole and rubs my tight channel, making my toes curl, and my eyes roll back. His lips are back on mine, a featherlight tease as his digits continue to ravage my insides.

My knees buck on a mewl, hips searching for more friction as I rock them against his fingers. His free hand creeps around my neck and squeezes, keeping me in place. I let out a desperate moan against the pillow.

"Fifteen days of …what? Mom's going to call you and ask how you've been doing, and you're going to tell her what? Dad's going to ask if you've joined the brotherhood and you're going to tell him *what?*"

Pulling me up with his fingers still in me, he lets my spread thighs sit on either side of his strong legs, my back arched forward. With my ass in the air and my face still on this pillow, he caresses the skin of my nape, tracing the shape of my spine until he joins his other finger at my ass.

"*What?*" He repeats on a hiss, followed by a sudden strike on my right ass cheek. I jolt forward when he crooks his finger, rubbing my prostate. I let out a moan of pain, of desire.

"What are you going to tell them, Régis?" He doesn't wait, but slaps me on my other cheek. I cry out, the pain a cruel sting to my skin, followed by the twitch of his finger.

"I—I—" My mind is swimming, and I let out another cry when he slaps me again. And again. And again. Rocking back and forth on his fingers, my ass is on fire, breath lurking in my throat.

"I don't know." I finally manage, then jump at yet another nasty slap.

"You don't know?" Arthur gives me an incredulous laugh. "I thought I'd made myself clear, little stepbrother. But perhaps you need a reminder?"

"No—" I whine. "Please." My ass is on fire, my cock hard as steel and dripping against my stomach.

Arthur caresses my aflame cheeks and I let out a shudder, trepidation building in my chest. "Please, don't. Not again."

"No? You say you don't like a bit of pain?" His hand slides in between my legs, and his thumb swipes up a bit pre-cum from my slit. "Hmm." I hear him sucking around his digit and letting out another shuddering breath. "Is that all for me?"

"No," I whimper, and he lets out a laugh.

Blanketing my back with his larger frame, I feel his wet cockhead prompt against my hole, then he slowly slides deeper between my cheeks, heading for my tunnel. Then he grabs me by the shoulders, and languidly pulls me back and into his lap, burying his cock deeper and deeper into my ass. I groan at the sensation, that intoxicating mixture of pain and pleasure. My ass feels hot against his pelvis, and our thighs connect.

"That's it, *chaton*. Clawing and mewling, and way too fucking proud for your own good. Your time of hiding is fucking gone. Now, one last time, what are you going to tell everyone who asks you who's taking care of you here at college?"

My head falls back onto his shoulder when I close my eyes. Full, I'm feeling so fucking full. I'm drunk on desire, on longing, as the heavy lit of craving is finally shattered to pieces, and its inside wraps around me. Holding close. Obsessive, dominant. Claiming.

"You," I whisper.

"Hmm." His hands reach for my hips and he starts grinding them into his lap for more friction. "That's right. I'm looking out for you. Now, ride your big brother, ride him like the little slut you are."

17

ARTHUR

Régis rolls his hips into my pelvis, the soft, hot skin of his nape brushing against my collarbone as he does so. His long neck is tilted up, beautifully arching as he gazes up at the ceiling, making those messy curls tickle my sensitive flesh.

I'm on fucking fire, cock throbbing inside the most gloriously tight and hottest tunnel I have ever fucked. My little stepbrother's ass. Dipping my head, I take in the handful of his round, perky ass cheeks, shimmering red by my hand, its tiny hole being invaded by my cock. It's one hell of a fucking sight.

I did that.

I slapped him, forced those words out of his mouth.

I am his protector, his guide through this darker world.

I am the one he'll turn to when things get too much.

Not his fucking dad.

Régis's nails dig into the skin of my thighs as he mewls. My lips trail the delicious curves of his shoulder blades, licking up the delicate lines of the skin right behind his ears. His skin is already glistening with a delicate layer of sweat, and its salty flavor mixed with that faint tease of eucalyptus and burned wood is intoxicating. I could clean his entire body with my mouth—lap up every single scent that is Régis.

He has left me fucking furious over the past days. For not coming back to me, even though I practically begged for it, for not needing more.

"I would have given you all," I rasp. Instead he avoided me like the stubborn fuck he is. Hiding in the library before dawn or in the fucking forest at sunset, making me feel conflicted as hell. I can't afford to be seen as anything less than strong. Not at college, and not with our brothers. I am the head of our family, the future leader of the Deverauxs. I shouldn't be dictated to by my little stepbrother, that little deviant who now moans raggedly while his ass keeps rolling, keeping my dick deeply buried inside his tight heat. But I believe that we have passed that phase. He's…fuck, he's been messing with my mind for way too long. I can't bear the thought of him hiding from me, of hiding his feelings from the world. His nails dig a little deeper into my flesh, tearing open my skin, making me wince at the exquisite sting. I watch my blood trickle down where it intermingles with Régis's flushed ass.

"Fuck, there's a good boy," I breath against the delicate dip under his ear, painting him with soft, open kisses. "Fuck yourself on my big dick. Get yourself off."

"Ugh—" Régis whimpers in reply, keeping his rhythm steady. More sweat leaks from his temple, where I eagerly lap it up, humming as I do so.

"Feels good?"

He doesn't reply, just keeps on grinding into my lap, breathing hard as he does so. When I crawl my hand around his tapered waist and touch his smooth stomach, I feel his muscles ripple under my touch.

"God, *chaton,* you're working so hard for me. Look at that. Taking my dick so well." He replies with an animalistic howl and his nails dig sharper into my skin. My fingers trace the line of his hard, strained cock, teasing the smooth flesh until I reach his balls. Velvety soft and so sensitive, judging by the way his wails become more urgent. He's close. Grabbing his hands, I yank them behind my neck, pulling him impossibly close. He lets me, for once unguarded and too slow to tense and rage, and push him face first onto the bed. I wish I could see his face, catch sight of those gorgeous blue eyes. So wide and innocent. Régis doesn't know how sweet he looks, how enticing his soft masculine features appeal to predators like me. With his hands immobilized, he falls onto the bed like a rag dog, ready for the taking.

And I fucking take.

One hand is around his cock, teasing his wet slit with my thumb while I pound urgently into his ass. I need this release so badly. After our first time together, and Régis's first time, I'd half expected him to come and search for me. Once again, I seemed to have underestimated the level of stubbornness my little stepbrother has.

"Please," he chokes, and his hips sluggishly move into my hand. I let out a chuckle, knowing that he hates it when I do that.

"Please, what, little slut? You need to come, hmm?"

"I, fuck—" He gives me another jerky roll of his lips, then moans.

"Tell me what you want."

He lets out a few curses and tenses his body. Fuck yeah, he's trying to regain control, trying to build up those guards, and it's sexy as fuck. Because I won't let him get there. Won't let him get up again and hide. Never again. My hand starts pumping his dick with a steady rhythm, and he wheezes.

"Tell me," I hiss into his ear. "What do you want? I'll fucking give it to you."

"I want to come," he finally cracks. Everything inside me

tingles at that small victory. My cock pulses, indicating I won't be lasting long either. "Please, I want to come."

"Yesss," I growl, stroking his cock frantically now. "Come with me."

His body shudders and convulses on a muffled shout, his dick pouring freely as his balls explode, followed shortly by my own mind blowing orgasm. Goosebumps erupt all over my skin when I collapse over Régis's body, caving his back and shoulders with my chest, as my chin lands in the crook of his neck. He's out of breath, panting heavily, face turned my way. His eyes are still closed when I drop a soft kiss on those lips of his, slightly parted and perfectly pink. Plush.

Fucking sweet.

"Come here." Getting up, I tighten off the condom and toss it in the bin, then grab him by his shoulders and nestle myself on my back in his bed, Régis tucked tightly against my chest. His cheek brushes against mine, eyes opening as he slowly blinks.

"I—hmm—" He yawns. Then he shifts his body, filling the curve of my side perfectly with his body. He sighs contentedly, releasing his breath in a whoosh of a tickle that lands on my neck. He does again, a soft buzzing sound that sounds much like a purr.

He has fallen asleep. And I'm left staring at him, wondering. There was something so fucking painful about hearing him sob, of watching those big, blue eyes red-rimmed from grief.

I dip my chin and gaze down, catching sight of Régis's unruly mop of golden hair and the side of his face—those curved lashes closed around his eyes, the straight nose with its slight curve at the end and those pouty lips. Soft puffs of air brush past them, making the long strands of his hair wisp at every exhale. He looks peaceful like this, and yet… "What the fuck happened to you, huh?" I ask the quiet air.

No one answers. No one ever told me about Régis's past. I know that it must have been bad, I'm not blind. Dad and

Nathatlie worked with lawyers and other experts for a while before they finally took his Dad to court. To prison.

I know that Régis had to go to a psychologist, and I also know he didn't go half of the time and stayed away, doing god knows what, during those hours.

Keeping my arm loosely wrapped around his tapered waist, I curl one of Régis's legs over my thigh to keep him in place. His face lands with a thud into the crook of my neck, his puffs of air now landing directly onto the sensitive skin of my collarbone. He doesn't as much as stir at the change of position. He won't talk to me about his past even if I had him at gunpoint. The realization makes something stir in my chest. It's...unusual.

People either give me what I want or...they give me what I want. Aside from the frustration, it's actually quite refreshing to be around someone different. Someone who keeps his secrets.

Brushing a curved lock out of his face, I squeeze his hold a little tighter. Yeah, he likes me to work for it.

I can do that. I don't care if he's off limits because he's my stepbrother, I'll deal with those consequences later. Leaning my chin on his soft hair, I hum for a bit, thinking, then whisper,

"I'll find out, *chaton*. I'll find out what happened to you."

That's easier said than done though. I make a few calls home to subtly inquire about Régis, but with our parents being so careful with him, I need to be careful and not draw any unwanted attention. Of how I've been sneaking into his room lately, claiming his bed and his body for most of our nights. It doesn't work, with Dad steering the subject back to myself and the business every single time. He wants to know if I've already begun preparing for the qualification presentation. Where I want to live after graduation. When I'm available to join him and the M&A team to go to Spain and visit the wineries we are interested in buying.

It's... a lot.

And the odd times I am lucky enough to get Nathalie on the phone, she doesn't elaborate, keeping their secrets to herself. My own planning is rigid as hell and doesn't allow me much thinking outside of my perfectly laid out road to my future.

Every morning I get my ass up before dawn, making sure I leave my little stepbrother's room before he wakes up, and creep back into my own bedroom. Sometimes Louis joins me for my morning run, although I only allow him to tag along if he can keep his mouth shut. I love my brother, but won't have his chatterbox around me too early. I need to focus. Need my well-built morning work-out before I dedicate the rest of the day to my studies. Hard work is paying off though, my weekly grades are assuring me that I'm by far the strongest of my year.

The pressure's high. Even though no words are exchanged, we both know the truth. I need to win the *Prix d'Honneur*, need to excel in every fucking thing I do.

It's a Friday when I finally stomp back up the stairs after classes have finished. I'm more than ready to traditionally kick off my weekend. Before, we used to do that with champagne and a blowjob, but I'll solely opt for the first one. Louis still gets his, and like the true brother he is, he cannot stop from reminding me of my old habits, and how I have turned into a boring douche.

Smug fuck.

He's got a point, though. I'm restless, can feel it in my fucking bones. There are too many balls in the air, too many challenges I need to get control of before they become a true menace. I had expected to spend more time with Dad now that I'm in my final year. Had anticipated being baptized more into the business by now. But he's holding off, and I'm unsure of why that is. And that feeling lingers, making me a little jerky. I don't get insecure, have never had a reason to feel that sensation since I've been protected by family and wealth my entire life. But this newly found sentiment is creating something that gets alarmingly close to discomfort.

Dad checks in regularly to ask about Régis, and despite what I tell my little stepbrother, I always feed Dad with the same information. Régis is doing well, integrating more and more and receiving excellent grades. And yes, after that one little gaffe which was nothing more than a misunderstanding, he has presented himself at the Initiation of the brotherhood and has performed his role.

Exceeding my expectations.

Fuck, my little stepbrother. I'll never admit it out loud, but that's where my real fucking problem lies. Because he's a walking liability. An unstable whirlwind of secrets that makes him erratic. He's unintentionally mysterious, his secrets much more obvious than he thinks. And still, he's a closed book who has somehow wrapped Amadou, Dad's bodyguard, around his little finger. I know he's filling his fridge regularly, but with a full operating canteen, I wonder why. I'll figure it out.

Julien has been tracing his paths, but apart from Régis spending his after school hours outside in the rainy forest, he is mostly in the library. Or in class. And since a few nights ago, in bed, with me. Naked, trembling, desperate for my touch.

That's right. No more waiting fifteen fucking days. My little stepbrother awaits me in his bed, every night of the week, just like I told him to.

Those moments have become an unofficial ceased fire between us, as if our rivalry is valid between the hours of six in the morning until eight in the evening.

It makes me fucking restless.

Because he is unpredictable.

I have spoken to his teacher, Montague, but the twink won't give away anything about Régis's subject for his presentation.

Unpredictable.

And yet…I can't stop myself. Can't stop myself from coming to his bed every night, from inhaling his enticing scent and wrapping my stronger hands around his delicate frame. From brushing my lips against those lush curls and purring into his ear. Because I love how he responds, whimpering even when he snarls at me to go away and leave him in peace. I love how he quivers against my hold, my cock buried deep inside his ass, and mewls for me to go on and never let go.

Never let go.

That's a long, fucking time.

"Arthur, hold up!" It's a Friday afternoon after class when I make my way up the stairs. Outside the storm is raging, screeching and roaring as it clatters against the arched, floor-to-ceiling windows that take up the entirety of the wall across from the stairs. A light flickers, right before I turn to face my brother. He's soaking wet, football shorts stuck to his thick thighs and his tee plastered against his wide chest.

My lips twitch at the sight. "Let me guess, football practice finished early?"

Shaking out his wet hair like a dog after a bath, he shoots droplets all around, grinning as he catches up with me. "Not even." Together we climb the stairs. "Coach makes us work really hard this year," he mumbles. Following the narrow hall toward our room, Louis leans against the wall, a shivering mess, while I unlock the door. By the looks of it, we are the first ones to arrive.

"Get in." Kicking open the door, I nod at him to go first.

He pats my shoulder as he passes me, his wet hand making goosebumps scatter across my shoulder. "Thanks, bro, I'm gonna head for the showers first thing."

Following him inside our bedroom, I watch Louis as he dumps his duffle bag in the corner, toes off his football shoes, then rolls off his knee socks. "Fucking hell, everything's soaking, fucking wet."

I huff out a laugh. "Yeah, gotta love an outdoor sport."

He grimaces as he hopscotches for balance, then tosses the wet socks right by his shoes. Lifting his hand to pull his shirt over his head, he says, "Yeah, well, let's just say that the others finished practice a little earlier than I did."

"Oh?" I frown. "What the hell did you do?"

Louis shimmies off his wet shirt, followed by his shorts, then tosses the whole lot in the hamper. In nothing but his boxers, he saunters to our bathroom, where he halts and turns over his shoulder. He shoots me a crooked grin, but I don't miss the slight flush on his cheeks. "Got a warning for bad behavior."

My brows shoot all the way to my hairline. "A warning for bad behaviour? Does that even exist? This feels like old school, dude."

"Yeah, well—" He shrugs, then walks inside the bathroom, clearly not wanting to elaborate. I'm about to call him out on it, when I hear the front door open. I turn around, hoping that it's Régis, only slightly disappointed when I catch sight of my cousin. Gaël hops in, gaze searching around. He grins when he catches sight of me. "You guys are already here? Sweet. I'm thirsty."

Deciding to leave Louis and his suspicious excuses, I walk back into the living room. "You got it." Grabbing two bottles of Moët & Chandon from the fridge, I stride back to the couch, where Gaël's already plopped down, his naked feet propped onto the coffee table. His green eyes flash when I hand him the bottle, the glasses already on the table.

We polish off our first glasses with random chit-chat about the week. Right as we empty our first bottle, Louis heads out of our bedroom, joining us. He's back in his normal black sweats and a Harvard University hoodie I don't recognize, holding a small, golden box that he passes to Gaël.

"Here, Aunt Marie-Louise sent you some new lotions and creams by the looks of it."

"Sweet." Gaël puts his glass aside, tears open the sides, then peeks inside. He smiles. "The new collection of edible lotions have arrived. Can't wait to try these on Dominique."

Louis lets out a huff as he pops the second cork. "Save me the details, bro." Then he sets the bottle to his lips and takes a large gulp.

"Dude," Gaël nudges him in his side and I laugh when my brother jerks, nearly dropping the damn champagne onto the floor. "We use glasses for those, you ass."

"Hey, it already comes in a glass." He takes another drink, then wipes his mouth off with the flat of his hand. "Fuck, I needed that."

"He got punished on the football field for bad behaviour," I specify. Gaël's eyes turn wide as they dart between me and my brother, as he lets out a snicker.

"Yeah, well, I'm not the one pounding into my little stepbrother's ass every night." Louis points the bottle in my direction, a dirty smile on his lips.

"You fucking ass," I growl. "I told you not to—"

"Oh, wait, what?" Gaël's eyes flash with surprise. "What?" He asks again when none of us answers. Louis has at least the decency to look guilty, and knowing him, those fucking words just slipped out of his scandalous mouth, but still. Fuck me.

"It's not like that."

"No? Then how is it?" Gaël asks.

"Well, we—" I stutter, ignoring their sniggers, mind rattling. Frankly, I haven't got a clue on how to finish that phrase. Because it's exactly like that, and when Louis's chuckles turn into a loud bark of laughter, I feel like flinging the entire chair right at him.

"So it's true," Gaël drawls as if tasting every word carefully. He waits a beat, but when I don't rush to convince him of the contrary, he lets out an amused huff. "And I told Dominique he was imagining things. Turns out that he was right."

"It's not like that, cous. Asshole," I mouth to Louis when he's finally recovered enough to fill up my glass. He sends me a wink in return. When he puts back the bottle, he leans back into his seat, folding his hands behind his head as if he's waiting for the show. Apparently, I'm not the only one who's not willing to take the bait, because Gaël takes a sip from his glass, then says, "You'll tell me when you know what it's like, okay? On a more serious note, our brothers are getting more and more restless."

I nod, perhaps a little too eager. "That teacher Montague sure as hell doesn't make himself popular by changing the selection criteria of the *Prix d'Honneur*. I also heard that he does things differently in the classroom." I haven't really, but I don't like the fucker. He's too close to Régis.

Gaël hums at that. Louis doesn't reply, but when I eye him, his cheeks are a little flushed.

"Well, we have another initiation planned for tomorrow," Gaël continues, hands folded together under his chin. "I've asked Dominique to play." He waits a beat, then continues, "I think we need to do things a little differently, if we don't want the guys to go for Régis. They all seem to be taken by the idea of getting their hands on the outcast of the group."

"He's with me," I snarl before I can think twice.

Gaël's gaze flickers with mischief. "Yeah, I know that now." He lets out a low whistle, eyes darting to Louis, then back to me. "Who would have thought? Still… and I know that you've made your claim and all that, but perhaps it's time to show the others too?"

Louis snorts. "Show the others? What the hell are you going to tell Dad?" He shakes his head. "He's Nathalie's son, man."

"I know that," I snap. Releasing a heavy breath, I rub a hand over my forehead. "This is exactly why I didn't want this to happen. It's too complicated, it's inconvenient."

"But you want him," Gaël deadpans.

"But I should fucking hate him," I huff in annoyance, nodding at Louis when he approaches with the bottle.

"But you can't have him," Gaël pries, his eyes hooded with that scrutinizing gaze. "Or...can you?"

"Let's keep him safe first," Louis decides. "Let's get the brothers to focus on charity tomorrow instead." He slides his phone out of the pocket of his sweatpants. "I'll call Dad."

"The brothers need to get laid. They need to let off some steam," Gaël adds. "Don't tell your dad that." Louis grimaces at that.

There's a short knock on the door. When it swings open, the wind swoops a window out of its hinges. It opens with a bang, filling the space with freezing air. My gaze flicks outside, toward the wailing tops of the large evergreens, shaking through the darkened air like it's the plaything of the devil himself, and can't help but wonder...is Régis out there?

"Oops, sorry." Our favorite sex toy comes walking in, a slender hipped beauty Louis and I hire every Friday evening. And while Louis still hires him, I merely watch, but don't participate. *Not anymore.*

Right now, he swings his silky strands over his tender neck, then gives me a doe-eyed smile. "Hi, gorgeous." That's right. He's my *previous* sex toy.

"Not him. Come here, baby." Before I can answer, my brother has swept the smaller male onto his lap. They both cackle at that, and my brother makes a show of cascading his hand down the escort's waistband where he grabs hold of a firm ass cheek. Gaël sends me an exasperated look as he hops up to close the window. "Delicious," Louis purrs. "Damn, sweetheart, you've got me all hungry again."

I am, too, and while the escort is cute and pretty, my appetite is solely focused on one single guy I can't wait to devour. Suddenly, a light cracks through the pitch-dark sky, electrifying the outside air. He better fucking not be out there. I growl at the thought, and before I think better of it, my phone is already pressed against my ear. That asshole better have his eyes on my kitten.

"Where the fuck are you?" I snarl the moment Julien picks up, earning a surprised gaze from all three men in the room. While I listen to Julien blabbering about being in the gym, Louis feeds our boy champagne from the bottle. With an annoyed huff, I go to the fridge and pull out another bottle.

"He's downstairs playing chess, Arthur. Jeez, he's really got you wrapped around his little finger, hasn't he?" Julien sounds properly annoyed, and it pisses me off.

"You better watch your tone," I threaten, refusing to let him make me feel like an even bigger idiot.

Julien splutters a reply, but I'm no longer listening. The phone vibrates against my ear, and I check the caller. It's Dad.

"Make sure he stays there and doesn't go out in the storm," I can't help but sneer, always needing to have the fucking last word. Slamming the fridge door shut with my hip, I turn around and toss the bottle at Gaël, ignoring the way his eyes flicker with amusement as he gets to work at opening our drink. "And Julien? Don't fuck this up."

Gaël pours me a glass and I follow him to the couch as I greet Dad.

"*Comment ça va, mon fils?*"

"Good." Sagging down onto the cushion next to Gaël, I grab hold of my glass and take a sip from my drink. Louis is working the escort's ass as he lets him drink some more from the bottle, and in my peripheral I see Gaël sitting cross-legged as he checks the contents of his box. The tiny bottles of oil clink sharply in the background as Dad debriefs his week. As it turns out, the due diligence report I worked on during the summer break helped our finance department with our final preparation toward yet another winehouse, this one located in Italy.

"We should soon be able to make an offer. I'll try and see if I can bring you with me, depending on the date."

My chest deflates a little as I relax into my seat. "That would be really cool."

There's some rustling in the background, then Nathalie gets to the phone. "Hi Arthur, how is Régis? Is he with you?"

"No, I'm sorry, he's not." This is only one of the countless moments that she's asking me this question, her disappointment thick though she never lets it out. Gaël looks up from his oils with a wicked grin and I roll my eyes at him. A few more hours, then my kitten will be back with me. In bed. "He's playing chess downstairs." She lets out an approving sound at that, sends me kisses, then Dad's back on the phone.

"I see that Louis just called me on my other phone, but I can't reach him." My eyes catch sight of my brother rolling the escort's hip over his own as he lets him ride his cock, his chest plastered against the guys's back. Our boy's head falls back and his eyes search mine as he bounces onto my brother's lap, giving me a salacious smile.

"No, Louis is busy. Football practice. But I know why he called you." I blow a kiss to the escort, then grab my glass and head for the bedroom. Kicking the door shut with the back of my foot, I amble toward the window. It's still howling outside, with heavy rain and stormy gusts coating the forest. "We discussed tomorrow's gathering with the brotherhood. There's been some tension. I can't put my finger on it, but the guys are agitated."

Like cats seeking their mice.

"Oh, explain?" Dad asks, sounding genuinely worried.

"Our brothers have trouble concentrating."

They want to hunt.

"Our brothers need a change."

They need to claim.

"Our brothers need to be motivated differently."

They need to fuck.

Dad hums. "To be honest, Elder Jacques mentioned something similar. And Régis has been attending our gatherings?"

"One so far. But Louis and I think that for tomorrow, it might be an idea to focus on charity instead." I empty my glass in one go while Dad contemplates my suggestion.

"It's too early, don't you think?" He finally asks. "Masks only go down after *Réinvention,* which is only in a few weeks time. Only then can you all communicate freely. Speaking of, Nathalie wants to make this year's Christmas even more festive by doing an outdoor seafood barbeque."

"That sounds great. Dad, why don't we invite a few elite members for tomorrow's gathering? They can talk about charity, and the importance of donations to the less fortunate. We can keep our masks on."

Dad lets out a long sigh. "Alright then," he finally agrees. "I'll see what I can do. I'll call you back when I find a few volunteers at such short notice. But right before Christmas, it won't be easy."

"Thanks, Dad."

I hang up and check the time. It's already nearly nine o'clock. We somehow still managed to fill the time with nothing but bullshit and bad jokes. Leaving my glass in the kitchen, I ignore the sound of Louis's grunts and smacking balls.

"Just got a text from Dominique." Gaël's still working on his oils, unbothered by the fucking going on right beside him, his phone discarded on the couch. "He'll head back in half an hour or so."

"Good." That means that I'll be waiting for Régis by then. Freshly washed and very naked. In his bed. "Dad will pull some strings for tomorrow evening."

"That's great. Oh, Arthur—" He calls out, right when I turn to leave. Turning over my shoulder, I jut my chin. "You've got to think of a way to get this approved, bro."

I narrow my gaze. "What?"

Gaël grins. "Don't play dumb on me. You and your little stepbrother."

"Oh, fuck off dude." Flipping him off, I want to turn for my bedroom, but change my mind at the last second. The master key gives me access to Régis's empty room within less than a second. On second thought, I prefer using his bathroom for my shower, just to rub it nicely into his adamant, pretty head that I'll have him anyway I like.

18

RÉGIS

A touch, slick and taunting, distorts the cool, concrete floor on which I'm kneeling. Grabbing the iron bars tight, I blink at the crumbling walls of my bedroom. Dad's shouting grumble echoes through the gravel as the entire place seems to collapse.

We're disappearing. No! The words get stuck in my throat, but the only sound that leaves my mouth is a long moan. My eyes flutter, and I squeeze tighter, knuckles turning white from the effort. It doesn't stop my room from dissipating into a void.

And I'm still here, panting like a dog when that slippery tongue repeats its pattern of lapping, slow and persistent, right through the crease of my crack. The iron cage is gone.

"Fuck," I choke. "Feels good." My gaze dips and time stutters as I rock into the touch and just let myself get transported back to my bedroom. Back to Monterrey Castle. Fuck, I was far, far away. But now that I've returned, I can't keep my eyes away from this magnificent view. Arthur's lying between my thighs, his veiny hands keeping my ass cheeks apart. His black hair's a disheveled mess of strands that fall over his forehead, between which he peers up through dark, thick lashes. His tongue peaks out and caresses my ass again, hands squeezing my cheeks as he spreads them further apart. "Oh, god." I blink again, awareness slowly returning. I jerk my hips.

He chuckles lowly, then dips his tongue further and inside my body. My knees shake as my hips jerk. "No escaping now. Look how you tremble for me. You like that, don't you, *chaton*?"

"Yeah," I admit in a whisper, still feeling vulnerable after my bad dream.

"I'm going to fuck those nightmares out of you." He flicks his tongue around the tight ring of muscle, and when I relax at the touch, he lets out a satisfied rumble. It's fucking sexy. And then he dips a wet finger inside me and I moan, craving the sting, that delectable cocktail of pain and pleasure, of being claimed and giving in.

"Yeah..." He rasps. "Take my finger like the good little slut you are. See how your ass is sucking it in, wanting more." He swirls it around a few times as it reaches deeper inside my channel. And then he hits my g-spot and I squirm in ecstasy. Another finger dives in, pistoning my tightness. Fisting my mouth, I mewl and buck, writhing on my sheets as Arthur has his way with me. When he finally rolls the condom around his rigid shaft and coats it with more lube, I shiver in anticipation. "Remove your hand, little stepbrother. I want to hear you scream."

He goes slow at first, easing me into the intrusion. But once he's filled me completely, he gives me a wicked grin that promises trouble. "Go on, claw at me. Hiss and arch your back and growl at me. Fight me." He grabs my leg and lets my calf rest on the crease of his elbow. Then he does the same with my other leg, before leaning his hands down beside the pillow, bending me in half, and my knees touch my chest. "*Allez*."

"You cocky bastard," I snarl, and his darkened, pupil-dilated eyes twinkle with glee.

"Yeah. Give me more."

I try to give his head a kick with my knee, but I can't put any force without being able to use my foot. My foot, that's uselessly dangling over his shoulder.

Arthur lets out an amused laugh, then pulls his cock entirely out of me. "Fuck, I like you like that, Régis." He gives me the shortest of moments and a filthy once-over, then he pummels back in. Hard. My hands grab hold of his sides as they hang on for dear life. He bows his head and his lips find mine effortlessly, brushing together in between puffs of air and moans of pleasure. With every thrust he hits my prostate, making my cock swell achingly, desperate for release he won't give me yet.

"Always fighting," he mumbles inside my mouth. "You've always been fighting me."

"That's because you're always challenging me," I breathe. "Always making me feel inf—oh, fuck—inferior."

"Yeah?" He pulls back his mouth just enough for him to look at me. Onyx eyes with the tiniest slither of gold. Fucking mesmerizing. "That's because I feel the need with you."

"Why?"

He crashes his mouth back onto mine, his lips wet and full as they rub against mine. It brings a jolt to my cock and I squeeze his sides a little tighter. "Because you are a threat, Régis." His eyes are back on mine, teeth coming out as they dug at my bottom lip. He rolls his hips firmly against mine, his huge cock filling the entirety of my ass, plunging that prostate mercilessly. "But look at that, your claws aren't sharp enough for me. You can't lock me out anymore."

I free my mouth from his teeth, then tilt my face to gain access to his neck, its flesh so smooth for my tongue. "And how's that?" I can't help but ask, then lap at the tender skin. Arthur shivers, then swears.

"Just like that, *chaton.* Just like that. But you won't have me."

What? I blink my eyes, but he doesn't say anything after that. He just fucks me, brutally, with unfaltering rhythm that makes me crumble as I pant for release, begging him with soft whimpers that sound pathetic to my own ears. I can't help it. I need it, need him, so fucking badly.

When he finally wraps his hand around my leaking cock, I can cry with relief.

"*S'il te plait*," I weep. "Make me come, I need to come."

Arthur presses kisses on my forehead, nose and both my cheeks. He takes my lip hostage between his teeth and nibbles at the sensitive skin.

"Come for me, *chaton*. Come."

I explode on a muffled cry, cock pulsing savagely while my hips jerk. It feels fucking amazing, violently so, as the orgasm rages through me. Arthur lifts his hands and presses them under my nape, splitting me even further in two as he pulls me in impossibly close. Fucking me so hard, his rhythm fast and hard, his abs rippling as he rocks his hips.

"You are a drug, baby," he snarls, his hot forehead touching mine as he keeps on going. "A fucking drug." And then he comes on a howl, his entire body shivering as he fills the condom with his cum.

We stay like this, panting heavily with our foreheads pressed together, our breaths intermingling as we chase more touch. More connection, our burning flesh touching in relief. When he finally releases my legs, he takes his time to massage the joints, bringing the blood circulation back. And then he pulls me close and against his back, arm wrapped around my waist. He often does that, rolling me onto my side and into him. It must be his favorite position.

"Today Christmas break starts," he finally says.

"Yeah." I'm not looking forward to this break. I'd rather stay here and focus on my studies, in peace.

"We're all going home," Arthur continues, as if he just heard my thoughts. He presses a kiss on my nape, then squeezes his hold around my waist tighter, letting out a satisfied sigh as he does so. "But Régis? We'll come back to Saint-Laurent for a short break in a few days. Just like we did last year."

"You mean when I caught that escort with his mouth on your dick?" I can't help but sneer. He chuckles lightly at that, the sound ticking my ear.

"Exactly. When we ended up in the forest with Julien."

"The guy in that cloak." The memory makes me shiver. "The first one I met and the lover of Dominique's older brother."

"Yeah." His voice is barely a whisper. He waits a beat, then, "But this year, you'll be coming for your pledge."

I don't speak, the earlier feeling of satisfaction slowly replaced by that usual sentiment of self-protection.

"You either pledge to the brotherhood or you leave college. You know this, right?"

I know this, but… "I wish things were different," I whisper. He doesn't speak for a moment.

"I know, I do too," he finally breathes.

Much later, when classes have finished for the day and everyone's about to head home for their break, I catch Maxime and Dominique chatting downstairs. Maxime's already in his woolen parka, his arm wrapped around his friend's shoulder as he barks out a laugh. When he sees me with my suitcase climbing down the stairs, he lets go of Dominique.

"I'm so jealous of you, you know that, right?"

Glancing between him and Dominique, I raise a brow. "Uhm…no?"

Maxime laughs. "Because you guys get to spend two weeks together! Not me, I have to fly up to Paris to spend time with my Mom and grandparents. Ugh." He leans in and squeezes both arms around me. "Life's not fair. Anyway, have a great one.

Luckily my grandma will be there too, and I can't wait to try some of those chess moves you taught me on her. See if she still wins." With a last shake of his hand, he heads off and follows two bodyguards who are carrying his luggage outside the castle and toward the parking lot.

"So..." Dominique turns my way, his dark hair styled in his usual messy look. "Are you looking forward to Christmas?"

"Is he right? Will you be joining Gaël?"

He smiles, then nods. "Yeah. Though my parents have agreed to join us for Christmas day. We will be going on a holiday then, just the three of us. When you come back here..." his voice falters. "I can't be here then."

My chest pangs as his true meaning clicks. Three years ago, almost to the day, Dominique's brother drowned. It happened the same night the Alpha Fraternarri rewrote history, as they like to call it. This is the brotherhood I am supposed to pledge my allegiance to. Here. On school territory. Because he wanted to reach his secret lover.

I dip my chin in understanding. We linger for a moment in one of those comfortable silences I've come to recognize and appreciate, a peaceful stillness that allows both of us to gather our own lost thoughts.

I can't even imagine what it would be like to lose someone I love as much as Dominique loved his brother. I...don't think I've ever felt that way before about anyone. I mean, I still speak to Dad every two days, but these days, he can only snarl at me. According to the prison doctor, he has gone into a depression and apparently my phone calls are the light in his days. I usually make them from my den in the stables, somehow feeling a little less guilty of the fact that I still can't visit him because of that restraining order.

Recently, the den has felt too small, cool iron cramping my limbs. Despite the books I keep in there, the place doesn't comfort me as much as the one at home did. It's too cold, too lonely out there, and I am increasingly apprehensive of cloaked figures huddling around. Maybe the promise of warm, firm hands wrapped around my body is too sweet.

I sigh inwardly. Maybe I'm getting too soft.

Arthur is right. I'm nothing more than a stubborn cat, clawing and hissing, but unable to stop him from circling me, backing me up, cornering me.

It scares the living shit out of me. His hold on me, the way he seems to make my defenses melt. No matter how much I fight him, no matter how much I snarl at him, he just laughs it away, only to come back with full force, rolling over my borders like he owns a goddamn army.

But I won't be defeated. I can't. If he sees what a pathetic sliver of a man really is hidden behind the veil that is mine, he will retreat.

All the people I love go away. And I will be alone again.

I need my iron.

Punishment stabilizes my troubled mind, keeps me in check. Orders are easy to follow.

I'll be good.

But secretly, I love this newer version of Arthur. Ever since he somehow claimed his space in my bed, he's started talking to me. He's been sharing some of his concerns, asking my opinion on mostly business matters. When we lie in bed at night, and he holds me tight, it's like the animosity between us is temporarily set to non-active. It's like my bleeding heart is not leaking for once.

Arthur pries his way inside my head. Makes me question things I never thought would be heard in the wide world. Me. My voice. He wants to hear its contents, wants to hear my thoughts.

"If you believe that all humans are equal, do you also believe that we should all be given the same chances?"

"What about criminality? Should we reintroduce the death penalty?"

"What punishment does your father really need?"

So far, he hasn't asked me what really happened between the four walls of our cramped two-bedroom apartment in Nîmes. I wonder if that's because he already knows, or doesn't care?

Yeah, Arthur makes me share things I never thought I'd say out loud with anyone one day, because I didn't think anyone would care.

I don't know if *he* does, or if it's simply part of his bigger game. I never know with my older stepbrother.

Next to me, Dominique clears his throat, his way of starting a conversation. "Did you bring your portable chess game?" The question makes me smile, taking the weight of my heavy thoughts, and I point backwards at the backpack I'm wearing.

"Of course. Which is why I'm so happy you'll be joining the Deverauxs."

He doesn't call me out on my little slip, and I decide that I don't care for now. After all, going to their big mansion by the sea wasn't my choice. Instead he huffs out a chortle. His eyes shine with something. Is it me, or is he also relieved?

"Oh, sweet. Then we won't get bored." His eyes glitter.

"Who mentions boredom?" We both turn our heads, only to find Gaël sauntering over in his obscene fur coat. Hooking an arm around Dominique's shoulder, he pulls him close. "The cars are here, *trésor*. I've arranged special entertainment for our journey." I don't miss the way he sends Dominique a salacious wink. "And I will promise you this, you won't be bored."

Dominique rolls his eyes dramatically.

Louis approaches us with that usual swagger, jaw working as he chewed gum. His shirt is only half tucked inside his pants and his tie is loosely wrapped around his neck. His cheeks are flushed. "Alright lovebirds, time to roll." When I look past his shoulder, I catch sight of Mister Montague and send him a clumsy wave that I regret instantly.

"Happy holidays."

His smile is small, the look in his eyes sincere. "You too, Régis. And the rest of your family." Sending me a final nod, he turns around and walks away, heading for the South Wing... which I think is a bit odd, but there's no time to think. The guys have started walking toward the outside parking, and behind my back, the castle already feels cold and empty. Not the kind of place I want to linger on my own.

Outside, three familiar SUVs are already waiting for us, Amadou and Didier chatting on the hood as we arrive. Upon our arrival, they jump up to help us with our suitcases. Our feet crunch into the gravel as we move forward surrounded by students getting ready for the break, eagerly wishing us happy holidays as we pass. Both Gaël and Louis casually greet their friends without slowing down as they make their way to the cars. I follow behind, the inner turmoil increasing with each step. I wonder where Arthur is, but I cut the thought short immediately.

"Mister Régis." Standing right by a shiny black SUV, Amadou waits for me with a warm, wide smile that makes me feel strangely comfortable. He reaches for my luggage. "It's good to see you again. I hope that the mini fridge was to your satisfaction."

Watching him put my stuff in the back of the trunk, I let out an unintelligible mumble, feeling both grateful and a little awkward about Amadou feeding my unhealthy habit. The one that has kept me going over the past month.

My thoughts shoot back to the stables and my iron corner of comfort, chest tightening with something sharp, something close to nostalgia. That place is mine. I created that, in honour of my past. Because of my inability to let go of my pain, of this desperate void of loneliness that seems to haunt me even in this place. Although its walls have been breached multiple times now.

Right before he can open the door, I grab hold of his upper arm and gently squeeze. Amadou's dark, chocolate gaze lands on mine. They look friendly, his eyes. Always have.

"Yeah. I mean, uhm… I don't know how you managed to get that sorted, but thank you." His smile widens and he dips his chin lightly.

"*De rien.*" He swings open the door and I sit down.

Right next to...

"Mother." My brain stutters, mind coming to a halt, before it slowly picks up in first gear. She smiles, green eyes glimmering like the matching earrings that dangle into the curve of her neck, where they meet with the scarf that's wrapped around like a colourful collar.

"I wanted to come and pick you up, *chéri*. To see how you are doing?"

In the front, doors are closed as Amadou settles in the driver's seat."Everyone's here. We're leaving," he announces. Turning over my shoulder, I watch Monterrey Castle slide deeper into the background until only the Christmas decorations in the garden are visible. Lights adorn the stone walls of the building, tracing some sort of shape that's still unclear because of the sun. I wonder what the castle will look like at night, deserted and lit up. A shiver brushes over my skin, leaving nerves in the pit of my stomach.

By the time I finally turn back, we have left school territory, our SUV following the one that transports Gaël and Dominique.

"I wanted to see how you are," she asks softly. "Since you haven't replied to my messages."

Rolling my lips, I wrap my hands together, fisting them into one ball. "I'm fine."

There's another silence and we both watch the car slowly

make its way through the forest. When we reach the main road, my mother asks, "Do you still call your father every two days?" When I don't answer, she lets out a heavy sigh. "What do you need from those phone calls?"

"My life?" I snap, regretting it immediately.

She shakes her head as if in denial. "I didn't mean it like that." Her voice has turned into a mere whisper. "Have you been sleeping in your own bed?"

The words are a blow to my heart, and my hands clench tight at the increasing pressure. "Uhm…"

"I know, Régis." Her voice breaks and she lets out another of those long sighs as she rubs her legs. "I spoke to your dad."

"What?" I snap my head, searching her eyes, but she's looking straight ahead, avoiding my exasperation.

"I don't think we've had such a heart-to-heart in a long time," she mumbles. "He told me about your punishments. Of where he locked you in, sometimes for hours. He's a sick man, Régis." When she finally turns, her eyes are wet with tears. Something fierce flickers through that emerald stare. "I didn't realize how sick he was until I talked to him." She sighs on a shudder. "I—I promised myself I wouldn't talk about how sorry I am. Not today. You know this, you know I would give all the money in the world to take back our past together. I know you've been in touch with this young graduate who wanted to take on your father's case. But I'm begging you, *chéri*, stop fighting us. Your father won't ever be set free again. He doesn't deserve your love, Régis. He's bad, and what he did to you was a sin."

My heart's galloping in my chest, and I press my hand against my ribcage to try and get it under control. It's no use. Hurt and regret make it beat too fast, fear adding that sting that always makes me aware of everything. Of danger. My mother grabs my wrist, and I try to pull back, the touch a burning sting that makes my chest heave. I don't want the touch, don't want it, it's not good… Then she curls her smaller hand around mine and squeezes a little. Something clicks inside of me, my flesh feeling hot and cold and heavy with sorrow.

"Breathe, my love."

Breathe. Arthur's husky voice echoes through my mind. My mother squeezes my hand again. I suck in a big puff of air that expands my entire ribcage expands.

Breathe.

I repeat myself, taking in big gulps of air that make the tremble in my head dissipate slowly.

"Are you feeling better?" She finally asks.

I swallow, then nod. "Yeah." My voice sounds a little raspy, but we don't care, both too busy staring down at our intermingled limbs. Time dips.

"So…" My mother shifts in her seat, leaning our hands onto her leg. "You have been sleeping in your own bed then?"

I shake my head, then slowly bring it back to a nod. "*Oui.*"

She hums, as if she was expecting that answer, then lifts her gaze until it burns onto my face. "With Arthur?"

"What?" My head snaps up, but I can't avoid the way my cheeks heat. Searching her eyes for something—anything—that helps me understand how on earth she can ask me this question. "This is—" Ridiculous. I want to yell. My cheeks heat with embarrassment and something close to anger. "Has he—" I cut myself off. *Has he told you?*

That fucking asshole.

Mom gives me a thoughtful shake of her head, then sags a little further back into her seat. "Alright, we'll figure this out later. Now, tell me about this presentation of yours for the *Prix d'Honneur.* I'm so proud of you."

I blink, unsure of what to say. A cocktail of emotions swim through my mind, too slippery for me to grasp and understand. Does she seriously know what I have let my stepbrother do to me? How has he been on my mind ever since I met him, and that I crave to have him near, despite my anxiety?

And if so, is she just parking that subject to discuss school instead?

"Useless boy. Get in there."

I wince at the memory, but can't help the way my fingers clench and unclench, missing the grounding feel of metal. I wish Arthur was here.

Swallowing, I force myself to keep up, to keep it cool, to stay strong. "Well, I told you about Mister Montague, who's been helping me."

"Yes?" She smiles, radiating a sense of relief I feel too. Talking about my studies is easy. I can do that. Running a hand through my hair, I clear my throat. "Well, he has convinced me to do things a little differently, without it being too innovative. So, instead of giving a traditional presentation in front of the board, with slides and all, I'll go for interaction. I am thinking of asking other students to read out quotes I'll randomly hand out to them, and to have them share their opinion on some of the topics to create a discussion."

My mother cocks her head in thought. "Do you know which other students will be there?"

"No. Why?"

"If you can find out in advance, you can adapt your questions to the most suitable student. To get a better debate rolling." And just like that, we have reached safer grounds. My mother is sharp in her questions as she challenges me for content. It's...nice. We discuss my presentation topics, then move to my classes, to the courses I'm taking on. She's curious, interested, and open-minded. I can really use some of that.

By the time we finally drive through the gates of the family property, the atmosphere in the car is light, and we've shared all kinds of topics. Student life, friends, but also new plants they have recently added to their floral collection. And when I hop around the corridors of the mansion a bit later, followed by Amadou and my luggage, only part of me is surprised to catch sight of the beautiful, giant white bird of paradise that's waiting for me inside my bedroom.

She did that. For me.

19

ARTHUR

Christmas this year is different from any of the ones we've celebrated before, and I'm not just talking about the dishes Nathalie has chosen—a seafood barbecue.

We're all crowded outside on the heated terrace, dressed formally in crisp white shirts underneath sleek black tuxedos. My stepmother looks angelic as she plays the perfect role of hostess, despite the other guests all being family.

Dad had some business relations over for an *apero* before, the champagne tasting that much better with a signed deal in our pocket. The second most luxurious wineries in Spain are now ours, and I'd be lying if I said I wasn't proud of the way I participated in the project. Six more months and I'll graduate. That should make me feel…elated, but something treacherous twitches in my stomach.

Personnel is setting up the piano by the pool under Dominique's scrutinizing eye, the sloping green grass melting perfectly into that mesmerizing sight of the Mediterranean Sea. Gaël has somehow managed to get his hands on Régis, who's looking uncomfortable as my cousin smears some oil onto the flat on his hand, most likely describing the function of yet another of his perfumed greases. He's a pro like that, an insistent motherfucker. Still, I grin at the sight, then turn, only to catch my brother's stare. Louis is talking to my uncle, but when I meet his gaze, he gives me a knowing smile. With a huff, I retire back into the house.

Last year's Christmas resembled a pitiful collection of family members who tried too hard to fit in two perfect strangers. The result? A strained diner that lasted for fucking-ever until Régis could finally excuse himself and head for his room. Only then had the fog dissipated and had Nathalie turn into the loving woman we know her to be.

Régis...

Through the windows I gaze back at the outside party. My little stepbrother is still talking to Gaël, and even from afar I catch his careful smile while my cousin talks to him in his usual smooth, seductive way. Gaël has always been a player, a blond-haired seducer with skillful hands. Hands that he only keeps on Dominique, ever since he openly and officially claimed him as his. By the barbeque, Louis, Dad and my uncle bark out a laugh at something, a comforting rumble I grew up with. Family. Love. Perhaps the biggest privilege I've ever had.

I've never questioned my upbringing, nor our family values and opinions toward the world. We all felt the same, thought the same, played the same.

A smooth chortle shoots my eyes back to Régis. He's smiling at something Gaël says, his head tilted back as he exposes his straight, white teeth and that adorable blush. My chest rumbles at the sight of those wavy, golden locks and his eager, blue eyes. I don't know what my cousin told him, but it has done the trick. His guard is down.

Grabbing two glasses of champagne from a held-out tray, I'm on my feet and ready for the door before I can think things through.

"Arthur." I startle from Nathalie's voice, coming through the kitchen. She's standing by the kitchen island, a purple kitchen apron covering most of her black dress, a glass of wine in her hand. Next to her stands Gaël's mom Marie-Louise who throws me a smile before she gets called out by my uncle. I watch her leave, then turn to face my stepmother.

"*Oui?*" There's something about the way those bright, green eyes look at me that makes me feel unnerved. A slither of nerves crawls through my spine, and I try to cough it away, but it won't stop freezing my back on its way up to my neck.

Nathalie gestures to me to come closer. "I've got you something."

I crack a smile, but it feels forced on my face. "I thought we already unwrapped all the gifts?" When I reach the island, my eyes fall to the picture she's holding in her hands. When she reaches up to show it to me, I notice that they're shaking.

"This is the only photo I have left of Régis."

My nerves turn into ice as I look at the image of a young boy with a mop of golden curls and a cheeky smile on his sweet, little face. In his hands he's holding a bouquet of wild flowers the size of his head, his two, small hands tightly wrapped around them.

"He always loved flowers," Nathalie breathes. "Those first years of his life, we often visited my parents, who had a huge garden. My mother would take Régis into the garden and they could spend entire afternoons out there, just being outside. Being surrounded by green."

I swallow, but bile forms a big lump in my throat, spreading a feeling of discomfort all the way from my throat to my chest.

He still does, I want to say.

"That's...nice," I settle with.

Nathalie smiles at me, her eyes glassy with unshed tears. "I know about the both of you, Arthur," she mumbles. My lips part in shock and I suck in a sharp breath, but before I can come up with anything to say, she waves with the image. "You don't need to say anything else right now, but my son is troubled. He has suffered a lot, he has—" She lets out a shuddering puff of air, and a single tear rolls down her cheek. With a manicured fingertip, she wipes it away and her lips curl into a regretful smile. "I am going to leave this photo on here for one hour. If you are serious with my son, you take the picture and keep it safe. We will figure out how we will do things. This must be as hard for you, as it is for me. If you're not—and believe me, I will understand—you leave the picture to me. I will take it back, carry it close to my heart, and we will never talk about it again." She nods my way. *"D'accord?"*

My chest heaves as I can just stare at her. Surely she can't mean that she knows, *knows*? "What do you—"

"Don't, Arthur. I know all about forbidden love, and we can work with it. But don't give me any lies." Dropping the photo onto the counter, her demanding gaze finds me. "One hour," she murmurs, and then she's gone.

I spend the next fifteen minutes in my bedroom, pacing around restlessly, allowing panic to rise, swell in my chest, and deflate again. A whirlwind of thoughts invades my mind but I can't see clearly anymore. How the hell does she know? Is she bluffing? Do I want her to bluff? Is there a way out for this forbidden connection that we both feel?

Régis is troubled. Does that mean she will tell me more about him if I put my cards on the table? Would Régis *want* me to put my cards on the table? Something suspiciously close to insecurity rumbles through my stomach, and I don't like it one single bit. Still, when there's a loud knock on my door, I jump, growling at the person who's caused me to startle.

"Chill, bro," Louis comes in, looking identical in his matching black tux and white shirt. "What the hell are you doing up here? I can feel your distress all the way in my own heart." I notice that his usual smile is not spread across his lips. Instead, his dark gaze eyes me wary. "Talk to me."

"It's nothing, man."

"It's Régis." He narrows his gaze.

Relieving the air in a big whoosh, I nod slowly. "Nathalie. She knows that something's going on between us. I have one hour to show Nathalie that I'm serious about him."

This time Louis's brows rise up to his hairline. "O-kay? Explain."

I tell him about the photo, of her implications, of the possible way out and I reiterate to him once more, why nothing further can happen between me and Régis. It's because of who I am. Of the expectations others have of me.

"You could have both," Louis mumbles, putting his finger exactly on the sore spot on my heart. "If you—"

"What? If I keep up our family's reputation?"

"I was going to say, if you can handle our little s-brother. He's going to need a lot of love." My heartbeat picks up into a steady ruffle at that thought, my body clearly already having made up its mind. "I think that Dad already made a start with forbidden romance by marrying a homeless woman." We both chuckle at that. "Your biggest challenge is Régis. You'll need to convince him that you want him." He lets out a cackle at that. "I still can't believe it, man. You are always so fucking furious whenever he's around."

"Yeah, well I'm still not too keen on the whole thing."

"Liar." Louis claps me on my shoulder, then pushes me toward the door. "And a bad one. Now, let's go grab that photo and enjoy today. The rest you'll figure out as you go along."

He looks sweet in that picture. Fucking *sweet.*

My phone rings again and as I clumsily try to retrieve it from my suit pocket, I nearly stumble against the sink. Fuck whiskey.

I check the caller ID. And fuck, of all people, of course it's Julien. I've got no time for that twink. If he's got something to say, he can send a text message. Fumbling the phone away, I hear the guys laugh outside on the patio. Dad, my uncles, Gaël and Dominique, and Louis.

"Get your fucking act together," I growl at my own reflection. My eyes are a little bloodshot and I make a face at myself. Clearly a lightweight.

Tucking the photo back in the inner pocket of my jacket that hangs loosely over my shoulders, I notice that the papillon is missing. I must have lost it somewhere before when we decided that the heated courtyard was the perfect spot to start a dance floor. My family isn't anything if not known for throwing a party. Some of our business relatives stayed a bit longer, despite it being Christmas, and Dad went all the way in opening a few bottles of 2015 Petrus that must roughly cost over three hundred euros a bottle. When someone proposed to play a game of poker, I couldn't refuse. Even won a few games. But when the whiskey got introduced...yeah, that doesn't mix well with my structural lack of sleep.

Then Régis went upstairs, and for me everything went downhill.

"Arthur! Have you fallen asleep, my man?" Gaël calls, banging on the door, too loud. He's clearly tipsy as well, judging by the way he grins at himself.

"I'm coming," I growl, sounding way too irritated. I'm feeling cold and petulant, and I don't want to be down here anymore. When I open the door of the bathroom, I catch sight of my cousin, who's leaning by the wall, a vague stare in his green eyes. Yup, he's drunk.

"Come on." I grab him by his shoulder and he giggles like a girl when he leans in to me, stumbling over his own feet. "Let's get to bed."

Gaël yawns loudly, then falls into another fit of laughter that makes me chuckle, as we visibly suffer to climb the stairs.

"Paracetamols and water, coming up," I hear from behind me. Dominique follows us up, and once we've reached the spacious hall on the first floor, he passes me a bottle of water and a strip of pills, before grabbing hold of his lover.

"Guest bedroom is in the right wing," I say, the words sounding like a slur of consonants. Fuck, I'm definitely drunk. Without watching them leave, I wobble to my bedroom, where I chuck down half the bottle and two pills. Then I take a hot shower, that makes me feel both drowsy and a lot better.

By the time I am dressed in a pair of sweats and a shirt, it's past one. Régis has gone to bed over an hour ago, so he'll be asleep. I don't care.

Creeping through the corridor, it doesn't take me long to get to his bedroom in the far corner. Tucked away in safety just like he needs. The door's unlocked when I turn the knob, and when it opens it shows me the sleeping silhouette of my little stepbrother. He's curled up into a ball and has placed multiple pillows against the back of his frame to make the sleeping space even smaller. I carefully put them onto the ground, then slip in behind him, pressing my chest against his back, locking a leg over his thighs while my hands wrap around his slender waist.

And then I breathe in, deeply, allowing my mind to come to a stuttering halt. I fall asleep with the scent of eucalyptus and burning wood in my nostrils, with his firm, warm skin on my fingertips.

It's a routine we pick up over the next few days. Much like the habit we started at college, we do our own thing during the day, only to find each other at night. Though something has definitely changed.

The picture I carry in my pocket.

Dad's daily meetings that prepare me for life after graduation.

And then there are Régis's daily trips. He goes back to Nîmes, I know he does. I fucking hate it, hate that he needs to go through this phase of confrontation with his past as part of his healing. Sometimes I wish I could cure him by simply cutting him open and taking out his hurt, bandaging the wound and stitching him back.

"I went to visit my grandparents grave with my mother," he tells me one night, a few days after Christmas. "It feels familiar to walk around the streets of my own neighborhood." He's lying like a corkscrew around my limbs, chest touching mine, his head tucked under my armpit, leg sprawled over my legs, his arm spread across my torso where our hands are squeezed together.

"But does it feel good too?"

Looking up, he blows a strand out of his face, eying me on a shrug. "Good? I don't know. It's just familiar."

"But does it like…I don't know, help you to feel better?"

"I'm not sure," he mutters, then rolls his head back into the curve of my arm.

"You can't always keep on going back in time." I'm a little hesitant, but when he doesn't protest immediately, I continue, "The time has moved on, things have changed, and you are still there. You're holding onto things that have disappeared." I squeeze his hand a little tighter as I focus on the way his heart beats furiously against my chest. "It's time to move on, *chaton*. Don't you think?"

He doesn't look up. Instead, my words bring silence. A tense one. One that can burst into a heated argument at any given moment. But as it lingers, the only sound the beating of his heart between my ears, I decide to give it another push. "Tomorrow we're going back to school for one day."

"I know," he mumbles, making me frown into the dark.

"You do?"

"Yeah, Louis told me."

Louis…my soft, cocky jock brother who seems to have developed a soft spot for our little stepbrother. The thought makes me smile.

"Alright, so you know what's going to happen then?"

He shrugs against my collarbone. "I guess. You guys are going to reconstruct an army to relive history?"

"Yes. 1789, the Revolution. Although in your case, I guess it might be your opportunity to rewrite your destiny."

I can feel his smile against my Adam's apple. "Yeah, you've told me this before."

"And I meant it."

This time it's him who gives me a little squeeze. "Some things…" He swallows against my flesh. "Some things are hard to change. And some people won't let go, you know? Even if you try hard. It's like they don't want to make that lost time, that past you're referring to, slip from their hands. They want to keep it…keep me."

"Yeah," I mumble against his golden curls, inhaling deeply, cherishing his scent. "I know. Just keep on wrenching away, and they'll eventually let go."

"I hope you're right." His breath tickles my flesh, and goose-bumps scatter around the delicate skin of my clavicle. He mumbles some more words, but they get lost against my flesh. I've heard them though. And they make my chest swell and bring a stupid grin to my lips. Who would have thought?

Mon coeur.

My heart.

PART III

CONCESSION

"Allons enfants de la Patrie, le jour de gloire est arrivé!"

Two rows of lined-up uniforms stood tall and proud in the cool forest. Apart from the faint brush of the wind through the treetops, and the sound of rustling fabric, no one spoke. They'd been prepared before, during their pledge. Pupils had turned into brothers, masks had been taken off and tension had slowly melted into relief. Students, they were students. Just students.

Now they were all here, outside, set up as an army. For the occasion, or for the thrill they'd put on their Venetian masks again, the glorious colours somehow matching the soldiers' hungry, determined gazes. Because in front of them, out there, in the pitch-dark, were the red cloaks. Exclusive sex workers who performed the role of commoners. What once had been played out, would have a different outcome today. Tonight, the elite wouldn't falter.

In front of them, the hint of movement, followed by a flick of dark red.

"Aux armes, citoyens. Formez vos bataillons..."

Monterrey Castle had become their safe haven, and had provided everything from shelter to a breeding place for the Alpha Fraternarii. And tonight, with their new brothers fighting at their side, they'd win the war.

"Marchons, Marchons."

They'd beat the stubbornness out of those who're supposed to obey, not to reign. They'd make them bend, then stumble to the ground. And then they'd show them who was in charge.

Réinvention.

Alpha Fraternarii, the most powerful brotherhood in France. We. Rewrite. History.

Every year again.

First there'd be the hunt, then the reward. Sex. Lots of it, their needs filled to the brim. They'd play and win, share their trophies, share them as they'd fuck them. Supremacy.

Aristocracy shall live on?

"Brothers of the Alpha Fraternarii, tonight's the night." Their

commander sat on a horse. His uniform, made of a blue coat, red piped with white collar and cuffs, white piped and red lapels, blue piped red cuff flaps and shoulder straps, white turnbacks piper red and brass buttons, matched the others'. It was the exact replica of what the elite soldiers had worn in the late 18th century. Riding on his horse, he took his time to look everyone in the eye. "We're all here."

Where are you?

I'm here.

"And they—" He waved with his rifle across from them. "Are out there, waiting to be found. They have been bad, and they know it. We'll hunt them down, won't we?"

There were cheers from the crowd. Two more horses appeared, their riders wearing identical uniforms and golden masks.

Where?

Here.

"This is for us all. Because we value traditions, show loyalty and respect. We respect!"

More cheers.

I'm scared.

"What are we going to do?"

"We'll hunt them down!" The crowd hollered.

"We'll make them yield and punish them." His horse reared with a loud neigh while the commander raised his arm to the air.

"Punishment, punishment."

Through the darkness I can barely see. Someone fires a musket and I cringe, fingers touching cold iron that very moment.

"Punishment, punishment!" They hooted.

"Make them yield." The commander shouted, followed by the eerie sound of movement.

The ground trembles around me.

The battle has begun.

Where are you?

All around them, brothers started running as they started the hunt. A cat and mouse game with only one outcome. A satisfactory outcome, in this case. Of fucking. All around them, everywhere. It would only take a matter of time for the battlefield to turn into one, deranged orgy. The elite would win, its weight heavier on the scale. Its power superior. Just like in real life.

They'd turned unhinged in the name of history.

My entire body trembles and I grab it tight, squeezing the unyielding, cold material as I stay still. If I stay silent, they won't find me. If I stay silent, he won't find me.

Except, he always did. Always found me, always punished me, always threw me in and dragged me out.

Always a punishment.

Someone howled and dove forward, another shouted in laughter. The best games in life were those which were cruel. Ones with a single outcome.

The musket fired, its sound a loud bang in the trembling forest as horses passed them by in a run. There were brothers everywhere, the first slaps and moans breezing through the woods. All around them, commoners were falling, showing their white flags in defeat before they'd get what was coming for them.

Carnage. Pleasure. The best fucking in their lives.

In the name of history.

20

ARTHUR

With a click of my tongue, the horse picks up speed, riding fast. We're practically flying through the shrubs and trees as I make my way through our self-proclaimed battlefield. Tonight's not as cold as last year's *Reinvention* by far, but still my body trembles as my gaze sweeps my surroundings.

"Where the fuck are you?" I grumble through gritted teeth.

Around me, it's a salacious mix of pure lust and pretend rage. Some soldiers are still marching around, laughing and joking as they call out what they're going to do once they find their red cloaks.

"Punishment." The word shifts through the air, where three other guys are bending over a woman in a red cloak. They have shifted up the delicate material to above her waist, showing off her naked ass as it gets plundered by one of them. I look away, the sight too familiar and not helping me to calm the fuck down.

There's something else though…

"Ssshh." I clack at the horse to calm down and steer us toward where a guy is standing alone, facing the lake. It's the same lake where Damien, Dominique's older brother, died exactly two years ago. He's turned his back to me, but when he hears me coming, he turns around, his mask already moved up to show me his identity.

"Julien?" I ask. "What the fuck—"

"You have to go to the stables." He stares up at me. "I've found something. I called you during Christmas break, but you never picked up. Come on." Without waiting for me to follow, he just starts running over the sandpath, back to where we came from, nearly running into the chariot that bumps over that same trail, the blue and yellow flag fluttering in its speed. Inside, I catch a glimpse of two guys fucking.

The speed of my heart picks up, matching the increased jog of the horse as I follow Julien through the woods.

When we halt in front of the deserted stables, he places a finger in front of his lips, gesturing to me to be quiet. There's a soft glance in his eyes, one I can't decipher.

"Two years ago, I lost my love. If you would know the number of times I begged for time to go back, for me to change its outcome." He inhales deeply, steadying himself and his emotions when his hand reaches out to grab the wooden porch. "I'm sorry, Arthur, and good luck. But I just couldn't let this happen to anyone else."

Pinching the bridge of my nose, I frown. My heart beats erratically. "What the fuck are you talking about?"

"You wanted me to find out about Régis. I never thought it would be like this." He takes a few steps from me, then halts and turns. "And don't put on your flashlight," he whispers, then he's gone.

As I peek inside the shed, something skids inside the back of my throat only to slowly descend, unfurling and tightening my chest in its wake. The place is cold, humid, but aside from that, it's empty.

No.

I strain my ears at the sound of the softest of sobs.

It's not.

My heart ruffles painfully inside my ribcage when I zoom in on the sound I'm so familiar with. My little stepbrother. I know it's him.

Unsure if I should make my presence known, I hesitate for a few seconds. "Régis?" I finally whisper, then jump at the sudden bang of the rifle.

"Punish them, soldiers!" Someone shouts.

The sobbing inside the stables increases in volume, and I can practically smell the bitter scent of fear.

"Oh my god." I stride inside the space, determined to comfort Régis and bring him back, but immediately bump into a brick wall. "What the..." I grumble, brushing the dull ache from my forehead before switching on the switchlight, despite what Julien said before. I can't see shit and frankly, hearing my little stepbrother sobbing, makes my inside capsize with worry. Still, as I make my way further inside, nothing prepares me for what lies before me.

Inside the shed, against the wall in the far corner, stands an iron cage. And inside is—inside is... I freeze.

"Régis?" He's curled up behind the metal bars of the cage. No, not a cage. It's fucking kennel. Meant for an *animal*. My heart thumps painfully inside my ribcage, fluttering and tightening and making me sick at the sight of my little stepbrother, who has been put inside this prison like some sick joke. "Who—who did this to you? I'll fucking kill them." In less than three steps I am crouched down by the kennel, my fingers already on the chain. "They even locked you up? What the hell. Tell me who did this, *chaton*. Tell me." Opening the door, I reach out for him with both hands. "Come here."

He coils away to the furthest corner.

"What the—Régis?" I frown. With my flashlight pointing straight at the ceiling, there's only a glimmer on my little stepbrother's face. But I see enough. "What's going on, baby?"

"Please don't punish me," Régis sobs, his voice deadly soft, barely a whisper spoken between us, as he repeats it again and again. It scratches my insides, making my chest ache and tense.

Realization hits me hard. He put himself in here. *He* did that. That...breaks my heart.

Régis' gaze drifts, even though his eyes are trained on me, most likely flicking through his own memories. Searching, but what is it that he recalls?

Exhaling on a deep shudder, I fight my increasing jumbling thoughts. This entire event is one big fucking trigger for my little stepbrother. Why did that couselor not raise a red flag to anyone in the family? Surely they must have talked about all of this?

Why didn't he tell *me*?

"I'm not going to punish you," I mumble, reaching a little deeper inside the kennel. "I promise you, I won't hurt you. But it's cold here, and you're shivering. Can I touch your hands to lead you somewhere safe?"

Fuck, he looks so incredibly fragile, a cloaked mess with his head tucked beneath velvet. That means he didn't even make it to the actual line-up, unless he's wearing his uniform under the heavy garment. He's still wearing the white mask adorned with flowers. The one I gave him.

"No, I—" I can feel his burning stare through the faint light. "I want you to u-understand. I'm broken. You—you..." He shakes his head, then drops his chin back to his chest in defeat.

Unsure of what to do, I stay put, my hands still lingering inside the cage, before I force myself to pull them back and carefully place them on the outside of the bars.

Silence lands over us as we sit there. Régis sits in his cage, and I am leaned on my hunches, guarding the entrance. At least the door's open, though he's still too far from me to comfort him.

We stay like this for I don't know how long. At a certain

moment, the outside noises dim, meaning that all soldiers have now moved on to their moment of relief. Meaning that the battle is over, and the horses will come back at some stage. I send Amadou a quick message to come and get us.

"Back at home, Dad used to throw me in a cage." The words are barely whispered. He pulls up his mask and slides it back against his forehead, sweeping the golden curl out of his face. "For punishment. I hated it. Hated feeling so helpless. Hated to be bad. But with time, I—I guess I got used to it. It meant that he was at home. He—he wasn't often at home, but when he punished me, I knew he was there. It meant I wasn't alone."

I gingerly slide my fingers over the bars and into his direction. This time he doesn't seem to notice, his chin still fixated on his chest as he continues his whispers and finally shares those horrific experiences.

"I don't even know why I'm telling you all this." His body shudders in an attempt to shrug, and my chest strains.

"I am here." Rolling my lips in concentration, I take those five extra centimers and cover my digits with his. He flinches, but doesn't remove his cold fingers. I exhale in relief.

"I was afraid of being alone," he finally continues. "But I was also afraid of him. You see, Arthur—" He looks up, blue eyes glassy with unshed tears. "I've been good, right? I joined the brotherhood, did what you all asked of me. But when they talked of p-punishment, my insides turned into ice."

"And you came to hide here."

Régis nods in confession.

I look around the storage space, once more realizing that I need to get him the hell out before anyone returns. "Is this where you go when you stay away for hours?" Bile rises in my throat, and I can't help squeezing my eyes as I await his reply.

"Yes," he murmurs. Something explodes in my chest. Oh fucking god, he must have been so alone. So afraid.

"I don't—" Looking up, I realize that my vision is unclear,

watery from tears that leak from my heart. This is fucking killing me. "Can you please, *please* promise me to stop doing that? We'll figure it out."

His body shudders. "I'm pathetic. Always afraid, always fighting everyone off. You don't—"

"No." My other hand reaches out before it connects to my brain and carefully grabs hold of his cloaked forearm. "This is not on you, Régis. That fucking bastard had no right to do those things to you." I pull him closer, surprised that his body moves forward and into my grip without a fight. It doesn't take much effort to haul him out of the kennel and into my arms. His large, wet eyes peer up at me, matching my own sadness. "He'll never hurt you again," I promise. I mean every fucking word of it.

Régis' smile is small and fragile, and his teeth are clattering. Still he wraps both his hands around my neck. I can't ignore the gesture of complete trust, and I'd lie if my chest didn't puff up because of it. To have him cling onto me like the true kitten he is, sniffling and opening up, fills me with the strangest feeling of honor. He's surrendering to me. My hands reach out around his nape and squeeze him tight.

Despite the tenderness of the moment, I can feel him smile against my cool skin.

"Is my big stepbrother softening up?"

My own lips curl up at the words, and a final tear drops down onto my cheek. I leave it there to roll down, then lick it away. My hands are full anyway, too busy scooping up Régis as I finally manage to drag him out of the kennel completely.

"Maybe?" I tease, then turn serious again. "But this is not how you go down, little stepbrother. My rival is strong, fierce, and a stubborn little fucker."

We stay hidden in the shed as we wait for Amadou to arrive. All the while I beg for my brothers to stay away. Régis doesn't speak again, but he has stopped trembling. I have placed my blue jacket over his shoulders, keeping the cloak tight around his huddled frame as he leans in and against my shoulder.

"Will you tell me everything?" I ask, breathing in his hair. I want to know more. I want to know fucking everything. "Please tell me everything."

He doesn't reply, just hangs against my chest, his chin against my clavicle. After what feels like a long and short period at the same time, headlights appear, pointing our way. Régis whines in my arms, but the moment he hears Amadou's voice, he ticks on my arm in the need to be out.

"This way, sirs." Without as much as a flinch at the way Régis is curled up into my touch, Amadou holds open the backdoor of the SUV.

"Thank you," I hum, sliding myself onto the leather seat with Régis tucked into my arms. I wonder if he has fallen asleep.

"Where to?"

"Home." Régis whispers, the sound muffled against my shirt. Amadou looks up, and catches my stare in the rear mirror. His brow creases. It's no secret that he has a special relationship with my little stepbrother.

"Home?" Without waiting for a reply, he puts the car in drive.

"By the sea," I clarify when the car bumps over the uneven path toward the main entrance of the castle. Judging by the other cars we pass over the sand lane, tonight's event has finished.

I dip my chin to face my little stepbrother, guiding his head for more comfort until he touches the backseat. His golden, wavy hair partly teases my shoulder, only to flurry up with the regular puffs of air that leaves from his plush, parted lips. Lips that disclosed most horrific experiences. Lips that haven't been kissed by anyone but me.

His long lashes adorn the upper part of his cheek. Cheeks that flush so beautifully when he's fighting me.

I love it when he fights me.

Reaching out, I gingerly brush some of his hair from his temple with the tips of my finger. His skin feels cool, frail.

I love it when he opens up to me.

"Are you sleeping?" I whisper. He doesn't react. Tracing the rest of his jaw, I can't help but go through the earlier events. I follow the shape of his nose, small with a slight upturn at the end, his other cold cheek, where I equally brush some honey strands away, then scoot a little closer and tuck him back against me. His head lolls a little, before it lands right in the crook between my shoulder and neck, its shape perfectly fitting the snug space. His hair tickles my nose and mouth, and he lets out a soft murmur, but otherwise keeps on sleeping.

"You scared me tonight," I whisper, wincing at my own words. Fuck, he better not hear me. Looking up, I catch Amadou's curious glance once more, and scowl back in return. The fucker had better haven't heard me.

It doesn't take us too long before we finally reach the sea. The gates open, and the SUV drives onto the gravel lane and toward our house. "Is my brother home yet?"

"No, sir. Didier is still out, waiting for him."

I frown. "That's a bit late, isn't it?" Checking my phone, I see that we're nearing three in the morning. It's not like Louis to go home this late.

"I don't know, sir, I haven't heard from them. Would you like me to check?"

"No, it's okay." With my free hand, I quickly shoot Louis a message. "Open the door for me."

Amadou rushes out of the car after he's parked it in the garage and opens my door, then steps aside so I can carry my little stepbrother outside and into the hall, then up the stairs and inside his bedroom. He has a nice room with a view of the sea. I bet Dad and Nathalie did everything in their power to make him feel at home. But if they know what truly happened in that house, they have some explaining to do.

"Do you need anything else?" Amadou asks once I've draped Régis into his bed and tuck him warm under his sheets.

"No. You may leave." I catch Amadou looking down at Régis, then back up at me, before he slowly blinks. Then, after a slight nod, he ambles toward the door and closes it behind him with a soft click.

He knows. He fucking knows. Yet I can't make myself to care. Instead I take off my jacket and the thick cloak, shimmy Régis' slender hips out of his pants, and leave him in his boxer briefs, the blanket snugly tugged up to his chin. Régis shivers, then murmurs some more, before he turns onto his side, his back toward me. When he scoots a little away from me, I accept the invitation, toe off my shoes and slide into the bed behind him while awkwardly getting out of my cloak, shirt and pants.

"I can't stay," I muse inside his ear. But I'll savour this moment.

He lets out the softest of replies, barely audible, but they make my insides rattle with contentment.

Merci.

The vibrating sound of my phone wakes me up from a restless sleep. Too short. Blindly grabbing behind me in search for the source of annoyance, I inhale another delectable whift of Régis—eucalyptus and burning wood, mixed with his own, unique scent—before I roll onto my back, phone in hand.

"Yeah?" I grunt on a rasp.

"Arthur? Where are you?" It's Louis. Blinking my eyes furiously, it only takes me a few seconds to remember. Last night, the hunt, the search, the cage... I shift my head to Régis. He's still lying on his side, his hair covering most of the chiseled features of his face.

"I'm at home, you?" Absent-mindedly, I brush them away.

Louis lets out a bark. "Yeah, I figured, but *where* at home? You aren't in your bedroom. It's eight in the morning, and Nathalie and Dad just got up. I suggest you do the same thing."

"Shit." Tossing my phone back on the floor, I lean in and slowly brush my lips over Régis's head, then press a kiss on his ear. "See you later, *chaton*."

I meet up with my brother in the work-out room, but other than attacking me with a few of his typical smart ass looks, he doesn't comment. In fact, we don't talk at all, simply focus on our training program in silence. It has been a short night for both of us, and judging by the way I catch his dark eyes staring into the void a few times, I reckon he's got a few thoughts of his own. We'll talk about it when the time is right, like always.

When I finish my last set of crunches, I get up, and grab my towel and bottle of water. "Catch you at breakfast."

The hot shower does the magic trick to my tense body, though my entire morning ritual is disturbed by my thoughts. I…I want to know more. About Régis's past, his therapy, this abuse he's been through.

When I come downstairs, Nathalie is already inside the kitchen, setting the table. When she sees me striding her way, her green eyes flare with something, but she blinks it away.

"Oh, Arthur, would you mind helping me set the table?"

Dad's sitting at the kitchen island, reading his newspaper. I can feel him look up at me in surprise when I reply, "Yeah. I fucking mind. You and I need to talk about something. *Now*."

"Arthur," Dad barks. "Watch your mouth."

"It's okay, Jean-Luc." Nathalie dismisses him with a wave of her hand, and smiles at me. Knowingly. "Sure. Follow me."

We head toward Dad's office.

"So, you two talked?" She asks immediately once the door

falls closed. I watch her take a seat onto the couch, gesturing to me to do the same thing.

"How can you be so calm about this?" I seethe, dodging her question since I'm not allowed to talk about *Reinvention*. "You *knew?*"

Nathalie watches me come closer, but it isn't until I take a reluctant seat across from her, that she nods. "Some parts."

"He made him get into a cage."

Her eyes glisten. "So he told me."

"He told you? And you didn't—"

"His Dad did."

Oh. We stare at each other in shock. Words form an utter mess inside my head, creating a big, dirty mess.

Nathalie lets out a long sigh. "He likes you. I can see it in the way he looks at you, hear it in the way he snarls at you."

"Now's not the time to discuss who he likes."

Nathalie cuts me off with a single hand. "You like him too. You took that picture, so I trust you're serious about my son." Her green gaze collides with mine, keeping me in place. "I know this is not the most conventional love, but I won't judge you for it. I hope that he will trust you and you'll do the same in return. Only then can you forge a stronger future out of the shatters of your past."

"I—" Glancing down at the fisted hands that lie in my lap, I overthink her words. Love. It's such a big word. I never thought I wanted to love someone, to claim that special person. I have no time for love. It sounds lame. Like one, big, fucking lie.

"It won't be easy to win him over," Nathalie continues. "But apart from bringing in the best help he can get, and talking to him, again and again, trying to make him talk, I don't know what else we can do. His Dad will never be able to see him again, and I know he needs time, but I really, really hope that he will trust you more than he trusts me."

"I hope so too," I admit. "Does Dad know?"

She smiles at that, then shakes her head. "Not yet. It's not my truth to tell. Besides, something tells me that he'll want you two to break the news to him."

The thought of telling Dad makes my shoulders clench. I inhale deeply through my nose. "I hope he won't take my future away." Fuck. My eyes jump back into hers. "Would he?"

"Never." Nathalie straightens her spine a little more, and something fierce blazes in her eyes. "You know, Arthur, I may not have been there for my son when he was young, but I'll be damned if I'm not there now he's older. If he accepts your love, I will support the both of you to the grave. Conventional or not."

"Oh, okay." I chuckle at that, a sheepish sound that definitely reflects my relief.

"Arthur." Nathalie stands, and I promptly copy her movements. "My sons, together." She giggles, then wraps her slender arms around me. "I wonder what surprises Louis will have for us. It can't get any more forbidden than two stepbrothers."

I laugh against her golden curls. "Well, never say never."

A soft knock comes on the door, followed by a voice. "Am I interrupting something?"

"Jean-Luc, *amour*," Nathalie lets go of me and gives me one final wink, before turning her attention to Dad. "Come, sit with me." I follow her once more, now facing both my parents when Dad moves to join her, looking as equally baffled as I do.

"We wanted to talk to you about Régis," she says.

Frowning, I flick from gaze back to Nathalie, wondering if I have somehow missed something. "What about him?"

"Well, we had a good conversation with Régis about his past few months at college. A personal conversation, right love?" She glances back at Dad, who smiles, remembering. "I know that your father asked you to guide Régis. We talked with him about that, and he wants you to continue guiding him. He feels a little lost without you." She smiles at me, knowing that she'd kept this from me before.

Elation, I feel fucking elation.

Dad, unaware, but always the leader in conversations, leans a little forward as he takes the word. "I know you're busy, son. School asks a lot from you, so does the brotherhood, and me. But Régis is family now too, and he doesn't have a lot of people he can turn to. He trusts you."

"Sure." The words leave my mouth in a hurried whoosh, its signification leaving me all sorts of giddy.

He wants me in his life. My little stepbrother wants more of me. Fuck, yeah, he can get it. Excitement coils down through my pumping vein, trickling south toward my groin. Not now, damnit. Not now.

Tonight.

Clearing my throat, I subtly place my hands between my thighs. "Of course I will continue to guide him."

"That's great," Dad nods. "Because he's actually adamant to leave today. He says he wants to study. We have covered all our business subjects over the past days, and I believe that you have deserved some time off from the holding's activities. For now." He winks.

"Yeah…sure." We all stand. "I'll go and get my stuff." Nathalie leans in for a kiss, and Dad gives me a hug and a clap on my shoulder. "We're both very proud of you. You prove to me every time that you have what it takes to succeed me and be the best CEO this family has ever known. Now, go back to college. Your brother and Didier are waiting for you by the car."

"And Régis?" I ask, even though I already know the answer.

"He's already left with Amadou."

Turns out, he hasn't. When I walk through the front door and head for the car, Amadou is still chatting to Didier, the backdoor open. I can't help but throw a victorious glance at Régis. *There.* It doesn't carry the same punch though, despite his fiery glare. Because something has irrevocably changed between us that night.

Once we're back at college, he spends most of his time in the library working on god knows what, but unlike all the other times, we sit together in the deserted, ancient place that houses thousands of books on thousands of shelves. He still won't talk to me though, his admission is more powerful than his words could ever be. And that evening he's waiting for me in bed, scooting over for me as I join him. And there, surrounded by nothing but the faint light of the moon, his body relaxes and slumps against mine, and he lets me in. And now he has voiced that out for the very first time, and accepts that he wants me close.

Fucking glorious, this triumph. And guess what? Count me in damn it, count me in.

21

RÉGIS

"You have given that subject an interesting turn," Mister Monatague hums when I finish my presentation. We're practising for the *Prix d'Honneur* that will take place tonight. "I am not a fan of last-minute changes, but this one really adds value to the overall vision on your chosen topic. I will comply."

"Great." Stepping aside from the desk that's been placed in front of the room, I fold the stacks of paper in one, thick pile and put them back into my backpack. "I'm relieved, because I really needed your approval." My hands feel clammy and my insides feel as wobbly as my knees. Mister Montague claps my shoulder with his hand.

"You're going to be just fine, Régis. You are extremely brave for doing this, for bringing on this topic and for defending it in front of a group of privileged directors."

"I guess." It comes out lame. Grabbing my bag, I head for the door. "So you'll be there? Tonight at seven?"

"I'll be there." My teacher offers me a comforting smile. "Make sure you eat and drink beforehand, and leave your nerves in your dorm." We both chuckle at that. He's right though, there's no need to be apprehensive about this presentation. I can recite the lines in my sleep, and have worked out the topic to the finest details. I have all my sources ready.

It should be enough to qualify.

My phone buzzes in my pocket, and when I catch the called ID, my nerves wring together in a tight ball. Fuck, it's Dad.

"I've spoken to the lawyer," he says flatly when we've been given our time. "And he says that he hasn't spoken to you since last summer."

"I—" My breath catches in my throat as my speed increases. Up the stairs, through the narrow hall, to our dorm.

"You've left your dad to rot in a prison!" Dad shouts ruthlessly. "You've left me to die! Have you already planned the funeral? Already ordered the headstone?"

The door clicks behind me as I make my way inside and toward my room. Louis is sitting on one of the couches in his football gear, chatting to one of his friends from the team by the looks of it. He gives me a funny look when I rush past, but I ignore him.

"Of course not. I—"

He won't let me talk. Too furious all together, like he usually was. Back at home, when he'd get lost in one of his tantrums, would be the moment he'd drag me to my bedroom and to the kennel.

"I have changed my will, you worthless piece of shit." He lets out a horrifying laugh. "Don't want your pathetic fingers to touch any of my stuff."

"Dad, I—" I close the door with my hip, then melt against the cool wood. "I—" Arthur is sprawled out onto my bed in nothing more than a pair of track pants. Bare foot, bare chested, his raven mop a tangled mess, a stormy look in his onyx eyes. He's furious. But that's not it...that's not it. My gaze slides toward the window, toward where the kennel has been placed. It's the same one I kept in the stables. He's put it there.

My heart thunders inside my chest as I eye my iron bars, and when Arthur slowly gets up from the bed, it takes all my strength not to run away from him. From Dad. Like some twisted horror version created in my mind that has tied them together, in a battle against me.

Useless boy. Get in there.

"I can't believe I trusted you, Régis, to get me out of here," Dad spews. "The lawyer says that the case looks tough." He's silent for a moment, and it's the exact moment for Arthur to approach me, his tall, sculpted, lithe body caving me in against the door. Tipping up my chin, he brushes his lips against mine and I shiver. "Or have you told your mother incriminating things about me? You little liar, that's what you have done." He rumbles through the phone. "As if you haven't destroyed my life enough."

I squint my eyes. *Do you want me to go inside the kennel?* I feel like asking. But my mouth tingles from the connection with Arthur's and my mind gets fuzzy because of this crazy hate-love connection that's slowly consuming me whole. I can't concentrate, and it makes me both tense and strangely careless. I'm not given an option to suggest anything though, because my big stepbrother easily captures the phone from my ear, while his other hand snakes around my neck, pinning me against the door.

"I suggest that you stop calling Régis from now on." His voice is nothing more than a hoarse rasp, but it's enough to have my knees buckle. Our eyes meet and when Dad barks an answer, Arthur's lips slowly curl into a cruel smile. "I said, I suggest that you stop calling Régis from now on," he drawls. His cold, dark eyes meet mine. "Starting *now*."

Making a show of disconnecting the call, he hands me back the phone, then lets go of my neck and strolls back to the bed.

"Does he still call you often?" He asks.

I watch him climb back onto the duvet, then spread his legs wide, his head supported by the headboard. He doesn't look at me, instead blinks slowly as his gaze slides toward the kennel.

"I still can't believe your father put you in that cage." His long, slender digits crawl around the waistband of his sweats, and I'm caught transfixed by its sensual sight. "And he locked it?" His eyes dance back to mine, I can feel its heady stare, and heat rushes to my cheeks. Still I can't look away, my mind a whirlwind. I clear my throat, that's choking up because of the truth hitting the cool air.

"Yes." I finally admit, my own dick throbbing beneath the navy-blue pants of my uniform.

"And you never fought him?" His hands slide to the sides of his waistband and dip the fabric down. His huge erection pops out and hits his navel. A soft whimper escapes my mouth and my gaze flicks up, only to meet his deviant stare. It's wrong to be so turned on by my big stepbrother, wrong to share this kind of information. Wrong to have told my mother that I wanted Arthur closeby. And yet, it feels so fucking right. Perhaps in its sick wickedness, his provocative way of talking to me, of always using his body as a weapon against my defenses, he manages to pass my defenses and get his hands on those details I usually don't share with people.

I do it with him. And despite everything, it feels good. Despite everything, I don't feel judged by Arthur.

"No," I finally breathe. "I thought that—" I wave my hand dismissively, unable to find the right words. Unable to even find the right emotion. "Perhaps he was angry at me for making my mother leave. Perhaps he had the right to treat me like that." My voice ebbs away, the words laced with uncertainty. I'm not sure if that actually makes sense. It used to, for years. Right now, not so much anymore. Still… "He doesn't deserve to be in prison. He's getting older and he…he's my dad."

Arthur bares his teeth, growling, "He's a fucking abuser, is what he is." We stare at each other. "What he did to you was wrong, Régis, prison is the right place for him to be. There's no fucking excuse for his behaviour." His charcoal gaze burns inside mine, setting my stuttering mind ablaze. "I put the cage inside here for you, because I don't want you to go into that cold forest to curl inside yourself. When you feel the need, you can do it here. And when you feel the time's right, we'll get rid of it, together with the horrors from your past. Okay?"

My eyes blink furiously, my lips unsure of what words to form. His are…yeah, I would like that.

I nod carefully. "Okay." I would fucking like to live without that cage one day.

Arthur palms his impressive length absentmindedly, visibly contemplating my words intermingled with his own thoughts, its sight salivating. Then he crooks a finger. "C'mere."

I hesitate, but only briefly, because I simply can't seem to defy him. Not right now, when I'm feeling vulnerable discussing this. When I come to halt at the bed and look down on his fingers cupping his sac, his smooth, tanned skin with that gorgeous trail of dark hair that connects both his cock and his sculpted stomach, I swallow.

"I know what you need. Crawl on the bed, little stepbrother. Crawl over here, then take my cock between those sexy lips of yours."

I do. I must have lost my mind entirely, a thick fog of lust temporarily taking over my senses. I want Arthur so bad, it makes my limbs tremble and my mouth drool. Fuck, he is quite the sight with his digits loosely caressing his wet slit before he slides them between my lips. "Suck on them, Régis," he rasps. I do, and he hums lowly, visibly satisfied. When he moves his fingers, he uses them to pinch my jaw and tilt up my head.

Licking my lips, I focus on his words, but trepidation creeps up through the cracks, making my thoughts go hazy. "Are you —" I tilt my head and nod toward the kennel. "Are you going to use it for punishment?"

His fingers under my chin press deeper into the skin of my cheeks, as his eyes shoot daggers. Then he bends my head, forcing me down until I am met with his leaking, throbbing cock. With my lips right by his crown, he compels me to look up again. "You want me to punish you?"

I don't answer, but feel my lips tremble.

Arthur brushes a finger over my wet mouth. "You want me to guide you into submission? Want me to train you in obeying your big stepbrother?"

Fuck. That shouldn't be hot, but I feel my own cock harden at the thought. His fingers leisurely trace the shape of my mouth, then he guides me even further. Down. Until my lips touch his wet slit and my breath hitches. Then he forces me to look up again. "If you want me to put you in place, I will gladly do so. But not like that, *chaton*. This—" The corners of his lips tick up cruelly, and he pulls me in and onto his cock. My lips spread as they wrap around his wetness, inhaling its heady, salty scent. "Is how I'll train you. How I'll punish you. This is how I'll show you how you are mine, Régis. By kneeling for me and worshipping my cock. By providing the perfect suction with your gorgeous lips. By your silence and obedience. That, my little stepbrother, is submission."

My veins sizzle with something fierce, making my own cock buck in my pants. And then my tongue curls around his hard shaft and I take his head deeper inside my mouth. Arthur groans, his fingers wrapping around the back of my head as he holds me in place. There's no time to panic when he glides deeper into my mouth, no time to gag on his rigid length as it claims my throat, because for some twisted reason even my body obeys. Relaxing my throat, I let him in, swallowing around him as his dick hardens even further, leaking his precum inside my throat. I hum at that salty taste, tipping my head forward to get more of him, more of this moment.

"Such a good, little stepbrother, Régis," he breathes. "You

take my cock so well." My eyes fly up to his, but when our gazes collide, I see no mocking. There's only heat radiating through the tiny slice of his dark brown iris, because his black pupils have taken over the rest of his eyes. Hungry, as he watches me feast on his cock, ravished by its taste, its texture, and the power he holds over me, but somehow doesn't use against me.

I let him.

"Come on, *chaton*, use your claws."

My nails come out immediately, scratching the warm skin of his upper legs as my head keeps on bobbing, led by his hand. Fuck, it feels good to rip him, to see blood on his flawless skin. To know that I have power over him as well.

"That's it," Arthur purrs. "Hmm, yeah, keep going." He drags his hand from my nape to my shoulder blades and squeezes, massaging the tense muscles as I keep on blowing him. "Fuck yeah, I'm going to..." His cum floods my throat and I swallow around the eruption, taking in all he's got to give. It's a lot, and when both his hands fly to my head and cup my temples to keep my mouth on his cock as he moans and hisses, he's got me perfectly encaved. It's like being in a small, refined area, with the focus on one, simple task.

It quiets my mind.

When I've fully milked him, I pull back and lick his crown clean. He drags his hold toward my face, cupping my cheeks with his larger hands, forcing me to look up.

"Hmm... that was perfect. Does that make you feel good?" His tone is soft, low, thick with that usual touch of hoarseness that I love so much. And his eyes...they seem to look right through me. Seem to know what's going on through my mind.

"Yeah."

There are so many things I should be rehearsing, not sucking my stepbrother's cock.

"Better," I admit carefully, "Though sometimes I wonder if

it's not just a trick." The confession makes me swallow hard, heart thumping fast. I can't believe I said that out loud.

Arthur gives me a stilted look and cocks his head. He waits a beat, before asking, "Trick?"

"Yeah," I mumble, suddenly feeling a little silly. "You know, like you don't mean it?" It comes out on a croak, followed by a shudder, when Arthur's fingers trail down over my chest, following the path of curves toward my belly button, to where my own cock is still hard and leaking, apparently not caring that my mind is trying to escape again.

"Well, this situation is quite the challenge," he finally admits. His digits circle the crown where my slit is oozing precum. My body trembles again, this time in pure heated anticipation. "There are plenty of reasons to declare the both of us crazy."

"Because we're stepbrothers?" The words come out on a restrained breath, Arthur's fingers tightening around my cock-head, swiping up the sticky mess I'm making.

He drapes his larger body over mine, then dips his head to level my eyes with his dark glow. "Hmm," he purrs in my ear. "That. We live in the same family. But also because we're both after the same prize." His hand forms a tight fist around my shafting. I swallow thickly, watching him watch the way my Adam's apple bobs. It somehow intensifies this need to challenge him again. His smug, handsome glare, all satisfied and content, doesn't do anything to make that less. My cock is throbbing, his pressing fingers making it difficult to fight the feral need to roll my hips and search for relief. My hard-on is raging, desperate. But there's something preventing me from giving in—this thrilling rivalry.

Arthur leans forward, raking me with his wicked gaze. "I think it's time to put some rules in place, little stepbrother." Placing his other hand on my thigh, he makes a show of dipping his gaze toward my straining cock that's currently held hostage by his hand. When he looks up again, his eyes are pupil-blown, glowing fiercely.

His mouth is on mine before I can take in the next breath of air. Soft, wet lips drag over mine, brushing together and bringing back those treacherous flutters in no time. They are everywhere in my stomach, despite his words, my body still wanting more from him. *Needing* more from him.

"No more calling Dad in prison," he whispers against my lips, followed by a soft kiss. "No more punishments in cages. Locking you up like you're a piece of meat." Another press of his mouth. "No more kept inside insecurity." He purses another kiss onto my lips, then slides all the way down. Leaning back on his haunches, he slides both hands over my thighs, before lowering his mouth toward my leaking cock. My gaze stutters when he presses a peck onto the wet crown, hips rolling up on its own volition.

Arthur chuckles lowly. "Hmm." He sweeps up the wetness, licking his lips when he's suckled it down. My knees start to tremble and I swallow away my moans. "Guidance." His tongue darts out and he laps some more at the crown. When his dark eyes meet mine he grins devilishly. "You want some more of my guidance." I moan, then tip my head back up, unable to look when his hot mouth wraps around my cock. I am so turned on that I won't last. "And I'll give it to you." My cock sinks deeper into his mouth.

"F-fuck—" I pant.

"That's right, little stepbrother. Fuck into my mouth, *chaton*. Take what you want."

Tentatively, I rock my hips a little forward. Arthur hums, sending a zip of desire through my spine. "More."

I do it again, and a string of whimpers escapes from my mouth. "I can't…oh, god, of, fuck…"

Arthur grabs both my ass cheeks and squeezes them deliciously, making me moan in desperation as he grinds me forcefully onto his cock. My eyes roll back, toes curling as hot, thick arousal consumes my entire body, spreading around like wildfire. This feels so fucking good. He hums in approval, and the low, raspy sound wracks me entirely, destroying the remaining defenses my heart keeps around. They crumble to the ground and my hips pick up his guiding rhythm, bucking forward and causing him to gag. It's the filthiest, hottest sound I've ever heard. I look down and catch sight of drool and spit rolling down the corners of his lips.

"Fuck, so hot." Smearing my fingers through the mess, his gaze flicks up and our eyes meet. And then he hums again, and I explode. I come on a howl, knees trembling and hips sluggishly rocking forward a few jerky last times. Fucking fireworks. Arthur's throat works around my cock, swallowing me down until I'm left a panting, sensitive mess. Only then does he get up, puts my dick back inside my pants, then stands up. Tilting my chin, I look up at him, unsure of what to say now. We stay in silence, but our eyes speak truths in their search for each other. Truths we can't even begin to describe.

Trust.

Safety.

Comprehension.

Attraction.

"The brothers will hold a celebration tonight after the presentations have taken place." He brushes a lock behind my ear. "I will take you. We go in initiation style, with cloaks and masks. They are restless, looking for a good fuck. Our escorts will be there as well." His fingertips brush under my chin, caressing the tender skin. "You will stay by my side the entire night. I don't want to share you." He waits a beat, as if waiting for my approval on that blunt declaration.

"I don't want to share you either," I whisper.

Arthur tilts his head to the side. "You won't," he finally murmurs. His fingers trace my bottom lip, before he finally lets go and walks away. "Mom and Dad are on their way here. We're meeting them for dinner at the canteen downstairs."

"Is it that late already?"

"No, but the canteen is open earlier today for those who present." He uses my bathroom and after he has flushed the toilet, he washes his hands by the sink, dries them, puts on his shirt, then uses my hairbrush to comb his wild, raven hair. When our eyes meet through the mirror, something has shifted yet again. I can feel it in the air, and it causes a shiver.

"That prize is mine, Régis. And mine only."

"Yeah, well, you've got to earn it first."

His eyes lock on mine and a small smile spreads on his lush, curvy lips. "Oh, I will, *chaton*." He straightens his clothes, runs another hand through his hair, then walks back inside my room and grabs his backpack.

"Shall we?"

22

ARTHUR

Dinner with Mom and Dad passes by in a blink of an eye, with Louis, Gaël and Dominique joining us. Instead of eating in the canteen, we spend most of our time in Dad's office, where we combine talk of studies and business as usual.

The atmosphere is pretty laid-back, despite tonight's presentations. I'm not particularly nervous—not to sound too much like the cocky asshole my little stepbrother makes me turn out to be, but I enjoy speaking in public. Plus, I know each member of the board. Not to forget that Dad's here with us, and even though I can understand his reasoning for not making me skip this part of the qualifications, there's no way on earth he'd let me fail this. Regardless of the quality of my presentation, which, conveniently, discusses the future of traditions.

I can't say that the same goes for Régis. Despite our earlier relaxation exercises on his bed, my kitten looks tense, his handsome features schooled into his well-practised aloofness. Louis tries to make him laugh a few times, but he's not rewarded with anything other than a few forced grimaces that have nothing to do with the quality of my brother's jokes.

Finally Louis gives up. He just gives Régis a hug and a

friendly pat on his shoulder, then announces that he will meet us in the presentation room. Gaël lets out a dramatic sigh, then points at the armchair that stands by the crackling fire.

"Alright, take a seat. Your shoulders come up to your nose, dude. That's no way to do a presentation." Régis stares at the chair, then at my cousin, who slaps on the armrest, holding a small bottle of oil in his hands. "Come on, don't be shy."

But Régis isn't shy, or perhaps that too. He's afraid. "I don't think—" I start, but Régis takes a slow step forward, in its wake brushing a hand over mine. Comforting.

"Perhaps it will do me good," he mumbles to himself. I don't miss the way Gaël's brows pinch, nor do I miss the way my own chest clenches with something dangerously close to pride. It's his way of coming out of his shell, step by step. And what's more precious, is the way he is including me. That little touch of reassurance, that tells me that is doing this for me. For us.

While Gaël babbles happily about the type of oils he's using, I take a final look at my presentation.

"Are you ready, son?" Dad asks, eying my notes as I flick them through. He's wearing his usual navy-blue suit with the crisp white shirt, the colors matching my own school uniform. His thick, graying hair is slicked back, revealing an angular face that matches mine and Louis'. So do his eyes, dark and intense, as he gazes at me. When I nod, he pats me on my shoulder, leaning in ever so slightly. "You know that this is purely a formality, right?"

I nod again.

"There aren't that many contestants, and I know that the board will let on a few more other students, since we did agree to modernize our traditions." Our gazes both linger at my notes, which cover exactly that theme.

"Do you also know who will win today?"

"No," he shakes his head slowly. "I don't have access to that information, nor can I direct it." I don't know why those words bother me, but something about them brings a tingle of worry in the pit of my stomach. My eyes flick back up from notes, and into Dad's. He's already gazing at me, searching.

"If you can secure my spot, surely you can secure one of my brothers as well?" I ask.

"Unfortunately it doesn't work like that, Arthur. It would be suspicious. But I'm sure that Régis will be doing just fine. Mister Montague has been sharing his debriefs, and they are full of praise." We both turn our gazes toward Régis, who gets out of his chair and pulls his clothing back in shape. The smile he shares with Gaël is more relaxed. The smile my cousin gives in return is definitely frank. Yeah, I believe that both Louis and Gaël have softened up for my kitten.

"If everyone's ready, then let's go," Nathalie says, phone in hand. She's been on the phone for the past thirty minutes, a glass of wine in hand, a small handbag tucked over the shoulder of her blush-colored dress. It's long, falling right above a pair of white pumps. She looks her usual classy self, but today there's also something stormy in those green eyes. Something tells me it had to do with her phone call. But I won't ask, because she's right. It's time to go and get ready for our qualification presentations.

In casual silence, we stride through the South Wing, following the trail of narrow corridors until we join the large reception hall. Around us, other groups of people are dotted around. It's a regular school evening, so some students are heading toward or leaving the canteen, whereas others make their way toward their evening activities. I greet a few of them with a clipped nod of my head, never really caring to engage in conversation. Especially not tonight, since my earlier anticipation is rapidly turning into something stronger, something hotter that's flooding through my veins as it does that usual trick it always does—preparing me for my win.

When we walk into the presentation room, two hosts by the

door in our navy-blue uniform colors greet us. Where one of them guides our family to where Louis and Dominique are already waiting for us, the other one walks us toward the front of the room. The other participants are already waiting, seated in order of presentations. I count ten of them. This is going to be a long night.

Turns out, it is. Most of the other presentations bore the fuck out of me. Me and Régis got separated when we were seated earlier, but when it's my little stepbrother's turn, I find myself leaning forward, fog leaving my brain while my eyes see clear again.

Régis's presentation is ... spectacular.

Everything from the way he magically makes his appearance strong and confident, to the subject he introduces. It's nothing like I've ever seen before, since he clearly hasn't chosen the conventional delivery. Rather than solely making use of PowerPoint, Régis hands out cards with texts and includes his audience, and even the board, in a clever way. Judging by their occasional surprised looks from behind their thick, metal glasses, the board shares my opinion.

Sitting behind the row of older, powerful men, sits Mister Montague. Alone. He has been there the entire evening, but I haven't given him much attention. Until now. There's something in the way he looks at Régis. His wild mop of strawberry blond hair has been slicked out of his face, making his forehead and the pair of glasses he wears on his nose, more prominently visible. He's older than I first thought. If I'd have to guess, he's somewhere around his mid-thirties. Still, he's an attractive guy.

As Régis quizzes the board with a series of rhetorical questions about different classes and the way that these have blurred over the past decades, Mister Montague's lips widen into a smile, and he nods his head absentmindedly, clearly engulfed in the topic. My nostrils flare at the thought that he might see the same beauty in my little stepbrother as I do, that he may try to get in my way of completely and wholly claiming my kitten, despite it being more than a challenge to do so. But when I flick my gaze to my family, there's something else there. Or should I say, *someone* else. Louis. Wearing my identical glare as he stares at Mister Montague. If looks could kill…

Blissfully oblivious, Régis strolls around, taking a few steps toward his PowerPoint presentation to underline a few words he put there in bold.

Goals.

Passion.

He reads them out loud, his voice a little shaken with emotion. "Our regular schools don't teach us how to identify our goals. How to describe them first, then structurally, step by step, work toward them. They don't teach us how to turn our feeling of passion into a weapon." He takes another few steps, until he's standing right in front of the board. "A weapon that creates the basis of everything. The reason why we want to succeed in the first place. Why we want that mansion by the sea —" His eyes dart to mine, blue irises turning a fiery shade darker in those few seconds we stare at each other. "Or that spacious penthouse in the city. We need our own, personally forged ammunition as guidance through our life. Through which we can braid knowledge that we have been fed with at schools, a way to actually make those dreams become true." He points toward the screen, then looks into the room.

"Goals and passion. Add education, and perseverance. That's another one that we're not taught enough at schools. How to be determined, how to work for our goals. For our passion. Students have become too sloppy, filling their free time with social media and gaming, teachers have become too lazy in motivating them to make the difference—" I suck in a deep breath and the room falls eerily quiet when one of the board members raises a hand.

"This is very impressive, Mister Deveraux. But this prize

focuses on Saint-Laurent, and how we can make this college more innovative. *Our* world."

Oh, fuck. Not good.

Régis swallows heavily, eyes darting between the board members, before they land back onto those who spoke. "Education concerns all of us. Education is the basis of a healthy society. It is the most powerful way to decrease crime rates, to fight racism—"

"Again, Mister Deveraux. How does that affect *our* world? The situation you so accurately describe is an issue public schools need to deal with. Yes, I agree, our students need passion. They need to be taught how to activate their knowledge of determination into one that is layered with numbers and analytics. But your description of our surroundings is not correct. You clearly have no experience with private institutions before you started your career." Someone sniggers around us, a soft, mocking sound that makes my blood sizzle.

"There's nothing wrong with a student questioning world education," comes a voice from behind, firm and fair as always. Dad.

"I would like to finish my presentation," Régis grates. "I would like to thank you all for your attention and presence, and hope that my topic, and my quality of presenting it to you, has been sufficient to qualify for the beautiful *Prix d'Honneur.*"

Only three of us can win tonight's qualifications, the final competition taking place in spring. But here's where it gets interesting. We are all brothers here, with three of us coming from powerful families. Four, if you include Régis, which I don't think the board will. Blood separates us, thank fuck for that.

Looking back at my family, I catch Louis's glare. He's sitting between Gaël and Nathalie—families are seated in the back of the room—and both my brother and cousin have a peculiar tense look on their faces.

They want Régis to win.

I can feel it. Can feel Louis's connection inside my own heart. Because despite their different ways of showing affection, they've grown to like my little stepbrother, despite him trying to snarl and claw at everything that comes too close. Perhaps he has more in common with us than he thinks. Because while we keep our inner circle a place of love and affection, we keep emotionally clear of practically everything and everyone that falls outside of that warm place.

Someone claps from behind me, and when I turn over my shoulder, I see that Dad has moved to stand. It's a standing ovation. One that is immediately picked up by Louis, Nathalie, Gaël and Dominique. It makes my chest constrict with the weirdest of emotions.

But fuck, do I love my people.

I want Régis to be part of my people too.

He's been in his bedroom for way too long, and it makes me feel all sorts of fucking ways. Apparently I'm not the only one, because around me, hanging on our couches, slumped beneath our black, silky cloaks, are Gaël, Dominique and Louis. We sit there in silence, listening to Régis crying inside his room. That sound...it's fucking constricting my insides, rolling them forcefully up into a ball that sits in my throat, like some big motherfucker I can't swallow away. I hate it.

"He did really well." Gaël finally says, watching as he rolls his mask between his thumb and index finger.

Louis nods. "Yeah, he did."

"I couldn't have done that," Gaël adds, and once more, the other two mumble in agreement.

"Even Monatgue told Régis that he was impressed," Dominique says, and again, they share a hum of agreement.

"Yeah, well, he was never going to win those qualifications," I snarl. The others blink at me. Annoyed, a brush a hand through my hair. "It's an interesting topic—"

For commoners. Fuck, does that thought annoy me even more. I growl, then jump out of my seat, and stride for his door. With a loud knock, I bang on it once, then twice.

"Régis, open up."

Of course he doesn't listen. When does he ever listen to me?

I shouldn't care. I should be fucking *happy* that he's out of my way. That he is not the rival I made him out to be. He lost, he *lost*. But the entire world now knows that the rules to this game have changed. Everything has changed. I have too. And I will win against the other two competitors, of that I'm sure. My little stepbrother definitely had the best presentation tonight. And that thought alone fucking pisses me off. He deserves better, but then, we all know that this life isn't about what we deserve.

I bang again on the door, ignoring my brother's attempt at soothing me.

"Go away!" He yells back.

Nope, not going to happen. "Open the door for me, Régis." I will get in his fucking room.

"I don't want to talk about it." Wrong.

Lifting my leg, I kick it with full force against the newly-built door, grinning when I hear a yelp from inside his room. "I'm coming for you, *chaton*." I kick the door again, the sound of splintering wood like music to my ears.

"Arthur!" My name leaves his mouth in a rush, and when I push my hand through the hole I created and open the door from the inside, it takes me exactly three seconds to locate my little stepbrother. My heart lurches as it starts to pump frantically.

He's still on his knees by the cage, hands connected to metal.

When he watches me making my way inside his room, he struggles to get up, but he's not fast enough.

"Not so easy when you've been sitting on your knees for the past hour, is it?" I spit, fury and sorrow intermingling. Regretting that my family convinced me into giving him space on his own. His traumatic past, together with this unhealthy obsession I have for my little stepbrother, create acid, and it's making me vicious and fast as I chase him through his room.

"It's time to take your loss like a man, *chaton*. Let is go. It's done." He jumps up the bed and digs himself over to the other side. Grabbing hold of his ankle, I drag him over the sheets and back to me, but his ferocious kick against my chest is more than I bargained for. He catches me in surprise and I let go, watching him dive onto the ground at the other side of the bed before I run around it.

"Oh, no, you aren't," I growl when he reaches for the door. The door that is broken, might I add, and I don't want to know what kind of amusement we've created for the depraved souls of my brother and cousin. "You're going to stay here and fucking talk to me."

"I don't want to talk to you!" He runs forward, but right when he reaches out for the knob, I jump and catch him by his wavy, golden hair. As I pull him back he yelps, then tries to get away, but his sadness doesn't stand a chance against my madness. I haul him by his arm and turn us around, then throw him onto the bed, pinning his hands with all my force above his head, forcing him to look at me. He writhes beneath me, both our chests heaving from the exercise, and despite the gravity of the situation, my cock roars to life, filling with a need to claim, to fucking own this guy.

His eyes are large and wet, and the deepest of blue. Tears still roll down his puffy cheeks, dribbling down to the corners of his mouth. When his tongue snakes out to lick them away, I dip my head and capture it with my own. He startles, and I dive further, forcing him back into his mouth, with my tongue curled around him. Régis stops fighting me a little, and with one hand I grab both of his wrists and keep them above his head, while my other drops, fingertips brushing past his soft, golden curls as they descend to his cheeks. They feel hot and cold at the same time, accompanied by the wetness from his grief. Stroking his tears away, I cup his chin, using it as leverage to tilt his face in the angle I want, and continue kissing him. Slow and demanding, the proof of who owns him. Who gets to know what happens inside that beautiful mind of his. Régis lets out a sweet mewl that has my cock weeping in my pants. It takes all my fucking willpower to pull back, especially when he chases my mouth, brushing his over mine, not ready to separate.

"Régis." My voice sounds gruff even to my own ears. He slowly blinks as his gaze travels up to meet my own. "Your presentation was amazing."

Fresh tears roll down his cheek, and I need to force myself not to lick them away and claim that luscious mouth of his again, and again. "It wasn't amazing enough," he breathes thickly.

"Yes, it was. But a world like this wasn't made to be changed."

His tongue darts out, licking his own salty tears as he takes in my words. "Why not?" He finally asks, sounding so innocent and young that it makes my chest flutter. "Why would we? We have everything we want. Power, money, we have it all. Why would we want to change that?"

And now I want you. The words echo too loudly in my head, where they repeat themselves like a broken record.

Want you. Want you.

Fuck, it makes my cock burn with the need to claim him. Again and again, until he realizes that he's not going anywhere without me. The thought is...disturbing, and strangely soothing at the same time. Weight falls off my shoulder at this admission that Régis is, like I always knew he would be, a problem. A threat to my future, yet, also... a soothing comfort. He is. Because I want to take care of him, protect him from anyone. Keep him closely tucked to my heart. Will he let me? Tonight will reveal that to me, I guess.

A knock on the door startles both of us and we look up from where we lay on the bed, we catch two amused pairs of eyes.

"You okay there, little stepbrother?" Louis asks, the tips of his lips curved into a smirk as his gaze finds mine.

"Yeah, yeah, we were just—talking." I don't need to look back at him to know that his face will be bright red.

"Exactly," I add in feigned annoyance, "And you were disturbing us."

"That so?" Gaël drawls, his blond hair tucked away under the hood of his cloak. "Well, we're sorry to ruin the party, but we've got a bigger one waiting for you." He wiggles his eyebrows suggestively, and under me, Régis snorts.

"We'll be there in five," I say.

"Okay. Someone will repair the door when we're out, so it should be fixed when we're back, for your next uhm...*conversation*."

When Louis and Gaël walk away—of course after making sure that we hear their loud cackles—Régis pushes me in my chest.

"Get off me, they can't know."

"Know what?"

Our gazes collide, his still a stormy blue filled with conflict. "That you...and I—" He bites his lip, then looks away. "Just, get off me."

"That we fuck?" I tease. "That we talk? They already know." Pulling off from him and onto my haunches, I let my fingers trail over his white shirt, tracing his abs and curves all the way to his hardened cock. He clears his throat when I brush my fingertips over it. "Actually, there's something I'd like your opinion on."

"What's that?" He eyes me suspiciously.

I chuckle, then slide off the bed. "Well, there are more topics I'd like your opinion on, but this is quite a pressing matter. Hang on." I open the damaged door, making a show of ignoring the inquisitive looks from my family members as I head for my own bedroom. My cock is hard and impatient in my pants, and I need to keep my thoughts free from anything sex-related that involves Régis to keep my control.

Grabbing my gear for the night, I head back to Régis's room, only to catch him pulling on his own cloak as well. He looks fucking delicious in it. All smooth and black, with those lush curls and clear doe-eyes glancing at me through the mirror.

"I need you to pay careful attention tonight."

Régis stills, my words somehow hitting its goals. "For what?"

I shrug, the movement a strong contrast from my searching gaze. I am worried. "For anything *off*."

He turns around in a rush of clothes, then gives me a nervous laugh. "Can you at least give me a clue?"

"No." Pursing my lips, I hold up the shiny, golden mask I hold up. "I'll be wearing this one tonight. You're a brother now, so you can make your own choices. Just know that during a celebration, there's a lot of fucking." Régis gulps. Sliding my hand down over my stomach and making sure he watches when I squeeze my hard-on, I add, "I want you to be the one I fuck tonight, *chaton*. But it's time you come and collect your prize yourself. No more little boy manners, Régis, not after that show you put on earlier tonight. So if you want me, you come and find me, before someone else does."

23

RÉGIS

The Atrium appears spine-chilling dark and foreboding as we make our way inside following the secret passage underground. I absorb my surroundings—the large plants, couches decorated with loosely dotted pillows, nothing more than curvy shapes, lit by the outside moon and cressets that burn fiercely all around us.

Just like my own blazing heart.

Thud. Thud. Thud.

Stepping inside the brightening room, I follow my fellow brothers, placing the torch I've been handed into the designated spot by the piano. Dominique's already playing, half of his face blindfolded by some form of thick silk with a pattern which replicates the delicacy of lace. Whatever it is, it's smooth and soft, like the tones coming from the instrument.

"Moonlight Sonata."

He told me this was his brother's favorite song. He must be thinking of him tonight. Dominique is wearing a black suit with a brooch of a white mask with silver curls on them, just like the one Gaël wears.

Claimed.

That...must feel nice. To be protected by someone, to be kept warm in the cold, to know that you're not alone when you fear you are.

"*Mes frères*." Elder Jacques calls out, thudding his cane onto the cool ground from the central place on the stage from where he looks down upon us. He stands in between two other black cloaks that also have white fur around the edges of their hoods.

The three white furred cloaks.

The three leaders of the Alpha Fraternarii at Monterrey Castle.

They carry identical masks of golden crows, its nose an obscene curve that leads all the way to the non-existent mouth of the bird. Unlike their usual masks, the shape of the bird reveals their own, curved lips. Around us, the crowd silences almost immediately, the melodic sound of the piano the only filler of the heady quiet.

"We're here, at this *soirée*, to celebrate. Because we have so much loyalty. Talent." His cane points slightly toward a part of the glazed wall, where a group of red cloaks are kneeling, their heads bowed, hair covered with their hoods, ready to serve as tonight's entertainment. "So much respect." Elder Jacques's voice is barely more than a satisfied hum, coming from a man who's used to getting what he wants.

"Yet you are restless." Monsieur Z speaks now. His raspy, high-pitched tone should be amusing, but in this context, it comes off as threatening. But it's not *off*, is it?

As subtle as I can, I shift my stance and look around, in search for shiny gold, but come up empty. Instead I catch the attention of a few brothers with white, matte masks and hungry eyes that pierce through the creepy holes. It makes me shiver.

"Hungry. You are looking for something different. We understand that, *respect* that." He takes a step forward. "And we will accommodate, mark my words. We have already introduced a first change when we convinced the board of Saint-

Laurent to accept a change in the qualification criteria for the *Prix d'Honneur.*"

My stomach wars against that piece of information, the earlier defeat coming back in full, sour force.

"But I realize that not all of you are interested in the chance to win the most prestigious prize of this college." The words leave his mouth on a sneer, followed by a sharp bark of laughter. A taunt. "Which is why we're also looking into different ways of making things a little more interesting. Perhaps we'd need to find a way to let in fresh blood? Hmm? After all, sex is power to our brotherhood." He thuds the cane once more into the ground, and as he eyes the crowd, his lips are curled into a vicious sneer.

Some brothers cheer under the Elder's salacious glare.

"Yes," he hums, finishing his inquisition until he stares back at the cloaked man next to him. "Perhaps it's time to find a different kind of balance."

The other Elder, Monsieur Z, nods, then grins before he takes over the lead. His gaze stares into the crowd, then he lips part on a sharp intake of air.

"It's all about balance," he agrees, and the same words linger in the expectant air as they increase in volume, until they finally smother the peaceful sounds of the piano. It makes me lose my grip, and panic settles into the pit of my stomach and makes me want to leave.

Iron. I need my iron.

No, you don't.

"Easy now." A hand wraps around my side, offering a comforting squeeze. "Just breathe in, you're doing fine." His voice, nothing but a private whisper behind his black and purple mask, is enough for my lips to part and to suck in a deep breath, clinging on to the heady air around us. Not, it's more. It's comfort. It's Maxime. A friend. A brother.

Around us, the crowd shifts in its attempt to give way, and

my heart frantically thumps in my chest at the sight of a shiny, golden mask.

Maxime drops his hand. "Remember, you're doing fine."

The piano picks up, but Dominique is no longer playing his brother's music. No, he has moved on to darker, more urgent notes. In the corner of my eye, red cloaks rise in one flowing sea of color, then take a united step forward.

Elder Jacques raises a dramatic hand to the sky. "We congratulate those who proved their value tonight and made it through the qualifications for the prize. May the best brother win!"

A cork pops too close to my ears, followed by the sizzling sound of its contents as it's being received with a loud cheer. Part of me wants to run, but the other, more forbidden part I've been trying to tame ever since I set foot in the Deveraux mansion, follows the shiny, golden mask as he makes his way through the crowd, followed by the two other chosen candidates. They wear equally shiny masks, but I quickly zoom out on them, instead focusing solely on Arthur. I watch him as he talks to someone else, then with both their hands adorned with a glass of champagne, they stroll over toward the far corner, toward Dominique.

When I shuffle on my heels, I notice that Maxime is no longer standing next to me. No, that same black and purple mask is now kneeled on the floor, facing me, surrounded by two brothers who carry white furred edges around their hood, their backs presented to me. One of them looks over his shoulder and catches my flitting gaze. *Monsieur Z.* He sends me a filthy grin, then turns back. I don't miss how he grabs the edges of Maxime's black cloak and pulls his black and purple mask a little up, freeing his mouth. He starts rocking his hips, head tipping back.

I look away.

Arthur was right, the crowd has gone feral. These brothers

are hungry for more, their need thick and toxic in the air, intermingling with the woody scent of incense that comes in small circles of smoke from each corner of the Atrium. That in itself is *off*. And it's both suffocating and arousing at the same time.

Devour or be devoured.

This is pleasure in the name of history, claimed by the filthy, wealthy, and privileged. And yet… red cloaks are scattered around us, used to fulfill the most devilish desires these guys have. Escorts more than willing to let themselves be used for the fat pay they will get. It's diametrically opposed to what I strive for, to what I was willing to defend in life. If only the board had let me get past those qualifications. Then I'd be able to use my voice and speak up, I'd be able to use my volume to teach and preach about those less privileged.

I'd be able to make a difference.

But these guys don't want any changes in life. They don't need one. They've got everything their heart desires—power, a gloriously carved out future and all the money in the world. This…this democracy we live in, is nothing more than an illusion.

And still we have a choice. I did. And with mine, I chose to live with Dad, to let myself be punished by him, to be locked away like a caged pet that didn't obey. In the name of destruction.

Destruction. Because that's what he used to accuse me of. Of having made my mother flee our house. I cried too much, was too loud, wanted too much attention. And for all those years, I believed that to be true. Not anymore. I'm fucking sick and tired of being devoured.

The thought leaves my mind in a whoosh, colliding against two cloaked brothers who approach me, their white masks ominous as they stare me down. My mind stutters, limbs ready to take a step back. I don't know who they are, though right now I wonder if that really makes a difference. Staring into the void of their masks, I guess it does. It's enough for me to make a decision on the spot. For the very first time in my life I wonder what it would be like to proactively *make* a choice. To choose a side and stay there, knowing that I made the right one, one that actually makes me feel *good.*

I want to feel good.

My cock fills at the thought of a shiny, golden mask and watchful, onyx eyes behind them. Of lush, raven strands and a chiseled jaw. Of words, spoken in that hoarse tone, that challenge me, that actually want to make me come out from my iron cage. That wants me to hear myself, because he wants to hear me too.

I turn around, presenting the two brothers my back as I search for Arthur. I scan the piano in the corner, but the only ones I see are Gaël and Dominique, who's still playing the instrument, though miraculously so. He sits on his lover's lap, his ass no doubt filled up, his head slumped back against the black cloak as he's being rocked forward.

It makes me grow hungry. A thought that would have put me off just a few months ago, yet after these moments spent with my so-called brothers, it doesn't feel that shameful anymore.

I can see the other brothers looking at me. I don't know why, but they do. Their gazes are sinister behind those masks as they take in my every move. The Great Hall is filled with salacious sounds. Grunts, moans, the wet slapping of flesh as it pounds into spread opened, willing holes. I walk through the crowd, toward one of the many glass panels that separates the rare species of plants they cultivate here, from the outside woods. Perhaps we are too, a rare species of privileged, who need to be kept separate from the rest.

In the far corner, right by a giant white bird of paradise, sits Arthur in an armchair. His legs are spread, and his masked chin is leaning onto his folded hands as he looks at me. Waiting. For a moment I just stand there, unsure, my new found determination easily beaten back into a pile of nothing. Part of me wants to go back to my bedroom and hide in safety. But my cage lost its hold on me the day my tormentor left, and no matter how hard I tried, that emptiness just wouldn't be replaced. Not by pain or anxiety. Until Arthur. After him, the emptiness was replaced by desire, fueled by rivalry. That, in its own turn, liquified into something more primal. Feral in its intensity, like Arthur's gaze burning my skin, yet somehow soothing my mind.

It's the longing for my stepbrother, infuriating and toxic, though more caring than I could ever have thought. Protective, the way he holds me when we meet each other in bed.

Forbidden, yet lustful.

Arthur tilts his head, watching me from behind his mask, as if beckoning me to come forward.

Then, as if the crowd has stepped aside to let him through, Elder Jacques appears by my side, stepping in slowly, those black, piercing eyes from behind his white mask focused on mine. He's clearly on a mission as he steps in closer, and with each impending shuffle of his feet, I wince a little further. Remembering what happened the last time he was this close to me, I feel my veins fill with ice. Would he want me to…

"*Mon frère.*" Elder Jacques approaches me and snakes long, cold fingers around my wrist, right under my cloak. The sudden touch feels like an attack to my skin and I flinch.

"*Monsieur,*" I mutter as softly as possible, not sure if I should reply, and not willing to give my identity away, assuming that he doesn't know who I am to begin with.

He gently pulls at my joints. "Shall we?"

My heart plummets, sweat breaking out on my forehead. "I—"

But before I can think of anything else to say, another brother heads our way, wearing a shiny, dark-blue mask, followed by the two other cloaked figures that also wear white fur around their hood.

Elder Jacques leans in, his masked face brushing my ear. "It seems like we are disturbed *again*," he mumbles. Goosebumps scatter all around my sensitive flesh and I jerk my head away from him. He lets go of my wrist, and with a nod to the blue mask he follows his other brothers back through the crowd.

My chest heaves from my pants, fear still rattling in aftershocks through my veins, as if my body hasn't gotten the memo. Or perhaps, it's a warning, that danger hasn't yet subdued. I gaze at the blue mask, and judging from the heavy stare that comes from the holes, he's already looking at me. This brother is enormous and has the darkest eyes I have ever seen. It's enough for me to turn on my feet and back away.

The armchair is only a few meters away from me, but it feels like an everlasting walk. And not just that...it's like we have fought our battles and he has surrounded my king with his own troops.

Check mate.

But this is a different kind of victory. It tastes enticingly sweet, and I'm not sure whose camp is in celebration. I'm feeling ecstatic, that I realize. Lighter, carefree. Because I want Arthur so bad it makes my blood boil and my stomach flutter. I'm no longer afraid of wanting him, or of being afraid of admitting it. My legs feel wobbly and my lips feel dry. Still I keep on walking.

My mind wonders how on earth I should start a conversation, or if he even wants to have a conversation, or perhaps he never wanted me to come over in the first place. By the time I halt right in front of his sprawled out form, my skin itches with nerves.

"There you are." Is all Arthur says, and then he reaches out both hands and grabs me by my waist, turning me around effortlessly as he pulls me straight onto his lap. I mentally collapse. All the built-up insecurity falls apart like a domino effect replaced with desire, syrupy and sweet. My dick fills as my chest shatters with feral need. So hungry…

"Are you wearing something under this cloak?" Arthur rasps against the crook of my neck, his fingers already busying themselves with the seam of my cloak. Pulling it away from under me, he now has free space to roam his fingers under the garment.

"Underwear," I grate.

"Hmmm." He purrs, as his fingers find the thin material of my boxers. He follows my spine up until he reaches the material of my tank top, letting out another long, low hum as he does so. "I needed to visualise that," he mumbles. "Needed to know what I was working with here. Thankfully, not much. It seems like my little stepbrother finally starts listening to me."

I let out a nervous laugh that quickly turns into a hiss when his hands grab both my ass cheeks and rub them firmly, rocking me onto his lap with languid, sensual movements. I lean back against his chest, just like I'd seen Dominique do before, and Arthur meets me at the curve of my neck, his lips on mine at my next inhale. They feel both rough and soft at the same time, his hunger obvious as he moves to lick inside. He nibbles at my bottom lip, laps at my upper lip, only to dive back in and suck on my tongue. The chase, the sensations, the fact that I'm sitting here, on his lap, with one of his hands around my throat while the other lingers on my cloak, has me moaning in starvation. I rock my hips into nothing, not being able to get enough friction, and it's making me work myself even further up into a frenzy. I growl in frustration.

Arthur smiles against my lips. "What do you want, *chaton*?" I watch with hooded eyes as he grabs a bottle of lube from the armchair and holds it in front of me.

"Yes," I breathe.

"Yes, what?"

I swallow, eyes darting from the bottle back to him. "I want that. I want you to make me feel something I've never felt before."

"Hmm," he croons, leisurely tracing the shape of my mouth with his tongue. The sensation makes my toes curl. "I can do that. If you ask me nicely."

"What?" I snap.

Arthur huffs out a wolfish grin, then squeezes one of my cheeks, making me squirm on his lap. "Beg, kitten." He lifts his hips in a roll, and his erection grinds against my ass, making me moan. Pleasure scatters all around my insides.

"I—Please—"

"Please, what?" Arthur's eyes are dancing. "Be specific, little stepbrother. Tell me what you want."

Something cracks inside me. But where I expect to feel humiliated by his request, I feel light. Clear headed. "Make love to me," I whisper.

Arthur takes my chin between his fingers and tilts it up until our eyes meet. His are pupil-swollen and dark with that faint ring of gold. "Good boy," he muses. He presses a soft kiss onto my lips. "I'm going to do just what you asked."

Uncapping the bottle with one hand, he pours a generous amount onto his two digits, then lets those fingers crawl under my cloak once more. "Lift your hips, Régis." I do as he says, and he easily pulls off my underwear and shimmies them down my thighs and knees until they land on the floor. Then those fingers are back, teasing my hole with cold, wet sweeps. I only have a few seconds to adjust to my initial surprise, before a slick finger dips inside. My muscles clench, but when Arthur pulls me closer to his chest to bring his lips onto the skin of my neck, I unclench a little. He licks and kisses the heated flesh under my ear, his raspy voice murmuring words of praise.

I want to be his good boy. The thought makes me practically

jump out of my skin, only to be soothed back in by his probing finger.

"Feel how you're sucking me in, kitten. Do you want me there? Want me to make you feel good?"

"Y-yes," I garble, panting. He hums in reply, then adds a second finger.

"Take it Régis, relax for me. I can't wait to feel your tight heat all around me again."

"Fuck, Arthur." My hips grind sluggishly when he hits my g-spot, white pleasure sparking to live in front of my closed eyes. His digits keep on going back and forth, widening my channel with every stroke, relaxing me and pleasuring me as they hit that spot over and over again. My hips buck and I moan freely now, my cock hard and throbbing beneath the silky layer of my cloak.

I don't know how long he keeps up his delicious torment, because I'm delirious with lust, riding his fingers and begging him for more. When he finally stands us both up to pull down his own briefs, I shudder in relief.

"Please, please—"

The blunt head of his cock probes against my hole and I push back in frustration when it takes too long for him to penetrate me. Arthur chuckles at that. "Nearly there, *chaton*. You better get your claws out, you know I love it when you scratch me. Mark me, Régis, and make it hurt."

And then the slick crown of his cock slides into me mercilessly. I barely have time to adjust, my muscles clenching with initial panic, only to unclench at the sound of his approving purrs.

"Let me in, Régis."

I surrender, pushing back against the way his cock slowly slides further into my tight channel until he owns me completely. "That's it, baby. That's it." His hand slides over my waist and upper legs, rubbing my flushed skin as he continues to fill me up. When he's all the way in, we both let out a shuddering breath. "Fuck, yeah," Arthur growls. His hand crawls up my groin and wraps tightly around the shape of my clothed cock, making me stifle a groan. We're just getting started and I'm already so hard for him.

"I want to show them all," Arthur mumbles against my ear. "Move, kitten. Ride my big cock."

"What do you want to show them all?" I have barely moved a few times, but I'm already out of breath. The angle isn't easy, the soft seat of the armchair not very helpful.

Arthur lets out a grunt. "How you are fucking mine, little stepbrother."

Without any warning, he moves out of the chair, taking me with him. He holds me up as he takes one, two steps, his cock still buried in my ass, then he pushes me forward and onto the ground. We're in a glassed corner, behind the piano. Yanking off both our masks, he looms over me. "Get on all fours, *chaton*. I'm going to fuck you hard now," he grumbles. I barely have time to do as he says, when he starts pounding my ass with fast, short thrusts. They are effective, pumping my prostate with every thrust, making me move forward as I moan and writhe, my eyes squeezing shut.

"Oh my god," I pant. My chest feels tight, filled with flutters and something else that lights up with every puff of air that brushes past my neck and ear. Arthur is everywhere, covering my body with his larger one, like he has done every night over the past weeks. Despite his words of rivalry, he's been protecting me, shielding me in his attempt to make sure that I won't need my iron.

Right now, he fucks me mercilessly, ungracefully unyielding as he pummels my ass, making pain and bliss melt together in an everlasting ache of desire. Thick, heavy, warm and solid. I never want it to end. But it will, embarrassingly fast, when he grabs hold of my cock. My painfully hard cock that is begging me for release.

"You want to come?" He croons.

"Yes," I pant. He yanks out of me and rolls me onto my back.

"Then mark me with your fingers," he growls. I grasp his thighs and squeeze, squeezing a little more when he moves back inside me. "Scratch me, *chaton*, and purr for me like a real kitten. Then I'll make you come."

I'm too far gone to care, too desperate for release. A growl emerges deeply from within me while I dig my nails in the flesh of his naked thighs. And fuck me if it doesn't do something to those flutters, if it doesn't somehow make my mind clear. It only takes a few rapid strokes before I come hard and with a un-kittenly shout. My release comes out in thick, creamy spurts, leaking onto Arthur's stomach and chest.

"Yesssss," he hisses. Two, three, four more thrusts and his face twists into an expression of pure bliss, and wonder. And he comes, lips parting and nostrils flaring. A faint flush colors his cheeks and he is the most beautiful sight I have ever seen.

Mine. My entire body buzzes at the thought.

Mine. My entire body buzzes with the sound. He's mine. Nevermind that we'll only get in each other's way and then hate each other for it. Nevermind that this beautiful thing we have - a blooming flower adorning my fantasies - might wither and die in the end. He's still mine.

24

ARTHUR

Something has irrevocably changed between me and Régis. Things have grown from a delicate breeze to a full blown whirlwind that seems to consume both of us with its searing heat and vortex; it has painted the sky and colored my life.

There's desire, lots of it. But that's not all. There's this insatiable hunger to discover more about him, to dig through his past and fight his fears, and if I could promise him that he'll never be mistreated again by anyone, I would. If he'd believe me.

One day.

Because Régis has me in a chokehold. Me, the person I was, the person I've always wanted to be, it's...I'm still *me,* and yet I'm different.

From the moment he openly gave himself to me during our last *soirée,* impaling himself on my lap and clawing at my flesh like the sweet kitten he is, Régis is everywhere. His soft, gentle self has found its roots somewhere into my existence, meandering around my mind and soul like the finest of flowers. And I can't wait to watch him bloom.

What colours will he have?

After he didn't qualify for the *Prix d'Honneur,* Régis's initial sadness has evaporated, and he seems to have forgiven life for being this narrow-minded. We have even stopped our ongoing back and forth bickering about it.

No, Régis no longer feels like my competitor, although I'm not sure anymore what he represents now. He has always felt like a threat to my future, and perhaps that's exactly what I should be worrying about. But I can't put myself through it anymore. We've passed that phase. Instead I want to understand this blossoming connection between us. My brain tells me to be careful, but my heart wants to nourish it, make it bloom. This unique, delicate coupling.

The entire family knows that Régis should have won those qualifications. My little stepbrother is intelligent and willing to learn. He's frank and has a heart for justice, and if it's within my power, I'll do anything I can to make sure that he qualifies next year. Having a heart comparable to his might not be a trademark that's highly valued in the brotherhood, but Deveraux Holding surely does. We allow our family members to flourish and want what's best for ourselves. But in the process we sometimes step over others, but we do what must be done.

We have spent every single night together since that heartbreaking moment I found him in the cage. That moment all the walls around my little stepbrother come tumbling down.

The moment my heart cracked wide open for him.

Perhaps I shouldn't have listened to him, but when Régis begged for the cage after our first night, I had it brought inside his room for him. I didn't want it there but it didn't seem right to judge him over his attachment to a piece of furniture. Especially one that was so intrinsically connected to a terrible part of his past. I had to allow him to heal in his own way, no matter how I felt about it. So I have done everything I can to prevent him from sleeping in it. How could he in the first place? The kennel is barely big enough for the size of a Mastiff, let alone a human being. Knowing Régis, he'd be too fucking stubborn to simply listen to me, so instead I have taken off the lock and have changed the position of the hinges. Now, the door can only be left in an open position, and inside I have put a few pillows and some of his books. The chess board stands on the floor next to the metal cage, and when I came into his room last night, I noticed that he placed some green shrubs around the metal bars.

No, my little stepbrother is not ready to say goodbye to the embodiment of his painful past, but I sure as fuck am ready to finish off the source of his venom. And though I may never understand how he could have ever forced himself to be inside that cage, I can only respect his silent wish to give him more time. And slaughter the monster he dreams of at night.

Right now I'm standing by the entrance to the canteen, leaning against the wall, arms folded in front of my chest. It's a quiet evening with not much going on. It's quiet inside the food court, rain pattering against windows that offer nothing but darkness and the reflection of four guys laughing and joking at the only occupied table.

Chess night.

Régis hasn't seen me yet, even though he knows I'm here to pick him up, since he's too engrossed in wiping that smug jock's ass in just a few immaculate moves. Yeah, my little stepbrother plays his chess game mercilessly and adapts on the fly, much like the way I play real life. The thought makes something clench inside my chest. Perhaps that's one of the reasons why we fit so well together.

"What a dick move," Jo grunts, his dark eyes flashing when Régis takes his bishop with his knight.

"Well, you had that one coming," Dominique snickers. He's looming over Régis's slight frame, eying the board with a hellish concentration from the looks of it. He has been a good friend to my kitten.

"I still vote for being able to pull back with my pawn," Jo mutters. "Just one, innocent step?"

"Uh uh," Régis teases, the sound making my nostrils flare. Is my *chaton* flirting with the dark haired football star? When Jo looks up with another one of those teasing smirks, a growl vibrates through my chest. Not on my watch.

Right as I want to step in and pluck Régis away from their game, my phone vibrates. Without even having to check the caller ID, I know who it is. Time to go.

"Boys," I bark, then saunter forward, to where Maxime and Dominique, both standing over the seated players, look up at me in surprise. I don't miss the way Dominique's ginger-haired friend winces a little when I get closer, just as I most certainly don't miss the way Jo jumps out of his seat to shield his friend. Hmm…interesting.

"*Chaton*, it's time to head out. Amadou is waiting for us."

For a hint of a second, Régis just sits there with his back my way, stiff and tense as a pole. Gone is his earlier casual demeanour as the true meaning of my words hit home.

It's time.

His golden waves have grown a little longer, practically reaching his nape when he tips up his chin and looks through the window to the darkened garden. Then he nods. It's a slow gesture of his head, followed by a heavy sigh that I can practically feel in my own chest.

Nathalie begged me to accompany Régis at all times, and even though he still doesn't reply much to her messages, they are in more frequent contact. But it's in me that his mother confides. I update her about his well-being, and in exchange she has promised me to secure my future if we will confront Dad.

Not if.

When.

Our future.

But first things first, starting with tonight.

"Tu viens?" I ask softly. *Are you coming?* When I feel Régis's friends watching me curiously, I bare my teeth at them. Fuck them all.

"Oui." His reply comes soft, but when he gets up and turns around to face me, he has slipped on his well-practiced mask. The one I don't want.

He straightens his jacket, then looks at Dominique. "Can you please bring the chess board upstairs when you finish?"

"Sure." Dominique pats Régis's shoulder in a timid gesture of affinity. "Well, good luck."

"Thanks. Bye guys."

They all mumble their replies, but I feel the tension. Good, that means he has told them.

That means he trusts them.

Reaching for him, I pull him close to my chest and kiss his forehead. "Hey you."

"Hey to yourself." He looks up, his eyes smiling. "Did you have a nice day?"

"I did. Busy. I didn't see you here for dinner?" I ask, cupping the back of his head against the crook of my collarbone. His golden locks tickle the thin layer of exposed skin right above my collar, his cheek warming my flesh and my relief. Yes, he must trust me, because he lets me guide him toward the exit.

Régis shrugs. "No, I ate early, then went to the library. I have this presentation for Spanish tomorrow, remember?"

"I do now. Sorry, I'm afraid my own brain has gotten some serious injuries after today's calculus test. Remind me to drop that subject for my final trimester."

Régis chuckles and presses himself even closer to my chest. My arm squeezes him tight, holding him in check as we make ourselves outside.

"Fuck, it's cold," I growl. The chilly wind seems to blow right through us, and it's making my bones rattle inside.

"And wet."

When Amadou sees us coming, he opens the door of the back seats, showering us with that calming smile that always seems to work so well on my little stepbrother. This time is no exception.

"Sirs." He waits for us to get comfortable, then shuts the door, only to take his own seat behind the wheel. If he's surprised to see me grabbing hold of my kitten and tucking him against my chest, he doesn't show. I should be more careful, really. For all I know, he could tell Dad. But when that chocolate gaze searches for Régis, followed by another of his reassuring smiles, my doubts melt. No. He wouldn't. They have a special connection and it's based on trust. "It's a forty-five minute ride," Amadou continues, "You might want to get comfortable."

Régis pushes himself a little deeper against my frame, and I pull him so close that he's glued against me, hip to shoulder.

"*D'accord*," he says.

Amadou hums, and the car pulls up and over gravel. "Good, then let's go."

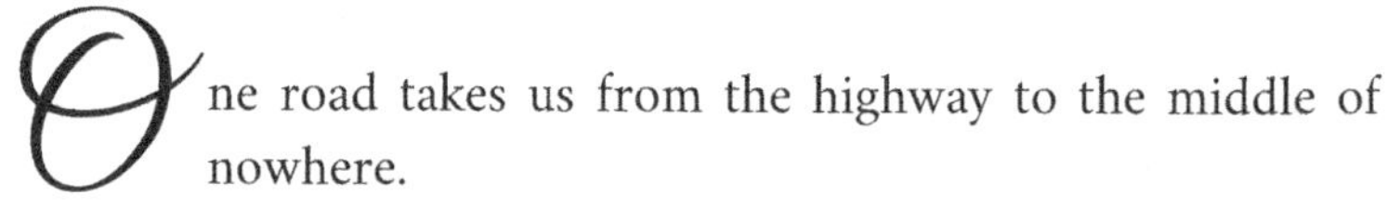

One road takes us from the highway to the middle of nowhere.

Toulouse prison is an immense block of concrete and barbed wire, of surrounding fields that appear abandoned. It's a big place, housing over 3,000 prisoners, making it one of Europe's largest prisons.

Amadou steers the SUV to one of the closest spots in the large, empty parking lot. When he turns off the engine we all just sit there for a moment in utter silence, waiting.

Régis's lighter frame is no longer brushed against my chest. No, he has moved over, away from me, to where he now sits with a rigid spine as he peers outside the window in front of him. There's nothing more than meters and meters of solid mass of misery, surrounded by cables adorned with spines to prevent inmates from climbing the walls.

Finally he turns to face me. Biting his lip, his gaze has become glassy. "I—"

Despite that ferocious flicker in his bright blue eyes, he looks so fucking fragile. It takes a lot for me not to scoop him up and press him tight against my own body, to warm his chilly bones, comfort his worrying mind and kill his demons. I'd slash them all, starting with the monster who's waiting for me inside that building across from us. The monster who keeps him up at night.

When Régis finally blinks, a tear rolls from his cheek and despite my earlier resolution, my hand shoots out. I want to soothe him so badly, brush his sorrow away, but another part of me hesitates. Because this moment is Régis's, and I'm just a passenger. Clenching my jaw I keep my hand lingering, in case he...in case he needs me. In case he accepts the comfort that I'm willing to give, even though this is very new territory.

I watch him swiftly brush his own tear away with long, agile fingers.

Yeah, I want him to need me. Because I'm a fucking goner for my little stepbrother.

Régis dips his gaze and looks at my hand, then reaches out his own, hesitant fingers. My heart is beating in my throat, pounding and pounding, as I wait for him to accept me. To accept us.

He takes in a deep breath, and whispers, "You could have found yourself an easier lover." His fingertips brush mine, and I stifle a sigh of relief. So much fucking relief.

The corners of my lips tip up when our eyes meet. "It's a bit late for that."

His digits caress the back of my hand, the touch featherlight. "You could have found someone who's not your stepbrother." His own delectable mouth pouts into the smallest of smiles, making my own lips curve a little more while my heart keeps on thundering.

"Now where would be the fun in that?"

His long, slender fingers curl over mine and squeeze. He cocks his head. "Someone who's not your competitor?"

"I prefer ally," I smoothe. He lets out a chuckle, the sound a little breathy. Perhaps he is feeling as relieved as I am.

"Have you lost your wickedness?" He asks. I suck in my bottom lip and his gaze drops to catch the moment. Then he flicks his eyes back to mine. "Well?"

"Oh, I can assure you, *chaton*, that I have not lost my wickedness. Nor my appetite for challenges. And I am determined to share all my deviant tastes with you. But—" I jerk my chin toward the looming prison. "There's someone in there who deserves the wickedness in me more."

Régis's fingers squeeze mine again while his chest expands from the deep breath he inhales. His body shudders when he exhales, and he nods. Then, "I'm ready. Let's get this over with."

I raise his hand swiftly while dropping a kiss onto the delicate, smooth skin before he can pull away. Then I let out a howl and rush to open the door. "That's the spirit." Régis scoffs behind me, but I ignore it. I'm too fucking elated to care. This is the moment I have been waiting for ever since I caught Régis trapped in his past in that horrifying cage. No, scratch that, when Régis walked into my life with that haunted look in his eyes.

Payback's a bitch, and I'll make sure that we'll fill our cups with that luscious potion of vengeance.

Security checks our ID, then searches us extensively before they let us deeper into the prison.

"I thought we came during visiting hours?" I ask Amadou, who leads our tiny group with confident strides, looking every bit the tough, protective bodyguard he is. Turning over his shoulder, he offers me a striking grin with shiny white teeth that light up his entire face. "You know your father."

"Visiting hour finished an hour ago," a young prison guard supplies from behind us. There are several other guards shielding us as we make our way through the corridors, where noises from inmates are slowly growing stronger with each turn. There's a banging sound, repetitive and threatening, accompanied by hoots and shouts. A buzzing sound echoes through the building, and I can feel Régis tense in my hand.

"It's just standard procedure," the young officer says. "It might sound a little scary when you're not used to it."

"What's happening?" Régis finally asks, when ahead of us, a group of officers come running through a different part of the corridor.

"Fight," the guard in the front says, then gestures to the door on the left. We all come to a stop. The rest of the wardens step away from us, and the guard with the keys in hand turns to face Régis.

"Mister Deveraux, you have ten minutes with him. He's restrained, so he can't hurt you."

Régis shudders, then lets out a restrained chuckle. "Why would he hurt me? He's my Dad." The guards blink at each other.

"Updated prison policy," the warden with the keys nods. "Also, just so you're aware, there are cameras everywhere, so you won't really be alone."

"Oh, I won't be alone." Régis looks my way. "My boyfriend will join me."

Boyfriend. Not stepbrother, or nemesis. Or, what was it that he called me that first time? Narcissistic punk, if I remember correctly. I want to call him out on it, make a joke or something stupid, but now's not the time. This is far more important. Him standing here, telling the whole fucking world that he belongs to me. That I am his boyfriend. I give myself an inner high-five and can't help the way my chest swells at the meaning. Unfortunately, the guard shakes his head at that moment.

"I'm afraid you are the only one who can go any further." His gaze sweeps over me, as if he's sizing me up. Uh uh, dickhead, you've got the wrong guy.

"I believe Jean-Louis Deveraux called to arrange this private appointment?" I say, tilting my chin as high as I can. The warden nods.

"He did. But—"

"And you still want to go against his arrangement?"

The guard hesitates.

"Allow me to introduce myself, I am Arthur Deveraux. Maybe I should give my father a call." This time the warden truly looks puzzled, his gaze darting back and forth between me and Régis. My inner devil purrs. "That—" I point toward Régis. "Is my stepbrother *and* lover. Now, I will visit his fucking crazy dad with him together."

"But—" The warden sputters, face flushing from embarrassment.

"You can always call my dad instead to clarify this little misunderstanding," I send him a wolfish smile, "But I can assure you that he won't be happy that his son was denied access. Not happy at all."

For a brief second, no one moves, the hoots and howls from the inmates the only sound in the air. Then the guard nods and jerkily moves to stick the key into the keyhole. "Very well. You can accompany your stepbrother. You have ten minutes."

The heavy, iron door opens with a barely audible groan, revealing a plain, white room with nothing but a table and four chairs. From my swift once-over I see that they are secured to the equally white concrete floor. Unable to toss any chairs around then, I conclude with a slight inward pout. How I'd love to create some chaos. Although, judging from the huddled form that sits at the table, both his wrists shackled to the top, there won't be much of a fight to begin with. At least, not the type of fight that's won with fists and punches.

A plastic cup of water has been placed in front of him, and just as I wonder why the hell personnel would give him any refreshments during our visit, Régis's Dad starts coughing. It's a throaty, dry wheeze that sounds as if he's sputtering up his entire fucking lungs, his body shuddering from the violent jerks. He's wearing a pair of grey sweatpants and a matching hoodie, slippers wrapped around his socked feet. His ankles are equally shackled to the table.

"Keep your germs to yourself," I snap as we make our way inside, fingers tightening, making sure to keep my little step-brother's smaller hand securely wrapped in mine.

"Dad," Régis chokes, and just as I think he'll wring himself loose from my hold to do something stupid like run over to the sick fuck and hug him, he lets me guide him to the other side of the table. As we take a seat, I catch the disapproving stare from a pair of equally blue eyes, before his face converts into a pained grimace. Régis's Dad juts his chin my way, then spats, "What's that? Is this your boyfriend? Didn't I teach you any better?"

Next to me Régis flinches, and my own jaw clenches with fury. I cross my ankles and push them firmly in an attempt to stay seated. But oh, do I want to stand up and let my fists have their way with that timeworn face. Régis squeezes my hand, before he replies, "No. You didn't teach me anything at all, Dad." His voice is soft, but he already sounds tired, and we haven't even begun. His father places both his hands on the table, the movement followed by a heavy rattling sound.

"You need to get me out of here, son," he pleads, his tone softer and more pliant now like a turned switch, much like his gaze. "It can be you and I again, my boy. We don't need anyone else. Your mother is fighting me, Régis, she is determined to punish me even further."

Those words make me explode. "Don't you dare speak to

him about punishment." My ankles pull free and I growl at him as I start getting out of my seat.

"Arthur," Régis whispers urgently, and I know that I should shut my fucking mouth, know that I should let my lover do this by himself, but fuck... it's hard. Squeezing my jaw tight with a pained groan, I sit back down and turn to face Régis, nodding in defeat. Across the table, his father's trembling. At first, I think he might be sick, but then I realize he's laughing. His entire body shaking, his face contorted into one of the most vicious scowls I have ever seen.

Here is who lives in Régis's nightmares. The monster himself.

His lips curled into a fine sneer, his brilliant eyes shooting frantic daggers. The man's a fucking psychopath.

"Régis, Régis, is that why you never came to visit me?" He tuts. Next to me, Régis shrinks, and I can feel him running for cover into his mind. The only way he has ever won a battle. "Because you were too busy with your *boyfriend*?" He lets out a disgusting chuckle.

"No," Régis wheezes next to me. This time I squeeze his hand, hoping that he'll find comfort in my touch.

"You know who he is, right? He's a fucking rat, son." He continues to shudder, mouth dropping open to let out a horrifying breathy chuckle. His eyes flash and the room goes cold. Next to me, Régis writhes in his seat.

"No, I never came because of the judge."

"The judge?" Régis's dad sneers, his previous mockery visibly replaced by something vicious. "The *judge?*"

"I think this is enough," I say, giving Régis's hand another, more urgent squeeze. "Come on, *chaton*, we're out."

"*Chaton?*" Régis's father barks out a chortle, loud and raspy and full of hate.

"Where did my son go? Who is this spineless little fucker—"

"You want to know where he went?" Régis jumps out of his

seat, my hand still glued to his. I scramble to follow him up. "You left him, do you remember?" His voice trembles, thick with loathe and fury. "Like you always did. Punished. Alone in that fucking cage. You left him to rot. Left him to hate himself and the world. But you know what? Someone opened that lock and got me out. Someone who wants me in their life, who wants to love and care for me."

Régis's father lets out a terrifying roar as he tries to get up, but thankfully locks into place by the shackles. He growls in protest, his hands fluttering against the table when he realizes they don't move any further. "You are a worthless piece of shit! You are not my son! You—"

"You're right," Régis booms. His father shuts up at that, instead gazing with a burning stare, and I hold my breath. "I am not your son, not anymore. I have filed for freedom, and together with the official statement from the psychiatrist who examined me after my mother came to rescue me from you, I will soon no longer be your child."

"Régis—" His father shudders, but my fierce fighter is not yet finished. With a wave of his hand he dismisses anyone from speaking.

"I don't want anything to do with you. Ever. You don't exist to me anymore, nor do I to you. I have erased you from my life. You hear me? I have erased you." He inhales deeply, lets the air out as they both stare at each other for what feels like a lifetime. In silence. "*Mon coeur,*" he finally says, squeezing my hand and encouraging me to follow him. "Take me home."

25

RÉGIS

The car journey back to Monterrey Castle feels awfully long and too short at the same time. My thoughts are scattered all around my leaking heart, though I'm feeling light. Relieved. Confused—although things are crystal clear at the same time.

I openly declared Arthur as my boyfriend and he accepted that role. Just like that, as if it was the most logical thing in life.

Although, that too, is a revelation. Arthur is the most obnoxious, cocky, privileged and determined guy I have ever met. But underneath all of that, he is also loyal and fierce, sexy and intelligent. And my goddamn stepbrother. My lover. Yes, Arthur is the love of my life.

I nibble on my lower lip while gazing outside as the car leaves the highway and turns for the miners village of Saint-Laurent. We pass rundown shops, a church, a bakery that is still open despite the late hour, and then we turn around the corner, disregarding the *Place de la Gare* and its empty train station as we head for the forest.

"Your father called," Amadou hums. Next to me, I feel Arthur move in his seat, and without hesitating, I grab his hand and curl my fingers around his. "He received a call from the warden," Amadou continues, and even without looking, I can feel his eyes on me through the rearview mirror. "He and Nathalie will be waiting in his office upon return. They have some matters to discuss."

I swallow, thinking of something to say. My stomach clenches as the tension rises in the silence that follows.

What if this connection that has been growing between us, will be cut off before our minds have time to connect any further? My chest tightens at that doomed scenario, making my thoughts spiral.

Get in there.

No! Never again.

"Are you alright?" Arthur's soft question makes me blink, clearing the fog from my mind. I lift my gaze only to meet his searching eyes. They are so dark, those thick, long lashes fluttering when he curls his lips into a small smile. "You are squeezing me to death here."

My eyes drop with a startle, and when I see my white knuckles cover his palm, I try to pull back and release him. He doesn't let me. Instead he puts pressure as he squeezes back while using his other hand to cup my face. His fingers trace the lines around my mouth then stroke my cheek.

"Your skin is cold, *chaton*. I'll take you to bed, warm you up, shield you from your fears. Would you like me to?"

Yes. So badly.

"We can't," I choke. My chest constricts, but I'm not ready to share my dread to have our little bubble of intimacy burst so soon. "We mustn't keep our parents waiting."

"You're right." Arthur's fingers on my face halt and he lowers his gaze, searching mine once more. "Is that why you're suddenly so tense?"

Releasing my hand from his, I turn them both into fists, frustration boiling up and spilling my words. "Aren't you afraid of what they'll say?" I pull my face free from his hold and blow a lost curl from my cheek before I look away in frustration. Outside the forest greets us, the bumpy road a sign that we are nearly at Monterrey Castle. "They know, Arthur. About us." Turning back to face my stepbrother, I feel a desperation that threatens to choke me. "They will separate us."

Everyone I love goes away. And I will be alone again.

My chest cracks and I breathe in harshly, but it's like oxygen doesn't reach my lungs. It stays high in my head, making me float. Making me sad, so fucking sad.

"Your mother already knew, Régis." Arthur's voice is low, calm, as he wraps his fingers back around mine and pulls me in once more.

"What?" I ask, bewildered. Arthur presses his hand against my shoulders and drags me, closer and closer, until my chin hits the curve between his neck and his cheek. And then his hand slides up and combs the hair in my nape calmly. I let out a heavy breath, then carefully wrap my own arm around his shoulder and turn my body as I allow myself to melt into his embrace.

"Your mother already knew," he repeats, like it's the most normal thing in the world. "She confronted me during Christmas. Gifted me with a picture of you, from when you were young. She promised not to tell Dad. We will have to do that now."

Pulling back slightly, I can only stare up at him. Arthur's hooded gaze is dark and mysterious, yet gentle like his touch. "But back at Christmas, we weren't together yet. I mean…how did she find out?"

He shrugs, then brushes the same stubborn curl out of my face with a smile, before he drops a kiss onto my cheek. "I love your hair," he mumbles instead, then presses his lips on mine. "We're going to be alright, little stepbrother, I promise."

The ominous towers of Monterrey Castle come into view as they stand out against the dark sky, welcoming us back home.

Some of the stones of the impressive building are lit up in golden lights, forming the shape of a crow.

I can't keep my eyes off it, as if the bird represents the mysterious, enticing veil of the secret brotherhood.

Alpha Fraternarii.

"We're here," Amadou announces after parking in one of the designated spots. Not wanting to keep our parents waiting much longer, we make our way out of the car and inside the castle, where he follows us in silence through the labyrinth of those narrow corridors, countless frames and endless golden sconces. After having taken this route numerous times, I actually start to find my way around here, the puzzle of passages slowly becoming a clearer picture.

We halt in front of Jean-Luc's office. My heart plummets, despite Arthur's little squeeze on my shoulder, followed by the soft kiss he presses onto my head. When he pulls away, his gaze lingers, just like the smile which instantly brings me comfort. He opens the door and right as we make our way in, we are welcomed by a barking laugh.

It's Louis. He's standing by the crackling fire, dressed in his football gear minus the shoes, holding a glass of champagne, laughing at something his dad just said. Jean-Luc, wearing his usual navy-blue suit that would match any of our school uniforms had we worn them tonight, accompanied by his thick, silvered mane slicked across one side of his face. He always looks so well-composed, in balance and ready to receive whoever wants a piece of him, every single bit the powerful, wealthy business magnet. He too, is holding a glass of champagne, looking relaxed and amused by Louis's outburst. On the coffee table tens and tens of different tapas have been placed, and the record plays a soft song.

"I can see that we're late to the party," Arthur grins, then gestures for me to go ahead and keep on walking. I do, the thought of him following me on my tail making my shoulders slump in relief.

Louis looks up and holds out his hand for his twin to clap. "There you are." He turns his gaze to mine and smiles. "Hi there, little s-brother."

"Hi," I choke out, swallowing. I let my eyes dart around until they've found my mother. She is standing by the window, her back toward the glass, wearing another of her usual, classy, long dresses. Her hair is pulled into a ponytail, making her smile even more prominent than I'm used to.

"Régis." She takes a few steps toward me, and when we reach for each other, our touch is a little hesitant, though genuine. I place a kiss on each of her soft cheeks, and let her cup my face and pull me in close. "I'm so very proud of you," she mutters, her fingers digging a little deeper into my skin.

"Son." Jean-Luc booms, and it isn't until Nathalie releases me, that I realize he is talking to me. I turn around, to where he is waiting for me to accept the glass of champagne he's offering. Behind me, by the fire, Louis and Arthur are casually chatting as if we haven't just come back from prison. Although that's not entirely true, because I don't miss how Arthur keeps a protective eye on me every now and then, checking in to see if I'm okay.

Am I? Are *we*? Okay? God, I hope we will still be, after tonight.

Accepting Jean-Luc's offer, I clink my glass against his outstretched one before taking a drink. Champagne still tastes a little too sour for me, but I suppose I'm starting to get accustomed to the taste. And something tells me that I need to if I want to survive in the Deveraux family, considering the number of litres they drink.

"So, Deveraux Holding successfully bought one of the largest champagne houses in the country," Jean-Luc announces. "And this is the result. Do you like it?" He chortles, then squeezes my shoulder affectionately as if he already knows the answer to that. He seems to be in a good mood. Will he still be when he finds out the truth about me and his son?

Part of me feels brave after what today put me through, the reckoning with my own dad. That was brutal, but I'm still here. And I want to claim my prize, damn it. The real prize.

My prize.

Arthur Deveraux.

"Come, sit," Jean-Luc gestures to all of us, then grabs a number of documents from the piano hood before moving to where my mother has already taken a seat on the couch, right across from us. It's exactly the same way we sat last time except that this time I find myself in the middle, with both my big step-brothers sitting on each side of me. Although only one of them possesses the sort of body heat that is addicting.

"I believe we have a few more things to celebrate today," Jean-Luc announces. "How did it go in prison today, boys?"

I can feel all eyes turn to me, and as I slouch back a little deeper, I try to formulate the right words. Part of me knows I should feel embarrassed. I'm not even sure if Louis knows I went to see Dad in prison, and I don't know what I think of him now knowing. But another part of me is done with that shame.

I'm still here.

"I went to visit Dad..." I hesitate, suddenly feeling uncomfortable with the wording. "To visit...*him*," I correct. "I went there to tell him that I want nothing to do with him anymore. That I will do everything I can in my power to separate myself from him. I don't want him to be my father anymore."

My chest shudders at my own words, but where I expect my heart to crack open and weep, there's a dullness instead. I have shed enough tears. I have suffered long enough.

Someone lets out a long puff of air, and when I drag my gaze up, I blink back at Jean-Luc. The older man smiles at me, a hesitant, trembling smile that's very unlike his usual self-confident appearance. The documents in his hand flutter when he waves them in the air. "From the day I realized that Nathalie had a son, I have wanted to have you in our family, Régis. Nathalie was the gift life gave me, and you are part of her. Of us. Words won't ever convey just how sorry I am for all you have endured. I know Nathalie hasn't told me everything about your past, but I pray that the two of you will be able to find a way to talk about things. Don't carry your burden by yourself, son. Life's too short to grieve in perpetuity." His gaze slides to Louis, then to Arthur. "Louis will be there for you too. As will Arthur..." He clears his throat, the tips of his lips quirking up. "I would very much like to be your father, Régis."

Silence follows his words. I expect someone to call him out on it, but when I turn to my right, I find Louis looking at me with that usual crooked grin on his handsome face.

"What do you say?" He asks. When I don't reply immediately, his grin widens. "Don't worry, little s-brother, Dad already discussed this with me and Arthur. This family has no secrets, right?" He winks in a silent challenge, and in a flash of memory, I'm back in the SUV when I had my first taste of champagne. My first touch of Arthur. When Louis had also challenged me. Back then I had no idea what was coming for me, but now I do. I am no longer that skittish kid who lived with his abusive dad.

"I—" Here goes nothing. Turning back to Jean-Luc, I hesitate, then take in a deep breath and puff up my chest. Then I blurt, "I'm in love with your son. I—I—"

"What?" Louis taunts next to me. "Why are you only just telling me now?"

"He doesn't mean you, you dickhead." Arthur grumbles, then raises our entangled hands for everyone to see. His scowl is on his twin, but I don't miss the mischievous twinkle in those onyx eyes. "He means me."

Louis chuckles and is about to say something in return, no doubt a joke of some sort, when Jean-Luc says, "I know."

All faces turn his way. His dark eyes dart between both me and Arthur as we wait for him to say something. He takes his time, continuing to stare at us in rapid intervals, until finally he parts his lips. He clears his throat, then casually drops the documents onto the table. I immediately recognize the official logo of the national government with the colors of our flag.

Adoption papers.

He lets out a long breath, then rubs his knees in thought. "I won't judge your love," he finally says and pinches the bridge of his nose. "After all, my own experience of falling in love with a homeless woman wasn't exactly conventional. Still our family accepted us, because they recognized our love. The same stands for you two today, Arthur and Régis." My mother grabs his hand, holding it in hers, just as I feel Arthur squeezing my own hand. Something in me unlocks. "But we are a well-known family, boys, and I need you to be sure. I can't make any controversial announcements only to have you back out afterwards. It's imperative that you two know—*feel*—that you are meant to be together forever before we share this publically. You're still young, and I wouldn't want to put that sort of responsibility on your shoulders. Perhaps we can work on a solution as a family for a little while while you see if this relationship is taking you where you hope it is?"

"I want to stay here in Monterrey Castle after I graduate," Arthur blurts.

Jean-Luc's eyes flit to meet his son's. Then he slowly lifts the papers from the table.

"The answer is yes, Jean-Luc," I breathe, before he can reply to Arthur. "I'd love to have you as my dad. Officially. But only if you can accept me as your other sons' lover."

Next to me, Louis barks out a laugh, slapping his knees as he bends forward with laughter. "Oh my god, the drama. I'm loving it! And you guys say that I'm the trouble maker." Grabbing the bottle from the wine cooler, he stands to top us all up. "Step son,

son, son-in-law, whatever the title, Régis." He halts to clink his own glass with mine, his charcoal eyes dancing with amusement and something else. It's affection, and it's making my heart swell in my chest. "I'm glad that you're a part of the family."

"I still can't believe how well that went, right? *Right*?" Bouncing through the damn corridors, we finally make our way from Jean-Luc's office to our own dorm.

Our dorm. Bedroom. Bed. Ours.

Next to me, Arthur chuckles raspily and grabs me tighter into his embrace. "Right. And I can't believe that you actually finished that final glass of champagne. If I'm not mistaken, you're getting the hang of it?"

I let out a snort then trip over my own feet, silently bracing myself to hit the floor right when Arthur's fingers dig into the bare skin of my nape as he hauls me upright. He pulls me to his chest. "What did you expect, hmm?" He purrs softly into my ear, making goosebumps scatter all around the flushed skin. "That I'd let my little stepbrother walk free? I'm nothing if not a man of my word. And I've told you numerous times that they all know that I claimed you." Clutching my neck tighter in his firm grip, he forces me to turn my face and look at him. His eyes are dark, with that hungry stare I've come to know. Pupil-blown, with a tiny ring of sparkling gold. His lips hover over me, his warm breath lingering right above my mouth. I lick my lips eagerly, excitement sizzling through my stomach, revelling in the way his gaze takes the movement in with a low growl.

"You're mine, Régis. My broken boy. My love. And I will melt all your fractures back into one, smooth shape of a heart." He leans in, closing the final distance between our faces. "My heart," he murmurs, making my chest tighten with a longing so strong it burns. And then he presses his lips against mine as he keeps my nape in check in his firm grip, licking his way inside with a tenacity that is new. It shows me that he too was nervous about tonight. He too was afraid that our blooming connection would not be approved.

Even though he would never admit it out loud, because Arthur Deveraux would never admit out loud that he is afraid.

Our tongues, teeth and lips tangle and play, nip and lick. In turn, it's making my knees buckle and my cock throb. My head is spinning and while it could have been the drink, I know for certain it's because of Arthur. And okay... perhaps a little bit because of the champagne.

"Take me back to our room," I beg against his mouth.

"Yeah?" Arthur spreads my clothed ass cheeks, then squeezes them, urging me to lift my hips. I do, and he hoists me up until my crossed legs hug his waist and my arms circle his shoulders. Pressing my cheek against his collarbone, I can't help the smile that curves my lips at the feel of his beating heart. Fast, impatient, eager thumps. "Are you hungry for me, little brother?" Arthur licks the shell of my ear and I shudder when I frantically nod, my cock throbbing in my pants. Too tight, everything feels too tight, too hard, too eager for release.

"Please," I wheeze. "I need you, *mon coeur*."

"I need you too, *chaton*. C'mon, let's go back."

Arthur starts making his way back to the large reception, and I pull my arms tighter around his neck for leverage. However, when we get closer to the canteen, I realize that we're not alone. Others could see us any minute now. I wiggle in his grip. "Perhaps it's better if you let me go. What if someone else sees us?"

"Fuck them," Arthur grunts against my ear. His nonchalance makes my heart billow, filling with a sense of pride and belonging. "You are mine." My hands tighten around his neck and I squeeze my eyes, deeply inhaling those words. I am his. A shock waves through my body, making my core tremble with the most primal sense of relief. I belong to him. I'm no longer alone, no longer in the dark. I am wanted by the one who carries my heart. And he is mine, my heart. *Mon coeur.*

I hear Arthur bark a few greetings when we make our final way to our dorm, but I don't open my eyes again, not wanting anyone to interrupt this moment of bliss.

Finally the door of our dorm slides open with a bang, hitting the wall, revealing soft sounds in the shared corridor. Dominique's playing the piano, and by the smell of it, Gaël has unleashed some of his oils.

"Eucalyptus," Arthur mumbles in my ear, as he kicks the door shut, then strides to my room, with my body still firmly kept between his hands. "Your scent."

"My scent?" I ask.

"Hmm. It smells like the forest. It suits you." Arthur places me onto my bed like I'm fragile, then looks down on me with a tender look in his eyes, that quickly turns wicked.

I frown. "What?"

"Nothing." He shrugs. "It's just that I have been thinking."

"O-kayy?"

Arthur huffs out a laugh, then toes off his shoes and starts to unbuckle his pants. I watch, mesmerised by the sight of those long, slender fingers opening the zipper and popping the button. When he slides his pants off his sculpted thighs, I ask, "What were you thinking?"

The material falls down his long legs and onto the ground as Arthur crawls onto the bed sliding in between my spread legs. My erection kicks against my restraints, and he must have seen, because a luscious smirk curls his lips. "Hungry?" He pulls off my shoes, then opens my pants with agile movements, dragging them and my socks down and onto the floor, leaving me in my very tight underwear.

"Maybe. But what were you thinking?"

He grins. "Curious much? You know me by now, I'm always

thinking. Of you, of me, of us. Of our future...." He tilts his head, eyeing my crotch, then licks over the cotton of my boxers, tracing a line over my bulge. "You told me that we should be more open-minded. The Alpha Fraternarii. Right?" His teeth peek out and latch on my boxers, tearing it to one side to give space for my cock.

"Yeah," I pant, unsure of where he wants to go with his words, and impatient to feel his mouth on my body. I'm so hot for him.

Arthur hums. "So, I may have told Elder Jacques that the Deveraux family supports the idea of giving other, securely selected, students an opportunity to prove their worth."

"Prove their worth?" I try to snort, but I stifle a groan when Arthur growls his victory and catches my hard, throbbing cock in his mouth the moment it plops free. "Fuck."

"Hmm," Arthur purrs and looks up. The sight of that handsome face, mouth filled with my cock, is enough for my body to shiver in hot desire. He snakes a hand around my girth, then pops off with one last lick that makes me moan. "If we get to chase them," he murmurs.

"What?" I'm dazed, but not dazed enough to catch that dangerous glimmer in my lover's eyes. "*What?*"

"Our brothers want to chase them. The new members."

"Will you?" I blurt.

Arthur chuckles, then takes my cock back into his mouth and shakes his head. He suckles on the crown, making my mind stutter, then whispers with his lips against my slit, "I already have my perfect little slut here." He flicks his tongue against the leaking head. "Don't I?"

"Y-yeah," I gasp.

Arthur grins, then leads my cock back into his mouth and all the way to the back of his throat.

"Oh, fuck, oh fuck," I sing. My toes curl and my eyes roll back as pleasure builds low in my stomach, making my balls draw close. "If you continue like this, I will come too soon. It's been a stressful night, you know?"

Arthur chuckles, then pulls back a little to lap around my cock. "My poor *chaton,* all that pent-up energy makes you want to come really soon? Uh uh, that's not going to happen. You're going to come when I tell you to and not a moment before." He suckles my cock right back between his plump lips and hollows his cheeks.

"Fuck," I groan and my hand falls down to his head. My fingers curl around a few strands of his thick, raven hair and I pull. Hard. "I'm gonna come." Arthur must see my inner battle, because the scorching look in his eyes goes together with wickedness, and goddamn sexiness as he once more pulls off my throbbing cock just to let his tongue play with the slit. I'm leaking for him, trembling in my hunger for release. And still he won't let me come.

Sitting back on his haunches, he barks, "Turn around." His hands grab hold of my sides and he lifts his own leg as he rolls me over and onto my stomach, my cock leaking onto the bed. He crawls over my back and reaches for my bedside table. "This is the last time we will use a condom. We'll get tested and cleared, then I can properly fuck you. *D'accord*?"

I can only nod against the pillow, while my hips rock sluggishly back against his hard frame. "Please," I wheeze, too fucking gone. Behind me I hear him uncapping the bottle of lube, the sound going in harmony with his sinister chuckle.

"Oh, you want me to finish what I started?" His fingers crawl over my ass cheeks, and I expect them to be wet with lube, getting ready to breach my hole, but instead, he squeezes my cheeks apart. "Spread them wider for me, *chaton*. Come here." Grabbing my hands, he places them onto my own ass and spreads my cheeks apart. I do as he says, following his instructions, rocking my hips in an attempt to relieve the pressure building inside of me while begging him to continue. "I like you like this, little brother, spread open and waiting for me." His tongue licks the crease of my ass and I jolt in surprise. "Hmm. You taste good. Keep on spreading them for me, show me your sweet little hole." He clasps my hands and I comply, panting when he licks me again. "This is mine, isn't it?" I moan in reply, and he chuckles raspily against the sensitive skin of my rim. "That's right, kitten. All mine." And then he dives in, lapping at my hole with rapid flicks of his tongue that have me babble in rapture and buck my hips. "Oh, you want more?" Planting his own hands on mine, he spreads me impossibly wide, and his tongue plunges into my hole, licking and nibbling as it goes impossibly deep. Moaning freely, I push my hips back frantically for more friction.

"Please," I pant. "Please please please. I need it so badly."

Arthur keeps on piercing that spot with his tongue, while his hands, still intertwined with mine, encourage my hips to rock back. And again, and again, until I go crazy with need.

"*Mon coeur*, please," I sob. That seems to do the trick, because he finally pulls back and releases my hands. Pulling me tight by my hips, he jerks me upward and onto hands and knees.

"So desperate for my cock." He taunts as he lines up behind me. "Your hole looks so fucking sweet, *chaton*. All opened up for me. You taste so good, baby. I could lick your ass every minute of the day."

"Fuck," I choke, his words making my cock lurch.

"Are you ready for your big brother?" He grabs a fist of my hair, then tips up my head, bringing it to his chest while the rest of my body is leaning on my hands and knees. "There's my sweet kitten." He nuzzles my cheek and neck, and places open kisses on the tender skin while he lets his cock slide in. Slowly, so tauntingly slowly, while he hums on my skin and soothes my heated flesh with his wet lips.

"Oh, fuck," I repeat on a sob.

"Hmm, exactly." Arthur glides in all the way, until he's fully sheathed. Only then does he let out a shuddering breath, the warm puff of air on my neck causing goosebumps. "You turned my life upside down," he muses against my skin. "The hidden little stepbrother. How on earth could someone hide you?" He slowly pulls back until only the tip of his cock is buried inside me. "I love it when you fight me." His fingers trace the lines of my back, following the bone of my spine all the way up to my nape. "But look at you now. Trembling with need, my cock about to wreck your ass, bringing you the best fucking of your life." The tips of his fingers are soft in comparison to his filthy words. He's right, I love the hold he has on me. "You're so clever, so good. Together we can make so much happen."

"Yeah," I mumble.

"I'll wait for you here in Monterrey Castle, where we can spend every free minute together. While you continue your studies, I'll work from Dad's office. We will have our own, private dorm here. Would you like that?" He slides back into my ass, but the movement is slow, sinful. It's Arthur's way of torturing me. He won't stop until I give him what he wants. Luckily I want to give him just that, everything he wants, because I want it too.

"*Oui*," I reply.

"Good." He traces his fingers down over my spine and caresses my ass cheeks and crease. "Look at that, filled with my cock. What a fucking sight you are. Perfection," he murmurs, his voice thick with aw. "We will rule Saint-Laurent together until you graduate."

"*Oui*," I moan, when he pulls back and slowly slides back in.

"You will win that prize before you graduate. I'll make sure of it. Would you like that?" This time when he slides in, his rhythm has picked up. It's still not fast enough, but when I rock my hips to encourage him, he slaps my ass with a *tssk*.

I halt and let out a string of curses that he laughs away. "*Oui*," I settle with. Arthur hums in satisfaction.

"That's a good reply. Then, we will get rid of the cage, get rid of everything and everyone who hurt you in the past." His rhythm picks up once more and this time I start panting. When I don't reply fast enough, he slaps my ass once more, harder, the impact making me hiss.

"*Oui*!" I squeak. Arthur chuckles.

"That's right, *chaton*. Because you are mine. Everyone here knows, and soon the outside world will know of our forbidden, filthy love."

"*Oui*."

"Now, let me show you how I satisfy my little brother. Hold on tight, my love."

26

ARTHUR

"Fuck, fuck, fuck," Régis sings when I slam right home and roll my hips against his like a snake. His hole clenches, squeezing me impossibly tight while his parted lips moan against the pillow. He's laying on his cheek, offering me the perfect view of his side frame, that golden hair and his angular, sharp features. They are covered with a softness that is so Régis, from the flushed cheek to the wide eyes. His tone is no longer raspy and his pleas have decreased into a string of unintelligible moans he lets out when I relentlessly plunder his ass.

"So fucking tight," I praise, and I lean in further on the palms of my hands as I capture Régis's puffy mouth. "So good," I murmur against his lips. They are wet and sweet when he presses them onto me, revealing soft words. He's once again begging for more though I don't think he realizes the sounds he makes, tempting me with those piercing eyes to bring him release. "You make me feel so good, little brother. So fucking good." Grabbing a handful of those luscious golden waves, I lift his head with his mouth still glued to mine. His hot, tight ass is still milking my cock. His hand flies to the back of my head and he squeezes my nape, keeping me in position. I growl, but while

I let him keep me steady, my lips are in charge, licking and nipping and dragging my tongue and teeth all around inside his mouth. When I bite onto his tongue, he lets out a yelp but his body shudders urgently. He's close.

"Is this what I'll be getting every day?" I ask against his lips. He lets out a smile, lips puffy and swollen, a glassy gaze in his eyes. "Fuck, baby—" My stomach tenses with a nearing orgasm, and my thrusts become sloppy as pleasure threatens to pull me under.

"S'il te plait," Régis begs. "Come."

And that's it. That's all it takes for me to lose complete control. I rock my hips and give him another few thrusts before my body tenses up. "Fuck—" My heavy balls combust and my orgasm rattles through me like a freight train, blazing mercilessly through my entire body. I come on a howl, body convulsing as I collapse above Régis. He whines, and with my after-orgasm brain still foggy, I pull out, then spin him around and onto his back. His gorgeous, weeping cock is hard as rock, veiny and wet and I don't hesitate. I swallow it down all the way to the back of my throat and suck like my life depends on it. Régis shudders and shouts, body shaking as he sobs and moans. And then he fills my mouth with his sweet release. I swallow it down, greedily, milking him frantically until he pushes me away. I leave a last lick on his slit, then press a kiss onto his lower stomach. Régis is still shaking when I come back up and take him into my arms, pulling us both under the blankets and turning to face one another. Bringing him even closer to my chest, I mumble, *"L'amour de ma vie."*

"And you are the love of mine," he muses, then yawns. "Can we go to sleep? I'm exhausted."

I turn my head, catching his hooded eyes through the dim light of the room. His face is close to mine, his scent blanketing my senses. Without a single thought, I lean in and rub my nose against his, making him giggle as he returns the gesture.

Outside the room the other guys are chatting as they get on with their whereabouts. It's only Thursday night, but right now it feels that all the nights of the entire week have been jammed into one, single night. "I was nervous too," I whisper into the darkness. Régis doesn't reply, his breathing altered to light, regular snores. "I'm just not used to sharing those feelings. I was afraid that Dad wouldn't accept us. That he'd take away my future, both with you and within the business. I don't know who I'd be without all that." I let those thoughts grate my mind while my eyes search around Régis's room. They land on the cage. The one he agreed to getting rid of.

"What was it like?" Régis asks, the words barely a whisper that make my ears strain with awareness. I don't think my love has ever asked me a question about me and the life I lived before we met.

"What was what like?" I prompt, needing to be sure that we are on the same page. Because I want to talk to him despite our fatigue, want him to know. About me. He can know everything about me. But I'm not the type to overshare. Never have been.

"To be the golden boy of the family? The one who can't afford to be nervous or make mistakes?" His head shifts and I can feel him looking at me.

Releasing a shuddering breath, I take my time answering. To be frank, I didn't expect him to ask this, though I should have. Régis is perceptive enough to have captured my earlier conflict despite my bravado. Because...he's right, I'm used to puffing up my chest and I know how I come across. I'm irreplaceable. "I don't think I realized that I always had to be the tough one until I met you," I admit. In my arms, Régis lets out a soft smile that makes his chest rattle against mine.

"No?" He asks, though he doesn't sound amused.

"No. Before I met you, I lived a pretty one-sided life. I was just... me. It was clear from a pretty young age that between me and Louis, I was the studious type. So when the time came, the family agreed that I would take over Deveraux Holding one day. There are only two other members of my generation, and both Louis and Gaël don't have any business ambitions. They agreed to me taking that place, and there I was."

"There you were," Régis repeats, his lips brushing against my neck.

"Yeah. Before, I didn't fear anything, never had to. We have always sheltered each other in the family, and having a twin makes that even stronger. Me and Louis, we are one. That changed when I met you, *chaton*. You made my heart tremble. I hated you that very first time I met you. Because you put me out of balance, made me feel things I had never felt before."

Régis' teeth nip in the skin of my neck, marking me in the softest, yet most persistent ways possible. It makes my body tingle with pleasure. He releases my flesh, then murmurs, "What things?"

"Oh, you want me to spell it out for you, yeah?" I tease and he chuckles, then takes my flesh back between his grip, and pleasure escalates to a sense of belonging. "You were sweet, Régis. Timid and snappy. A feisty mystery. So beautiful. I guess I wanted you right away, but I didn't want to. I was afraid that you'd take my life away."

Régis lets go of my skin again and laps at the sting. "That I would replace you?" He asks, hot breath against the mark.

I shrug in the dim light. "I guess."

"Hmm." He settles himself against the crook of my neck, curling a leg over another as he gets comfortable, clearly wanting to be as close to me as possible. "I would never want to take over your future. Together, yes. But not without you. I'm nothing without you, *mon coeur*." One of his arms rounds my waist and dips his head, squeezing his chin against my chest. And then he lets out a satisfied hum. "Thank you for sharing this with me."

"You're welcome."

"I like wicked Arthur, but I like nervous Arthur too," Régis teases, making me grin.

"Don't get used to him too much, little brother. He'll rarely come out to play."

Régis giggles, and I kiss his head, pressing him impossibly close. *"Fait de beaux rêves, chaton."*

"You too," he replies almost immediately, making my eyes close with a soft smile. Smart ass.

Something has changed. I can feel it the moment I walk into Régis's bedroom, and catch him sitting at his desk, instead of hanging with the guys outside in the shared lounge, ready to celebrate Gael's birthday. At first I think he's studying, which shouldn't surprise me. But when I come closer, I realize something is missing.

The cage.

"Where is—" Did he get rid of it? Or did he simply move it? No, he got rid of it, I realize in a flash. Without telling me. That should make me proud, that should make his fierceness even more radiant, but selfish me feels left out. Why wouldn't he share such an important moment with me?

He must see me staring, because Régis huffs out a little laugh. It's a sad one, though, mingled with relief. I recognize that smile. It's the one I've become to notice when he's about to say something important. When his big brain has been stewing, and he has been agonizing over the words for too long.

"It's still here," he finally says, then with a sigh, points toward the closet. "But I think it's time. I think I'm ready to let go." The doors are ajar, and when I take a closer look, I catch sight of the glimmering steel. He has shoved the cage inside, though it won't exactly fit. The damn thing is too big to just fucking throw away, and just the right size for him to keep crawling inside. A growl forms its way in my throat as the thought splashes through my core, its instant fury making me a little light-headed.

"I want to ask Amadou," Régis continues, his voice soft, and careful. "I trust—you trust him, right?"

I reply with a single nod.

"I want him to take the cage somewhere far away. I can't do it by myself." His voice falters and I take that as my cue to slowly close the gap between us. He's still sitting at his desk when I reach him, and take hold of his hands. Mine clasp around his, the smooth texture caressed by my bigger frame.

"You don't want to know where the cage goes?"

He shakes his head.

"But you don't want the cage destroyed?"

"No." His voice is weak and strong at the same time. Insecure and determined. "I can't bear the thought that the cage is no longer there. But I don't want it in my life anymore. Because—"

"Because you have me now." This time I definitely growl, the sound making Régis smile through his rising sobs.

"Exactly."

I pull my little stepbrother out of his chair and against my chest in one smooth movement, then press us close together. "You feel that?" I mumble in his golden hair. "You feel how my heart beats for you?"

"Yes," he breathes, then sobs once more. It's not from sadness, I know. His arms curl around my shoulders and press me closer. It's from something so much more. Something we share, like some precious treasure.

"The only people I trust with my life are my family. Amadou is part of my family," I mumble.

He nods against my neck, his hair tickling my ear. "Call him. Ask him to come over. Let me do this, *mon coeur*." He pulls back, his blue eyes large and proud. "Let's do it now. *Allez*!" He insists, when I'm left fumbling with my phone.

"You're such a bossy babe," I complain, smiling when he mouths *but you love it.* I give Amadou quick instructions, and it takes him literally not more than three minutes to come bursting through the front door of our dorm, where the party has already begun.

"You're joining or what?" Louis whines from the kitchen when he sees us, a whisk and bowl in hand. No one flinches when we walk past carrying the metal cage toward the exit. No one flinches in the corridor when we carry it all the way through the narrow hall and down the stairs, through the reception area and to the parking where the SUV is waiting. Amadou opens the trunk and we place the cage inside. It's not until he closes the trunk that I feel the invisible weight lifted.

"I trust you," Régis tells Amadou. "Please take it somewhere, far away."

Amadou dips his head gracefully. "Thank you, Sir Régis. I will." When he looks up, his dark eyes land on mine, that warm glow scorching in its recognition. His lips tick up.

"Régis?"

Someone calls from behind us, and Amadou's gaze shoots up and behind us, only to flash at the sight of Régis's friend, Maxime. He approaches in a slow jog, his ginger hair flopped to one side, his freckles glimmering like tiny spots of gold. He's an attractive guy, though a little too gullible for my taste. When he sees us, he smiles, but his face flushes violently when he catches sight of Amadou. Turning back over my shoulder to sweep my gaze over our bodyguard, I'm only half surprised to find his eyes dark and dangerous, pupils dilated and *starved.*

"I—I thought the party was upstairs?" Maxime stammers, eyes darting between the three of us.

"It is." Régis says. He gives Amadou one final nod, the cage inside the trunk one final stare, then I watch him turn his back to both and sling an arm over his friend's shoulders. But he doesn't move. Instead he hangs on with a rigid spine as I watch

Amadou get in the car. He doesn't leave until I gesture for him to go. Only then, once the car slowly pulls off and through the gravel, does Régis turn over his shoulder. I can feel his burning gaze from here. We stand there, the three of us, until the car leaves our sight. Maxime doesn't ask anything, making me appreciate him just that little bit more. Now's not the time to talk. And so we stay there, in silence, until finally Régis clears his throat. Leaning into him, I brush my lips against his ear and whisper, "It's done."

When we make it back upstairs and into our dorm, I peel Régis away from Maxime, and with a growl in his ear, I push him toward our bedroom.

"I need you for one more minute."

"I hope you'll need me for more than that?" He teases, but lets me willingly pull him back inside his room. Once the door is closed, I lean a hand on it and drop my head, inhaling deeply as I'm briefly lost in my own jitters. I've been waiting for a fitting moment to give this to him.

"I've got you a gift," I say, then flit my gaze to his. He looks surprised.

"A gift? But it's not my birthday."

"Come here."

He follows me through the room, letting out some sputters on how I have made myself at home in his space. I open a drawer and take out a oak cube.

Régis eyes it warily. "What's that box?"

"It's not a box. Look." I sit us both down on the bed, then place the gift between us. "Open it."

He does, fumbling with the tiny iron hinges before they finally click. "Remember when I called the cage a crown of steel?" The words leave my mouth on a whisper and I lace my fingers through his. I don't know why this makes me so nervous, but it does. I want him to love this and to understand my intention. I want him to accept it.

"I do," Régis breathes, and together we open the gift.

It's a chess board.

"I want to be your king of steel, *chaton*."

"My..." His face flushes and he dips his gaze when he discovers the metal chess pieces.

"You're so strong, Régis. You got rid of that cage. *You* did that, my fierce and proud boy. That cage, that reflected your past. This—" I gesture to the pieces that Régis now inspects one by one, their silver color glittering in his eyes. "This can be our army." With a growl I lunge forward and capture his mouth with mine. His lips are already wet, already waiting for me, impatient for our touch. Brushing our mouths together, I revel in his soft sigh, chest pounding with a sense of reverence. "*Our* future," I mumble against his lips.

Pulling back to gauge his reaction, I catch the moment his lips curl into a beautiful smile. Relief, happiness, infatuation, it's all there in those piercing clear eyes. It's breathtaking. "We'll share an army of steel."

"I love it," Régis breathes, then leans forward to place his own hands over mine as we hold the iron chess pieces, and his mouth is back on mine.

"Let's play now, *chaton*. Come on, let me beat your glorious army and fuck you for the rest of the evening as my reward." My tongue darts inside his hot mouth and circles around his, flicking and playing while my body heats up.

"Not now," Régis pants, "There's a birthday celebration outside. They're waiting for us." When he sees the desire in my eyes, he pulls back with a taunting smile, then places a final peck on my mouth. "I know. I feel the same. But later. First we celebrate with the others." He stands up before I can, giggling when I try to grab him with a whine but hit the air instead, a playful smile curving his luscious lips as he looks down at me. "Are you seriously pouting?"

"No." I get up with a grin, knowing it'll be a permanent

feature on my face tonight because he has just made me the happiest asshole on earth. Then I pull him into me one last time before collecting the chess pieces into their little bag, fold the wooden board neatly around it and put it onto his desk. "I never pout."

"Liar." Régis pats me on my ass, then flees to the door on a jog, cackling as he opens the door before I can get to him.

"You're gonna pay for that."

"I didn't know you enjoy cooking?" Régis asks my twin when he's standing right by him in the tiny kitchen corner of our shared dorm. Sprawled out on the couch are Dominique and Gaël, the latter wearing a birthday crown that is brightly colored and has 22 written on it.

"*Enjoy*?" Louis closes the fridge with a push of his hips, holding two bottles of champagne as if they were arms. "I am the fucking best you can get here in college." Handing out one to Régis, he hands the other one off to me. "Get your ass to work, bro." Louis's gaze darts between the both of us. "Fuck, *bros* I meant. Not fuckbros. Damn, this shit got so complicated." Tossing the bottle my way, he chuckles at his own joke, then turns back to his pans. He's making Boeuf Bourguignon upon request from our birthday boy.

"Nope, it didn't get complicated." I watch Régis struggling to open the bottle of champagne, and pull him in, right when the cork pops, and the fizzy drink shoots out of the bottle and against Régis's chin and cheek. His eyes turn wide in surprise, and from the couch comes a loud concert of cackles from Dominique and Gaël. I don't hesitate, but slurp the drink right off his face, making an obscene sound as I do. "Our little brother is mine, and mine alone."

"Oh, get out of my kitchen you filthy love birds." Louis

snatches the towel from his shoulder and shoos us away, but not before he grabs the bottle out of my hand. "You can keep him!" He sings when Régis and I burst out with laughter as we skitter away and back to the couch.

"Oh, you filthy *chaton*." I continue to lick Régis face even when he's lying onto the couch, although my tongue is now solely focused on his mouth. Hmm, those sweet lips. I wouldn't mind taking him back to his room and fucking him senseless, but the door opens and in come Jo, Maxime and Julien, who is pouting as he follows the others. Across from me, Dominique flies out of his seat and wipes off invisible dust from his hoodie, before making his way to his friends.

They exchange pleasantries and smile as they catch up on plenty of things. Louis fills up their glasses and Gaël puts on some music. I decide to help my brother in the kitchen, and when I turn over my back I'm relieved to find that Régis is chatting to his friends, shielded by Dominique. Or is it him who's shielding Dominique? My gaze finds Gaël, who is carefully watching his boyfriend while talking to Louis at the same time. My twin's phone buzzes, and when he picks it up from beneath the white cooking apron he has put on for the occasion, he frowns. Then his face flushes.

"Are you okay?" I can't help but ask.

He shrugs. "Yeah, it's just, uhm—"

"What?" Gaël now also asks, frowning.

Louis shrugs again, but the movement falls flat. "Nothing. It's for homework." Then he pockets his phone and turns around, presenting us with his back.

"Homework?" I mouth to Gaël, whose brows are still pinched, making his painted eyes look even more like a cat. My brother never cares for homework, which is why Dad arranged private teaching sessions with the new teacher Régis speaks so highly of, Mister Montague. Oh…

"Arthur?" Régis takes that moment to call me out. When I

look up, I catch him staring at me with a playful grin. The chess board has been put out onto the coffee table and the others are sitting around it, holding their glass, and their breath as they gaze between us. "Wanna play a game?"

"With you?" I rasp. Hmm…

"Of course."

I cock my head. "What will I get when I win?"

He smiles, cheeks flushing with excitement. "Me," he breathes. "What will I get when I win?"

"Everything you want, *chaton*."

He blinks, then his smile grows wider and he gestures to the board. "Game on."

27

AFTER

There were four of them. Elected by the brotherhood here in Monterrey Castle.

Four masks.

Gold.

Silver.

Copper.

Bronze.

Four brothers to cause chaos. Four brothers to create carnage.

"You voted," Elder Jacques said, and leaned onto his cane. The golden crow faced them all in a secret salute, before it was raised into the air, back to the four chosen ones. "You voted for *them*. And with them, you voted for a modern, strong, respectful Alpha Fraternarii. Born in the past, aged through time, surviving the future. *Le roi est mort...*"

"*Vive le roi!*" They all shouted.

Anticipation rolled thick around them, like foggy clouds filled with dread, and lust.

A lot of lust.

There were 4 potential members looking to join our ranks.

"Welcome to our candidates," Elder Jacques spoke, directing his low rasp to the students who formed a line right in front of him. They were dressed in black suits with an equally black shirt tucked beneath their jackets. The Elder dipped his chin in acknowledgement to the four waiting individuals. "You have been carefully screened, your profiles accepted by our brothers, and even though you don't know exactly what we stand for, you have agreed to participate in a mind-altering experience, with the possibility of earning a permanent membership. To what?" The Elder crooked a dark smile that forced a harsh line under the dark curves of the mask that hid his nose and upper part of his face. "You don't know yet. Perhaps you know them." He gestured to the brothers who stood dotted around them, dressed in their usual cloaks and white masks. "Perhaps you share classes with these gentlemen, without knowing their double life." He let out a harsh chuckle, then pointed his cane forward. "Perhaps not. Who knows? Most of you will have the evening of your life, only to return to your dorms after tonight and continue to live your life as you know it. One of you will stay. One of you will be given the chance to join us." A dipped silence. "Do you want to join us?"

"Yes, sir," the four mumbled, their gazes flickering between the Elder and the four masked men who stood right across from them. Waiting.

"Good. We will explain the rules, but all I can say is this, you'd better run fast."

ACKNOWLEDGMENTS

This was always going to be a difficult story to write. But as I started to dig deeper and deeper into the life of Régis, uncovering trauma and so much sorrow in that young man's mind, I needed a filter. And what a filter you gave me Charlotte, along with so much appreciated feedback. I'm so thankful for our evenings texting back and forth, checking in on how Régis would feel in specific situations, and about how he would deal with them. Trauma is such an ugly beast, and we fight it all in our own way.

Thank you Char for your honest words. They put me back on track on multiple occasions. My amazing alpha and trooper, Nicole. You have become my right hand and rock over the past months. Thank you giving me so much of your valuable time by reading Crown of Steel, and by getting my author's account out there. Bookstagram is like a jungle to me, but you easily manoeuvre us through it. Thank you for being by my side. Jen, my friend. For reading. For believing. For sharing your words of wisdom, your empathy and your kindness. Thank you for giving me a piece of your big and kind heart.

Heather, my editor. For reassuring me after yet another sleepless night. For always being present when needed, despite the fact that we live so far apart. Thank you for complimenting me on my growth as an author, and for guiding me through these stories.

Thank you to my Street Villains! The coolest street team in book world. :-) And to Charlotte and Nicole. One is my creative outlet, the other is my rock. Your presence has pulled me up when I felt down, and has made me shed tears of joy and sadness at the same time. Thank you for digging with me.

A big thank you to my family. To my three beautiful boys. Thanks to you Jordan, I know last year wasn't easy. Thanks to you Kim, for sprinkling all your sunshine over me. And thank you Mom and Dad, for all the wine and evenings spent together, talking about my stories. Thank you for being so open-minded and curious. I love you all to the moon… and back.

Lastly, thank you to you, my dear readers. Thanks for picking up my books. Thank you for loving this unconventional world. I appreciate you all!

THE UNDENIABLE SERIES

You like m/m romantic suspense set in a mafia world?

Start the Undeniable Series here

S***hameless*** is the first book in the series. It's a gritty, epic enemies-to-lovers with a seasoned bully and his blushing prey. It's filled with twists and turns and contains plenty of action and suspense.

F**lip the page for a sneak peek**.
(TW: murder)

PROLOGUE

The sound of heavy rainfall dripping onto the antique windows of the abandoned church created an ominous atmosphere that was as dark as the night outside at this hour. In this part of Manhattan, the streets were filthy, despite the fresh smell of the rain that had wiped out the usual stink of rubbish coming from the huge dumpsters. Trash bags were discarded freely by careless business owners and residents.

No, it was not the weather to be outside in. But there were always those who were in need of their fix. In need of their cash. In need of their lay.

The woman in his arms should have been out now, selling her cocaine, doing her duty, and providing for her family. But she was a fallen angel, a beauty in disgrace. Ripe for the taking.

Saint George's Church let out a long chime that shook him out of his reverie and back to the task at hand.

They were on their second date and Carol had never been more in love, nor more enchanted by this man, who was so different from the American guys she'd dated before. He was well-mannered and soft-spoken, his foreign accent a constant reminder of all the things she'd wished to discover in life one day, and she was determined to exorcize whatever coldness haunted him, replacing it with her growing love. If only he would let her.

She was so intoxicated by him—this charmer, who'd literally just walked into her life—that she failed to see the red flags that were slowly but steadily smothering her. The ones that were indicating that something entirely different was about to happen.

His hand on her shoulder was warm and familiar. It shouldn't bring her such comfort, yet it did. She leaned into it, consumed by his smell, and that voice that was now leading her deeper into her own mind, bringing her back to moments lived that she had forgotten about.

He'd brought her to one of the few abandoned churches in Manhattan tonight. It had been easy to get in, surprisingly so. They'd climbed all the way up to the gallery above the narthex, where a pipe organ had once stood. Over the last few hours, they'd shared a bottle of wine, had some snacks, and had made out. Carol was ready for more, but instead, they'd once again talked about her life. With him, she felt no shame, no fear. Where her lips were usually sealed, she found them open in his presence, sharing her deepest secrets. Especially like this, when his enchanting voice made her drowsy and compliant.

"Carol, can you hear me?" he purred. She soothed even further into its smooth melody, only vaguely registering the rope that was being loosely pulled around her neck.

"Yesss," she slurred, nuzzling her face onto his chest. God, he felt so good, so warm and reassuring. She raised a hand to touch his dark curls, loving how they slid through her fingers like loose sand.

Ever since she'd come to Manhattan, her life had taken her on a wild ride, but joining the Business was probably the best thing she could have done. Dealing C was easy for a crime organization that already had a marked territory. Being the family business that they were, they provided full protection if she performed well. Which she hadn't done recently, since she'd fallen into that common trap of becoming her own best client.

"Your family must miss you," her French lover mused, and in the fog that was Carol's mind, she briefly wondered which family he was referring to. The one that had abandoned her when she was sentenced to prison, or the one that had prevented her from going in the first place? She wanted to ask him, but he continued, "My family wants what your family has. You know that?"

"No," Carol mumbled sleepily.

"I know." His finger trailed along her cheek, and Carol couldn't prevent the sigh from spilling from her lips. "I'm here to take what your family has."

"Take," Carol stammered lazily in reply, then blinked her eyes with heavily dilated pupils.

His fingertips teased her chin, then dipped further down to the rope on her neck as he murmured, *"C'est ça."* That's it.

He leaned in for her willing lips while his other hand took out the phone that was safely tucked away in the pocket of her coat.

"Now the fun begins," he murmured to himself, and then pressed play on the voice recorder on his phone. With his free hand, he tucked Carol's sand-colored hair behind the ears of her narrow face. Before, it had been full and thick, but too much cocaine had gotten rid of the fine strands like a lawn mower, leaving some parts of her skull practically uncovered.

"Viens." Come.

Leaning heavily on him for support, Carol scrambled to her feet, cherishing that grounding grip on her shoulder. She eyed him with a glassy stare, her lips slightly parted.

Barely an hour ago, she'd been looking at him with lust and heat, wanting him to touch her. He smirked into the darkness. That was what they always wanted, his perfect victims.

He'd tried before and had failed to set foot on American soil by infiltrating American companies. The promised land where they'd be free from all those who were no longer part of their family. Because they'd forged a new one. Though all of them, including his own family, underestimated him and his mission. He'd show them his true devotion and the tables would turn. Both organizations he'd targeted for the cause hated each other's guts. And it was kind of funny to see how they ran around each other in circles, avoiding contact. Both organizations were full of weak lackeys, making it easy to reach his objective, and unless they wanted to negotiate, he'd continue his murderous path until he hit his destination.

"Tonight, you're going to make me so happy, Carol. You know why, don't you?" She gave him a sweet, confused smile in return.

He nudged her gently to take a step forward until she was standing on the edge of the platform above the empty nave of the church. From here they had a perfect view of all the rows of pews that hadn't been taken out, despite the church being out of service for a long time. Even the altar was still there, with its beautiful statues and paintings portraying a suffering Jesus Christ.

Without removing his hand from Carol's shoulder, he stroked her hair once more before he started tightening the noose around her neck. She sighed into the warmth of his soft touch and he even went as far as moaning gently in her ear as he rubbed his growing erection into the crack of her ass. She was face to face with doom, and she hadn't even realized. Just the thought of it made him horny.

Aware of the fact that they'd be listening, he decided to continue the charade and mumbled into the voice recorder, "We're here at Saint George's church, me and Carol. Aren't we, baby?"

Carol moaned something that vaguely resembled a yes, and

he let out a soft chuckle and pinched her ass. If only she had a dick, he would have started their closing scene with a quick fuck. But women didn't do it for him. And his love was waiting back home.

"We'll come to America and take what you have. Until you let us in and give us what we want, no one will be safe from us." His voice dropped to a whisper and he pulled the noose tight around Carol's neck, then tilted her head to drop a soft, last kiss on her cheek. After he'd reassured himself that the other side of the rope had been firmly knotted around the connecting pillar, he gave Carol the subtle push she needed.

The woman let out a surprised gasp as she plummeted down into a free fall, grasping at the emptiness, plunging toward death. The sound filled the quiet of the church and brought him out of his own trance, and he gave himself a moment to revel in the usual rush of adrenaline. Below him, dangling in the open air, he felt Carol coming back to her senses, but it was too late. Too late to change her destiny.

"Adieu," he whisper-mumbled into the phone recorder. *"Notre famille arrive. Soyez prêts."*

With that, he placed the phone on the floor, ready to be found by the Business.

"Our family's coming. Be ready."

ABOUT THE AUTHOR

Nothing with Lola Malone is what it seems. Although it's true that she loves writing romantic suspense and good wine, when you read her books, don't be fooled... her men are naughty and hot, shy and determined, and her plots twist and turn. But just when you think you've seen it all? You haven't. Lola creates stories in a unique world that's filled with culture, art, fashion and gorgeous men.

Below are my socials. I love to connect with readers! Join my FB readers group, my IG, or just drop me a message.

ALSO BY LOLA MALONE

The Initiation Series

Crown of Disguise (book 1)

The Undeniable Series (MM Mafia)

Shameless

Fierce

Obsessed

Infuriated

Made in the USA
Middletown, DE
02 July 2024

56434395R00243